D0970328

IT'S NOW OR NEVER

Two young women's lives are destined to intertwine in 1950s' Liverpool.

Liverpool, 1955. Actress Dorothy Wilson is offered her first major part in a feature film. But her boyfriend Sam wants her to settle down and start a family. Meanwhile, Lynne Donegan is bringing up her daughter on her own, eking out a meagre living as a dressmaker. The two women's lives are destined to intertwine in ways they could never imagine.

A Selection of Recent Titles by June Francis

IT HAD TO BE YOU
SUNSHINE AND SHOWERS
PIRATE'S DAUGHTER, REBEL WIFE
THE UNCONVENTIONAL MAIDEN
MAN BEHIND THE FAÇADE
MEMORIES ARE MADE OF THIS *
IT'S NOW OR NEVER *

* available from Severn House

IT'S NOW OR NEVER

June Francis

Severn House Large Print
London & New York

This first large print edition published 2014
in Great Britain and the USA by
SEVERN HOUSE PUBLISHERS LTD of
19 Cedar Road, Sutton, Surrey, England, SM2 5DA.
First world regular print edition published 2014 by
Severn House Publishers Ltd., London and New York.

British Library Cataloguing in Publication Data

Francis, June, 1941- author.
  It's now or never.
  1. Actresses--Fiction. 2. Single mothers--Fiction.
  3. Liverpool (England)--Social life and customs--20th
  century--Fiction. 4. Large type books.
  I. Title
  823.9'14-dc23

ISBN-13: 9780727897329

Prologue

Cheshire: 1942

Lynne sat feeding her baby, thinking of the child's father and wishing life could have been different. It was no use relying on her mother to help her, but Nan could just come up trumps if the letter reached her in time. Her grandmother must be well into her seventies, but was indomitable and still working. Lynne was almost out of her mind, worrying that the staff would talk her into giving up her baby. One nurse had spoken of babies being found on doorsteps or even in bins on the streets of Liverpool because their single mothers had been unable to cope. The voices could be so insidious, going on and on in her head, insisting that Lynne and her baby would be better off if the child was adopted.

She forced back tears and buried her face in the crook of her daughter's neck, thinking about the last time she had seen Robert. They had kissed in the shadow of the Liver Birds, not caring whether anyone was watching them. She remembered how a breeze from the Mersey had scooped up the skirt of her best dress, so that the brightly coloured floral fabric had wrapped around his navy-blue trousers as if nature was determined to keep them together. She had not

5

said *Goodbye* because in her head it had sounded so final. Instead, as he had turned away, she had whispered *Tarrah* and blown him a kiss. It still hurt to think that she would never see him again.

'Will yer stop crying!' snapped the other girl in the room, whom Lynne only knew as Dot.

She was standing over by the window that looked on to the drive of the large Tudor-styled house that had once been a rich woman's home. 'We could all weep if we wanted to, but what's the bloody point? I can't wait to get out of this place and start my life all over again.'

'You've made that clear since I first clapped eyes on you,' said Lynne, staring at her. 'And I'm not crying!' she added through gritted teeth.

'Well, that makes a change,' said Dot in a mocking voice. 'Since the day we gave birth, yer've been whingeing.'

'I have not!' retorted Lynne, her blue eyes glinting with annoyance. 'And even if I had, I don't see what business it is of yours.'

'It gets on me nerves.'

'Well, you won't have to put up with it much longer, will you?' Lynne said. 'You'll be out of here today.'

'Yeah, thank God! I'll be free to do what I want!'

Lynne was having difficulty believing that Dot could really be as hard as she made out. How could any mother, having held her child in her arms, bear to be parted from it? And yet...

She cleared her throat. 'I don't know why you didn't just try and get rid of yours early on if that's how you felt?' she said, flicking her

6

auburn hair back over her shoulder.

'Too damn scared, kid,' snapped Dot. 'I remember overhearing me mam gossiping with a couple of the neighbours in hushed voices about a girl in the next street to ours. She damn well died.'

A shiver went through Lynne. 'Poor girl!'

'Yeah, poor bitch.' Dot heaved a sigh.

There was a silence.

Lynne murmured, 'I don't think it was just fear that prevented you. Perhaps you felt the same about your bloke's baby as I did about Robert's. She's all I have left of him since his ship was torpedoed. Even if I'm forced into giving her up for someone else to rear, I'll know that somewhere in the world there's part of him still alive.'

Dot's throat felt suddenly tight and she wished Lynne would shut up. She tried to close her mind to the image of her son's face, his perfect little body, his tiny fingers that the nurse had told her could be double-jointed. *Just like his father!* Still, she'd given him away now. He had a mother who wanted him, as well as a father. It would have been a big mistake to tell Sam that the comfort they had sought from each other had resulted in a baby. The day of her best friend Carol's funeral had been horrible for both of them. Sam had been in love with Carol and when she had been killed in an explosion, he had been broken-hearted. She had been too young to die, just as Dot reckoned she and Sam were too young to marry and become parents. She took a deep breath. She had done the right thing having her son adopted. It was much better for the three of

7

them. Especially if she was going to achieve her dream of being a famous actress one day.

She squared her shoulders and tilted her chin and there was a hint of amusement in her voice when she eventually spoke. 'Bloody hell, yer a real romantic, Lynne. I would have thought after what you've been through, all that stuff would have been knocked out of yer. Mine's gone now and at least I've made two people happy. I just came to say tarrah, what with us having given birth within minutes of each other.'

'Where will you go?'

'I'd rather not say ... and to be honest, I hope you and I never meet again!'

One

Liverpool: 1955

Dorothy Wilson ran up the steps of the Lynton Hotel on Mount Pleasant, a short distance from Lime Street. As she furled her umbrella, she hoped the snow would not stick or bang would go her plans for tomorrow. She was looking forward to seeing Sam and his stepmother. Once inside the vestibule, she rang the bell. Within moments she heard hurrying footsteps approaching from the other side of the glass panelled door and recognized the proprietor, Kathy McDonald, a pleasant looking middle-aged woman wearing a tartan skirt and Fair Isle twin set.

'What a terrible evening it is, Miss Wilson,' she said, opening the door and beckoning her inside before closing it quickly. 'You must be freezing.'

'You can say that again,' said Dorothy, shivering. 'What's for supper?'

'Irish stew, so there's still enough in the pan for you and our American guest who's newly arrived.'

'A Yank!' Dorothy could not conceal her surprise. 'Now I might expect to see one of those if it were Grand National week, but in February?'

'He's here to find someone,' said Kathy,

smiling. 'Which reminds me. There was a telephone call for you from your agent. Poppy Jamieson? She said she'd ring back later.'

Now what could Poppy want? Dorothy had told her after she had finished her last job that she needed a commercial or a film rather than theatrical work, as they paid more. If she was to achieve what she had set out to do here in Liverpool, directing and producing a social history of very special women of the city, then she needed more money.

'Did she say what time she'd ring?' asked Dorothy.

'She said that she'd give it an hour, which would be anytime now,' said Kathy.

As if on cue, the telephone in reception rang. 'Perhaps that's her now,' said Dorothy.

Kathy lifted the receiver. 'Lynton Hotel.'

Dorothy watched and listened and then took the receiver from her. 'Hello, Poppy. What can I do for you?'

She listened to her agent's words with a mixture of excitement and apprehension, only to say when she finally managed to get a word in, 'I'll think about it.'

'Think about it! Is that all you can say, Dorothy dear? This is the chance of a lifetime! You can't possibly turn it down. There's money to be made and I must have your answer tomorrow.'

'I need a bit more time than that!' exclaimed Dorothy.

'The day after, then,' Poppy conceded, 'but you're taking a risk leaving it that long. This is

10

what you've talked about since you first came to London.'

'I wouldn't argue,' said Dorothy, feeling all of a dither, 'but things change.'

'If you have any sense at all, Dorothy, my dear, you will terminate your relationship with your policeman and return to London where you belong.'

'Liverpool is my hometown!'

'Was. You should never have gone back there.'

There was a click as the phone went down. Dorothy frowned as she returned the receiver to its cradle and stared into space.

'Bad news?' Kathy's tone was sympathetic.

'No, it's good news, but it's made my life more complicated than I could ever have imagined.' Dorothy hoped she didn't sound dramatic as she turned and headed for the stairs. 'I'll just get changed and be down shortly,' she called over her shoulder. 'I'm really looking forward to that Irish stew. I could eat a horse!'

Once in her bedroom, she wasted no time removing her outdoor clothes and hanging them up. She wished there was a radiator on which to place her gloves and hat but the hotel did not run to such luxuries. Instead she put a couple of pennies in the meter and switched on the electric fire.

She sighed, thinking Poppy was right, of course: she should have stayed away from Liverpool. Only two years ago she had been offered a leading part in a play to be shown at the Royal Court. For years she had slogged her guts out, first working in an ammunition factory during

11

the war. The factory work paid well and there were perks, such as cheap nylons and make-up. Her wages had helped pay for elocution lessons, which allowed her to follow her heart, first into unpaid work in a Manchester theatre to gain experience, which led to walk-on parts and speaking roles in repertory theatre. She sighed, remembering the sheer hard work of those days, as well as the fun times.

There had been men, of course, but nothing serious. She still did not know whether to regard it as good luck or bad luck that Sam Walker had spotted her coming out of the stage door of the Royal Court one evening. Months later he had been in the audience at the Playhouse when she had been appearing there in a costume drama. When he had come backstage and asked her if she would accompany him to the evening do of the wedding of a female colleague in the police force, the years had rolled back, reminding her of the May blitz in 1941 and the day of her best friend's funeral.

Dorothy closed her eyes tightly. She was not going to dwell on that day now. If she did it would open a whole can of worms. She went over to the wardrobe and removed a pair of warm slacks and a cashmere jumper. The latter she had bought with some of the earnings from a part she'd played in a drama series on the radio. It had led to her getting her first film role in a Glynis Johns' vehicle, *Mad about Men*. It had only been a tiny role, but what fun it had been spending time on location in Cornwall.

As she dressed and reapplied lipstick and face

powder, she found herself thinking about two American films in particular: *Roman Holiday*, introducing a new star called Audrey Hepburn along with the famous Gregory Peck. The other was *Three Coins in the Fountain*, which had also been shot in Italy in glorious Technicolor and had introduced two young foreign actors, Louis Jourdan and Rossano Brazzi, to British audiences.

She gazed at her reflection dreamily, thinking how it only took one good film for a career to take off. Now here she was being offered an audition for a co-starring role in a film set in Italy and Scotland. She could hardly believe it and knew she would be a fool not to seize the opportunity that her agent reckoned was within her grasp. She had been asked for especially by the woman in charge of casting.

Dorothy glanced at her watch, grabbed a cardigan and the key to her room and hurried downstairs. Once in the dining room she chatted to Kathy's teenage daughter, glad of the distraction from her thoughts.

After her meal, Dorothy went into the smoking lounge to have one of the five cigarettes she limited herself to each day. Contrary to what some doctors had claimed earlier in the century, they really weren't good for the throat, but the odd one definitely helped with the ol' nerves.

She went over to the window and, raising the bottom of the curtain, gazed out. The snow was still falling in fat flakes and already the road and pavements were covered in the white stuff. She imagined basking in the sun in Italy and warmth spread through her body. Perhaps she could per-suade Sam to holiday abroad, driving the pride of his life, a second-hand Austin A40 Somerset he had bought last Christmas. He had wanted them to get engaged but she had told him she was not ready for such a commitment, so he had bought a car instead and she had promised that she'd reconsider his proposal next year.

She thought of their plans for tomorrow. Would Sam still have it in mind to visit his step-mother on the Wirral? This latest snowfall could change things, always assuming his job didn't. Sam was a detective sergeant, in line for promo-tion and if involved in a case, he could so easily cancel arrangements at the last minute. Maybe he would ring this evening if that was so? She finished her cigarette and decided to call it a day and go up to her room and read in bed.

But once in bed, Dorothy found that she could not concentrate on the words on the page and her mind began to drift. She had always wanted to be an actress, ever since she had run down the aisle of the Pivvie in Tunnel Road during a showing of *Cinderella* when she was five years old. The ambition had burned brightly in her ever since: she had even given her baby away without even telling its father, Sam, that she was pregnant because her heart had been so set on becoming an actress. Her stomach performed a somersault. She had certainly never thought she would get pregnant: that only happened to other girls. Her mother had been terribly upset and then became exasperated when her daughter refused to name the father, so she had arranged

14

for her to go away to a relative, who knew of a charity home in the Cheshire countryside where unmarried mothers could have their babies. Apparently it had been founded by a rich female philanthropist who had an interest in 'fallen women'.

Dorothy had hated the place but it had been preferable to giving Sam the news that he'd got her in the family way. After all, she wasn't the only one with ambition. Even then Sam had been determined to follow his father into the police force. They had both met with success but the ultimate dream was still just out of reach. Hers was to be famous and his to climb to the top in the police force but he also wanted a stay-at-home wife and family. If she mentioned Poppy's phone call and what it entailed, he would be far from pleased. He had told her that he loved her, and what woman would not be attracted to Sam? He was a dish, with fair hair and brown eyes and was amusing and clever. *Never mind his having a good body as well.* The temptation to try out for the role of wife and mother was there but was it enough? What the hell was she going to do?

She stifled a yawn and knew she must get some sleep. Hopefully, after a good night's rest, the picture would be clearer. The book slid from her fingers as she closed her eyes and drifted into sleep. She dreamed she was back in that home in Cheshire, reliving the birth of her baby and her final mocking exchange with the girl who had shared her room. As the images filled her mind, Dorothy found herself regretting her

15

harshness and longed to have wished Lynne and her baby daughter good luck.

'I wonder what happened to them?' she murmured.

Two

Roberta Donegan was hurrying past the hospital on Myrtle Street, wishing that on this day of all days her mother had not arranged for them to meet at the milk bar in Lycee Street. Her cheeks were flushed with cold and several snowflakes landed on her nose. Her auburn fringe curled damply beneath the rim of her navy-blue school hat. She wore a blazer over a cardigan, beneath which she was clad in a gym slip, blouse and tie. Above her knee-length grey stockings, her legs were goose-pimpled and her feet were freezing in clumpy black leather shoes.

She would have felt even more chilled if it were not for the navy-blue and gold striped school scarf which she had shoved inside her blazer, criss-crossing the ends so it kept the worst of the cold from her chest. Her mother, Lynne, was always fretting about keeping warm because she had suffered from pneumonia when Roberta was a toddler and even her grandmother had a bad chest, mostly due to the Woodbines of which she'd been so fond, but her Nan's wheezing and chesty cough played a daily, rattling

16

warning of the pitfalls of not looking after yourself.

Thinking of her great-grandmother made Roberta feel sad and tears pricked her eyes. Dear Nan, who had led such an interesting life and had so many tales to tell of her days as a dresser in the theatre. The one that Roberta liked best was about when she was a tiny baby and had slept in a box which Nan and Lynne had carried with them from place to place on their travels with the repertory theatre. It had all come to an end just after the war, when her mother had fallen ill.

Suddenly Roberta slipped in the snow and her heart jumped with fright. *Concentrate on where you're putting your feet*, she told herself. She thought how it would have been so much simpler for her to catch the number 25 bus outside school as usual and go straight home. That way she and her mother could have visited a local cinema instead of one in town. The thing was that Lynne enjoyed coming into town and so this evening was really to be a treat for both of them. It was Roberta's own fault, of course, that she was late, having forgotten to tell Lynne that the whole class would be kept in for detention that evening. Her mother was bound to be worrying because she was overprotective of her only daughter.

Roberta guessed that it could not be helped because like many a war widow, her mother had brought her up without the help of a husband. There had certainly been no help from Robert Donegan's side of the family, but maybe that

17

was to be expected. After all they lived on the west coast of Ireland and her mother had never met them. As for Lynne's parents, her father, Nan's son, was dead and Lynne never spoke about her mother, except to say they had lost touch. Instead she had told her daughter more than once how she and Robert had fallen in love at first sight in an air-raid shelter here in Liverpool and, after a whirlwind romance, had married before his ship had sailed off into the blue – only for it to be torpedoed in the Atlantic.

Suddenly Roberta felt herself slipping again and she only just managed to save herself from landing flat on her back by grabbing hold of a convenient lamp post. She swung round as she hung on, so she ended up facing the way she had come. It was then she saw the man. Hastily, she dug in her heels and managed to bring herself to a halt. Her heart felt as if it was bouncing about in her chest. For an instant her fingers itched for paper and a stick of charcoal, despite not being able to clearly make out his features due to the brim of his trilby shadowing the upper part of his face. Could it be the same man she'd seen outside her school on Grove Street earlier? She was sure he'd been wearing a black trilby and gaberdine mackintosh but was this one as tall? She hoped that she was mistaken in thinking that he could be following her and wasted no time going on her way.

After a few minutes she decided that instead of crossing into Hardman Street when she reached the Philharmonic Hall, she would turn into Hope Street at the other end of which loomed the yet

18

unfinished Anglican Cathedral. If he went straight on down to Lycee Street, then she would know that she was wrong in thinking that he could be following her.

She strained her ears for the sound of his footfall crunching in the snow and yes, there was definitely someone walking behind her. She resisted glancing over her shoulder and her fingers tightened about one of the straps of her satchel. It was getting dark and the street was deserted. She considered risking running as fast as she could to get the hell out of there and then saw light shining through a window. She felt a flood of relief because it came from the coffee bar where Betty Booth, a student at the Art School, worked part time as a waitress. Due to Roberta's love of art she and the older girl had struck up a friendship.

She decided to take refuge inside. But before she could do so, the door opened and a woman in police uniform and a man came out. Roberta recognized him as Lenny Colman, a man in his early thirties, of medium height with a mop of thick brown hair, the owner of the coffee bar. The two were talking and then the policewoman noticed her. 'Were you wanting to go inside, love?' she asked.

'Yes, but...' Roberta hesitated and glanced at Lenny. 'Is Betty in there?'

'No, you've just missed her. She's got visitors this evening and has gone home a bit early,' said Lenny.

'Oh!' Roberta could not conceal her disappointment. Then she realized that the policewoman was exactly the person she needed in the circumstances. 'Perhaps you can help me, Constable,' she said, dropping her voice.

'What is it?' asked the policewoman.

'I think I've been followed from school by a man. There was one hanging around outside the gates.'

'I see.' The policewoman casually glanced up and down the street before asking, 'Can you see him now? There's a man walking in the direction of the cathedral and another in a doorway on the other side up towards Hardman Street, lighting a cigarette.'

Roberta, feeling safer now that she had company, glanced in both directions. 'I can't say for certain that it's either of them in this light. I can see they're both wearing a trilby and a mackintosh but that's all. I'm not much help, am I?' she said wryly.

The policewoman smiled faintly. 'Did you get a good look at the man outside school?'

'Not good enough to sketch a likeness, and when I spotted the man on Myrtle Street, the brim of his trilby cast a shadow over the upper part of his face.'

The policewoman glanced at the badge on Roberta's blazer. 'I see you're from Liverpool Girls College. What's your name?'

'Roberta Donegan.'

'You're a bit late going home from school, aren't you, Roberta?'

'Detention,' she said succinctly, hoisting her satchel higher. 'I shouldn't even be here in Hope Street. I'm supposed to be meeting my mother in

20

the milk bar on Lycee Street. Anyway, I decided to test whether the man was following me and when I decided he could be I realized I could take refuge here.'

'You thought Betty could telephone the police?' suggested the policewoman.

'Yes, until you appeared with Lenny and I discovered she wasn't here.'

'Has she mentioned anything recently to you about a man hanging about outside here?' she asked.

Roberta shook her head. 'No, but it's not unknown, is it? A friend of mine said they come to eye up the girl students a-and...' She paused, a blush on her cheeks, remembering talk about a man exposing himself.

The policewoman eyed her sympathetically and Lenny said, 'He's a bloody nuisance and if I get my hands on him...' His voice trailed off and he obviously altered what he had been about to say when he continued. 'Anyway, now Constable Walker is aware of your little trouble, kid, she'll sort it out.'

'Too right I will,' said Constable Walker firmly. 'It's not pleasant for young girls to be scared to walk the streets at this time of evening.'

'I remember Nan telling me that she used to wear big hatpins and she kept one in the lapel of her coat,' said Roberta. 'She was ready to use it if she was attacked when she left the theatre in the dark.'

The policewoman smiled. 'I'd recommend carrying a small pepper drum with you.'

Roberta nodded. 'Mam worries about Teddy

21

Boys ... which reminds me, she'll be waiting for me.'

'I'll walk with you down to the milk bar just to make certain that you're OK,' said Constable Walker. 'See you, Lenny!'

He raised a hand and said, 'See you around, Hester.'

'You'll tell Betty I'm sorry to have missed her,' said Roberta.

'Sure, kid,' he said.

Roberta thanked him and then turned to Hester. 'I really appreciate this, Constable.'

'Right, shall we go?' Hester set off in the direction of the Philharmonic Hall and Roberta fell into step beside her. 'Tell me what you and your mother are doing in town?' asked Hester.

'I'm celebrating my thirteenth birthday, so Mam's giving me a treat. We don't often get the chance to go out together because we don't like leaving Nan alone. She hasn't been well recently but she insisted – and seeing as how Mam was feeling flush because several customers have paid their bills, we're going to the flicks. A neighbour is going to keep Nan company while we're out.'

'What does your mother do?'

'She's a dressmaker – a really good one! She gets that from Nan who used to be a dresser in the theatre because she was mad about the stage. But Mum's always been handy with a needle and she also designs stuff as well as use other people's patterns. She actually started out as a seamstress for one of the costumiers in Bold Street. Anyway, if you're ever in need of a new

22

outfit, styled individually at a decent price, then you know where to come,' said Roberta, a hint of pride in her voice.

Hester chuckled. 'You're not one to miss an opportunity, are you, Roberta?'

'My friends call me Bobby. Mum's name is Lynne.' She changed the subject. 'I love art, myself. Have you seen Betty's paintings on the walls of the coffee bar? I'd like to study art, just like her. Do you know that she's going to Italy?'

Hester smiled. 'Yes, I do. I'm friends with her half-sister, Emma. Also Betty is a friend of my half-sister, Jeanette. She told me all about how excited Betty is about her trip to Italy because Betty wants someone to take over her flat while she's away and Jeanette wants to be that person. She's visiting Betty this evening, along with the music group who will hopefully be playing at my wedding. One of the members is Italian and he sings like a dream.'

'I'd like to hear him and I'd love to go to Italy and study art,' murmured Roberta dreamily. 'I like portraits best but I'd enjoy seeing sculptures as well as the architecture. Rome, Venice, Florence.'

'I believe Betty is hoping to visit all those cities but she's going to be based in a seaside town called Castellammare di Stabia on the Bay of Naples.'

'So she told me.' Roberta's expression was rapt. 'Apparently it's about ten miles from Sorrento and has archaeological sites and spas and a castle. I've been told the scenery is sensational. Mount Vesuvius is the other side of the bay. We have a copy of a painting on a classroom wall called "Faithful unto Death". The original painting by Edward Poynter is in the Walker Art Gallery.' She drew breath. 'I tried to copy the Roman soldier's expression but it gave me nightmares! I dreamt I was trying to escape when the volcano erupted and Pompeii was destroyed.' She stopped abruptly. 'I'm babbling, aren't I? But you have to admit that coping with snow seems pretty tame in comparison.'

Hester smiled. 'You're certainly enthusiastic. I suppose Betty told you that there's a painting by her father in the Walker?'

'Yes, it's of the Mersey and shipping. It's interesting but I prefer paintings of people,' said Roberta with a shrug. 'But don't go telling Betty that. She thinks her father's the bees' knees and wishes he hadn't been killed at Dunkirk.'

'She believes she takes after him,' said Hester, and changed the subject. 'Do you have any brothers and sisters?'

'No, I'm an only child. Mum's a widow, same as Nan. My father was a sailor and his ship was torpedoed in the Atlantic. We share a house in Lombard Street, off West Derby Road. We were lucky getting it. Nan's cousin lived there so we moved in with her after the war. She died not so long ago. Do you know the area?'

Hester smiled. 'Yes, as it happens. I live within five minutes' walk of Lombard Street. How's that for a coincidence? Also, our Jeanette works part-time at the milk bar where you're meeting your mum. It's a small world.' She came to a halt on the corner outside the Philharmonic Hall.

'Can you see any sign of the man who might have followed you?' she asked.

Roberta gazed about her for any sign of a man in a raincoat wearing a black trilby who might look suspiciously like the one she had seen. 'I can't really say. There are several men about, but...' She sighed. 'You must consider me terribly indecisive.'

'Don't worry about it,' said Hester. 'I'll have a word with your mum and make a couple of suggestions. It's possible your suspicions could be right, little as we'd like that to be true.'

Roberta thanked her and they turned and headed down towards Lycee Street. 'Mum's not in favour of me going to Art School after I finish grammar school. She'd like me to do teacher training. She sees it as being a respectable and well-paid career.'

'Thinks artists aren't respectable, I suppose,' said Hester seriously. 'There are those who regard women being in the police force as unacceptable.'

'Well, they're wrong,' said Roberta firmly.

For several moments they walked on in silence and then the girl asked, 'Have you seen the film *Three Coins in the Fountain*?'

Hester said that she had and they continued to talk about films, Italy and art. What with being engrossed in their conversation, Roberta didn't notice if they were being followed or not. It seemed to take no time at all to reach their destination.

They entered the milk bar and a woman immediately stood up, leaving an empty plate and

25

cup and saucer on the table where she had been sitting. She clutched a handbag and a book. 'Where have you been, Bobby?' she asked, hurrying towards them. 'What's happened?' She gazed in alarm at Hester.

Her daughter did not reply but smiled delightedly at Lynne, pleased with her because she was wearing her favourite coat of russet tweed, flecked with green and styled in the new A-line. On her neat little head she wore a mustard-coloured felt hat with a cream artificial flower tucked in the brim. What Roberta did not approve of was the metal-rimmed spectacles which made Lynne look older and studious and concealed eyes which were a stunning blue.

'Constable Walker, this is my mother, Lynne Donegan,' said Roberta.

'Mrs Donegan,' said Hester, offering a hand. 'Don't you be worrying. Your daughter hasn't done anything wrong.'

'I'm glad to hear it,' said Lynne, looking relieved. 'Not that I thought for one moment that she'd broken the law.' She shook Hester's hand. 'Perhaps you'd like to explain, Constable Walker?'

They dropped hands. 'Your daughter thought she was being followed, so I decided I'd best keep her company and deliver her to you,' said Hester.

Lynne stared at her daughter in dismay. 'What does Constable Walker mean *followed*? Who was following you? It's not a lad, is it? You're far too young to get involved with boys. What about your schooling?'

Bright colour flooded Roberta's face. 'You're obsessed with the idea of me getting involved with boys, Mam. Cross my heart, it was a man and I don't know where he went but I reckon he was scared off by the sight of Constable Walker.' She darted a smile at Hester. 'You don't know this but she lives near us and knows Betty Booth and is a friend of her half-sister, Emma.'

Lynne sighed. 'I'm confused. Where did you meet Constable Walker? What's all this about Betty Booth?'

'We met outside the coffee bar where Betty works,' said Hester. 'Your daughter told me that she thought she had seen a man loitering outside her school and that he might have followed her. I suggest, Mrs Donegan, that you have a word with the headmistress. Better to be safe than sorry.'

'Thank you, Constable Walker. I'll do that,' said Lynne, her brow knitting. 'I thought Liverpool would be a safer place once the war was over but it seems I'm wrong, what with these Teddy Boys to worry about, and recently I've heard of several shops being broken into. I think I'll have to resort to doing what we did in the war and carry a hat pin with me.'

Hester smiled. 'Roberta told me you're a widow.'

'Yes, that's right,' said Lynne smoothly. 'I presume you're not married, Constable Walker, or you wouldn't be in the police force, doing an excellent job, no doubt.'

'It's good of you to say so. I followed in my father's and brother's footsteps. They're both in

27

the force, although Dad will be retiring soon and I'll be leaving as I'm getting married at Easter.'

'How lovely!' exclaimed Lynne. 'And where will you be living? It's so difficult to get a house, what with so many being destroyed during the bombing.'

'I'll be moving to Whalley, a village further north. My mother died when I was only young and I was evacuated there for part of the war. That's where I first met Emma and my future husband and I will be renting her cottage as she married Betty's cousin and has moved to Formby.'

'I've never lived in a village,' said Lynne. 'It'll be a big change for you.'

Hester agreed. 'I have been spending a lot of time up there recently due to the cottage being renovated and I've had no time to do anything about my wedding gown.' Hester paused. 'Roberta told me that you're a dressmaker.'

'Yes!' Lynne hesitated. 'Perhaps you'd like one of my business cards. I know a lot more brides-to-be are buying their gowns off the peg these days but if you'd like—'

'Something special!' Hester smiled. 'Yes, I'll take one of your business cards, Mrs Donegan.'

Lynne rummaged in her handbag and produced a card and handed it to Hester. 'Just drop by any time. I'm home most days and if I'm not there my grandmother will be. You can leave a message with her and let me know if I can be of help to you. Just be patient if she can't get to the door quick enough. She's not been well recently.'

'Thank you,' said Hester, pocketing the card.

'Did you make the coat you're wearing?'

'Yes,' said Lynne, smiling. 'Do you like it?'

'I do. I like the cut and the material.'

'It's a favourite of mine,' put in Roberta, winking at her mother. 'I keep telling you that you're talented, Mam.'

'She certainly is,' said Hester, her eyes twinkling. 'It's been a pleasure meeting you both.'

'And you, too. Thank you for helping my daughter.' Lynne glanced at Roberta. 'And now we'd better get a move on, Bobby. It's later than I planned for us to be going to the pictures.'

'But I haven't eaten,' protested Roberta.

'You'll have to put up with having some popcorn in the pictures,' said Lynne firmly. 'Think of Nan. She'll worry if we're late getting home.'

The three left the milk bar together but parted outside with a tarrah.

Roberta thought that her mother was now bound to ask her about the man, but to her surprise Lynne only said, 'Not now, later. We're going to have to rush if we want to get to the pictures before the big film starts.'

'So can you describe this man?' asked Lynne when the lights went up for the interval at the cinema.

The question took Roberta by surprise, as she'd expected her mother to discuss the film they had just seen. She wanted to forget about the man and drool instead over Rossano Brazzi who had played the Conte in *The Barefoot Contessa*. It had been such a sad and dramatic story which had ended with him killing the wife he'd

29

believed to be unfaithful, unaware that she was actually carrying his child. Sometimes Roberta felt sad about her mother having been widowed during the war at such a young age. It would be fine with her if Lynne were to meet someone else and marry again but the years were passing and it had not happened.

'Well, cat got your tongue?' said Lynne.

Roberta offered the packet of Butterkist to her mother and considered what to say. Her fear had vanished and it was difficult to recapture her earlier mood when she had caught sight of the man in Myrtle Street.

Lynne took only a few pieces of the toffee popcorn as it had nearly all gone. 'I'm starting to think you made it up.'

'That's not true!' Roberta's voice was indignant. 'He wore a black trilby and I tell you what, Mam, it reminded me of the black Stetsons worn by the baddies in cowboy films.'

'He didn't have a six-shooter strapped to his hip, did he?' asked Lynne drily.

Roberta grinned and hunched down in her seat. 'You're making a joke of it but it wasn't funny at the time. Anyway, I told you I didn't get a close enough look at his face to describe him. Constable Walker took me seriously, anyway.'

'I liked her,' said Lynne.

'You'll like her even more if she decides to employ you to make her wedding gown.'

Lynne could not deny it. 'The money would come in very handy. I wonder how many bridesmaids she's having and whether she'll consider me making their dresses, as well?'

'It would be great if she did. Maybe there'd be enough money for me to go to Italy, just like Betty Booth.'

'You can forget that for a start,' said Lynne firmly. 'If you were going to go, I'd want to go too and we can't afford it. You'll have to wait until you're working and earning. Besides, right now Nan has to be our priority. She's been good to us both, so we couldn't leave her.'

Roberta looked into the empty packet of Butterkist. 'The popcorn's all gone and I'm still hungry.' She glanced at those queuing up to buy ice cream from the usherette at the front of the stalls. 'Can I have an ice cream?'

'No, they cost at least twice as much in here as a shop.'

'But you ate half my Butterkist and I bet you had tea and cake in the milk bar while you were waiting for me.'

Lynne could not lie and instead said mildly, 'I wouldn't have dared talk to my mother in that tone. She'd have given me the back of her hand for giving her cheek.' She dug into her handbag and produced a couple of coins. 'Go on, get an ice cream, but I want a lick.'

'You're not a bad mother.' Roberta smiled and took the money and kissed Lynne's cheek before going to join the queue. When she returned the first thing she said was, 'What was your mother like, besides sounding more Victorian than Nan? You never mention her.'

'That's because she was a bad mother,' said Lynne, only to wish she had not said that because her daughter would want to know why.

31

'Did she beat you?'

'She kept a cane under the sideboard but it wasn't that I hold against her,' said Lynne honestly. 'She seldom used it but she threatened a lot.'

'Then what was it?' Roberta persisted.

Lynne thought about Ellen, the mother who had told her not to expect any help from her when she had poured out her troubles. One would never have thought there was a war on, with lovers being parted all the time, never to see each other again. She had sometimes wondered if Ellen had ever loved Lynne's father. He had been a brave man, and died rescuing three children from a house fire. Nan had certainly loved her only son and it was that love that bound her and Lynne together. Ellen, on the other hand, had never even shown any emotion when her husband's body was brought home and had lain in a coffin in the front room. Afterwards Ellen had found herself a job and pretty well left Lynne to fend for herself.

'I think you've forgotten why your mother was so bad,' said Roberta, rousing Lynne from her reverie. 'Is she dead now?'

'I've no idea. I've told you in the past that I lost touch with her. She could be,' said Lynne, remembering how angry she had been with Nan when she discovered that the old woman had gone to visit Ellen while Lynne was seriously ill with pneumonia. Apparently Nan had wanted to give Ellen a last chance to make up the rift between her and her daughter because there was a real possibility that Lynne could die. As it

32

turned out Ellen had left Liverpool not long after the war ended. Her next-door neighbour couldn't say where she had gone. When Lynne recovered from the pneumonia, her anger and pain went deep. How could her mother show such little interest in her own flesh and blood? She had rejected not only her daughter but her granddaughter too.

'I can see I'm not going to get an answer and the lights are starting to dim,' whispered Roberta, offering the choc ice to Lynne.

She took a small bite before saying, 'I could never talk to her. Not like you and I and Nan talk to each other. Now shush!'

Roberta fell silent.

Lynne thought *Thank God!* but the B feature could not hold her attention and she found her mind wandering. She had been blessed in Nan. She thought back to that day in the home in Cheshire when her grandmother had come charging to the rescue. She had been up north in Preston when Lynne's letter had caught up with her and had wasted no time responding to her granddaughter's plea to come and help her. The old woman had shed tears when she had seen the baby and said, 'You're both coming with me.'

One day Lynne was going to have to tell her daughter the truth about her birth. So far she and Nan had kept up the pretence that Lynne was a war widow. It had saved any awkwardness and embarrassment during her daughter's growing years. Lynne had taken Robert's surname, believing her daughter was entitled to use it. Good ol' Nan! What would she have done without her? Suddenly Lynne needed to be home to see for herself that her grandmother was OK.

'Hi, Nan! Did we wake you up?' Roberta kissed her great-grandmother and then rubbed her rosy cheek against the old woman's wrinkled one.

'You're freezing,' wheezed Nan. 'Is it snowing again?'

'Was, but it's stopped now,' said Lynne, smiling down into her wrinkled face, before bending to pick up the shovel in the scuttle at the side of the fireplace. She flung the glistening lumps of coal on to the slumbering embers and returned the shovel to its place before sitting in the armchair the other side of the hearth opposite Nan. 'You been all right? Did Miss Draper come for her costume?' she asked, removing a glove.

'Aye, she'd rather have spoken to you than me but she was satisfied with the alterations and paid up. I put the money in the cocoa tin in the sideboard.' She rubbed her hands, the knuckles of which were disjointed and painful looking. 'So did you enjoy your evening out?'

Mother and daughter exchanged glances. 'It was fine, Nan,' said Roberta. 'Would you like a cup of tea or cocoa?'

'Cocoa, and I wouldn't mind a conny-onny butty,' she said. 'And I need the lav.'

'I don't know how you can eat them, Nan,' said Roberta, hanging her blazer on the back of a straight-backed chair. 'Condensed milk is so sweet that it'll rot your teeth.'

'Haven't got many teeth left to rot,' chuckled Nan. 'But the ones I've got have lasted me a long time. And while I think of it, you should be wearing more than a blazer, luv. What happened to the gaberdine mackintosh I bought you?'

'I'm growing out of it, Nan. The sleeves are too short.'

'That's as maybe, but you could still wear it, until you get another,' said Nan. 'Now what was that look about, the two of you? I'm not completely blind. Now help me up!'

Lynne and Roberta placed an arm beneath the old woman's armpits and heaved her to her feet. 'You'd best slip your coat on,' said Lynne. 'It'll be freezing down the yard.'

'Well, fetch me it then, there's a luv. Where's the torch?' asked Nan, gazing about her.

'In the back kitchen where it always is,' said Lynne 'It'll be slippery out there, too. I'll come with you.'

'I don't want to be any trouble,' said Nan, staggering slightly and needing to rest a hand on the armchair.

'But you will be if you slip and break a limb,' said Lynne.

Nan sighed. 'I wish we had an indoor lavatory.'

Roberta handed a walking stick to her as Lynne fetched her coat and said, 'So do I, Nan.' She moved to open the door to the backyard. 'I bet there wasn't always an indoor lav in some of the digs you stayed in when you were a dresser.'

'No, but I met so many interesting people.' Nan linked her arm through Lynne's as they stepped outside.

Roberta wondered if her mother would tell

35

Nan about the man once they were out of ear-shot. Yet she was forever saying they had to keep things from the old woman as they didn't want her worrying.

The whistling kettle drew her attention and she made a jug of cocoa before slicing bread and taking a tin of condensed milk from the cupboard on the wall. After spreading it on the bread, cutting it into squares and placing it on a plate, she opened the back door, thinking the two women seemed to have been ages. She was aware of voices coming from the bottom of the yard. She caught the sound of her name and then that of Constable Walker and Betty Booth and then Nan's voice floated on the breeze to her. 'I knew a bloke called Booth before the war.' Roberta smiled, thinking about all the people her great-grandmother had known and hoping that, having met Constable Walker, more business would come her mother's way.

Three

Dorothy could hear a ringing in her ears and, without opening her eyes, she stretched out a hand and switched off the alarm clock. Then she pulled the bedcovers over her head and lay still; remnants of her dream still lingered. What was the date? Yesterday it had been the eighteenth, so it must be the nineteenth. She had gone into labour on the evening of the seventeenth but her baby had not been born until the eighteenth, so yesterday had been her son's birthday. It had also been that girl Lynne's baby's birthday. Had she been able to keep her daughter? Had her grandmother come up trumps? Were both children still alive?

She felt a sudden chill. Sam must never know she had given his son away. She could imagine only too well his reaction. She had never intended to see him again. Then it happened and she discovered he had matured into an extremely attractive man with a charm that she had been unable to resist. At the time of their first proper date, she was scarcely ever in Liverpool, so she had not visualized their relationship developing into something serious so quickly.

She groaned as there came a knock on the door and the maid's voice reminded her that she had wanted to be called at eight o'clock prompt in case she hadn't heard the alarm. 'Breakfast will be ready within half an hour,' she added.

Dorothy asked if there had been any more telephone calls for her. The reply was no. She stifled a yawn and asked after the weather and was told it had stopped snowing but everywhere was white. Even so, the sun was struggling to break through the clouds.

Thanking her, Dorothy threw back the covers and slid out of bed. She saw to her toilette before donning underwear, including a suspender belt and stockings, beneath russet corduroy slacks, a collared cream blouse and a green and brown patterned twinset. She brushed her lightly perm-ed hair that was the colour of ripening wheat until it shone. Then she sat on the bed and slip-ped her slender feet into a pair of highly polished brown brogues. Last of all, she picked up her handbag and went downstairs.

There was only one other person in the dining room and he appeared to be absorbed in reading some papers from a file as he ate his bacon and eggs. She estimated that he was in his mid-twenties.

'Good morning,' she said.

He lifted his head and blue-grey eyes took her in from her shiny hair to her polished brogues. 'Sure is a cold day out there,' he said.

She could see the admiration in his rugged face and was gratified. It was all part of the job, look-ing her best whatever the time of day or place.

'You're the American visitor,' she said.

'Sure am! And you're the English actress if

38

I'm not mistaken.'

'How did you guess?'

'The beautifully modulated vowels,' he drawled. 'I have to admit that sometimes I find it difficult to understand what these Liverpudlians are saying but I suppose I'll get used to it again. I remember what it was like from my days over here after the war.'

'Were you at Burtonwood air base?'

'That's right. For the Berlin airlift in 'forty-eight.'

'So what brought you back?' asked Dorothy.

'Doing favours for various people, my dad included. I'm planning to go to Scotland while I'm over here, too. You ever been there?' he asked.

'I could be going later this year,' replied Dorothy, feeling a stir of excitement. 'I believe the scenery is stunning.'

'My grandfather came from Argyllshire, so I thought I'd mosey on up there,' he said, putting down his knife and fork. 'It's on the west coast and you're right about the countryside.'

She was about to ask him what part of the States he was from when Kathy entered the dining room. They broke off their conversation and he picked up his cutlery and resumed eating his breakfast while reading at the same time. Several other guests came in during that time and so the opportunity slipped by for Dorothy to satisfy her curiosity about him for he rose from the table before she was finished and with a smiling nod in her direction he left the room.

A short while later Dorothy saw him pass the

window. He was wearing a black trilby and a beige gaberdine mackintosh. She smiled, reminded of a private detective from an American gangster movie. As she passed Kathy in the lobby, she asked the American's name.

'Stuart Anderson! He's from California.'

'The Sunshine State and home of Hollywood,' murmured Dorothy. 'I bet he's wishing he'd made the trip here in summer.'

'Apparently he intends to be away from home well into the summer. He'll be visiting the continent in connection with his work,' said Kathy, clearing a table.

'And what would that be?' asked Dorothy.

'He's an architect.'

Dorothy wondered if he would be visiting Italy but did not bother asking, for she had to get cracking. If she'd had any sense she would have asked Sam to pick her up here. She went upstairs to change her shoes for boots and to put on her sheepskin coat and woolly hat and gloves. She remembered to put a notebook and a couple of pencils, rubber and pencil sharpener in her handbag. If they were still to visit his stepmother on the Wirral, she would need to make notes as Grace was someone she wanted to feature in her film about Liverpool. Fingers crossed it wouldn't snow again and that she would choose the right moment to break the news to Sam about the need for a trip to London for an audition.

There might not have been another snowfall but the street where the Walkers lived had not been cleared and that fact gave Dorothy cause for

40

concern as she rested her shoulder against the front door jamb watching Sam. 'Do you think it's sensible using the car in this weather?' she called.

Sam glanced up from beneath the peak of the cloth cap he wore on his tawny head as he shook ashes and cinders from last night's fire on to the frozen snow in front of the Austin A40 Somerset that was his pride and joy. 'I don't know what you're worried about, Dot. Once we reach the main road, we'll have no trouble. The engine's running a treat and I just need to make sure the tyres get a grip as we set off. We'll be fine, don't you worry.'

'I hope you're right,' she murmured, wishing he wouldn't call her Dot. She glanced at the neighbouring kids who had created a slide the other side of the road, so that the surface of the compressed snow shone icily in the sunlight as one of them ran at it and went shooting along, arms outstretched. The next one to go was a girl with ginger plaits dangling from beneath her pixie hood. Dorothy found herself thinking of auburn-haired Lynne and her daughter from the home for unmarried mothers and was annoyed with herself. She had to stop thinking of that place or she would drive herself mad.

Sam's imperious voice interrupted her thoughts. 'Go and get your coat and hat and chivvy our Jeanette up! Remind her not to forget the spade and the sacking I placed by the kitchen door!'

Dorothy nodded, glad that Jeanette was coming with them. Normally Sam's half-sister work-

41

ed Saturdays but the owner of the milk bar was going to a wedding, so had closed the place. Dorothy liked the girl because she was always welcoming and friendly towards her.

She went through into the kitchen where she found Jeanette pouring boiling water into a Thermos flask. 'Now that's what I call using your nous,' said Dorothy, thinking Jeanette was as unlike Sam and his sister, Hester, as could be, petite and dainty, whereas they were tall and strongly built.

Jeanette shot her a smiling glance. 'I thought if we were to get stuck in the snow, a hot drink would go down a treat.'

'You're right, it would,' said Dorothy, 'but let's hope we won't get stuck. What about milk, sugar, tea and coffee?'

'In the shopping bag along with a bag of broken biscuits which were dead cheap. Mother's carer, Beryl, is bound to have a hot meal waiting for us, though.'

'You've thought of everything.' Dorothy smiled, ignoring the shopping bag on the table and instead picking up the spade and sacking by the door. 'Sam said not to forget these.'

Jeanette said, 'That's our Sam for you. He studies every eventuality and Storeton *is* in the countryside.'

'I thought it was close to Bebington,' said Dorothy, frowning.

Jeanette hesitated. 'Pretty much, although I remember walking from Bebington railway station and it was a heck of a walk. The trouble with country folk is they think nothing of walking for miles. Anyway, no use in worrying about that. There'll be a lovely roaring fire when we get to Mam's place.'

'She does know I'm coming?' said Dorothy, heading for the front door.

'She has an idea that you might be. I hinted that our Sam had it in mind to bring you. I told her that you were keen to ask her questions about her life.' Jeanette followed Dorothy out of the kitchen, carrying the oilcloth bag containing the flask and provisions. 'She met Carol, Sam's first girlfriend, and knows that she was your best friend,' Jeanette continued. 'Mam's really pleased that both of you have a chance of happiness this time around. It's the same for her and Dad. It could have so easily been Mam who was killed in that explosion but fortunately she survived even though she lost her memory, as you know, and was left crippled. For so many years we thought she was most probably dead.'

'But fortunately she wasn't,' said Dorothy, smiling, 'and those missing years are what I'm interested in.'

'I'm sure she'll talk to you about them but she also has lots of interesting things to say about when she was young.' Jeanette smiled. 'But I'll say no more. I know she'll be excited to meet you; I've told her Sam talks about you all the time.' Jeanette winked at her and smiled but Dorothy felt a moment's unease, especially if she was going to be grilled about matrimony by Sam's stepmother. She tried to brush it aside. 'I think there'll be enough in the way of weddings to look forward to with Hester and Ally's big

43

day. It doesn't suit everyone to rush headlong into marriage and leave their careers behind.'

'No, I'm sure that's right,' said Jeanette hastily. 'And I'm sure that Mum admires women with ambition.'

'But Hester had ambition. I can't help wondering if she'll be happy giving up her job in the police force to become a housewife in a country village,' said Dorothy.

'She loves Ally and they're both not far off thirty, so see no reason to wait,' said Jeanette, putting the shopping bag by the front door and going back for her outdoor clothes.

Dorothy put down the spade and sacking and followed her up the lobby. 'Thirty's not that old!'

Jeanette said, 'Sorry, I was forgetting you're older than Hester. I have to admit that the only career I'm interested in is marriage and motherhood. I certainly wouldn't want to go out to work for the rest of my life. I'm looking forward to marrying my Davy, having my own home and children.' She put on her hat. 'We'd best get cracking or our Sam will be telling us off.'

For once Jeanette's words irritated Dorothy but she tried not to show it. 'As far as I'm aware there is not currently a law against chatting, so DS Walker will just have to wait until we're ready,' she said lightly. 'Just remember, Jeanette, that marriage can be a wonderful thing but it's not ideal to be too dependent upon or subservient to one person. The suffragettes fought for equal rights for women and we should be grateful to them. I'll never forget the arguments that used to go on in our house between my mam and dad over money.'

Jeanette sighed. 'It's Aunt Ethel who's held most of the purse strings, at least where I'm concerned, for as long as I can remember. That's why I want my own place. Dad won't give his permission for me and Davy to marry yet. He thinks I'm too young and should wait until I'm twenty-one. I'm planning on asking Mam to get to work on him to persuade him to change his mind. I'll settle for a wedding next year. I'll be nineteen at Christmas. Right now I'm determined to live in my friend Betty Booth's flat when she goes to Italy during the summer holidays, although I could do with finding someone to share the rent with me.' She eyed Dorothy carefully. 'You wouldn't like to do it, would you?'

Before Dorothy could say that she might not even be in Liverpool, they were interrupted by Sam shouting, 'Will you two stop nattering? I'm ready to go!'

'Coming,' sang Jeanette, hurrying down the step which she had cleared of snow first thing that morning. She climbed into the back seat. 'Let's escape before the old witch wakes up.'

'Aunt Ethel is not going to want to come in the car with us on a day like today,' said Sam, taking the spade and sacking from Dorothy and placing them in the boot.

'She's panting to see the place where Mam's been living,' said Jeanette.

'Well, she's going to have to wait,' said Sam, holding the front passenger door open for

Dorothy. She climbed in and thanked Sam sweetly. 'My pleasure,' he murmured, kissing her on the lips before closing the door and going round to the driving seat.

'Here's hoping,' muttered Dorothy, crossing her fingers.

'Have a little faith, woman!' he muttered, raising his brown eyes heavenwards before setting the car in motion.

Dorothy glanced over her shoulder and Jeanette winked and crossed her fingers as well. The tyres crunched through the cinders and ashes and they were on their way. They conversed little as they motored into town, although it was as Sam had said and the main roads had been cleared. Even so, Dorothy and Jeanette thought it best not to distract him from his driving with chatter.

All was well until they came out of the Mersey Tunnel at Birkenhead and were heading towards Bebington. Then the car skidded on a patch of black ice, sending Jeanette's and Dorothy's hearts into their mouths as they were flung forward. With some skill, Sam managed to allow the vehicle to go with the skid and not to brake. Even so they were all shaken when at last they were able to continue with their journey in comparative safety.

Dorothy rubbed her forehead where she had banged it on the windscreen and wondered aloud whether Sam had actually ever taken a proper course of driving lessons.

'What a thing to say to a police detective sergeant!' he protested, looking hurt.

'I bet there are thousands on the road who

haven't taken a driving test,' said Dorothy, still feeling shaken.

'If that's a snipe at me,' said Sam, 'you can get out of this car now and walk the rest of the way.'

'I was just making a comment. I can drive but have never sat a test,' said Dorothy.

Sam glanced at her before giving his full attention to the road once more. 'The government suspended the need for a competency test for the duration of the war. Lots of people got into vehicles without having a test.'

'I remember plenty who were no worse than some drivers seen on the roads today.' Dorothy folded her arms across her breasts. 'Road hogs who are utterly mad and go far too fast.'

'There you go again,' said Sam, sighing. 'I think you want a walk. Perhaps I should stop right here and you can get out.'

Dorothy arrowed him a challenging look. 'If I thought you really meant that I would.'

'Who said I didn't mean it?' he teased.

'Will you two stop!' cried Jeanette. 'I can't help thinking how handy it is that Dorothy can drive. If we were to get stuck, we'd need your strength to push the car to get us moving again, Sam. I wouldn't have the foggiest what to do if I had to get in the driving seat,' she added.

'No woman is driving my car,' said Sam. 'Lots of things went on during the war that shouldn't have done and women driving is one of them!' He winked at Dorothy to show there were no hard feelings.

Her only response was to ask, 'Are we nearly there?'

'We've just passed a sign for Bebington, so it can't be that far,' said Jeanette.

'I'm glad you're watching where we're going,' said Sam, looking relieved. 'Dot, have a look at the road map and see where we turn off.'

'Pretty please,' she murmured.

'Get lost,' he drawled.

'One of these days I just might do that,' she said, reaching for the map.

'But I'd always manage to find you,' said Sam as he rested his hand on her knee. His proprietorial tone irritated Dorothy and made her feel even more on edge. Sooner or later she was going to have to tell him that she was going down south for an audition. There! She had made up her mind without consciously being aware of it until now.

It was not long before they were driving through Bebington and were soon descending a hill. There were fields and hedges on either side and the tyres slipped a couple of times but Sam drove cautiously and managed to keep control of the car.

'My stomach feels as if it's tied in a knot,' murmured Dorothy.

'How d'you think mine feels?' said Sam. 'This road is that narrow that I'm praying that another vehicle doesn't come from the opposite direction.'

'One of you would have to back up,' said Dorothy.

'I had worked that out myself,' said Sam drily.

'Let's not think about it,' Jeanette intervened. 'Isn't the countryside pretty, what with the trees and fields shimmering white where the sun's catching crystals of snow. I can understand why Mam doesn't want to move away from this area to the bomb-damaged streets of Liverpool. On the other hand, it's lonely and it would be a pain to be cut off by the weather.'

'It must be miles to the nearest theatre or cinema,' said Dorothy. 'I'd hate it.'

'You're allowed to hate it,' said Sam, 'because we're not going to live in the countryside.' Without taking his eyes from the road, which had began to climb again, he added, 'We'll be living in Liverpool when we're married. There's several theatres there and plenty of cinemas for you to visit. I'll be the breadwinner and you can please yourself which one to patronize.'

'But what if I really, really, want to continue acting?' asked Dorothy.

He glanced at her. 'I'll need you at home. We've already discussed this. If I want promotion I have to take my job extremely seriously. Sometimes it's a matter of life and death for people. In your case it's make-believe. I know this Liverpool film you want to make is different, but even so ... once you've done that and got it out of your system, I'd rather you didn't go back to acting. I'm sure you'd be able to find an amateur dramatics group locally to get involved in just for fun.'

Dorothy could feel her ire rising. 'You think I'll have time? I thought you expected me to be the little wife at home, warming your slippers and cooking your meals.'

'Sounds good to me,' he murmured. 'But

49

you've missed out looking after the children.'

His words seemed to hang in the air and Dorothy felt suddenly sick.

Jeanette blurted, 'Look, this is Storeton coming up now!'

'Bloody hell, it is small,' said Sam, driving even more cautiously as he glanced at scattered buildings and a row of cottages. 'Which house is Grace's?'

'There's more of it. There's Little Storeton, as well,' said Jeanette.

Dorothy, glad of Jeanette's interruption, took several deep breaths, relieved that they had almost arrived at their destination. 'So which house is it?'

'It's an end one. Go slowly, Sam,' murmured Jeanette.

'I can't really do anything other than that,' he muttered.

She pointed out an end sandstone house. 'Some of these are three hundred years old. I bet you didn't know that!'

'They look it,' said Dorothy, who much preferred modern houses, having grown up in a small Victorian terrace with cold running water and the lavatory down the yard.

'Here we are,' said Jeanette.

The car had scarcely come to a halt before she had the rear passenger door open and was climbing out. Dorothy followed her like a shot. As they made their way up the path to the house, a curtain twitched in the front window and before either could knock, the door opened.

'We weren't sure you'd manage to get here,'

said Beryl, beaming at them both. She was an athletic-looking woman in her forties. 'It's good to see you. I take it this other young lady is Sam's intended?'

'Yes, this is Dorothy,' said Jeanette, kissing the older woman's cheek. 'And Dorothy, this is Beryl, my mam's nurse and friend.'

'I hope my arriving unexpectedly is all right?' said Dorothy, offering her hand.

Beryl shook it. 'We were half-expecting you to turn up if Sam and Jeanette were able to come. Grace is going to be delighted to meet you and she can't wait to see Sam after all these years.' She stepped aside. 'You two go on in and get a warm. Lunch won't be long. We decided to be prepared in the hope you would get here.'

Jeanette led the way into the living room that overlooked the front of the house. Grace's attractive, strong-boned face lit up at the sight of her daughter and she set aside her crochet and held out her arms. 'Come and give me a hug, love!'

Mother and daughter hugged each other and then Jeanette sat on the pouffe beside Grace's wheelchair. 'How are you, Mam?'

Grace's green eyes twinkled. 'All the better for seeing you – and who's this you've brought with you? Am I right in thinking it's Miss Dorothy Wilson, not only Sam's young lady but the famous actress?'

'You flatter me, Mrs Walker,' said Dorothy, shaking hands with Grace. 'It's a pleasure to meet you.'

'Likewise, and please call me Grace.' She

51

patted Dorothy's hand. 'Now where's Sam? I've been expecting him for this past month.'

'He's always tied up at work, that's the trouble,' said Dorothy, glancing towards the doorway.

'Just like you,' said Sam, entering the room. He ducked his head to avoid a beam. Then getting down on his haunches in front of his stepmother, he took one of her hands and raised it to his lips and kissed it. 'You must be able to imagine how good it is to see you.'

Dorothy felt an unexpected ache in the region of her heart as she watched them. It was obvious the older woman was lost for words. With a tentative hand, she reached out and touched Sam's face. 'You were only a lad when last I saw you and now you're a man and so big and strong.'

'I always hoped I'd see you again but I didn't expect to see you in a wheelchair.'

Grace sighed. 'I do believe that some things are meant to be and it's certainly given me a different perspective on life. I think I've always been a touch selfish.'

'But wouldn't you say that some of that was due to your upbringing?' said Jeanette, frowning.

'I notice you don't deny I've been selfish?' said Grace softly, covering her daughter's hand with her own.

'I think we can all be selfish up to a point,' said Jeanette. 'It's hard to draw the line between selfishness and the need to do what's absolutely necessary to get what you want in life without hurting those you care about.'

'That's very true,' said Dorothy, avoiding looking at Sam as he rose to his feet and moved aside and perched on the arm of an easy chair. She felt a tap on the shoulder and glanced at Beryl who indicated that she sit down on the chair that she had placed the other side of Grace's wheelchair.

So Dorothy sat down, eager to talk to this woman about her life and the accident that had left her crippled. The cost of the sacrifice not to make contact with your husband and daughter, hoping they would believe you dead because you didn't want to be a burden on them. Had it had its compensations? If it had, then surely there must have been regrets as well? Such as not seeing your only child grow up. She thought of the son she had given away. She had never regretted doing so and must not do so now because what good were regrets?

If she had told her mother that Sam was the father of her child, she would have been round at his house like a flash, insisting to his father that his son marry her. Dorothy had never wished to trap Sam any more than she wanted to trap herself. She loved acting; it was her life's blood and she had no desire to play at it as Sam suggested.

'Tell me about your upbringing, Grace?' asked Dorothy.

Grace grimaced. 'It will shock you. I'd enjoy hearing more about your life, which is so very different to what mine has been.'

'I'd rather hear about yours,' said Dorothy

53

boldly. 'I'm sure Jeanette has told you about the film I want to make about women of Liverpool.'

'Oh, yes! But it's my mother you should put in your film, not me,' said Grace.

'The suffragette and believer in free love,' said Jeanette, smiling at her mother.

Grace shook her head at her. 'Don't mention *free love* to me. Love has its price and it's not always those who practise it that have to pay.'

'Can you explain that?' asked Dorothy, taking her pad and pencil out of her handbag.

'Do you have to, Dot?' said Sam, frowning.

Before Dorothy could respond, Grace said, 'I don't mind talking about my mother, Sam. If you don't want to listen, go into the kitchen and Beryl will make you a hot drink.'

'I'll come with you,' said Jeanette swiftly. 'I've heard it before and I agree with Mam – my grandmother, Lavinia, was a great character.'

'OK,' said Sam, and vanished into the kitchen with Beryl and Jeanette.

'So?' said Grace, staring at Dorothy. 'I presume you might have guessed that my mother went to prison for her beliefs and was force-fed?'

'Was she in Walton prison?'

'Yes, but she gave birth to me in a prison hospital in Manchester.'

Dorothy's eyebrows shot up. 'What about your father?'

'He was no longer on the scene. My mother believed in free love at the time and so did he.'

'So who brought you up?'

'I was fostered and my mother kept her eye on

me, not that I was aware of it at the time. She kept me secret from her father who was a cotton broker. He was a rich man, a widower, and he left her all his money. Later she caught religion and became something of a philanthropist,' said Grace softly. 'I didn't know any of this for years.'

'And so you should have lived happily ever after when you were rescued by Sam's father, married him and gave birth to Jeanette,' said Dorothy, scribbling away.

'I wasn't in love with George,' said Grace frankly. 'He was a lot older than me but I grew fond of him. We could have had a contented life if it hadn't been for his aunt Ethel, but the least said about her the better.'

'Did you ever meet your mother?' Dorothy could not resist asking.

'Oh yes, eventually, and I forgave her.' Grace continued with her story and then faltered and smiled wearily. 'Enough said if I add that we wouldn't have this cottage if it wasn't for my mother and she left me an annuity when she died.'

Dorothy realized Grace was getting tired and closed her notebook. 'Thanks, I really appreciate you telling me some of your, and your mother's story. Other people's lives always amaze me.'

'We all have a story to tell,' said Grace seriously. 'As I said earlier I'd be interested in hearing about you.'

Dorothy wondered what Grace would make of her story but she was not about to unburden herself and tell it. Instead she said, 'Do you know that Jeanette wants to rent a flat? A friend of hers is off to Italy in the summer and she needs someone to take over paying the rent while she's away. Jeanette's eager to spread her wings a bit but the difficulty is that she can't really afford it. She's trying to find someone to share with her but so far has been unlucky.'

Grace looked surprised. 'She hasn't mentioned it to me.'

'Perhaps she will today.'

'It would do Jeanette good to be independent. Her father is a little too possessive where his daughters are concerned.' She jutted her chin. 'I need to make up for the years when I wasn't there for her, so the least I can do is to talk to George about giving her some financial help and for him to see that his little girl is grown up. I think it could be a mistake making her and Davy wait until she's twenty-one.' Grace smiled. 'Will you be at Hester and Ally's wedding?'

'What's this about Hester and Ally's wedding?' asked Jeanette, entering the room carrying a tray.

'I was just asking Dorothy if she will be there,' said Grace, looking up at her daughter.

'The way our Hester's carrying on, she'll be getting married in last summer's frock,' said Jeanette. 'She still hasn't done anything about our outfits. She's too wrapped up in Ally and checking how the renovations to the cottage are getting on.' Jeanette handed a cup of coffee to Dorothy and then placed the tray across her mother's lap before removing her own cup and sitting on the pouffe. 'But when next I see her,

56

I'm going to give her a nudge.'

'That sounds sensible,' said Grace, sipping her coffee. 'And what about you, Jeannie? Dorothy was telling me about your friend's flat.'

So Jeanette told her all about it and also suggested that Grace and George should have a word with Emma's husband, Jared Gregory, about building an extension to Grace's cottage.

'You do realize that if your father moves out here and you're living in the flat, Sam will be left all alone with Ethel?' said Grace.

'Yes, but it would save me looking for a house for when I marry Dot,' said Sam from the doorway. 'You and Ethel get on OK, Dot, don't you? She likes you. We could even get married this year instead of next. What do you think?'

Dorothy could feel panic rising inside her as Sam so neatly mapped out her future. She visualized having to give up her career and being stuck with Ethel until she went senile and died.

'I find it amazing,' said Grace.

'What d'you find amazing?' asked Dorothy faintly.

'That anyone could get along with Ethel without wanting to throw a screaming fit,' replied Grace. 'I think you're best waiting, Sam, to see what your father says before you start making plans.'

Dorothy murmured agreement, feeling grateful towards the older woman whom she already admired for her courage and honesty. She thought about what she had told her about having met her mother and forgiven her for having had

57

her fostered. Knowing Sam, Dorothy knew he would never forgive her for giving away his son, so she could never tell him.

Four

Betty watched as the youth went over to the jukebox and wasted no time choosing a record and putting a coin in the slot. The latest catchy hit from Rosemary Clooney and The Mellomen, 'Mambo Italiano', caused two teenage girls sitting at a table a few feet away to stop talking and stare at him. She remembered Tony playing the same record on Friday and he had sung along with the music. It had been decided there and then that he would sing that song at Hester and Ally's wedding. He was a handsome lad with dark Italian looks that were as unlike this boy's as black from white. Yet she could not help thinking that this youth with his flaxen hair and attractive cheekbones and firm chin would draw the girls in a few years time like moths to a candle. She knew from the badge on his blazer that he was a pupil at the Liverpool Boys' Institute, as was his companion, Chris, one of their regular customers, who she guessed must be a couple of years older.

At that moment Chris caught her eye and she took a pad and pencil from her overall pocket and went over to the table where the other boy now joined him. 'What can I get you?' she asked.

'Coffee and a bacon butty,' said Chris before turning to his friend. 'What about you, Nick?' he asked.

'A banana milkshake and a bacon butty.' Nick glanced up at Betty from brown eyes that reminded her of treacle toffee.

'So you're Nick,' she said, writing down his order. 'You're new here. Welcome!'

'Thanks,' he said, flushing slightly.

'I told you they were friendly here,' said Chris, grinning across at him.

'We are as long as you don't burst into song too often or dance on the tables,' said Betty. 'At least not before the boss gets an entertainment licence. I keep telling him it could make his fortune but will he listen?' She smiled and left them alone and went through into the kitchen.

'Two bacon butties,' she said, stifling a yawn and resting her back against a table. 'We have a new customer. Friend of Chris.'

'The lad who goes to the Institute and lives Prescot Road way?' said Lenny, getting out the bacon. 'He has ambitions to be a reporter.'

'Your memory is improving, boss,' teased Betty.

'Don't you be smart with me, Ginger,' said Lenny. 'Light the gas for us, there's a love.'

'I wish you wouldn't call me Ginger. I know my hair's red but even so...' She lit the gas. 'I wouldn't mind so much if we were licensed for dancing...' She regarded her boss hopefully.

'You find me a Fred Astaire to perform here

59

and I'll apply for a licence,' replied Lenny, placing the frying pan on the stove.

'I wish you would and I wish you'd come and listen to the group play.' Betty resumed her position against the table and stared at him.

'I'll think about it,' said Lenny, who was a bachelor and lived alone in the rooms above the coffee bar. Betty had no idea if he had ever had a serious girlfriend. His behaviour was always circumspect where she was concerned. He interrupted her thoughts by saying, 'By the way I forgot to tell you that after you went on Friday, that girl who thinks you're God's gift to art came here, believing she was being followed.'

Betty watched as he laid four slices of bacon in the frying pan and said in injured tones, 'I thought you liked my paintings! I know they're not Picasso or Turner but you said they brightened the place up. Now, you're beginning to sound like my cousin, Maggie. At least I don't have to put up with her insulting me now she's moved out of the flat.'

'I do like them but you must admit that girl is a real fan of yours.'

'I presume you are talking about Bobby Donegan?'

'Probably. I can't remember all their names.'

'Was she being followed?'

'Not so you'd notice, although there were two blokes out on the street and she was definitely frightened. So Hester Walker took her under her wing.'

'She couldn't have anyone better,' said Betty, straightening up. 'I suppose I'd better get out there and make the lads' drinks. That bacon smells so good I'll be snatching it out of the pan if I stay.' Despite her words, she still lingered. 'Do come and listen to the group,' she said persuasively. 'It would pay you in the end. You'd have this place packed out with teenagers most evenings.'

'Which would mean me working longer hours and having to take on more staff,' said Lenny. 'Anyway, why should you be bothered? You'll be off to Italy in a few months.'

'Hopefully,' said Betty, crossing her fingers. 'I still need a definite yes from Jeanette about taking over the flat for those weeks while I'm away.' And on those words she left the kitchen.

As she made the boys' drinks, the door opened and a man entered. He stood there in the doorway, his eyes scanning the room. For a moment his gaze rested on Betty's face and then moved on. She had been about to take the drinks over to Nick and Chris but now she waited to see whether the man would stay or leave. She was suddenly aware that Nick was staring at him with such a look of dismay that she wondered if he knew him. Then the man removed his trilby and went over to a table and sat down.

Betty picked up the tray and went over to the boys' table and placed their drinks in front of them. 'Bacon butties will be ready soon.'

'Thanks,' they chorused.

She was about to walk away when Nick said, 'Do you know that man, Miss Booth?'

'No, never seen him before in my life. I thought you might by the way you looked at

61

him.'

'Before he removed his hat I thought he was my uncle.' Nick scowled. 'I'd go mad if he discovered I've started coming here.'

Betty was tempted to ask why, but at that moment, Chris said, 'He's signalling you.'

She excused herself and went over to him. 'Can I help you?'

He stared at her from grey-blue eyes. 'A black, sweet coffee and have you any doughnuts?'

His voice was pleasant but his accent took her by surprise. 'You're an American!' she blurted out.

'Is that a sin here?' he drawled.

She coloured. 'Of course not. It's just that we don't get many Americans in here. And I'm sorry but we don't have any doughnuts. I can get you either a nice Eccles cake, an iced bun, a toasted teacake or even a chocolate cake.'

A smile lit up his craggy features. 'An Eccles cake and I like them warm. I remember them from last time I was over here.'

'You've been to England before?' She clicked her tongue. 'Now that's a stupid question. Of course you have, otherwise you wouldn't remember Eccles cakes. Tea or coffee? Damn, you said coffee!' Without another word, she walked away, wondering what had come over her. Maybe it was because he reminded her of a detective in film noirs such as *The Maltese Falcon.*

She delivered Nick and Chris's bacon butties to them and left to serve her American customer a steaming black coffee and a warmed Eccles cake.

62

'Is there anything else I can help you with?' she asked.

'Information?'

Good God, perhaps he was a detective! 'What kind of information?' Betty dropped her voice.

'I'm looking for someone with the surname Graham. A mother and daughter. I wondered if the girl came in here.' He took a mouthful of coffee before adding, 'The daughter of the proprietor of the hotel where I'm staying suggested I try here.'

'I can't say I know anyone called Graham,' replied Betty. He looked disappointed. 'I could ask around,' she added. 'Do you have a first name for the girl?'

He shook his head. 'I know only that the mother's name is Lynne.'

'I'll see what I can do.' She hesitated. 'Is there any rush for this information? I mean – how long are you over here for?'

'I'll be going up to Scotland for a week or so in a few days and then I'll be back here.'

'Well, that gives me some time,' she said. 'May I have your name and the address where you're staying in case I need to get in touch?'

'Stuart Anderson and I'm staying at the McDonalds' place on Mount Pleasant,' he replied. 'And your name?'

'Betty Booth and you'll find me here except when I'm at college or at home.'

'You're a student?' he asked, sounding truly interested.

She nodded. 'Art student.'

At that moment someone called her name and

she excused herself. When next she had a chance to talk to him he had gone but the money and the bill were there on the table with a generous tip. She picked them up, wondering when next she would see him.

Five

It was Monday morning and Dorothy had still not told Sam about Poppy's telephone call. Neither had she phoned her agent. She and Sam had a date for that evening and she knew that she must speak to Poppy before then. She could not risk him talking her into changing her mind. She did care for Sam so she did not want to relinquish her relationship with him but she also wanted the part in the film. As Poppy had pointed out only too clearly, getting this role was the chance of a lifetime. She sighed, thinking good men were hard to find, but she had to make that call now or she might never get such an opportunity again.

She imagined that when he found out, Sam would either blow his top or go all quiet and that meant he was so deeply angry and hurt that he could not risk showing his feelings. There was even the possibility that he might decide to call it a day between them. She felt depressed at the thought because, although she was certain life would not be a bowl of cherries being married to

Sam, she could not imagine being married to anyone else. Still, she had to make a move and so she reached for the telephone.

At that moment it rang and Kathy popped her head out of the dining-room doorway and said, 'Would you mind getting that, Dorothy?'

She lifted the receiver and recognized her agent's voice on the other end of the line. 'So have you made up your mind yet?' asked Poppy. 'I've been waiting for your phone call. You do realize this is too good an opportunity to miss?' she repeated for what must be the tenth time.

Dorothy took a deep breath. 'I know. I'll do it.'

'Good! Then you'd best be on the next train to London. I'll meet you at Euston,' said Poppy.

They spoke a little longer and then Dorothy replaced the receiver and turned away, colliding into Kathy. 'So was it for you?' asked the proprietor.

'Yes, it was my agent! I have to go to London but hopefully I'll be back late this evening. If not I'll give you a ring,' said Dorothy. 'I just need to change and pack a few things.'

'Is it about a part?' asked Kathy.

'Yes, an audition for a film,' replied Dorothy, feeling a surge of excitement.

She ran upstairs, singing, and came face to face with Stuart Anderson who tipped his trilby to her. 'Good morning. You sound happy.'

'I'm off to London to audition for a film part, can't talk now,' she cried, hurrying past him. 'I have a train to catch.'

'Good luck! See you again sometime.'

'Hope so. I'd enjoy a chat about California,'

65

she called over her shoulder.

She reached her room and wasted no time changing and packing a few things, thinking she would ring the Walker household later that day. Someone was bound to be in and they could give Sam her excuses for breaking their date this evening.

The telephone was ringing as Jeanette entered the house, treading on the folded *Echo* as she did so. She snatched up the newspaper and rushed to pick up the phone. It had only been installed recently and even if she heard it, Ethel seemed not to know how to handle calls. 'Hello, Jeanette Walker here! Can I help you?' Her father had told her to give the number first but she had not committed it to memory yet.

'It's Dorothy! Can you give Sam a message for me?' said the voice on the other end.

'OK! Fire away,' said Jeanette, reaching for the pencil and pad on the small table that held the telephone.

She was just replacing the receiver when the front door opened and Hester came in. 'Who was that on the phone?' she asked.

'Dorothy! Do you know where Sam is? She had a date with him but isn't going to be able to make it.'

'He's not going to be able to make it either. He said he was going to ring the hotel and let her know.' Hester hung up her navy-blue great coat and hat and ran a hand through her flattened brown hair.

'She's not at the Lynton,' said Jeanette. 'She's

in London.'

'London!' Hester pulled a face. 'He isn't going to be pleased.'

Jeanette nodded. 'You can say that again! He's going to be furious when he knows she's auditioned for a film part.'

Hester gave a low whistle. 'I thought she wasn't going to go after any more film roles but concentrate on producing the Liverpool film she has her heart set on.'

'Apparently the casting director asked for her specifically.' Jeanette changed the subject and smiled at her half-sister. 'I'm glad you're home. I've missed seeing you the last couple of days and Jimmy needs to know if you definitely want the group to play the evening of your wedding?'

'Yes, I do! I thought I'd made that clear,' said Hester, opening the living-room door. 'Where's the old witch?'

'I don't know. I've just got in myself.' Jeanette hung up her coat. 'I can't see her being in the kitchen getting a hot meal ready for us.'

'Since Christmas she seems to have forgotten how to cook,' said Hester. 'I bought some sausages on the way home and there should be potatoes and onions in the vegetable rack.' She handed a shopping bag over to Jeanette. 'Put that in the kitchen for me. I need to go up and change.'

'OK! I'll see to the vegetables.'

There was no one in the kitchen, so Jeanette decided that Ethel was either in her bedroom or had gone out. Although goodness knows where she would go to at this time of day, and with

67

snow still on the ground, too! She put on the kettle and set about peeling potatoes.

The potatoes were boiling by the time Hester came downstairs and Jeanette was frying the sausages and onions. 'D'you know what time Dad will be in?' asked Jeanette.

Hester shook her head. 'Best put his dinner in the oven.'

'What about Sam?'

'Same. He might have had something in the canteen but he always has an appetite.' She took out a tin opener and opened a tin of garden peas. 'So what kind of day have you had?'

'OK. There's something else I want to talk to you about.'

'What is it? You look serious.'

'I was wondering when you're going to do something about your wedding dress?' said Jeanette, moving the sausages round in the frying pan and stepping back as fat spat out.

'Soon,' murmured Hester, opening the *Echo* that Jeanette had left on the table and beginning to read an article on an inside page. 'I'm considering having it made.'

'By whom?' asked Jeanette, sounding surprised. 'I thought in the short time you have, you'd buy one off the peg.'

'I had thought of it but changed my mind. I helped this girl the other day and her mother happens not only to be a dressmaker but lives in Lombard Street.' She glanced at Jeanette. 'What d'you think of that?'

'Sounds promising. What's their name?'

'Donegan! Lynne is the mother and Roberta is

68

the daughter. The girl knows Betty Booth and had stopped at the café because she thought she was being followed,' said Hester. 'Do you ever notice anyone suspicious hanging about outside the milk bar?'

'You mean a man?'

Hester nodded. 'Unfortunately the description she gave wasn't of anyone out of the ordinary. Now if he'd been dressed in a clown's outfit that would have been something.'

Jeanette smiled and reached for the potato masher, as Hester put on the pan containing the peas. 'So when are you going to visit this Mrs Donegan? And will she be making my bridesmaid's dress as well if you decide for definite to employ her?'

'Maybe! I thought I'd drop by in the morning.'

'That sounds sensible,' said Jeanette, draining the potatoes. 'I suppose you'll be buying your headdress and veil from a shop?'

Hester nodded. 'I'll be going shopping with Emma soon and will have a look then.' She stirred the peas in the pan with a tablespoon. 'There's going to be a programme on television to do with the Easter bride. It's not only about clothes and the wedding day but setting up home. I'd enjoy watching that if only we had a telly.'

'Perhaps we should have a word with Dad, although it could be all change in this house this year what with you getting married and me moving into Betty's flat during the summer.'

Hester's eyes almost popped out of her head. 'You're not telling me that Dad's agreed to that!'

'Not yet but he will because Mam is going to get to work on him. She's also going to talk to him about getting an extension built on to the cottage and his staying there.'

'What's our Sam had to say about it?'

'He's talking about taking over the rent book for this house and marrying Dorothy earlier,' said Jeanette, wielding the potato masher.

'Can you see that coming off?' said Hester, removing the pan from the heat and getting out plates.

'Not right this moment,' said Jeanette. 'But then Dad's not going to move in with my Mam immediately, is he?'

'So we could rent a telly and all chip in for the rental for the next couple of months,' said Hester, her face brightening. 'I'll talk to our Sam. He might continue with the rental because surely he's bound to want to watch Dorothy's documentary when it's eventually made.'

Jeanette frowned. 'You know what his attitude's been ever since she first voiced that idea. Anyway, I wonder how long it's all going to take before it's ready to be shown, now she's auditioned for this film role.'

'Let's forget it for now,' said Hester. 'I'm starving!'

Ethel came in while they were eating their dinner and switched on the wireless without saying a word. Jeanette took the old woman's plate of food out of the oven and placed it on a tray and gave it to her.

Several hours later Sam arrived, just as Hester and Jeanette were on their way to bed. 'Any food?' he asked, scrubbing his face with his fists and yawning.

'You look shattered,' said Jeanette sympathetically.

'I'll survive. There's been a spate of robberies in the Old Swan and Tuebrook area. A couple of post offices and a shop have been broken into.'

'That's bad,' said Hester, frowning. 'Anyone hurt?'

'Not so far,' replied Sam, sitting down and easing off his shoes. 'Have there been any phone calls?'

'Dorothy phoned,' said Jeanette. 'You probably know that if you've been in touch with the hotel.'

His head lifted slowly. 'She wasn't at the Lynton. Apparently she's gone to London. What did she have to say?'

'That she was sorry,' said Jeanette, darting a glance at Hester.

'At least she phoned,' said Hester swiftly.

'Who took the call?' asked Sam.

'Me,' said Jeanette.

'Then she didn't phone until this evening.' His voice was expressionless. 'Did she say whether she got the part or not?'

'No, but she sounded tired. I wrote down what she had to say and left it by the phone,' said Jeanette.

'There weren't any messages there.' Sam glanced at Ethel who was dozing in the chair. 'I bet she took it and threw it on the fire. You might as well tell me what it said, Jeannie.'

'She was sorry but her agent told her that the

71

casting director had asked specially for her to audition, so she felt that she couldn't say no.'

Sam was silent but his face told them what he was feeling and thinking. Hester went up to bed and Jeanette fetched his dinner and then scooted upstairs, having decided she had enough to cope with, thinking about moving into Betty's flat if her father agreed, without worrying about Sam and Dorothy's love life.

The following morning Hester wasted no time: after waving Jeanette off and giving downstairs a quick tidy, she left the house. The rest of the household were in bed as her father and brother were on later shifts and Ethel never got up early these days.

She crossed Whitefield Road and paused outside Skelly's Printers and thought that she must visit there on her return journey and order her wedding invitation cards to be printed. Opposite the printers was Barker & Dobson's sweet factory.

She took a deep breath, thinking there wasn't anything quite like the smell of chocolate and boiled sugar and mint. She remembered being told the story behind the discovery of one of the firm's most popular sweets, the Everton toffee mint, by a boyfriend who had been a football fan. It was said that even Queen Victoria had a fondness for the striped humbug with toffee inside. It seemed incredible to think that the original toffees had first been produced in a tiny shop way back in 1753 when Everton was just a village. It just went to show that some good things last and the sweet had even provided

Everton football team with its nickname, The Toffees.

Hester headed on up Lombard Street where, once a week, she visited the dairy there. The owner kept cows in the back and she purchased buttermilk from him for her father who'd had a taste for it from childhood. Having done that she crossed the street to the number on the business card and banged the knocker.

She waited, tapping her fingers on the railings that enclosed a small tiled area overlooked by a bay window. The movement of a net curtain caught her eye and she realized that she was being observed. Was that because Lynne Donegan was being extra cautious, thinking her daughter just might have been followed home? She waved a hand and the curtain dropped.

Moments later the door opened and a smiling Lynne stood there. 'It is Constable Walker, isn't it?'

'Yes,' replied Hester. 'Go on, say it! I look different out of uniform.'

'You do, but I can still tell it's you,' said Lynne. 'Do come in!'

She opened the door wider, pressing herself against the lobby wall to allow her visitor to pass. Hester wiped her feet on the coconut mat.

'I hope all is well with you and your daughter and she hasn't had any more scares. Have you spoken to the headmistress at her school? You can't be too careful these days.'

'Not yet, but I will,' said Lynne hastily, leading the way into the parlour where a small coal fire burned in a tiled fireplace.

Hester glanced about the room which contained a Singer sewing machine on a table, four dining chairs and a single comfy chair, over the arm of which lay a garment with a needle and thread hanging from it. In the alcoves either side of the fireplace were shelves containing various objects, such as reels of cotton and material samples, tin boxes and box files, as well as what could be pattern books. Beneath the shelves were cupboards.

'Would you like a cup of tea, Constable Walker?' asked Lynne.

'Call me Hester,' she replied. 'Yes, I'd love a cup of tea.'

'Then perhaps while I make a pot, you'd like to look at my portfolio of wedding gown designs.' Lynne removed the garment with the attached needle and thread and placed it on the table. 'Please sit down.'

She took a file from a shelf and put it on the arm of the comfy chair. 'I'll be back soon. Will you be needing a trousseau as well, because if you do...'

'I'm not sure yet.' Hester smiled at her and sat down and picked up the portfolio.

Lynne left her alone and hurried to make a pot of tea, thinking it was probably best if Nan stayed out of the way until Hester had left. Her grandmother was still in bed, so Lynne decided to take her a cup of tea and tell her she had a prospective customer. Hopefully, Hester would see a gown she liked in the portfolio. The household needed every penny they could get what with Roberta at grammar school and Nan not

74

able to help Lynne the way she used to do.

Hester lifted her head from her perusal of the designs she had been presented with and listened as light footsteps went up the stairs. Then she heard the murmur of voices overhead and wondered who else was living in the house beside the daughter. Then she remembered something having been said about a grandmother.

It was not long before she heard footsteps descending the stairs and a few minutes later Lynne appeared, carrying a tray with two lovely delicate china cups and saucers patterned with dark red roses. There was a matching milk jug and sugar basin, teapot and side plates, as well as a plate of buttered scones. She poured out the tea and told Hester to help herself to sugar and a scone.

'What a lovely tea set,' said Hester, helping herself to sugar.

'It belongs to my grandmother and it was her mother's before her. It's Victorian.'

'How old is your grandmother?'

'She's admitted to being over eighty but she has to be a lot older than that, although I don't know her exact age. She's in bed with a bad chest.'

'I left an old lady in bed, too,' said Hester, stirring her tea. 'My great-aunt; she's physically fit but we think she might be starting to go senile. It's a worry.'

'Nan's mind is as sharp as a needle,' said Lynne. 'It's her body that's letting her down. It's not just her chest; she has bad rheumatism, as well. Do help yourself to a scone.' She pushed the plate closer to Hester.

'These look home-made. I don't have much time to bake myself, although I enjoy doing so. I'm hoping to do more of it after the wedding when I move up to Whalley.'

'Nan used to love baking but my daughter does some of it now, when I don't have time,' said Lynne, moving a chair away from the table so she could sit closer to Hester. 'Will you have to give up your job when you get married?'

Hester sighed. 'Yes. I love my work but my future husband is from the area where we're going to live. He came out of the army a few months ago and is a motor mechanic and has started his own business. My friend Emma, who owns the cottage we're renting, used to sell teas and light meals during the better weather, so I'm hoping to carry on doing that. I think I mentioned she lives in Formby now but not that she's having a baby.'

'I bet she's thrilled.'

'Yes,' said Hester, smiling. 'She and her husband, Jared, both want children.' She paused. 'How old is your daughter?'

'Just thirteen,' said Lynne, accepting the change of conversation. 'I worry about her because she's my only.'

'So you definitely will speak to the headmistress about the man hanging around outside the school?'

'Yes, of course,' said Lynne, although she was not looking forward to doing so.

'Girls that age are so vulnerable and some men can be swines. One can't be too careful,' said

Hester, a shadow crossing her face. 'Is there a school friend she can come home with?'

'No, there isn't anyone, although my daughter tells me a whole crowd of them get on the bus together from school.' Lynne hesitated. 'It's her getting off at the other end that is the problem. Perhaps I should go and wait outside school for her.'

Hester agreed it might be an idea, finished her scone and drained her teacup.

'Did you see anything you liked?' asked Lynne, touching the floral wallpaper-backed file.

Hester nodded. 'There's several I quite fancied but I'd want some alterations if I decided to use your services.'

Lynne's mouth set firm. 'Tell me what they are and I'm sure we can work out a new design together if necessary. An original dream of a wedding gown like no other.'

Hester felt a rush of pleasure. 'When you speak like that I must admit that it makes me want to have a go at something different. It sounds fun. What about material?'

'That depends on what you're prepared to pay. Silk, for instance, doesn't come cheap.'

'I was thinking of ivory figured satin.' Hester hesitated before adding, 'I feel at nearly thirty that white is a bit...' She blushed and did not finish.

The blush caused Lynne to wonder if she was no longer a virgin but that was none of her business – and who was she to criticize anyway?

'White doesn't suit everyone,' she said softly. 'It seems to me that there's a hint of warmth in ivory that isn't there in white. When you consider that at the beginning of the century, and even during the last war, there were lots of brides who chose to marry in their Sunday best because they couldn't get the clothing coupons. Besides it was much more sensible to make or buy a dress or costume that you'd get more wear out of.'

'Is that what you did?' asked Hester.

'No.' Lynne glanced down at the open portfolio and lied glibly. 'Nan worked in the theatre as a dresser and was able to get her hands on a lovely gown from a play that had been on the Royal Court. It was in the Edwardian style and made of blue voile over white satin and trimmed with lace flowers.'

'It sounds lovely,' said Hester enthusiastically. 'Do you have a photograph?'

'No, everything happened in such a rush because Robert's ship was due to sail in two days.'

'What a shame! How long did your grandmother work in the theatre? My brother's girlfriend is an actress and has done a lot of theatre work.'

'Absolute years! She married late and then was widowed in her forties and was left with a young son and had to go out to work. Then when he married, she joined a repertory company. After Robert was killed and my daughter was born, we travelled with her and I helped her out with the costumes and much else besides. My daughter slept in a drawer when we were in digs.' Lynne changed the subject. 'What's your brother's girl-

78

friend's name, although I don't suppose I'd recognize it? She was probably after my time in the theatre.'

'Dorothy Wilson. She's done a lot in theatre but has also been on television and in a film,' said Hester, putting down her cup and going over to Lynne and looking over her shoulder at the design she had turned to in the portfolio.

'The name sounds familiar.' Lynne presumed she must have seen the name in the theatre and film reviews in the *Echo*.

Hester bent forward and turned a page. 'Now this is the one I was thinking about. I really like the neckline and the way the bodice hugs the waist before the skirt flares out. But I don't like all those little bows; too fussy for someone my size.'

Lynne glanced up at her and, as she was accustomed to guessing sizes, said, 'I reckon you're about five foot seven. Am I right?'

Hester nodded. 'My future husband is only two inches taller, so I'd wear low heels.'

'That makes sense,' said Lynne, setting aside the portfolio. 'Listen, would you like me to sketch a design without the bows and get samples of material for you to look at? I go to a suppliers near T J Hughes in Stafford Street. If you give me your address, I could pop an envelope through your letterbox with the design and samples inside.'

Hester smiled. 'I'd appreciate that.'

'Will you be having a honeymoon?' asked Lynne.

'We're not sure about that yet. If so it would

probably be just a couple of days up in the Lake District. Were you thinking I might want a going-away costume?'

Lynne smiled. 'It's usual. You could take my portfolio with my personal designs home with you if you like?'

'Thanks, that would be lovely.'

'Another cup of tea?' asked Lynne.

'No thanks. It's time I was going,' said Hester. 'I've more shopping to do and work later.'

Lynne stood up and took a slip of paper and a pencil from the mantelpiece. 'What about your address?'

Hester reached for the pencil and paper and wrote it down. 'I'm only five minutes away.'

So you are, thought a pleased Lynne.

After she had closed the door behind Hester, Lynne went upstairs to her grandmother's bedroom. 'You ready to get up, Nan?'

The old woman gazed at her from faded blue eyes. 'So, have you a new customer?'

'I think so,' said Lynne slowly. 'She seemed interested and I'm going to get some material samples and do a drawing, redesigning a gown slightly.'

'Well, that's promising.'

'She's friendly and seems to know what she wants.' Lynne perched on the side of the bed. 'Apparently her brother's girlfriend is the actress Dorothy Wilson. Does it ring a bell at all, Nan?'

Nan's hands twitched on the bedcover. 'Can't say it does. But I remember your mention of the name Booth the other evening. I knew an artist called Booth, used to paint the scenery at one of

80

the theatres in Liverpool. It was owned by his grandmother if I remember right.'

'Perhaps he and Betty Booth are related. She's studying art. I can't say I know of any other Booths,' said Lynne, helping her grandmother out of bed.

She wasted no time assisting Nan on with her vest, drawers, corset, lisle stockings, underskirt, tweed skirt and a blue twin set. But it wasn't until the old woman was settled in front of the fire that Lynne brought her a warm soapy flannel for her to wash her face and hands and brushed her scanty white hair.

'So did she say anything more about the man who followed Bobby?' asked Nan.

'Yes, she advised me again to go and speak to the headmistress about him hanging around outside the school.'

'Better safe than sorry,' said Nan.

'That's what Hester said,' murmured Lynne, knowing she could not escape getting in touch with the headmistress, Miss Palmer, who had not been at the school when Lynne, herself, had been a pupil.

She decided she would go that very day and catch a bus to T J Hughes. She would go to the school before visiting the wholesalers in Stafford Street for material samples. She could take a short cut that would take her to Myrtle Street and then round the corner into Grove Street.

As she went upstairs to change it was as if butterflies were doing a dance in her stomach. The thought of stepping inside the school walls again made her feel as gauche as a schoolgirl.

She had always feared the worst when told to report to the headmistress's study.

It was only when Lynne was putting on her best hat and coat that it occurred to her it would be sensible to telephone the school first. What if Miss Palmer was not there? What if she thought that Lynne was being overprotective of her daughter? But she had to do what Hester advised, rather than let something horrible happen to Roberta or any of the other girls.

Lynne checked the money in her purse and then raided the cocoa tin and took out several pennies. Having checked the school telephone number, she kissed Nan, told her where she was going, and left the house. She used the red telephone box on West Derby Road and her heart beat fast as she waited for a person at the other end to pick up; she scarcely ever used a telephone. She thanked God that the headmistress's voice was clear and precise and prayed that she, herself, would not stumble over her words as she explained her reason for calling.

The headmistress listened without interruption and then she said something that almost took Lynne's breath away. Apparently a man wearing a raincoat and trilby as described by Roberta had visited the school. He was an American and was trying to find a mother and daughter called Graham. He estimated that the daughter would be about thirteen years old and the mother was an old girl of the school. 'I told him there was no pupil with the surname Graham here,' she concluded.

It took Lynne all her self-control not to blurt

out that her maiden name was Graham. Instead she thanked the headmistress, replaced the receiver and left the telephone kiosk. Who could this American be? Was it possible he was searching for her and her daughter? For a moment Lynne thought of telephoning the headmistress again to ask if he had told her the woman and her daughter's Christian names but that would mean using up more money. Surely it was just pure coincidence that he had been standing outside the school and had walked in the same direction as Roberta?

Lynne sighed, no longer in the mood to go into town. Tomorrow would be soon enough to go to the wholesaler's. She would just buy something to eat for their evening meal and return home.

When she arrived back at the house, Nan expressed surprise at seeing her so soon. 'I changed my mind and decided to telephone the headmistress instead,' said Lynne.

'And what did she have to say?'

Lynne told her. Nan was silent, chewing on her gums. A sure sign, thought Lynne, that she was bothered. 'What is it, Nan?'

'I'm wondering if your mother could have sent him,' she wheezed. 'And when are you going to tell Bobby the truth about you not having been married to her father?'

'My mother!' Lynne was so astounded that the tin of baked beans she had just removed from her shopping bag slipped from her fingers. She bent to pick it up and placed it on the table and stared at her grandmother's wrinkled face, wondering if her mind was starting to go.

'You're not the only one who has a secret,' said Nan, chewing on her bottom lip.

'What do you mean my mother could have sent him?' demanded Lynne.

'Ellen went off with a Yank. An officer!' Nan sniffed.

'Are you telling me that she met a Yank during the war and married him?' cried Lynne.

'Yes.'

'How did you find out?'

'When I visited to tell her you were at death's door. The next-door neighbour told me how he used to come and see her and stay overnight. Apparently, she used to go dancing with him. He was stationed at Burtonwood air base and, when the war was over and he had to return home, they were married and she sailed off on a liner with hundreds of other GI war brides. Not caring a damn about those she left behind. Selfish cow!' added Nan, rearing her head and glaring into the distance as if she could see her daughter-in-law in her mind's eye.

'Bloody hell!' muttered Lynne, who seldom swore. 'I wondered where she went. But I can't understand why she should send this Yank over here?'

'I did write to her after I fetched you and Bobby from the home, telling her that you were both with me,' wheezed Nan.

'So she knew that much but made no move to get in touch. That says how much she cared about us,' said Lynne hoarsely. She began to pace the floor. 'I don't get it, Nan. Why should she send someone to find us after all this time?

That's if it is her who is behind this.'

'You'll only find that out if you get in touch with this Yank,' said Nan, her eyes alight.

'How am I going to do that?' cried Lynne.

'He's probably staying in a hotel in Liverpool somewhere.'

'But which one? There are loads of hotels in the city centre.'

'You could go asking.'

'I don't know his name, Nan! Anyway, I don't want to have anything to do with my mother. She wasn't there for me when I needed her.' There was a bitter note in Lynne's voice.

'Perhaps she regrets her actions,' said Nan.

'I don't care if she does' said Lynne, stopping her pacing and going back to unpacking the shopping. 'She's nothing to me. We've managed without her all these years and we'll carry on doing so. Not a word of this to Bobby, Nan,' she warned.

'But what if the man who followed her is this Yank?'

'We've no proof the man she mentioned was following her or that he was a Yank,' said Lynne, exasperated.

'I believed she was followed but how did he know she was the right girl?' muttered Nan. 'Maybe your mother had kept a photo of you at that age?'

'No way! Anyhow, you're not going to tell me that he could recognize my daughter from an old photo of me,' groaned Lynne, flinging the shopping bag on the sofa.

'Little as you like it, love, the family resemblance on your mother's side is strong.'

'Then why didn't he show it to the head-mistress if that were true?'

'Maybe he was shy?'

Lynne shook her head. 'He's an American and from what I've heard of them, they aren't shy!'

'He could have lost it but had an idea what you looked like! Easy enough to work out why he'd think twice about speaking to a teenage girl. Could have been concerned about frightening her by approaching her on a dark street?'

'He did frighten her!' Lynne sighed. 'You've almost got me convinced now that he is who you think he is.'

'So what are you going to do?'

A shadow crossed Lynne's face. 'I'm going to stick with what I said earlier. Although perhaps I should tell her about Hester Walker's visit.'

Nan looked thoughtful. 'It mightn't be a bad idea if you meet Bobby from school. It could be that he might try again and the school is his only lead.'

'And if you're wrong and it's not him?'

'Then our girl needs protecting.'

Six

'Hi there, Mrs McDonald!'

The proprietor looked up from the guest register and smiled. 'Hello, Mr Anderson! All packed for your trip to Scotland?'

'Sure am!'

'Have you had any luck in your search yet?'

'I'm going to give it another shot before I catch the train this evening.' He tilted back his trilby and smiled down her. 'At least I won't have any trouble tracing my pa's kin up north. He's kept in touch with them. If I have no luck today with Lynne Graham, I'll try again when I get back here before I leave for Europe.'

Kathy sighed. 'I envy you going to Europe.'

'Don't!' he said. 'It's going to be all work!' He winked at her and was about to walk away when he paused. 'Have you heard anything from that actress? What's her name...?' His brow furrowed.

'Dorothy Wilson,' said Kathy. 'Yes, she telephoned to say that she was staying on in London for a few more days.'

'Did she have any luck getting the part she was after?'

'She didn't say and I had no time to ask her. She was in a hurry, going to the theatre with some friends.'

'But she'll be back before I go to Europe?'

'I should imagine so,' said Kathy.

'Good looking woman,' he said. 'See you later.'

Stuart left the hotel and headed in the direction of Hope Street. He had it in mind to visit the coffee bar again. It was Mrs McDonald's daughter who had put him in mind of trying the place. Apparently it was really popular with some of the students and pupils from the nearby colleges and schools to gather because of the jukebox. She had given him the names of some other places, too. He had tried all of them but without any luck. Unfortunately he had mis-placed the photo of Lynne that his father had given him. He thought about the red-headed waitress, Betty, he had spoken to and wondered if she'd had any luck in discovering Lynne and her daughter's whereabouts.

When he arrived at his destination he was glad to find a vacant table because they were filling up swiftly as it was late afternoon and school was out. The jukebox was belting out a song he did not recognize and he guessed the singer was British. He felt out of place because he was definitely the oldest person there and he could not see Betty, only a blonde waitress who was obviously rushed off her feet. Then the door opened and the redhead entered. Instantly he recognized her and, raising a hand, managed to catch her eye.

She mouthed, 'Just give me a minute!' Then she disappeared into the kitchen, reappearing shortly wearing an overall. She came over to him. 'Good afternoon, Mr Anderson. I regret to say that I've no news for you. It's a pity you haven't a photo of the Grahams you're looking for.'

'I had one of the mother as a girl but I've misplaced it.' He smiled wryly. 'I can see I'm going to have to get in touch with Pa and ask him to send me another. It's whether it'll arrive in time before I leave for Europe.'

'You're going to Europe!'

He nodded. 'Sure am! A few days after I get back from Scotland. I'm catching the train up north this evening.' He paused and glanced about him. 'Look, I'd better order something. The other waitress is giving you a dirty look. Bring me a coffee and an Eccles cake.'

'Will do,' she said and hurried off.

A quarter of an hour passed before she returned with his coffee and Eccles cake as she had taken several other orders on the way. 'I'm sorry to keep you waiting and I won't be able to linger,' said Betty regretfully. 'You can see how busy we are at this time of day. I'd have liked to have asked you about your trip to Europe. I'm visiting Italy, myself, in the summer.'

His face lit up. 'I'll be spending some time in Italy. Are you going because of your art?'

'Yes, I'm hoping to be there for six weeks.' She placed the bill in front of him. 'Are you interested in art?'

'Sure am, but I'm mainly going for the architecture. I'm planning on being in Europe for at least three months,' said Stuart, spooning sugar into his coffee. 'Then I'll be back in Liverpool for a brief time before sailing home. Hopefully we'll be able to talk some more then.'

'That's if I don't have news for you when you get back from Scotland,' said Betty. 'If you manage to get a photo from your Pa that would be a great help, I'm sure.'

He agreed.

She wished him a safe journey to Scotland and hurried away, thinking that even if he had come later when the rush had died down, she would not be able to spend time speaking to him. Emma had stayed last night, having come to Liverpool to go shopping with Hester, and would be going home this evening so Betty couldn't linger.

Roberta slung her satchel over a shoulder and parted from her school friends on the corner of Grove Street. As she hurried past Myrtle Street children's hospital, she was thinking of Betty, hoping she would find her at the coffee bar. It was the first chance she'd had to go there in days because her mother had been meeting her from school. Apparently Lynne had decided that she wanted to make certain *that man* was not hanging around. She might have done the same today if Nan had not been so chesty that morning, making Lynne decide to get in touch with the doctor. Roberta was worried about Nan, too, but told herself that the old woman had suffered one of these bouts before and got over it. What she needed was some warmer weather.

At least Roberta was free to do what she

wanted and that was not only to visit the coffee bar but the Central Library in William Brown Street as well. She needed to look up some information for an essay. The pavements were now clear of snow and ice, so it did not take her long to reach Hope Street. She peered through the window of the coffee bar and saw that it was busy, but, having caught sight of Betty, wasted no time going inside.

A harassed-looking Betty glanced in her direction. Instantly Roberta made her way towards her but before she could speak, Betty said, 'Listen, I can't talk now. I'm rushed off my feet. If it's anything important, could you come back about six o'clock and I can give you ten minutes.'

'OK! I have to go to the Central Library anyway, so I'll see you later.' Roberta left the coffee bar, thinking that she only wanted Betty's advice about perspective for a sketch she was working on but she would make the effort and come back at six o'clock. Hopefully Lynne and Nan would not worry about her when she was late.

Once inside the library, Roberta found herself a table in the Local History and Records department and after taking a copy of *King Cotton* from a shelf, she sat down. She made some notes and had almost finished going through the book, which was about Liverpool's connection to the American cotton trade, when she heard the murmur of boys' voices and glanced round.

She noticed two youths sitting at the next table. One looked slightly older than the other, was maybe fifteen and had dark curly hair. He

91

was talking in a low voice to the younger one who was fair haired and appeared intent on what the other one was saying. She had a feeling that she had seen the older one before.

Suddenly as if sensing they were being watched, the fair-haired one looked up. For a moment their eyes met. Then he nudged his friend who looked in her direction. Instantly Roberta lowered her gaze, not wanting to be caught staring, but she had seen enough in those short moments to notice that the uniform he was wearing was that of the Boys' Institute on Mount Street, next to the Art College, which was just round the corner from Hope Street, near Mount Pleasant. No doubt she recognized the older one from the coffee bar but the fair youth was new to her. She decided she could not afford to waste any more time thinking about them after glancing at the clock on the wall. She would spend a bit longer on her research but then she would have to leave if she was to speak to Betty.

Despite trying to concentrate on what she was doing, she was aware when the lads stood up and heard the dark one call the other Nick as they made their way to the exit. Soon afterwards she left the library and hurried across town. It was beginning to get dark by the time she arrived at the coffee bar.

Betty was just putting on her coat. 'Perfect timing,' she said, slinging her shoulder bag on her shoulder. 'How d'you feel about walking up to my flat with me? My cousin, Jared, is dropping by to pick up Emma, who's been staying with me so as to do some shopping with PC

Walker. You've met her, haven't you?'

'Yes, she was kind to me when I was followed by a man the other week. She's been to see Mam and probably she'll be making her wedding dress. I liked her.'

'I heard about the man from Lenny. It must have been really scary,' said Betty.

'It was but I haven't seen him since, thank goodness.'

'Anyway you don't have to go home on your own. Hester Walker is probably still at the flat and Jared will be giving her a lift home. I'm sure he'll be willing to drop you off at the same time with her living so close to you.'

'That sounds great,' said Roberta, pleased at the thought of getting a lift.

Betty donned her woolly hat and scarf and they set off in the direction of the cathedral. 'So what was it you wanted me for?'

Roberta told her and for five minutes or so they discussed perspective. Then they talked about Italy and Betty mentioned the American who had visited the coffee bar earlier. 'He's going to Italy but first he's off to Scotland this evening.'

'Why's he in Liverpool?' asked Roberta.

'He's searching for someone,' said Betty, giving her a sidelong glance. 'Do you know anyone called Graham? He's looking for a woman called Lynne Graham and her daughter.'

Roberta gaped at her. 'Mum's name is Lynne and her maiden name was Graham!'

'You're joking!' exclaimed Betty, coming to a halt.

'Honestly, I'm not!'

Betty groaned. 'Why didn't I think of asking you before? I seem to have asked everyone else who's come in to the coffee bar!'

'I haven't been in the coffee bar for several days as Mam's been meeting me from school because of that man following me!' They stared at each other. 'Perhaps it was him!' said Roberta.

'Was he wearing a gaberdine mackintosh and a black trilby?' asked Betty.

'Yes!'

Betty gnawed on her lip. 'I remember thinking he reminded me of an American detective in a film noir.'

Roberta put a hand to her mouth. 'Then it is him! I wonder who he is and what he wants with us?'

'Wait!' exclaimed Betty. 'I'm not so sure they are one and the same. Mr Anderson told me it was the daughter of the proprietor of the hotel where he's staying who suggested he try the coffee bar in his search.'

'Is that the American's name? Anderson?'

'Yes, Stuart Anderson, and he's been staying at a hotel on Mount Pleasant. Does his name mean anything to you?'

'No. What's the name of the hotel?'

'I don't know! He just told me he was staying at the McDonalds' place.' Betty frowned. 'Anyway, you're not going to find him this evening. He was catching a train but he'll be back next week. You have a word with your mother about him and see what she has to say. Maybe she'll recognize his name.'

'I will! I mean, how many women called Lynne Graham are living in Liverpool? And as for my being followed from Liverpool Girls' College – Mum was a pupil there.' She stared at Betty. 'But who was the man who followed me if it wasn't him?'

'Maybe you weren't followed and it was just a coincidence that you saw a man dressed in similar clothes who was going in the same direction as you,' said Betty.

When they reached Gambier Terrace, Betty stopped in front of a house and took out a key and opened the door. Roberta followed her inside and upstairs to the top floor. A door was flung open and a pregnant woman stood there. 'So here you are,' she said, smiling.

'Yes, here we are,' said Betty, kissing her on the cheek. 'Bobby, this is my half-sister, Emma Gregory. Emma, this is Roberta Donegan, known as Bobby to her friends.'

'How d'you do?' said Emma, holding out a hand. 'Do come in.'

They shook hands.

'Did someone say the name Donegan?' asked a female voice.

Roberta followed Betty and Emma into a large room and noticed Hester over by a window that reached almost from floor to ceiling. There was also a man standing by the fireplace.

'Hi!' said Roberta, smiling at Hester.

Hester returned her smile. 'Have you seen any more of that man?'

Roberta glanced at Betty. 'We've some news about him. You explain, Betty.'

95

'What's this about?' asked Jared, who had dark brown hair and an attractive weather-beaten face.

'In a minute,' said Betty, putting on the kettle. 'I'm desperate for a cup of tea.'

'We've not long had a cuppa,' said Jared. 'So we won't linger too long if I'm to run Hester home.'

'You don't have to run me home,' said Hester firmly. 'I can catch the bus.'

'Oh yes, he does,' said Betty quickly. 'I've promised Bobby a lift home, seeing as how she lives near Hester.' She turned to Jared. 'You will give her a lift, won't you?'

'Yes, of course,' said Jared. 'Now what's this about a man?'

Betty spooned tea leaves into the teapot as she told them about Stuart.

Hester asked, 'How old is he?'

'Mid to late twenties, I'd guess,' said Betty.

'America entered the war in December forty-one,' said Jared. 'I'm pretty sure they didn't come over here until forty-two but the majority would have left by forty-six.'

'He was over here but I doubt he'd have been here during the war or met Bobby's mother,' said Betty. 'Otherwise he would have known her married name.'

'The Yanks were back at Burtonwood base in forty-eight,' said Jared.

'I think it's his father who knows about Bobby's mother and that she had a daughter,' said Betty. 'I forgot to say that he mentioned his pa gave him a photograph of Lynne when she

96

was a girl.'

'That doesn't help us to know whether the father met her during the war or afterwards,' said Emma.

'Can't say I remember setting eyes on any Yanks at any time,' said Roberta. 'Although I remember Mum talking about the Russians starting World War Three and finish us all off by exploding the atom bomb. I must have been about six at the time.'

Jared said, 'Instead the Russians set up a blockade of the Allies' road, rail and canal access to their sectors in Berlin, so the Allies had to airlift supplies in. You can read about it in the library if you're interested, Bobby.'

'I am interested,' she said, thinking suddenly of the two youths that she had seen at the library and wondered what they'd been researching.

'Anyway, enough of this,' said Emma, accepting her husband's hand to get up from the sofa. 'Time to go, for all of us.'

Roberta expressed her gratitude to Betty for all her help.

'That's OK,' she said warmly. 'I'll be interested to know what your mother has to say about Stuart Anderson.'

'I'm interested, too,' put in Hester. 'Your mention of the McDonalds' place on Mount Pleasant reminded me that my brother's girlfriend stays at the Lynton Hotel when she's in Liverpool. The proprietors might know the McDonalds. At the moment she's in London but should be back soon. If I see her, I'll ask about them.'

Roberta thanked her, impatient now to get

home and speak with her mother. She was dropped off first and it came as no surprise to see the front door opening as she crossed the pavement.

'Whose was that car you've just got out of?' asked Lynne, her face pale in the light from a street lamp. 'I've been worried about you.'

'Sorry, Mam. It's Betty Booth's cousin's car,' said Roberta. 'How's Nan?'

'Better than she was this morning,' said Lynne, closing the door behind her daughter. 'How come he gave you a lift in his car?'

'He was picking up his wife from Betty's flat and Hester Walker was there. He was dropping her off, so he gave me a lift too.'

'What were you doing at Betty's flat? I thought you were going to the library?'

'I went to the library but I called in at the coffee bar afterwards,' said Roberta patiently. 'And guess what, Mam, there's a man searching for us who has been in the coffee bar.'

'What!'

Roberta dropped her satchel on the floor and shrugged off her blazer and hung it up. 'He's a Yank and his name is Stuart Anderson and he's looking for a Lynne Graham and her daughter. What d'you make of that?' She watched the colour drain from Lynne's face. 'Are you OK, Mam? I didn't mean to upset you.'

Lynne fumbled for the doorknob behind her and stumbled backwards as the door opened. Roberta grabbed her arm and only just managed to prevent her mother from landing on the floor. She helped her to the sofa and sat her down before kneeling in front of her.

'Do you recognize that surname, Mam? Was his father here during the war? Apparently this Stuart was over here during the Berlin airlift.'

Lynne glanced at her grandmother and then murmured, 'Fetch me some water, Bobby?'

Roberta glanced at Nan and then back at her mother. 'I will in a minute but I want answers first. Tell me who he is and why he is looking for us. I think you know.'

Nan gripped the arms of the chair. 'Did this Yank say where he was staying?'

'In a hotel on Mount Pleasant. I don't know which one but Hester Walker said that her brother's girlfriend stays at a hotel on the Mount when she's in Liverpool. When she comes back from London, she's going to ask her if she's knows the proprietors whose name is Mc-Donald.'

'This has nothing to do with this girlfriend,' said Lynne, who had gained some of her colour. 'And I've never met any Americans called Anderson and that's the truth. Have you had anything to eat, Bobby?'

'No,' she replied, determined not to allow her mother to change the subject. She was sure Lynne was hiding something from her. 'You mightn't have met him but you recognized his name.'

'Why d'you say that?' snapped Lynne.

'Because of your reaction! I'm not daft, Mam. He's looking for you and me. Why?'

'I don't know,' said Lynne, sounding huffy. 'I'm not clairvoyant.'

'I know you're not, but why are you getting so

annoyed? He must be on the level if he's giving out his name. And I haven't forgotten seeing a man hanging about outside school. How would he know not only that I was a pupil there but that you'd attended the same school if someone who knew of us hadn't told him?'

Nan cleared her throat noisily. 'I think you should tell Roberta the truth.'

'Nan, don't,' Lynne appealed, stretching out a hand to her.

Roberta's gaze darted from one to the other and her stomach seemed to tie itself into a bow. 'So I'm ... I'm right! There is something ... something you've been keeping from me,' she said. 'Is ... is this Yank my ... my father?'

'Good God, no!' cried Lynne, starting to her feet. 'I thought you were good at arithmetic!' She folded her arms across her chest and began to pace the floor.

Roberta watched her. 'Sorry! But what did Nan mean about telling me the truth?'

An agitated Lynne shot a look at Nan, who said, 'Sorry, love, but you knew it would come to this one day.'

Roberta's heart was thudding and her knees were trembling. 'Will you tell me what this is all about? Is it that you're not my mother?' she asked through stiff lips.

'Don't be daft! Of course I'm your mother!' cried Lynne, her eyebrows snapping together. 'I could have had you adopted but I fought against it. You ask Nan!'

A bewildered Roberta looked at her elderly relative. 'What's she trying to tell me, Nan?'

'That she wasn't married to your dad when she gave birth to you,' said Nan.

Roberta could not speak for several moments. What was her Nan saying – that she was illegitimate? She needed air and breathed in deeply, watching her mother all the time.

'There was a war on,' whispered Lynne.

'But ... but you married him afterwards, didn't you? I mean, you're not a Graham like Nan but a Donegan and so am I,' said Roberta.

Tears swam in Lynne's eyes. 'He ... he was killed before we could be married.'

'But ... but you're a widow!'

'No, I'm not,' said Lynne fiercely. 'I took your father's name because I thought we both had a right to it.'

Roberta sat down abruptly. Her head was spinning with so many differing thoughts that she felt giddy and sick. None of them spoke for what seemed an age and then the world seemed to steady for Roberta. 'But you loved him and he loved you?' she asked.

'Of course!' cried Lynne. 'But we were both very young! I was only seventeen when you were born and by then Robert had been killed.'

'Only seventeen,' muttered Roberta. 'That's only four years older than I am now!'

'Exactly,' said Lynne. 'And I wouldn't recommend getting into trouble at that age, love.' She patted her daughter's knee. 'Although I wouldn't swap you for all the tea in China.'

Roberta blinked back tears and was silent for a long time while her mother and great-grandmother watched her anxiously. Then she took a

101

shuddering breath. 'What has this Yank to do with us then?' she demanded.

'Tell her the rest, Lynne, love!' urged Nan.

Lynne flashed her an exasperated look. 'But we don't know for certain that it's true.'

'Tell her!' ordered Nan.

'Bloody hell, Nan! I wish you'd give me a minute to gather my thoughts,' said Lynne, pushing back a hank of auburn hair.

Roberta waited impatiently.

Lynne sighed. 'Stuart Anderson could have been sent by your grandmother.'

'My grandmother!'

'My mother, your grandmother Graham! She threw me out when I told her I was having a baby.'

'That's horrible!' cried Roberta, her expression fierce. 'It's a good job you had Nan.'

'Nan was on her travels, so you were born in a charitable home for unmarried mothers in Cheshire,' said Lynne.

'So that's what you meant when you spoke about having me adopted?'

Lynne nodded. 'I wanted to keep you and so did most of the mothers who gave birth to healthy babies who were in there. Though I remember one girl who seemed glad to be rid of her baby. Fortunately for me Nan turned up in the nick of time and so I was able to leave the home, carrying you in my arms.' Lynne eased the lump in her throat. 'You and Nan helped me get through the trauma of losing Robert,' she said huskily.

Roberta took a deep breath. 'You really loved

him.'

'I've told you so,' said Lynne, shaking her head at her daughter. 'Being wartime there were probably thousands of women in the same dilemma. We all had to find different ways of dealing with it.'

'There's no need for you to feel ashamed, Bobby, love,' said Nan breathlessly. 'You or your mother! She could have had you adopted as she said but the pair of us found a way around that and we've managed, and although it's been difficult at times, we have no regrets,' she wheezed. 'You brought a lot of love with you.'

'I'm ... I'm not ashamed,' said Roberta, tears sparkling on her eyelashes. 'I ... I feel proud of the pair of you.' She tilted her chin.

'No one else need know you're illegitimate,' said Lynne, touching her daughter's knee.

'But what about the Yank? He's looking for Lynne Graham and her daughter and you seem to think he's connected to your mother,' said Roberta. 'Obviously he doesn't know you've taken the name Donegan? Did your mother know that my father had been killed?'

'Oh, yes! I told her but it made no difference. She went on to marry a Yank and sailed off to America! I can't believe she's had a change of heart after all this time,' said Lynne, glancing at Nan. 'So perhaps we'd be best forgetting all about her and this Stuart Anderson.' She wiped her damp face with the back of her hand. 'Now let's have some tea.'

'No, Mum, you can't just leave it like that,' cried Roberta.

'Yes, I can,' said Lynne, rearing her head. 'I want nothing to do with my mother. Now I don't want to hear any more about it from you,' she added firmly.

Roberta opened her mouth to protest but then closed it. There was no point in arguing with her mother right now. They'd all had a shock and needed to calm down.

As Roberta helped set the table for the evening meal, her head still buzzed with the events of the day. If she had not decided to go to the library straight from school and called in at the coffee bar, she would have been none the wiser about the Yank and her own status. Illegitimate! Her stomach trembled as she imagined the younger Lynne's panic at finding herself *in trouble*. She could not picture herself in such a situation but guessed if it were to happen, then her mother would not be in a position to reject her. Fancy having your own mother do so, she thought, feeling hurt for Lynne. Roberta thought about how fortunate she was that her mother had wanted her and had been able to keep her and felt sorry for all those mothers and babies who had not been so fortunate.

Seven

'Nick!' called Kenneth Rogers.

The youth lifted his fair head from the books spread out on the table and hesitated before standing up and heading for the top of the stairs. 'D'you want something, Dad?'

'Of course I do, son, otherwise I wouldn't be shouting you.'

'It's just that I'm doing my homework.'

'Leave it for a moment. I won't keep you long. I just need your help to move these planks of wood that came in this afternoon. A customer could fall over them where they are and injure themselves.'

'Coming!' shouted Nick, and clattered down the stairs to the shop below.

Kenneth looked relieved as Nick seized hold of the end of one of the smoothly planed planks of pinewood and between them they carried it into the storeroom behind the shop. They repeated the action several times before the man with greying hair eased his back and then sat down on a chair, stifling a yawn. 'Will you check whether all the doors are bolted top and bottom?' he asked.

'Sure,' said Nick, thinking he no longer needed a chair to stand on to do the job. He had grown three inches in the past few months and was now

105

taller than Kenneth. The youth was made up about that because his dad had told him that his nickname had been Titch when he was at school and he had been bullied.

There were some big lads at the Liverpool's Boy's Institute where Nick was a pupil and the thought of having to run the gauntlet of passing them in the playground or on the way there and back to school used to fill him with dread. Then he had met Chris who was two years older than him and who started coming into the shop to buy a pound of nails, a length of two by four, or a bag of cement, sand or plaster for his father who was a DIY enthusiast. The youths had struck up a friendship and Nick was no longer as wary of the bigger lads as he used to be and tried to give as good as he got.

Kenneth smiled at Nick as he returned from bolting the doors. 'Now how about putting the kettle on for a nice cup of tea?' said the man, getting slowly to his feet.

Nick nodded, thinking that his father had aged since his mother, Muriel, had died eighteen months ago. It was a bloody shame, just when life seemed to be going so well for them. She had been so proud when Nick had passed the eleven-plus and found real pleasure in buying his school uniform. He remembered her saying, 'I can just see you being a doctor or a teacher one day.' He felt that tightness in his throat and chest whenever he thought of her but at least he and his father had both survived their second Christmas without her. Although it would have been better if Uncle Dennis hadn't turned up on the day for the turkey and all the trimmings. But being family meant they had to put up with him, since the Rogers brothers' father had died two years after their mother.

If Muriel had been alive, Dennis wouldn't have got his foot through the door because they had never got on. She had considered her brother-in-law selfish and spoilt and had told him so to his face. In response he'd said that she was one to talk, adding that she lived in cloud cuckoo land. Nick could not understand why he had said that to her because he'd always considered his mother one of the most sensible people he knew. As for his uncle, he loathed him. Even when Nick was a small lad, Dennis had attempted to undermine his confidence. When he had made little gifts of wood for his grandparents or taken the drawings he had done in school to show them, Dennis always found fault with them. When Nick passed the eleven-plus, his uncle had told him not to get above himself and that it had been a fluke him passing the examination.

Nick had tried to ignore him but it was not easy because he also made comments about Nick being double-jointed, calling him a freak. He could only be thankful that his uncle lived in Wales, although for how much longer was a question that kept rearing its head. Recently Kenneth, who was the older brother, had talked about the need to sell the house in Flintshire where Dennis still lived.

Nick sighed as he spooned tea from the wooden caddy he had made for his mother into the fat-bellied brown teapot that Muriel had used every day until the last week of her illness. If only she was still alive. After she had died, Kenneth had been wont to say *At least she didn't suffer too long.* But how long was too long to suffer? Nick wondered, taking two coronation mugs out of the cupboard as he heard Kenneth climbing the stairs.

When his father entered the kitchen, Nick thought, not for the first time, how they did not look a bit alike. He remembered asking his mother whether he took after her side of the family. She had hesitated and then nodded, telling him that she had been blonde when she was a girl but her hair had darkened as she grew older. The fact that her eyes were blue and Nick's brown might be thought unusual with his hair being fair but, she had added, her Uncle Fred who had been killed in the Great War had been just the same.

Then there was Nick being double-jointed. It had to be a throwback to her grandfather who had been an acrobat in the circus. He smiled, remembering how his mother had always loved Bertram Mill's circus pitching the big top in Newsham Park, and the pair of them had always gone together. For weeks afterwards Nick had wanted to be a daring young man on a flying trapeze. He had grown out of that but he was still good at gymnastics.

'How about a couple of rounds of toast, beans and sausages for supper?' suggested Kenneth, breathing heavily as he sat down.

Nick rested a hand on the well-scrubbed table.

'That suits me, Dad. I might as well do it now and finish my homework later.'

'If you're sure you don't mind,' said Kenneth earnestly. 'I have some paperwork to do.'

As Nick took the frying pan from a cupboard along with a saucepan, he thought how much easier life had been when they had lived in the semi-detached house in West Derby, but after his mother had died, Kenneth had decided to sell the house and move into the rooms over his hardware shop on Prescot Road. He had said it would be more convenient. Nick had not argued, guessing that the real reason was because Kenneth could no longer bear living in the house without Muriel. Sometimes Nick thought it would have been better if they had stayed there because there were so many happy memories tied to that house but his father had seemed unable to see that.

As they sat down to their simple meal, Kenneth said, 'I was thinking now the snow has gone that we should visit your Uncle Dennis instead of him coming here so often.'

Nick's fair head shot up. 'Do we have to?'

Kenneth nodded. 'I have important matters to discuss with him concerning the house and there's a particular piece of furniture that Father left me I want to make sure he hasn't sold.'

Nick searched for an excuse. 'I've school work to do, Dad. I need to prepare for exams.'

Kenneth pointed his fork at him. 'No excuses! I want your company. You haven't visited the house since your grandfather's funeral. I want my share of that house. Our Dennis thinks he can go on hogging it but I'm not going to allow it.

I'm the eldest and he should listen to me. But does he? Does he, hell!' He paused. 'But I take your point, we won't go just yet. We'll wait until the Easter school holidays. The traffic will be murder on the bank holiday Monday, so we'll go the following Wednesday afternoon. Is that clear, son?'

'Yes, it's clear,' muttered Nick, making a sausage butty. 'Although I still don't see why I have to go with you. He hates me.'

'You're imagining it.'

Nick knew he wasn't imagining it. 'He's always poking his nose in my business, too,' he said beneath his breath.

Kenneth stared at him. 'He's just interested because he's got no children himself.'

Nick did not believe that, and was convinced that his uncle was trying to catch him out doing something so he could complain to Kenneth about it. 'Why d'you need me?'

'I need your help to carry that piece of furniture I mentioned.'

Nick looked surprised. 'Aren't we going in the van?'

Kenneth hesitated. 'We are but I can't lift it in and out on my own.'

Nick thought that Dennis could help Kenneth put it into the van and he'd be here to help him lift it out. He came to the conclusion that his father was making excuses because he really did want his company and so he resigned himself to accompanying him to Wales in a few weeks' time.

'I'd also appreciate your help in the shop

during the Easter holidays, not just Saturday mornings,' added Kenneth. 'It'll be yours when I go.'

The words *go where?* sprang to Nick's lips but he kept silent. This was not the first time his father had mentioned his passing away since he had become a widower. Sometimes it was almost as if he couldn't wait to join Muriel. That thought bothered Nick because although it was true that he'd never been as close to his father as he had to his mother, they had managed to rub along quite well.

He really hoped that his father had plenty of years in him yet, although Nick could see the day when they would not agree about his future. Kenneth was set on Nick following in his foot-steps and there was no way Nick wanted to spend his life working in the hardware shop. He might enjoy woodwork but he longed to do something much more challenging. What that something was he didn't know yet. He was fond of his father and respected him for being a hard worker but Nick could not forget his mother nurturing ambitious plans for him. If she were here now she'd be telling Kenneth that it was a waste of their son's education if all he was going to do with his life was to work in a hardware shop. She and Nick would have ganged up on Kenneth and eventually he would have caved in. As it was, Nick knew that he was going to have a struggle to do what he wanted in life and it was going to be that much more difficult than when his mother had been alive because his uncle was bound to put his oar in.

Eight

Dorothy gathered together her overnight bag and the shopping she had done while in London. In a few minutes the train would terminate at Lime Street. She was tired and doubted Sam would be there to meet her. She had telephoned the Walker household earlier in the day but he hadn't been there and, unable to make sense of anything Ethel said, she wasn't at all sure the old woman had understood her message for Sam.

He would not be in the best of moods, anyway, when they met, what with her having spent more time down south than she had originally planned. As well as seeing her agent and having the audition – which had gone brilliantly – she had taken time out to see old friends. She was going to tell Sam that she had only been told yesterday that she had been given the part and that was why she had stayed in London longer. At least it should please him that she would be able to attend Hester's wedding because filming would most likely not start for another two months.

The train came out of the tunnel and ran into the station. Even before it came to a halt, she was making her way to the nearest door. When she arrived at the hotel she was greeted warmly by Kathy, who informed her that Mr Anderson

112

had returned that day, too.

'He'll soon be off to London for a couple of days,' said Kathy, smiling. 'Then it's the Continent, taking in France, Italy and Greece. He was hoping to hear about the mother and daughter he's been looking for when he got back but there's been no phone call for him.'

'I was just about to ask if there had been any for me,' said Dorothy.

Kathy shook her head. 'I'm afraid not. How did the audition go?'

Dorothy's face lit up and she told her all her news before going upstairs to change. Some of her excitement evaporated as she thought of Sam. She was disappointed he had not telephoned to see if she was back and was filled with a sense of foreboding. What if Sam was so furious with her that he didn't wish to have anything more to do with her? No, she couldn't believe that. He had said he loved her and he had come round after some persuasion to her making the documentary set in Liverpool. Surely she could persuade him to see the positive aspects of her having won this film role? But what to do right now? Should she ring the Walker household again? What if he was there and didn't want to speak to her? Perhaps she should change and go to the house and try to talk to him. And if he wasn't there, then maybe Hester or Jeanette would be home and she could talk to them about Sam and try to gauge his feelings before she saw him. First, she had better dolly herself up.

She wasted no time claiming the bathroom and having a bath and then she took her time choosing what to wear, deciding on a frock she had bought in Bond Street. It was of green and orange jersey silk with a boat neck, three-quarter sleeves and floaty skirt.

Would he notice the dress was new? If so she could always tell him that she had bought it with Hester's wedding in mind and was trying it out. Perhaps it was a bit too summery and posh for just a visit to the Walker household, but she could put on a warm coat and it would make her feel more confident. She fixed her hair and applied fresh make-up. She reckoned that she was going to have to look really alluring to calm Sam down when she told him her news. Surely when he heard of the money she would be earning, he would be glad for her? She could tell him that part of it could go towards the cost of their wedding. The rest would go to making her documentary.

To Dorothy's relief the door was opened by Hester. 'So you're back at last,' she said.

'Don't sound like that!' groaned Dorothy. 'Is he home?'

'No, he isn't. You'd best come in.'

Dorothy stepped over the threshold and Hester closed the door behind her. 'You should have rung.'

'I did earlier in the day!' cried Dorothy, following Hester up the lobby. 'Your Aunt Ethel answered but I confess she sounded confused. Even so I hoped she would have told you and Sam.'

'No, she didn't. As for Sam, he's really busy at the moment but you can be sure I'll let him know as soon as I see him that you're back,' said Hester. 'Here, let me help you off with your coat.'

Dorothy thanked her and they went into the sitting room where a fire was blazing away and the television was on. Ethel was sitting in an easy chair, toasting her toes on the hearth and gazing at the tiny black and white screen.

'You've got a television!' cried Dorothy.

Hester smiled. 'My idea. I persuaded the whole family that we should have one and could afford it if we all shared the rental costs.'

'Even your great-aunt Ethel?'

'I just told her to hand over her purse and she did.'

'You amaze me,' said Dorothy.

'It amazed me, too, because she's always been tight-fisted, but she's getting that way she doesn't know what money is.'

'Poor old soul,' murmured Dorothy.

'Yes, it is a bit sad seeing her like this but I don't really want the old Ethel back. She could be a right so-and-so,' murmured Hester.

Dorothy thought that perhaps she should try and start up a conversation with the old woman. 'Mind you don't get chilblains having your feet too close to the fire, Ethel,' she said.

Ethel ignored her.

'She's becoming very forgetful and muddled but she loves the television,' said Hester. 'Cup of tea?'

'Yes, if you haven't anything stronger,' said Dorothy, sitting on the sofa.

'Sorry.'

'That's OK. I can do without.'

'In need of Dutch courage?' asked Hester, going into the kitchen.

Dorothy followed her. 'I knew Sam would be angry with me but I had no choice.'

'It's your business, not mine,' said Hester, crossing back and forth between the larder and the cooker.

Dorothy leaned against the table. 'I couldn't turn the part down. It's brilliant and so well paid.'

'I'm not saying anything,' said Hester hastily. 'But you know what he's like. He sees himself as the breadwinner.' She faced Dorothy. 'Have you had anything to eat?'

'No! I just washed and changed and came straight here.'

'I'll fry you egg and bacon,' said Hester.

'Thanks,' said Dorothy gratefully.

Hester smiled. 'That's a lovely dress you're wearing. Buy it in London?'

'Where else! I hope Sam likes it. I thought it would do for your wedding. How are the arrangements coming along?'

'Fine. I've been getting loads of ideas from TV programmes about the Easter bride and home-making.' Hester hummed the Wedding March as she put the frying pan on the stove. 'And I've found myself a dressmaker!'

Dorothy's eyes widened. 'I thought you were considering ready-made.'

'Changed my mind. She's really good. I'll be taking our Jeanette along to see her this week to be measured up for her bridesmaid's dress and to choose the material.' Hester melted a knob of lard and then took out two rashers of bacon and put them in the frying pan. 'So, will you still be here for my wedding?'

'Of course I will!' said Dorothy positively. 'Haven't I just told you I bought this dress with your wedding in mind? I wouldn't miss it for the world.'

'When does filming start?'

'Well after Easter,' said Dorothy. 'Part of it is to be shot on location in Italy.'

Hester nearly dropped an egg. 'You're going abroad!'

Dorothy giggled. 'That's where Italy is.' At that moment the kettle began to boil so she moved it off the hob and made a pot of tea.

'Thanks,' said Hester. 'You'd better make Aunt Ethel a cuppa, as well.'

'OK! I'm just so excited.' Her eyes sparkled. 'You must know how I feel, Hester. You enjoy your job.'

Hester glanced up from the frying pan. 'I wouldn't argue but if I had to choose between the job and Ally, then I'd choose him.'

Dorothy's expression sobered. 'Are you getting at me?'

'No, it's your life. As long as you know what you're doing and it doesn't all blow up in your face.' She put down the egg and turned the bacon over which spat out fat, causing her to lick her hand where it landed.

'You think I'm risking what I have with Sam to make this film,' said Dorothy, frowning.

Hester said, 'Aren't you? You know what he's

117

like.'

'Yes, and he knows what I'm like,' said Dorothy firmly. 'If he loves me, he'll want me to be happy.'

'That works two ways.' Hester sighed.

'I really want to go to Italy and he could take a week's holiday and spend it with me over there.'

'Maybe,' said Hester, forking the bacon on to a plate. 'I know someone else going to Italy this year.'

'Who?'

'Betty Booth, my friend Emma's half-sister.'

'Emma whose cottage you're renting?'

Hester nodded.

'I know someone going to Italy, too. An American who's staying at the Lynton.' Dorothy poured tea and sugared all three cups.

Hester paused before breaking the egg into the frying pan. 'Name wouldn't be Stuart Anderson, would it?'

Dorothy looked startled. 'How have you heard of him?'

Hester smiled. 'It's a long story. I was going to ask you the name of the proprietors of your hotel. Whether it was McDonald and, if not, could you ask if they knew anyone of that name in the hotel business on Mount Pleasant.'

'Well, you have your answer,' said Dorothy, smiling.

'So, what's he like?'

'He seems a nice bloke. He's just returned from Scotland.'

'Well, when you return to the hotel this evening, tell him that help is at hand.'

118

Dorothy stared at her. 'What d'you mean?'

'He's been looking for a mother and daughter and I think the mother is my dressmaker.'

'You're joking!'

'Cross my heart! I'll get in touch with her in the morning,' said Hester. 'You can tell him that.'

'Can't you give me her address?'

'No, I have to speak to her first,' murmured Hester. 'Now tell me what you want me to say to Sam if he doesn't get in until after you've gone?'

'That I'm really sorry I've missed him and give him a kiss for me and ask him to ring me at the Lynton,' said Dorothy.

So with that agreed, she ate the meal Hester had cooked for her. They discussed weddings, London fashions and films. Sam still had not arrived home two hours later so Dorothy left.

Hester had been impatient for her to go because she had decided that despite the lateness of the hour, she would visit Lynne that evening. She wasted no time doing so but the door was not answered immediately. Eventually, though, a harassed-looking Lynne opened it. 'Hester! What are you doing here?'

'Sorry to disturb you at this time of night,' said Hester, 'but there's a couple of things I need to say to you.'

'Is this to do with the material for your wedding dress?' asked Lynne, her eyelids drooping. 'Because I've already bought the fabric you've chosen and I also have some samples for your sister's dress. I was going to drop a note through your letterbox to ask the two of you to call in

119

tomorrow evening. I'd like to check your measurements again before I start cutting.'

'That's fine. I'll come about seven,' said Hester gratefully. 'But the main reason I called was to tell you that Stuart Anderson is staying at the Lynton Hotel. I'm sure your daughter told you about the conversation we had at Betty's flat, so I thought you might be interested.'

'Yes, I ... I see,' said Lynne slowly. 'Thanks for letting me know.'

'My pleasure,' said Hester, smiling. 'My brother's girlfriend, Dorothy, told me that he's a nice fella. I wouldn't put off speaking to him, if I was you. He'll be off to Europe any day now. Goodnight!'

Nine

Lynne closed the door and went back upstairs to her grandmother's bedroom. 'Who was that at the front door?' asked Nan.

'Hester Walker, whom I'm making the wedding dress for,' she said, toying with her fingers. 'She told me the name of the hotel where Stuart Anderson is staying.'

'So what are you going to do?' asked Nan. 'If you don't go and see him, you'll never know why he was trying to find you.'

'No, I won't,' murmured Lynne, gazing into the distance. 'Unless...'

'Unless what?' asked Nan.

'Nothing,' sighed Lynne, kissing her grandmother and wishing her a good night's sleep. As she was about to leave the room, she added, 'Not a word of this to Bobby.'

The following morning after Roberta had left for school and Lynne had left Nan tacking the hems of a couple of skirts for a woman in the next street, she caught a bus into town, still in a state of indecision. She had decided long ago that she was well rid of her mother, so why allow herself to be persuaded to find out whether it was her mother who had sent this Stuart Anderson?

She found the Lynton, almost opposite the YMCA building. As she stood at the bottom of the steps looking up at the shiny brass plaque next to the door, she wondered what if her mother wanted to see her and Bobby? The very idea made her feel churned up inside and she almost turned tail and ran. Then she told herself not to be so cowardly. Nobody could force her to do what she didn't want to do. She tried the door and found it led into a vestibule. The inner door, which was half glass, was locked but there was an electric bell in the door frame. She pressed it and a few moments later she heard hurrying footsteps. Through the glass she could see a woman coming towards her.

'Can I help you?' she asked on opening the door.

'Are you the proprietor?' asked Lynne.

'Yes, I'm Kathy McDonald. Are you wanting a room?'

'No, but may I speak to you for a moment?'

'Certainly. Would you like to come into the lounge?'

Lynne followed her into a room to the right of the hall.

'Please sit down,' said Kathy. 'You look worried. How can I help you?'

Lynne took a deep breath. 'I believe you have a Mr Anderson staying here.'

'That's right.' Kathy stared at her. 'You wouldn't be the woman he's looking for, would you?'

Lynne hesitated. 'It's possible. Is he available?'

'I'm afraid not.'

'Oh!' After building herself up to face him, Lynne felt deflated. 'I shouldn't have come. I told myself that I wasn't going to have anything to do with her. Forget I was here.' She stood up and made for the door.

'Wait!' cried Kathy. 'He's a very nice man. Why don't you leave your phone number and I'll have him ring you.'

'I don't have a telephone,' said Lynne, facing her.

For a moment the proprietor was silent, then she said, 'Listen, have a coffee with me? Mr Anderson has gone for a walk – to clear his head, he said, and verify his travel arrangements, so he's unlikely to be back just yet.'

Lynne hesitated and gripped her hands tightly in front of her. 'I wish I knew what was best to do. Has he spoken to you about why he wants to find me and my daughter?'

122

'I think that would be best coming from him. He was here in 'forty-eight at Burtonwood air base, you know.' She paused. 'I'll make us some coffee and you can think about what you'd like me to say to him when he returns – that's if you really don't want to see him.'

She left the room, leaving Lynne twiddling her thumbs and wondering whether to get out of there while she had the opportunity. She got as far as the reception when she heard the doorbell ringing. Thinking it could be Stuart Anderson returning, she felt herself panicking and then Nan's voice in her head told her not to be such a ninny. She took a deep breath and went and opened the vestibule door.

A man stepped into the hall and she stumbled backwards. His hand shot out and he grabbed her arm and steadied her. 'Are you OK?' he asked.

Brown eyes gazed into hers from what seemed a great height and she felt really odd. Flustered, she stammered, 'I–I'm so–sorry. I–I didn't ex-pect you to enter so swiftly.'

'There's no need to apologize,' he said, smil-ing. 'You're not Mrs McDonald, so you must be one of the guests.'

'No, I'm not,' she said. 'Are ... are you?'

'No, I'm picking someone up.'

'Then you're a taxi driver?' She paused. 'No, that can't be right.'

He grinned. 'Why not? I could be a chauffeur with a Rolls Royce outside waiting to whisk someone off to Knowsley Hall to have lunch with Lord Derby for all you know.'

She smiled. 'If you drove a Rolls, I don't think you'd be picking up a guest from here. More likely the Adelphi.'

'You're right, of course! I was just teasing you.'

Lynne smiled. *What a nice man*, she thought. *Handsome, too, and a nice voice.* But not the American accent she'd been expecting. 'I take it that you're not Stuart Anderson?'

'No, Sam Walker.'

'Oh!' Her jaw dropped and then she cleared her throat. 'You're Hester's brother!'

He looked surprised. 'That's right. Who are you?'

'I'm the dressmaker! Hester's dressmaker, I mean,' she added hastily.

'What are you doing here? Hester's visiting you this evening, isn't she?' he said, taking in her appearance with one sweeping glance from head to toe.

Having put on her best clothes, Lynne hoped he hadn't found her wanting and then remembered he had a girlfriend and her spirits drooped.

At that moment the baize door that led to the kitchen opened and Kathy McDonald came through, carrying a tray. She paused and then came forward. 'Mr Walker, can I help you?'

Sam removed his trilby. 'I've come to see Dorothy.'

'I think she's up in her room. I'll just take this through into the lounge and then I'll go and fetch her,' said Kathy.

'I was hoping to speak to her privately,' said Sam in a low voice.

She stared at him. 'We don't allow male visitors in the bedrooms, Mr Walker, so if you wish to have a private conversation you'll have to use the dining room as I'm serving coffee in the lounge to this lady here.'

Lynne had never been called a lady in her life before and she had to smile. 'Mrs Donegan,' she said. 'Mrs Lynne Donegan. Perhaps I can take the tray while you fetch Mr Walker's friend.'

Kathy handed the tray to her and then hurried upstairs.

'I think I might have shocked you both,' murmured Sam. 'I should have assured her that my intentions are strictly honourable.'

'It's really none of my business,' said Lynne, flashing him a smile and carrying the tray into the lounge where she set it down on a coffee table. She did not realize until she was seated that he had followed her into the room.

'I wouldn't mind a cup of coffee,' he said, pulling up a chair and sitting, facing her. 'This Stuart Anderson. I have a feeling my sister has mentioned him but I was a bit distracted. I've heard your name, too. Wasn't your daughter being followed a few weeks ago?'

For a few moments she had forgotten he was a policeman. 'That's right. I thought it was possible that Mr Anderson was the man following her.'

'Do you know why?' Sam's brown eyes were intensely curious.

She hesitated.

'You're thinking it hasn't anything to do with me,' said Sam, picking up the coffee pot and

125

beginning to pour. 'How d'you like yours, black or white?'

'I seldom drink coffee.'

'White and with sugar then,' he said, pushing the basin containing sugar cubes towards her.

She murmured her thanks and thought the proprietor was going to have to fetch another cup. She dropped in four sugar lumps and sipped her coffee before saying, 'It's possible that he's come from my mother. She married a Yank but we lost touch.'

'So he's come to give you news of your mother? Are you glad about that?'

She was silent, watching as he reached for a biscuit. 'I haven't spoken to my mother since 1941,' she said abruptly. 'Not once has she tried to find out how we were getting on.'

'You found that hard?'

She felt tears well in her eyes and now she was wishing he would go away. Why had she told him that? Probably because he was a policeman and used to giving criminals the third degree, dragging information out of them that they'd rather keep to themselves.

'Sam!'

The voice startled them both and instantly he put down his cup and rose to his feet. 'Dorothy!'

Lynne gazed at the attractive blonde standing in the lounge doorway with a smile pinned on her scarlet lips. Then she saw the smile die.

'Who's this, Sam?' asked Dorothy.

'Mrs Donegan, Hester's dressmaker. She's here to see Stuart Anderson.'

Dorothy took a deep breath. 'Sam, perhaps we

should go out and eat somewhere to have our little talk, which means I need to go back to my room and get my coat and hat.' She hurried back upstairs before he could say anything.

Her rudeness made Lynne feel uncomfortable.

'More coffee?' asked Kathy, breaking the silence.

Lynne shook her head. 'No thank you.

'I should have introduced you and Dorothy properly,' said Sam.

'It doesn't matter,' said Lynne lightly. 'My grandmother used to work in the theatre as a dresser and for a short while after my daughter was born, we both travelled with her.'

'You're saying you're used to the odd ways of actresses?' said Sam.

She smiled and stood up, facing the proprietor. 'I must go. Please, Mrs McDonald, let me pay for the coffee?'

'I wouldn't hear of it,' she said firmly. 'But do you have to go before Mr Anderson returns?'

'I must. I have work to do.' Lynne took a card from her handbag and handed it to her. 'I'd appreciate it if you could give that to him. Tell him I'll be at home this evening. Thank you again for the coffee and your kindness.' She turned to Sam. 'Goodbye, Mr Walker, it was nice meeting you.' She left the hotel, almost wishing she had never come.

Ten

Dorothy felt light-headed, remembering she had forgotten what Hester said about her dressmaker possibly being the person Stuart Anderson was looking for. Why did it have to happen now? After all these years, to meet that girl Lynne again and for her not only to have a connection with the American, but also with Hester!

Yet surely if Lynne had recognized her then she would have made some comment? Not that Dorothy had given her time to speak. Hopefully she had not recognized her but if they happened to see each other again, then Lynne might begin to question whether they had met before. She wondered what the other woman was saying to Sam right now and whether it had been a mistake leaving them together the way she had.

She could feel a headache coming on, so took a couple of Aspro with a glass of water. She put on her new red coat with the black fur collar and a small neat black hat with a half veil. With a trembling hand she applied more lipstick. Then, taking a deep breath, she picked up her handbag and went downstairs.

Relief flooded through her because there was no sign of Lynne, only Sam standing in the lobby, looking rapt in thought. For once she

128

hoped he was thinking of a case: a series of robberies perhaps, or a juicy murder. She cleared her throat and he raised his eyes to where she hovered on the stairs.

'You look well, Sam,' she said, smiling.

'So do you. Obviously you enjoyed your time in London.' His tone was cool and he made no effort to walk over and swing her down from the stairs as he might have done once.

'I wish you'd been there, Sam.' Her lips quivered. 'I really missed you. I'd have liked to have introduced you to my agent and shown you London.' She walked over to him and kissed him but he did not respond and her heart sank.

'I'm not a great one for shopping,' he muttered. 'That's a new coat, isn't it?'

Her eyes widened. 'Sam, I have to dress smart, it goes with the job.'

'You're saying your public expect it of you,' said Sam, taking out a packet of cigarettes. 'Smoke?'

She hesitated and took one. 'Don't let's light up until we're out of here. Kathy McDonald is of a mind that the smoke impregnates the furnishings and colours the ceiling and paintwork.'

Sam put the packet of Players away. 'Let's go to the Philharmonic pub. I'm hungry and we can get something to eat there.'

'OK, it's not that far to walk in these heels.'

Sam glanced down at her black patent leather, high-heeled, open-toed shoes but made no comment as he opened the vestibule door and indicated that she go before him.

When they reached the pavement Sam lit their

129

cigarettes and she linked her arm through his and they smoked in silence as they walked in the direction of Hardman Street.

Only after they had finished their cigarettes did she say, 'Please, don't be angry with me, Sam. It was essential that I stayed in London. I wasn't just enjoying myself, you know!'

'So what were you doing that was work, besides the audition and discussing the part with your agent? Going to the theatre, shopping, seeing old friends?'

She knew that tone of voice and her fingers tightened on his arm. 'Believe me, Sam, one has to do these things. Liverpool is in the sticks when compared to London and I needed to hear all the gossip.'

'Lynne Donegan's grandmother used to be a theatrical dresser,' said Sam.

'Lynne Donegan, who's she?' asked Dorothy with feigned innocence.

'The woman you were rude to by charging back upstairs without saying a word. Hester's dressmaker! Don't pretend you didn't notice her. She certainly noticed you.'

'Most people do,' said Dorothy, sounding amused. 'But they can be so gushing.'

'I don't think she's the gushing type. If she stared, it's possible that she recognized you from years ago.'

Dorothy's heart seemed to jerk against her ribs. 'Did she say where?'

'I told you her grandmother was a dresser and Mrs Donegan and her daughter travelled with her,' said Sam.

'So possibly she saw me in some theatre or other,' said Dorothy, stretching up and kissing Sam to conceal her relief. 'Let's forget about her for now? You mustn't be cross about my getting this part, darling.'

'Darling!' murmured Sam, his eyes narrowing as he gazed down at her. 'You've never called me that before.'

'Well, you are my darling,' she retorted. 'And the money will come in really useful when we tie the knot, without you breaking the bank.'

'I'm not interested in your money,' said Sam. 'I can support both of us. I just want to know when you're going to give it up and settle down.'

She hesitated. 'I want to make this film and produce that documentary set in Liverpool. If you love me, surely that's not too much to ask for?'

'Two can play the love game,' he said, as they arrived outside the Philharmonic pub, a marvel of Victorian architecture. 'If you love me...' he began only to be interrupted.

'Miss Wilson, it's good to see you!'

Sam stared at the man who was blocking the entrance to the pub.

'Mr Anderson!' Dorothy's hand tightened on Sam's arm. 'I didn't expect to see you here!'

'Did you know this place used to be a gin palace?' said Stuart, jerking a thumb in the direction of the ornate facade of the public house.

'Who told you that?' she asked.

'The barman! He was filling me in on some of its history. I'm discovering different stuff about Liverpool from the last time I was here.' He grinned. 'I also dropped by at the coffee bar further along Hope Street which wasn't there at the time, too. No swell jukebox. I was hoping to talk to the waitress about the mother and daughter I'm trying to trace but she was at college.' He pulled a face. 'I should have thought of that.'

'You've just missed the mother, Mr Anderson. She was at your hotel,' said Sam.

'Darn it!' said Stuart.

'She's left her business card with Mrs Mc-Donald,' said Sam.

Instantly Stuart's expression brightened. 'I'd better get back there right away. Thanks, Mr...?'

'Walker! Sam Walker.'

The two men shook hands.

'It sure is a pleasure coming across you like this, Mr Walker,' said the American.

'Listen, Mr Anderson, is this about her mother?'

'Why d'you ask that? Has she mentioned my stepmother to you?'

'When she heard an American was looking for her, she considered it likely that it had to do with her mother.'

Stuart sighed heavily. 'It sure is grief to my father that he should only have learnt about Lynne's existence after Ellen was at death's door.'

'So her mother is dead?' Sam frowned.

Stuart nodded. 'I'd best say no more right now.'

'I understand.' Sam hesitated before saying, 'Tell me, Mr Anderson, what line of business are you in?'

'I'm an architect with my pa's company. I haven't long finished my training, what with having spent time in the air force. Pa wanted me to try and find Lynne and her daughter and ask them to come over to California,' said Stuart. 'Not straight away, mind. He also wanted me to make the most of my time this side of the Atlantic and spend some time in Europe, looking at the architecture and seeing what's being done to replace the buildings that were destroyed during the war.'

'That sounds interesting,' said Sam.

'I'm really looking forward to it, especially now I know I can send Pa the news that he's been waiting for.' Stuart smiled. 'I'd best be off now.' With a wave of the hand, he hurried away.

'Well, that was informative,' said Sam, pushing the pub door and holding it open for Dorothy.

'You can never forget you're a detective, can you?' said Dorothy with a sigh.

'I'm interested in people.' He gazed down at her with an unfathomable expression. 'You think there's something wrong with that? I thought getting to know about people is part of your line of work, too.'

'Yes, but...'

'But what? I haven't anything against the Yanks,' said Sam. 'They might have been overpaid, oversexed and over here but Dad's always said that we wouldn't have won the war without them.'

'Our country's up to its eyes in debt to them,' said Dorothy.

Sam did not argue. 'But they never dropped bombs on us and killed my girl,' he said, going on ahead and finding them a table.

Dorothy caught up with him and sat down in the chair he pulled out for her. 'You still think of Carol as *your girl*?' she asked.

'I was thinking of then. What are you having to drink? Gin and tonic?'

'I might as well, seeing as this used to be a gin palace,' she murmured.

'You always have a gin and tonic,' said Sam.

He returned shortly with their drinks and, after placing them on the table, excused himself. She presumed he was going to the men's lavatory which was supposed to be really something, designed at a time when it was mainly men who frequented this place. He was away longer than she liked and she began to feel on edge, thinking of Lynne and his conversation with Stuart Anderson. She drank her gin and tonic much too quickly and it was a relief when he returned, bearing a tray with two plates of steaming food.

'I hope you don't mind me not asking what you'd like?' he said, smiling. 'But I had to go into a different room for the food.'

'I would have liked to have been asked because I need to watch my weight but this looks good,' she said, feeling suddenly in a better mood because he was smiling at her in that way she always found so engaging.

They did not talk while they ate. Having gone through a war when food was in short supply and often tasteless, such a meal was to be savoured. Only when they had finished eating

134

did Dorothy ask, 'Do you ever talk about Carol to anyone else?'

'No.' He offered the packet of Players to her. 'I'm not really in touch with anyone else who knew her.' He paused to light her cigarette. 'Look, Dot, I didn't mean to hurt you, if that's what I did, when I referred to Carol as my girl. Those days are gone and now we've the chance of building up a good life, the two of us together, if that's what we both want. My difficulty is in not knowing for certain that it is what you want. This career move on your part...' He paused to light his own cigarette and inhaled before adding, 'There's our Hester and Jeanette both desperate to get married while you don't seem in any rush.' He sighed.

Dorothy felt enormously guilty and reached out to him. 'I'm sorry! Sometimes I don't understand what drives me, myself.' She covered his free hand with hers. 'I do want us to have a life together but there were years when we weren't in touch and I was building up my career. You have to admit, Sam, that you'd hate to give up your job and stay at home and do housework.'

He smiled and squeezed her hand. 'There's no argument about that.'

'I know but times are a-changing. Two wars have seen to that and thousands of women did men's jobs then and discovered they liked earning their own money and didn't want to stay at home, either alone or with the children.'

'Someone has to do it. You have to remember that I was brought up with a mother who was ailing all the time and couldn't cope with all that needed doing and so Great-aunt Ethel moved in. She took over and my life was hell.' His expression was grim. 'Can you blame me for wanting a wife who's a homemaker and who'd be a caring mother to my children?'

'I don't blame you, Sam, but as I said, a lot of women want more than that these days.'

'I realize that and it's why I'm being patient and letting you do your own thing before we get married,' said Sam.

She felt a spurt of anger. 'You're letting me? Well, that's really generous of you, darling.' She stubbed out her cigarette in the ash tray.

'You know what I mean,' said Sam harshly. 'I've had to accept you putting your career before me. It's not surprising that I'm feeling bloody frustrated.' He stubbed out his cigarette and stood up.

'Where are you going?' she whispered, aware of listening ears.

He rested his hands on the edge of the table. 'I'm going to the lav,' he murmured. 'Think about what I've said while I'm gone.'

Suddenly the remembrance of that afternoon when they'd had sex filled her thoughts and she grabbed his sleeve. 'Did you ever do it with Carol?' she whispered.

He did not pretend to misunderstand what she was talking about. 'She was saving herself for marriage,' he said beneath his breath.

'I should have done that instead of having sex with you,' said Dorothy with a wry smile. 'But I needed comforting and I couldn't resist you. You were very attractive even then, you know!'

'We took a terrible risk,' said Sam, meeting her gaze. 'Have you ever told anyone what we did that afternoon?'

'Of course not! It was our secret.'

For several moments they were both silent.

'Did that dressmaker talk to you about her fella?' asked Dorothy abruptly.

Sam blinked at her. 'What's she to do with this?'

'She's about our age and hasn't she a teenage daughter?'

'Did Hester tell you that?'

Dorothy nodded. 'We all thought there was no tomorrow during the war, just like in the song.'

Sam straightened up. 'I've been standing here long enough. I'll be back soon. Don't go away!'

She stared after him, thinking about his mention of being frustrated. He probably didn't give any thought to her being sexually frustrated, which she would be if there hadn't been a couple of other men in her life – not that she had ever gone all the way with them – and for her having been so set on succeeding in her career.

She sighed; she had to think of a way to bring him around so she could have her cake and eat it. She really wanted to do this film, and besides she was committed because she had signed a contract. What she hadn't told him was that the company also had the option of her appearing in another film if she made a good job of this role.

When Sam returned to the table with another gin and tonic for her and a coffee for himself, she said, 'I was just thinking.'

'I've been thinking too, but you go first,' said

137

Sam.

'I'll forget about making the documentary and we can get married earlier.' She waited for him to say *That's great!* but he just stared at her for several long seconds.

Then he said, 'You had your heart set on making the documentary about the women of Liverpool.'

She sighed. 'I know but your happiness is of more importance to me.'

'You really mean that?'

She nodded and waited and still he did not say the words she expected of him. He sipped his coffee and when the cup was empty, said, 'I'm going to have to go soon.'

Exasperated, she said, 'A case, is it? One nobody can solve but you?'

'That's right,' he said, his eyes gleaming. 'I'm determined to make inspector this year.'

'So it's all right for you to be ambitious but not me?' she blurted out.

Sam looked startled. 'Why are you saying that? It's you that's just made the decision not to make the documentary so we can be married sooner.' He hesitated. 'Could it be that you've something else in mind?'

Her heart seemed to flip over. *Surely he couldn't read her mind?* 'I don't know what you mean, Sam.' She adopted an injured tone.

He was silent but continued to stare at her intently and then said abruptly, 'I really am going to have to go.'

'I'll walk part of the way with you,' she said, getting to her feet.

They went outside.

'Why can't we just live in the moment?' she asked abruptly. 'I won't be starting filming until after Hester's wedding.'

He gazed down at her. 'I had been thinking that we could spend a couple of days away together.'

She smiled. 'You mean as Mr and Mrs Smith?'

He grinned. 'No, I didn't think you'd want to risk that when you've this film coming up. See how self-sacrificing I am? I was thinking more of a trip to Whalley where Hester and Ally are going to live after they're married. I've never been there and I'd like to see the cottage. I've been told it's lovely country round about.'

She was disappointed. 'You want to stay in the country? I'd prefer Blackpool.'

'I'd prefer you not to go swanning off on location to Italy. I think I deserve to choose the location for us having a break together if you're going to have what you want.'

She knew he had a point and so, reaching up, she stood on tiptoe and placed her arms around his neck. 'All right, we'll do what you want, darling Sam.' She kissed him.

Slowly his arms went round her waist and the kiss deepened. Then he released her abruptly. 'I'll wangle a couple of days off soon and we can take the car and have fun together.'

'What if it snows?'

'One can have fun in the snow.' He tilted her chin and kissed her lightly. 'I'll be in touch.'

'OK!' She watched him stride off down Hardman Street, thinking of two whole days in a country village and with little sign of spring.

139

Still, there would be opportunity for plenty of canoodling and perhaps Hester and Ally would be there and she got on with them both. One thing was for certain and that was that they were unlikely to bump into Lynne up there.

Eleven

Lynne could not settle. She was supposed to be working but had so far done little beyond hemming the two skirts on the sewing machine that Nan had tacked. She kept stopping and thinking, not only of Stuart Anderson and whether he had been given her card, but also of Hester's brother and the effect that he'd had on her. She had never really looked at another man in that way since Robert had been killed and so it really bothered her that she should find Sam Walker so attractive. Especially as he was dating that actress, Dorothy Wilson, who could knock socks off Lynne when it came to allure.

The sound of someone at the front door caused her to almost jump out of her skin. She broke a thread and swore silently before rising from her chair. Going over to the window, she lifted the bottom of the net curtain and peered out.

Standing outside on the step was a strange man. The fact that he was wearing a black trilby and a belted raincoat was enough for her to drop the curtain and sink on to a chair. She had not expected him so soon but there was nothing for it but for her to go to the door and let him in. After all he had come all the way from America to find her and Bobby. Taking several deep breaths and smoothing down her skirt and hair, she hurried to the front door.

For several moments both of them just stood there, staring at each other. Then a slow smile lifted the corners of Stuart's mouth and he said, 'You're like your mother.'

'Only in looks. We aren't a bit alike really,' she could not help saying.

'Well, I wouldn't know that, Lynne, this being the first time we've met.'

'Of course, you're right,' she said, feeling slightly embarrassed. 'Do come in.' She held the door wide. 'Although, I doubt this house is what you're used to.'

'I know why you say that,' he said, stepping over the threshold. 'You watch too many American movies.'

'You're telling me that America doesn't have everything bigger and better?'

'Nope, and you shouldn't be ashamed of where you come from. My grandpa was a first generation American. His pa came from Argyllshire from what was just a stone croft in the hills.'

'I'm not ashamed,' said Lynne, tilting her chin. 'May I take your coat and hat?'

'Thanks!' He took them off and handed them to her. Underneath he was wearing a Harris tweed suit in a heather mixture, a cream shirt and a beige and brown tartan tie. His hair was thick and wavy and she was reminded of a big friendly woolly dog.

'No kilt?' she said with a hint of humour.

'I admit I was tempted.' He chuckled and changed the subject. 'I was beginning to think I'd never set eyes on you. If it weren't for Betty at the coffee bar and your daughter...'

'Roberta,' said Lynne. 'I named her after her father. May I offer you a drink? Only tea, I'm afraid. Unless you like Camp coffee with chicory essence?'

'Camp coffee will be fine. I remember having it when I was over here after the war. You know it was a Scotsman who invented it?'

'Of course, it has a picture of one on the label.' She led him into the parlour. 'I think we'll talk in here. My grandmother is in the other room and she's asleep. If she wakes, then she'll keep interrupting while you're talking.' She waved him to a chair and excused herself.

She was back in a jiffy and they settled facing each other with cup in hand. She was surprised at how comfortable she felt in his company, despite feeling slightly apprehensive about what he had to tell her. 'Well?' she asked.

'I never expected to return to Liverpool,' he said after a hesitation, 'but Pa was set on finding you and your daughter.'

'Not my mother – is she dead?'

He nodded.

A tremor went through her and unexpectedly she felt a lump in her throat.

'Sorry, but I gather there was no love lost between you.'

She nodded.

From a pocket he took a photograph and handed it to her. 'Your mother married my father and this is them and me with my grandparents.'

Lynne gazed at a younger but recognizable Stuart with her mother, Ellen, who was smiling, a man who had a faint resemblance to Stuart and an elderly couple. They were posed against the backdrop of a white painted house with a garden that appeared to be full of flowers as well as several trees that she thought were orange trees.

'How did she die? Was she ill? She looks so well in this photograph.'

'No, she was mauled by a bear while she and Pa were camping in the Rockies.'

Lynne could not believe it and had an urge to laugh. 'I can't believe my mother went camping! She wasn't that kind of woman.'

'People change,' said Stuart, sipping his drink.

'I wouldn't deny that, but my mother – camping!' This time an incredulous laugh did break from Lynne. 'It's impossible that she could have been killed by a bear. What did it do? Hug her to death?' She clapped a hand to her mouth. 'I shouldn't have said that, what an awful thing to say!'

'You're in shock,' said Stuart, starting to his feet. 'Have you any brandy?'

She shook her head. 'I'm all right, honestly. Just allow me a few moments to take this in.'

They were both silent for what seemed an age and then Lynne said, 'Mother told you about the old school, I suppose, and that I was a pupil there?'

'She'd kept a photograph of when you were a

143

school girl.'

'She kept that photograph!' Lynne could scarcely believe it.

'Pa believes it was because she was so proud of you winning a place at her old school. Your name and that of the school and the date were written on the back of the photo. I brought it with me and then I misplaced it. I found it again when I was in Scotland. I'd used it as a marker in a book of maps.' He placed the photograph in question on the table in front of her. 'Pa was really shocked when he discovered she'd kept you and your daughter a secret from us all that time but he kept his feelings to himself because of the state she was in.' A shadow crossed Stuart's face. 'I was sorry when she died as she was kind and always interested in what I was up to. She told me that she'd always wanted a son.'

Lynne felt a once familiar ache inside her. 'I know! She told me that to my face. I don't think she realized how much it hurt me. Nevertheless, thank you for letting me know she kept my photograph.'

Silence.

Lynne smiled. 'I'm glad you went to the coffee bar and spoke to Betty Booth. My daughter really admires her. Fancies herself as a would-be artist and enjoys sketching people. I'd like her to be a teacher and earn a regular wage.'

He smiled. 'Pa would say that most parents want what's best for their children.'

'It's true. He sounds a sensible man, your father,' said Lynne.

Stuart nodded. 'He'd like to meet you and your

daughter.'

'Oh,' Lynne was taken aback. 'I don't think...'

'There's no rush for you to decide,' said Stuart hastily. 'I'll say no more on that score right now. I rather threw that at you.' He leaned forward. 'Tell me ... Miss Booth ... does she have family?'

'I don't know a lot about her,' said Lynne. 'I have a feeling my daughter told me that her father was killed in the war and that her mother is dead. She has her own flat and several cousins. I think one of them is married to a friend of Hester Walker. She's the one who told me where you were staying.'

Stuart stared at her. 'I think I met her brother today. I certainly met a Sam Walker who was with the actress Dorothy Wilson.'

'What do you think of her?' asked Lynne casually.

'She sure is a knockout and he's a good-looking guy.'

'Yes, one could say they make a perfect couple,' said Lynne brightly.

'Looks are only skin deep,' he said seriously.

'My mother always thought they were important.' She sighed. 'It feels strange knowing she's dead and that there's no chance of me ever seeing her again.'

'If Pa and I had known, I could have visited you and your daughter when I was over here in 'forty-eight,' said Stuart, reaching out and touching her hand. 'At least I can tell you that I do have something of hers for you.'

'What?' asked Lynne, surprised.

'A couple of pieces of your mother's jewellery

145

that Pa was determined you should have if I found you.'

'Really?'

From an inside pocket Stuart took a small pouch of soft damson leather and handed it to her. 'She brought them from England and wore them every Sunday. She told me they were Victorian and from the port where Dracula landed in England.'

Lynne wasted no time loosening the draw-strings of the pouch. When she tipped it upside down, out slid a necklace of silver and jet beads and matching silver and jet earrings. 'I remember these,' she said, a smile curving her lips. 'Mother told me they had been in the family for years. The stones were found on Whitby beach and it was there that they were made into jewellery.'

'She told me that it was famous for its jet.'

'Yes, it was very popular with Victorian women when they were in mourning. She didn't often wear them, just on Sundays and for my father's funeral.' Lynne let the beads run through her fingers, remembering her mother telling her that the jewellery was worth a bob or two. 'I really do appreciate you bringing these to me. You will thank your father for me, won't you?'

'You could thank him yourself. Pa would sure love to meet you and your daughter. He thought that if I found you that maybe you could come back with me after my trip to Europe when I return to the States in a few months' time?'

Lynne sighed and said regretfully, 'I'd like to and I'm sure Roberta would, too, but I couldn't

146

leave my grandmother and she's not well enough to travel so far.'

Stuart looked disappointed. 'Well, when the pair of you are able to come, let us know. You don't have to worry about the fare, we'll take care of that.'

Lynne was touched. 'That's kind of you but I couldn't accept.'

'Why not? We're family!'

She smiled. 'I appreciate you saying that. Shall we just wait and see? And could you do me a favour and allow me to keep this photo of you and your family and my mother, so I can show it to Roberta?'

'Sure you can. I have the negative back home. I can also let you have the photograph your mother kept of you.' He reached into a pocket and took it out.

Lynne placed the other photograph on the mantelpiece before taking the one of her that her mother had kept all these years. She gazed down at her younger self and tears pricked her eyes. 'I wish she had told you about us earlier and we had met in 'forty-eight. I wouldn't have carried so much hurt and anger around with me for so long,' she said unsteadily.

He squeezed her hand. 'Well, we've met now and Pa and I don't want to lose touch with you and Roberta.'

She nodded. 'If we can't visit your father just yet, we can write.'

He agreed and released her hand. 'And now I must go. I can see you're busy and I've a lot to do before leaving tomorrow. I'll send you a postcard from the different places I'll visit and God willing I'll be back in a couple of months.' He stood up and leaned down and kissed her cheek. 'Until the next time, Lynne.'

'Until the next time,' she echoed.

She walked with him to the front door and waved him off. Their time together might have been short but it had been good. Her mother's death had come as a shock but at least she could be grateful to her for not forgetting about her completely and for providing her with a step-brother. She had always wanted a brother and it might prove useful for her daughter having family connections in America. This evening she was going to a friend's house straight from school, so Lynne decided not to tell Nan about Stuart's visit until Roberta arrived home.

Stuart's visit was still playing over in Lynne's head when Hester arrived that evening. She led her into the front room and helped her off with her coat, asking after her sister.

'I'm sorry, but Jeanette couldn't make it.'

'What a shame.'

Hester agreed. 'She did give me her measurements if you wanted to buy the material and just allow a bit extra in case they're not perfect.'

Lynne nodded but decided she would do no cutting until she measured Jeanette herself.

'I spoke to our Sam,' said Hester, smiling. 'He told me that he bumped into you at the hotel. Then shortly after he and Dorothy met Stuart Anderson outside the Philharmonic pub and told him about seeing you. What I want to know is whether the Yank came to visit you?'

Lynne wondered what else Sam had told his sister about her but did not ask, telling her instead about Stuart's visit as she took out her tape measure.

Hester's eyes widened. 'Goodness me! Perhaps your mother was once a girl guide and went camping when she was younger.'

'She never mentioned it. Anyway, she wouldn't have been taught what to do if she confronted a bear in the wild.' Lynne shuddered. 'When you think we regard bears as cuddly.'

'I know. Our Jeanette loved her teddy bear.' Hester held out her arms so Lynne could measure her bust.

Lynne continued with her story and Hester marvelled. 'Such generosity! It's a pity your mother didn't think of inviting you to California, all expenses paid. She might not have gone camping.'

Lynne giggled, although she knew that really what had happened wasn't the least bit funny. It must be nerves making her behave the way she was. 'Poor mother and my poor stepfather! Anyway, let's stick to the matter in hand. You've a good figure and I'm really looking forward to seeing this gown finished. I bet your future husband counts himself a fortunate man.'

Hester's eyes softened. 'I think I'm the luckiest woman alive. Ally's kind, understanding and has a great sense of humour.' She paused. 'Our Jeanette is hoping to get married next year, so there could be more work for you in the future. It's no use passing my wedding gown on to her.

It would need altering too much. I can give her five inches in height and she's slimmer than me. She takes after her mother. Whereas Sam and I take after our father.' She glanced at Lynne. 'What did you think of my brother?'

'You're lucky having him for a brother,' said Lynne before she could stop herself. 'I mean, except for my father and Robert, I've had little to do with men. At least having a brother means you grow up used to men's ways. I was only young when my father died.'

'You must come to the wedding,' said Hester, taking Lynne by surprise. 'You don't have to worry about buying a wedding present. Your work on this dress is enough and I don't expect a reduction either. I can afford it.'

Lynne felt a rush of pleasure. 'That's kind of you. Are you sure you want me there?'

'I wouldn't ask if I didn't. Do come! I bet you don't get out much to have fun, what with a teenage daughter and an old granny. Will Bobby be OK looking after your grandmother?'

'Oh yes, they get on well together. I'd like to see you married.'

'Then come! Unless you feel it would be wrong, what with you just hearing about your mother's death?'

'That wouldn't stop me going,' said Lynne. 'I grieved for the loss of my mother years ago. I suppose the famous actress will be there?'

Detecting the note in her voice, Hester darted her a look. 'Don't you like her?'

Lynne flushed as she rolled up her tape measure. 'I don't really know her.'

'Sam said that she was rude to you.'

Lynne felt a quiver go through her. 'Really! Well, she did kind of ignore me but maybe that was because she had to go back upstairs for her outdoor clothes.'

Hester looked thoughtful and only said, 'Anyway, you must come to the wedding. I'll send you a proper invitation. Now can I see my material?'

'Of course!'

Lynne fetched the parcel and unwrapped it on the table. She watched as Hester fingered the ivory brocade satin with a rapt expression on her face. 'I really like it,' she said.

'You'll look lovely. You won't know yourself when you see yourself in the finished gown,' said Lynne, thinking of those brides whose bridal finery she had created in the past. It always gave her a thrill when brides saw their reflections in the mirror.

'I hope you're right,' said Hester, touching her cheek with the fabric.

'Of course I'm right,' retorted Lynne, smiling. 'Now how about a cup of tea?'

'I don't mind if I do,' said Hester, wrapping the material in its brown paper again.

Hester was just on her way out when Roberta arrived home. They exchanged greetings and then said goodnight and parted.

'So is she happy with the material for her wedding dress?' asked Roberta.

'She chose it, so of course she is,' said Lynne, feeling suddenly overwhelmingly weary.

'Cocoa?' asked her daughter.

151

'Thanks!' said Lynne, flopping into an arm-chair. 'I've something to tell you both. I had another visitor today.'

Nan and Roberta stared at her. 'Well, tell us?' asked her daughter.

'Stuart Anderson!'

Roberta gaped. 'What did he have to say?'

'His father was married to my mother.'

'Was!' exclaimed Roberta.

'She's dead.' Lynne told them all about her meeting with Stuart. They showed suitable astonishment and amazement.

'I wish I'd been here,' sighed Roberta. 'Do you think he'll send us a postcard from Italy?'

'Of course,' said Lynne, smiling. 'He said he'd send us several postcards and I wouldn't be surprised if he sent Betty Booth one too. He seemed interested in her.'

'It's a pity they won't be in Italy at the same time,' said Roberta.

Lynne smiled. 'Now d'you want to see the jewellery?'

Nan and Roberta watched as Lynne emptied the necklace and earrings on to her lap. 'They don't look much,' said Roberta, disappointed. 'Like shiny bits of coal.'

'Looks can be deceptive,' said Nan. 'Made in Whitby and it wouldn't surprise me if that's where some of your ancestors came from. Thousands and thousands of people flooded into Liverpool during Victorian times by sea or rail. It was the place to find work with ships coming and going, bringing tobacco and sugar and cotton and exporting goods across the Atlantic and to all parts of the Empire. Houses were being built at a rate of knots but there were also the emigration ships carrying people out of Liverpool, too.'

'All right, Nan! We get the message that you were a girl in Liverpool's latter Victorian heyday,' said Roberta, reaching for the necklace on Lynne's lap. 'So this is your inheritance, Mam. Pity it's not gold.'

'Jet's rare and valuable,' said Nan.

Roberta said, 'Perhaps you should sell it, Mam. I like the idea of going to California. I could sing that song "California, here I come".' She left the room to make the cocoa.

Nan and Lynne winked at each other.

'So you've an invitation to go to America,' wheezed Nan.

Lynne was silent a moment. 'I'd like Bobby to go. But I don't like the idea of my stepfather paying for us to travel all the way to California. If I sold the jewellery then she could still go but she'd need a whole new wardrobe.' She paused. 'I've had another invitation too – from Hester Walker. She's invited me to her wedding.'

'That's great! You don't get out enough,' said Roberta, catching the tail end of what Lynne was saying as she came in from the back kitchen with a steaming jug of cocoa. 'You're going to need a new dress.'

'You think?' said Lynne.

Roberta and Nan stared at Lynne. 'You want to knock them all dead, girl,' said the old woman firmly.

As she was drinking her cocoa, Lynne had an

153

idea. 'Bobby, I want you to go into Central Library and look for a particular book for me some time soon.'

'What's it called?' she asked.

'I can't remember off the top of my head but it'll come to me,' said Lynne, her eyes gleaming. She only hoped that what she had in mind was not beyond her capabilities.

Twelve

The following Saturday Roberta left the bus in Lime Street and headed for the Central Library. She wondered if she would see those youths from the Boys' Institute again and, sure enough, the fair-haired one was there. She remembered his friend calling him Nick. He was consulting a book and making notes. As she searched the section on books of costume and fashion, she could not help glancing at him and wondering if his friend would be joining him.

She took two books from the shelf and went over to a table and sat down. Able to borrow only one of the books, she delved into her knapsack and removed a sketch pad and a couple of pencils. She opened the book on fashion through the ages and began to sketch several drawings of women's undergarments from the beginning of the century. The other book was the one her mother had wanted and she would take that home because it contained Edwardian fashion plates of some really eye-catching gowns.

Engrossed in what she was doing, it took her ten minutes or so to become aware that she was being watched by Nick. As she looked his way, he swiftly lowered his head and carried on writing, so that all she could see now was his profile, but she had seen enough to cause her fingers to itch. *I like the shape of his skull*, she thought, turning over a page of her drawing pad and, in a few swift strokes, she had a recognizable sketch of his head.

She heard the sound of a chair being pushed back and glanced up and saw that it was him making the noise. *Was he going or just exchanging the book for another one?*

He did not return to the table so she presumed he had left the library. She grimaced, thinking that she would have liked to have more time to make a better drawing of him. Hopefully she might spot him again here at the Central. She did a sketch of a bust bodice and decided to call it a day, as she wanted to drop in at the coffee bar. She had the library book stamped and left the building, heading across town to Hope Street, having arranged to meet a classmate there but she was also hoping to see Betty.

Every table appeared to be taken and most of the customers seemed to be talking at the top of their voices whilst Tennessee Ernie's 'Give Me Your Word' came from the jukebox. She spotted Betty and waved to her. After a minute or two the older girl came over to her.

'I know what's brought you here,' Betty

155

smiled. 'Jeanette told me that your mother had a visit from the American. Apparently he's your mum's stepbrother.'

'Yes, I'm really chuffed about it for Mam's sake. They had a really good talk and his father would like us to visit. He sent her some of my grandmother's jewellery. Apparently it's real jet and was very popular in Victorian times.'

'He sounds a nice man.'

'Mam certainly liked his son. I wonder with *him* being her stepbrother, whether I should call him Uncle Stuart,' murmured Roberta. 'Anyway, he's going to send us postcards from Europe and we'll be seeing him when he gets back here.'

'Well, I'm glad he turned out to be a respectable person,' said Betty, her eyes twinkling. 'Anyway, I'd best get on with my work.'

'You haven't seen my school friend, Thelma, have you? I'm supposed to be meeting her here,' said Roberta.

Betty nodded. 'She came in, looked around and went out again.'

'Damn,' muttered Roberta. 'Trust her to be early and not wait.'

'She might come back,' said Betty.

'But there's nowhere to sit!'

Betty glanced around. 'Those two girls over there by the mother-in-law's tongue look like they'll be going soon. It's a table for four, so you might have to share. But go over there now and hover.'

Roberta did as Betty suggested but someone else had the same idea and they both arrived at the table as the girls stood up. Roberta stared at him, recognizing the fair-haired Nick from the library. She placed a hand on the back of a chair as the girls moved away and he did the same. They both watched the other as if waiting for them to speak. Then he nodded at her and pulled out a chair and sat down; she placed the knapsack containing the library book and her drawing pad and pencils on one of the unoccupied chairs and he put his knapsack on the remaining empty chair.

He picked up a menu card and began to study it. She read the reverse and then leaned back. She had only enough pocket money to buy a hot chocolate and so decided to wait and see if Thelma returned before ordering.

Several minutes passed and still he appeared absorbed in the contents of the menu. She decided that he was either avoiding looking at her or, like her, was delaying the moment when he would need to order because he was also meeting someone here. Maybe the friend she had seen him with last time in the library? Which reminded her of the book she had taken out for her mother. She removed it from her bag and placed it in front of her.

He lowered the menu a couple of inches and their eyes met and then he brought the menu up to his face again. She had an urge to giggle but managed to control herself by opening the book of Edwardian fashion plates. She intended picking out the outfit that she considered would suit her mother best.

She turned over a page, only to start when a voice from across the table said, 'Aren't you the girl from the library?'

Roberta glanced across into eyes the colour of treacle. 'Shouldn't you have blue eyes?' she blurted out.

'You're not the first to say that,' he muttered.

'It's usual with fair hair.'

He shrugged. 'So what? Well, are you or aren't you?'

'You know I am, unless there's something wrong with your eyes. That's twice we've seen each other. I didn't know you came here.'

'Well, I do. What's your name?'

'Roberta Donegan, although I get called Bobby by my friends and Mam and Nan.' She smiled. 'I know yours is Nick because I heard your friend speak to you the time I saw you both in the library.'

He nodded. 'Where d'you live?'

'D'you know West Derby Road?'

'Yes.'

'Well, off there. Where do you live?'

'Prescot Road. My dad has a hardware shop. What about your dad?'

'He was a sailor and was killed in the war. My mum's a dressmaker.'

'My mum's dead.' Nick glanced down at the menu.

There was a silence and Roberta was tempted to ask if his mother had died recently but she decided it might upset him.

'Are you ordering anything?' he asked abruptly.

'I'm waiting for a friend, then I'll order,' said Roberta.

'So am I. How long d'you plan on waiting?'

'Probably half an hour.'

'That's two of us then.'

She looked down at the fashion book and turned a page.

He cleared his throat. 'D'you often come here?'

'When I can, I come straight from school in Grove Street early evening. I like to look at the paintings on the wall. You do know Betty the waitress painted them?'

'No, I didn't.'

'They're of Italy.'

'I thought so.' He rested his arms on the table. 'I noticed you seemed to be drawing something in the library.'

She flushed but then decided he couldn't possibly have seen the sketch she had done of him. 'I was copying some pen and ink drawings from another book for Mam. She's going to a wedding and she wants to make an outfit that'll knock people's socks off.' She paused. 'What were you writing?'

'I was making notes for an essay on ancient Rome.'

'Are you doing Latin for O level?'

'I want to. I enjoy it. You?'

She grimaced. 'I'll probably drop it. I'm not that brilliant at languages and we have to make choices for GCEs soon. I have to choose between History and Geography. I prefer History, so I hope to do that. I also want to do Art, of course, as well as English, Maths, Chemistry, Biology and French.'

He smiled. 'I'll probably do technical drawing as well as the other subjects we have to do. I also like music and Dad has a fiddle but he never plays now.'

She thought he had a really nice smile. 'I like music, too. How d'you feel about Frank Sinatra singing "Three Coins in the Fountain"?'

'Prefer Frankie Laine as a singer. He has a really powerful voice.'

'Have you ever been to Rome?'

'Heck no! You?'

She rolled her eyes. 'I wish! The nearest I've got to it is the picture house. *Quo Vadis*, *Roman Holiday* and *Three Coins in the Fountain*.'

He laughed. 'Have you ever been in the international library at the Central? It's circular and in tiers, just like a Roman amphitheatre.'

'I've looked through the doorway. I bet it's not easy finding exactly what you need if you don't know the name of the book you're looking for in there.'

'There is that but it's divided into countries. Besides, I enjoy finding things out.'

'I presume you don't mean just trying to find a particular book but solving puzzles and mysteries, as well.'

'Yeah, I enjoy a good whodunnit.'

The door opened suddenly and both their heads turned to see who entered. A girl came in. 'Your friend?' he asked.

Roberta shook her head. 'I think I'll just go outside and see if she's coming. Will you look after my stuff?'

He nodded and picked up the menu card once

160

more.

She went and had a look outside but the only person she could see was a man wearing a mackintosh and a black trilby. She found herself staring at him, reminded of the one whom she had thought had followed her from school. Since learning about Stuart Anderson she knew better. Even so she hadn't forgotten the conversation between Lenny and Hester that evening about men who came to eye up the girls and sometimes expose themselves.

She went back inside, just as Betty approached their table. 'Hi, Nick! Are you ordering?' she asked.

'I was waiting for Chris but I suppose I'd better order if I want to keep this table,' he said. 'I'll have a coffee and a currant bun.'

Betty looked at Roberta. 'What about you?'

'I'll have drinking chocolate.' She placed a hand on Betty's arm. 'By the way, there's a man outside watching this place.'

Betty frowned. 'Are you sure?'

'Would you believe me if I told you he was wearing a mackintosh and a black trilby?'

'What!' Betty hurried away.

To Roberta's surprise, Nick stood up and went over to the window and peered out. Then he came back with a scowl on his face.

'What is it?' asked Roberta.

'My blinking uncle! I was hoping he wouldn't discover this place.'

'You mean he's followed you here? I thought I'd seen him before but you weren't here that time.'

Nick's scowl deepened. 'He could have been hanging around outside school and I didn't notice him. He's always wanting to know what I'm up to. Let's forget him.'

'I would,' said Roberta, noticing that Lenny had come out of the kitchen. 'I bet a pound to a penny Lenny's going to see him off.'

Nick's expression altered and he stood up and went over to the window. He came back grinning. 'He's scooted.'

'I bet he won't be back in a hurry,' said Roberta. 'Lenny will warn him off and threaten him with the police.'

Someone put money in the jukebox and 'Mambo Italiano' flooded out. Roberta tapped her fingers in time to the tune and carried on turning the pages of the book. Nick took one from his haversack. She glanced at the dust cover as he opened it and noticed it was slightly torn and that the title was *The Mysterious Affair at Styles* by Agatha Christie. Of course she had heard of the famous crime novelist but she hadn't read anything of hers, preferring historical novels by Jean Plaidy because she felt she learnt from them. Somehow they brought history alive in a way that textbooks didn't. She had also recently read *Little Women* by the American writer Louisa May Alcott.

She found herself thinking of her grandmother Graham being killed by a bear in the Rockies. It felt peculiar knowing that her own flesh and blood had survived the war, only to go all the way to America to be killed by a bear. She glanced down at the open page of a model in a gown that would have been fashionable when her dead grandmother had been young.

At that moment Betty arrived at their table. 'Do you two mind moving your books?' she asked.

Roberta put hers away but Nick did not even lift his head. Betty placed the mug of hot chocolate in front of Roberta. 'There's yours,' she said. 'Thanks for letting me know about that bloke. I don't think he'll be back.'

'Good.'

'I think I'll tip Nick's drink over his head,' said Betty.

Immediately he looked up and smiled at her. 'Sorry.' He bookmarked his page and put the book away. Betty placed his order in front of him and the bills on a saucer in the middle of the table. 'You know, I thought all you young people came here for the jukebox but you seem able to ignore it,' she said.

'I like live music,' said Nick. 'The jukebox is OK if all you want are the top of the pops but what if you prefer to listen to country and western or jazz? There's not much of that, is there?'

Watching his earnest face, Roberta gave in to temptation and took out her sketching pad and pencil and turned over the pages and began to improve on her drawing of him.

'I suppose it's a thought.' Betty glanced at Roberta. 'What do you think?'

'What?' asked Roberta, without lifting her head.

Betty moved so she could look at what the girl was drawing and then shot a glance at Nick.

'That shows promise,' she murmured, then walked away.

'What is it you're drawing?' asked Nick, looking across at Roberta.

'Nothing!' She closed the book and stuck it in her knapsack and reached for her drinking chocolate.

His eyes narrowed. 'Rubbish is it?'

'Yes,' she murmured.

He rolled his tongue round the inside of his cheek. 'You're telling fibs. Betty said it shows promise. Why don't you want me to look at it?'

'It's of women's underwear,' said Roberta glibly, taking a sip of her drink.

He flushed to the tip of his ears. 'You're kidding me!'

She smiled sweetly. 'As if I'd do a thing like that.' Reaching inside her knapsack she tore a page from her pad and passed it to him. 'Nothing saucy but fashionable at the time.'

He looked at it and then grinned and passed the page back to her. 'It reminds me of those bathing suits women used to wear to go swimming in the sea from bathing machines.'

'That's right.' She dropped the page into her knapsack.

He bit into his bun and hesitated before asking, 'D'you want half? You look hungry.'

'No, you ... you eat it all,' she said. 'I'll save myself for my dinner. I don't want to get fat.'

He eyed her. 'You're not fat. I'm always hungry. Dad says it's because I'm growing so fast. I'm going to be much taller than him.'

Roberta took another mouthful of the hot

chocolate, which was delicious. 'I never knew my dad, but I know I don't take after him. As it is I can't say that I really miss him, although, of course, I'd have liked to have known him.'

'I see what you mean.' He took another bite of his bun and glanced towards the door. 'Here's Chris.'

She stared at the dark-haired youth who had just entered. 'I'd better drink up if you want this table to yourself,' she murmured. 'It doesn't look like my friend's coming back.'

'No, don't rush yourself,' said Nick hastily. 'There's room enough for all of us.'

Chris came up to their table and stared at Roberta. 'Who are you?' he asked bluntly.

'Her name's Bobby,' said Nick.

'Funny name for a girl,' said Chris.

She stiffened. 'My full name is Roberta. I'm named after my dad who was a war hero,' she retorted, removing her knapsack from the chair next to her. 'I suppose you're named after Christopher Robin out of *Winnie the Pooh*!'

Nick grinned.

Chris smiled lazily and sat down. 'Very funny. I was named after a saint if you must know.'

Roberta nodded. 'Saint of travellers.'

Chris ignored her and rested his elbows on the table. 'So how long have you been here, Nick?'

'Not long. Dad had me not only carrying stuff backwards and forwards this morning but was wanting me to memorize the price of everything. He was showing me the account ledgers. Then my uncle turned up and he was in an ugly mood, so I left them arguing and then...'

'What about?'

'He's lost his job and is in debt because he's been gambling. Dad was hopping mad with him but at least my uncle has now agreed to move out of my grandfather's house so it can be sold. Dad wants to plough his inheritance into the business. The only problem with a sale going through is that my uncle just might think he can move in with us,' said Nick.

If only Mum had been so lucky as to be left a house instead of a jet necklace and earrings, thought Roberta, reaching out a hand for her bill. 'I'd best be going,' she said. 'Bye, Nick.'

He looked up and smiled. 'Tarrah!'

She went over to the counter where Betty was ringing up an amount on the till. When it came Roberta's turn to pay, Betty surprised her by saying, 'How d'you feel about coming along to my studio flat next Friday evening? You can have a look at my other paintings. You've never seen my earlier stuff, have you? You could ask your mum to come as well and to bring some patterns. I'm going to need some new clothes for Italy.'

'I'll see what Mam has to say,' said Roberta, delighted at the thought. 'It depends on Nan. What time do you want us to come if we can?'

Betty told her, adding, 'Our Emma might also have some business for her. She's been saying she could do with a couple more smocks and maternity skirts.'

'Great! I'll tell her,' said Roberta.

When she arrived home it was to find Hester and Jeanette Walker there. Lynne had put in a lot of time on the wedding gown and Hester was having a fitting.

'You look lovely,' said Roberta, proud of her mother's skill with her needle.

Lynne smiled. 'I'm really pleased with the way it's turned out.'

'So am I,' said Hester, gazing at her reflection in the full-length mirror with a wondering expression on her face. 'I can't believe it's me. Although, I don't know about my being lovely.'

'You look beautiful,' said Jeanette, slipping her arm around Hester's waist and giving her a hug.

'And once you have your headdress and veil on you'll look like a princess,' said Lynne.

'You'll certainly give Dorothy a run for her money on the day,' said Jeanette. 'You've met our famous actress, haven't you, Lynne?'

'We weren't introduced,' said Lynne lightly, bending to adjust a fold of the full-length skirt of the wedding gown. 'But yes, I did see her.'

Hester and Jeanette exchanged glances but made no comment.

'I think Nan would enjoy meeting her, what with her having worked in the theatre,' said Roberta.

Lynne was about to say that Dorothy Wilson might not be interested in talking to an old lady when Hester said, 'I'll mention it to Dorothy when I see her next weekend. She and Sam are having a couple of days away in Whalley.'

Lynne felt a twinge of envy but made no comment as she helped Hester out of her wedding gown. Then while Roberta made a pot of tea, she showed Jeanette the candy-pink taffeta she had purchased for the bridesmaid dress.

'It feels lovely,' said Jeanette, touching it lightly. 'I can't wait to see what I look like when it's made up. How long d'you think it will take?'

'Not long,' said Lynne. 'I'll check your measurements and you can come for a fitting, say Thursday.'

'Thursday will be fine,' said Jeanette.

'Will the family be seeing you then, too?' asked Hester, buttoning up her blouse.

Lynne looked at Jeanette in surprise. 'Are you going away somewhere?' she asked.

Jeanette chuckled. 'Yes, I'm leaving home to share Betty's flat. I'll be looking after it for her when she goes to Italy, so we both decided that I might as well move in earlier since Mam has persuaded Dad to help me with the rent and that it's a good thing for me to have a bit of independence.'

Roberta was about to mention Betty inviting her and her mother to the flat but decided it was best to keep quiet about it until she had spoken to Lynne.

She brought up the subject after Hester and Jeanette had left. Lynne waited until she had finished before saying, 'What about Nan?'

'You can ask Her Next Door to keep her company,' said Roberta, almost dancing with impatience. 'It's business, Mam, as well as me getting to have a look at Betty's earlier work and hopefully what she's doing now.'

'OK, I'll have a word with Nan and Her Next Door,' said Lynne. 'Now, did you get the book for me from the library?'

Roberta handed it to her and tore the pages of underwear from her sketch book and gave her them, too. Lynne glanced at them and smiled. 'You are a clever girl, although I'm not sure I'll be wearing that corset.'

Roberta perched on the arm of the easy chair. 'Won't you need to so you get the right silhouette?'

Lynne pulled a face. 'We'll see.'

'You are excited about the wedding, aren't you, Mam?'

'Why shouldn't I be? It's ages since I've been places where I felt a need to dress up.'

'Have you ever thought of getting married again?' asked Roberta casually.

Lynne's fingers tightened on the book. 'I don't get to meet men and besides who'd want to take me on with a daughter and an old granny?'

'Is that the only reason or is it that you haven't got over my dad?'

Lynne sighed. 'Why are you asking me this all of a sudden?'

Roberta shrugged. 'I just wondered.'

Lynne's face softened. 'This isn't because of Stuart's visit, is it? I do like him but that doesn't mean I could ever see him as a potential husband. Anyway, he's younger than I am,' she said, thinking of a different man altogether.

Roberta dropped the subject and instead thought she would do a little more work on her drawing of Nick, wanting to catch his expression exactly right. She would take the finished article with her when she and Lynne visited Betty's flat to show her.

Thirteen

'Because you're mine, the brightest star looked down on me...' sang the dark-haired youth, clad in a black crew-neck sweater with matching black trousers.

Lynne, who was standing over by the window in Betty's flat, where there was a fantastic view of the cathedral and beyond that the Mersey, was nursing a glass of Babycham. She had not realized that hers and Roberta's visit to the flat would turn into a party with music. She guessed the lad was not much older than her daughter, who was perched on a pouffe with her sketch pad on her knee, gazing at him. Apparently he was part Italian and was good looking with curly hair that was almost as black as the jet jewellery Lynne was wearing. In a few years time he would be a real heart-throb and would have his pick of the girls.

Hopefully her daughter was only seeing him as subject matter for her pencil but Lynne doubted it. Roberta was getting to that age when boys were starting to become interesting, which meant she was going to have to keep an eye on her. She had discovered a drawing of another boy in the drawing pad when she had taken her daughter's gym clothes out of her satchel the other evening.

The song came to an end and he said, 'And how about a burst on the banjolele?' Grinning, he picked up the instrument.

'Not that, Tony,' groaned the girl, who had been introduced as Betty's cousin, Maggie, and had come with Emma.

'What's wrong with the banjolele?' asked Betty.

'It reminds me of George Formby and he's so old-fashioned.'

Emma, who was seated comfortably on the large sofa, said, 'I don't see anything wrong with the banjolele or George Formby. He's one of our own, a Lancashire lad. His films and his comic songs always made my grandad burst into fits of laughter.'

'Oh, Emma, he's gormless!' cried Maggie.

'Well it made him rich,' put in Lynne. 'I read an article in the *Echo* about him. I wouldn't mind his money.'

'Some of his music is swing,' said Tony, his brown eyes gleaming, 'and I enjoy playing swing.'

'I'd like to jive,' said Maggie. 'Couldn't you play Bill Haley and his Comets' hit from last year?'

'If you want to dance, then you'd be best putting out your ciggy or you'll burn someone waving your arms about the way you do,' said Betty.

Maggie sighed. 'You're always getting at me. That's why I moved out. What with that and your boasting.'

Tony began to thrum the strings of the banjolele and played a few lines of 'Leaning on a Lamp Post'. Jimmy, the leader of the music group which was to play at Hester's wedding, picked up his guitar.

'Well, you did the right thing, Maggie,' said Betty mildly, determined not to be provoked. 'Only you left me with a bit of a problem, what with me going to Italy. Fortunately that's been solved by Jeanette.' She glanced at Lynne and changed the subject. 'Did you bring your pattern book?'

'I put it on the table,' replied Lynne.

'Oh, that's yours, is it?' said Maggie, smiling at her. 'There's some nice designs in it. I had a quick look. I wouldn't mind you making me a costume for when I go to Charm School in London. A dress and a jacket was what I was thinking.'

'You're going to have to join the queue,' said Betty. 'I'm first to have Lynne's services because I'll be off to Italy before you go to London.' She turned to Lynne, who had moved over to the sofa. 'I'll be staying with Tony's relatives for most of the time, so I'll be based in Castellammare di Stabia, not far from Sorrento.'

'That's a cue for a song,' said Tony.

'Were you born in Italy?' asked Roberta, glancing up from her drawing.

He nodded. 'So was Poppa and therein hangs a tale.' He played several swift chords on the banjolele before stopping and saying. 'I fancy a coffee and a bite to eat. I'm prepared to make it myself. Is that OK, Betty?'

172

'Of course, put the kettle on,' she said, perch-
ing on the arm of the sofa and turning a page of
the pattern book. 'Do you think your stepbrother
will visit that far south, Lynne, on his European
travels? I'd like to know what he thinks of the
area.'

'I honestly don't know,' said Lynne. 'Perhaps
when I get a postcard from him, he might give
me an idea of his itinerary.'

They began to talk in low voices as they
looked at the patterns of summer wear.

Tony went over to a cupboard and took out a
container of coffee as well as a tea-caddy.
Roberta put down her sketching pad and went
over to him. She had it in mind to draw an Italian
background to the sketch she had done of him so
was interested in his story.

'I'd like to hear that tale you mentioned?' she
said boldly, the faintest of blushes on her cheeks.

'What tale?' asked Tony absently, glancing
over at Maggie who was moving the paintings
leaning against a wall about.

'You said that you were born in Italy so how
did you end up in Liverpool?' asked Roberta,
wishing that Maggie would not distract him. She
had to confess that the other girl was pretty, even
if she seemed at odds with Betty. What was
Maggie doing now messing about with her
cousin's paintings?

Tony glanced down at her. 'You really want to
know?'

'Yes, unless it would bore you?' she said,
giving him all her attention and thinking the way
each syllable rolled off his tongue caused her

173

heart to flutter.

He smiled and shook his head. 'I never tire of talking about it.' He paused to spoon instant coffee into a couple of mugs. 'My poppa was in the Italian navy when I was born and his ship was bombed in the Med.'

'So your father was a sailor like mine,' she interrupted.

He frowned. 'I doubt exactly like yours. Poppa was taken prisoner by the British.' She opened her mouth to say hers had been killed but the look in his eye caused her to clam her lips firmly shut and Tony continued, 'Because he spoke fairly good English, he was taken to India with a whole lot of Italian prisoners and acted as a translator. When an armistice was signed by Italy and Britain, my father and many other prisoners were asked if they would like to go to Britain and help with the war effort.'

'So he did,' blurted out Roberta.

'Who's telling this story?' demanded Tony.

'You,' she said meekly, thinking she might be going off him when she had just started to be fascinated by his dark good looks and voice. 'Sorry.'

'I should think so. You're as bad as my little sisters. They're always butting in. Anyway, Poppa ended up in a POW camp over here. As he wanted to get to Italy to find me and my mother, he knew he had to escape and thought to get help from his mother's relatives in Liverpool.'

'I presume he escaped?'

Tony sighed. 'Of course, but he was injured on the way here.'

'Your poor poppa!'

This time Tony only said, 'Then due to the bombing, he couldn't find the house of his aunt, so he went to the priest's house. And that is how he met my stepmother.'

'But how did he find you? And what about your mother?' asked Roberta.

'Sadly my momma had died and I had been put in an orphanage run by the nuns. Anyway Poppa came to Italy despite the Germans and managed to find me and he smuggled me into England.' He paused. 'That's the short version.'

'How fascinating!' exclaimed Roberta. 'Your father could write a book.'

Tony chuckled. 'Oh, he isn't one to boast about his bravery. I do it for him. Of course, it is sad that my momma died but I don't remember her at all.'

'My father died before I was born,' said Roberta, switching off the kettle. 'But I'm proud of him because he must have been brave to be willing to die for his country.'

'Now Betty, she is proud that her father was an artist, not that he died at Dunkirk,' said Tony, glancing her way.

Betty lifted her head. 'I heard that. It's only because I would have preferred him to stay alive. If he hadn't been killed we would have gone to Italy together and he'd have taught me so much about art.'

'You can't be sure of that,' said Maggie, glancing towards her as she picked up a canvas. 'What's this supposed to be?'

Betty passed the pattern book to Lynne and

175

went and took the picture from her cousin and held it at arm's length. 'I can't remember. I think I was exploring colour.'

'There's certainly enough colours in it,' said Lynne, staring at the painting. 'I like it. They're what I call warm colours.'

'It's not a bit like the one your dad painted that's in the Walker art gallery,' said Tony.

'I was experimenting.' Betty held out the picture to Lynne. 'Here, you can have it if you want?'

Lynne seized it in both hands and said delightedly, 'I've never had an original painting! Thank you.'

'What about my sketches?' asked Roberta. 'They're originals, Mam. You can take your pick.'

Lynne smiled. 'I know I can. I suppose I inherited my skill for design from your Nan but when it reached you it developed differently. You could make an excellent art teacher.'

Roberta sighed and exchanged a look with Betty, thinking she would understand how she felt about that comment.

But it was Emma who spoke next. 'What did your great-grandmother do?'

'She worked in the theatre as a dresser,' said Roberta.

'Betty's mother and mine were involved with the theatre in an amateurish way,' said Maggie, lifting up another painting. 'Why is it you've never wanted to follow in your mother's footsteps, Betty?'

She took the painting from her. 'Mam never

talked about those days. She was proud of my dad's skill as a painter because he made money out of it! I suppose she encouraged me because she believed I'd inherited his talent and could make money, too.'

'Well, I'll tell you this,' began Maggie, 'I don't think you did inherit his talent.'

'What d'you mean by that?' asked Betty, frowning.

'I mean...'

'Enough, Maggie,' said Emma, a warning note in her voice. 'I don't know why there has to be this rivalry between you and Betty.'

'That's what girls are like,' said Tony. 'Now my sisters...'

'Boys can be just the same and it's not just in families that one gets rivalry,' said Roberta brightly. 'Now who wants coffee and who wants tea?'

'I'll have tea.' Lynne smiled at her daughter before turning to Emma. 'What do you want?' she asked the woman who was nervously twisting her wedding ring round and round her finger. It made her wonder whether Emma knew what was behind that rivalry between the cousins. She felt sorry for her, thinking she shouldn't have such squabbles to bother her when she was pregnant. Fortunately the subject was dropped and the conversation moved on.

Roberta would have liked to have discussed Betty's pictures with her but she had either forgotten her reason for inviting her to the flat or she did not want to talk about art because of Maggie's words. She was almost glad when it became time to go home, although she had enjoyed the music. She wondered what Nick would have made of it. Perhaps not his style if he went for country and western or jazz.

It was Emma who remained talking to Lynne and Roberta at the door a bit longer than expected. 'I'm sorry about that spat earlier,' she said in a low voice. 'It's what happens in families.'

Roberta glanced at her mother, thinking of her grandmother Graham, but Lynne did not mention her; instead she placed her hand over Emma's and said, 'If you need a listening ear...' Then she stopped.

No doubt she had remembered that Emma had a husband to confide in, as well as her close friend, Hester. Roberta linked her arm through her mother's and they left.

Only later did Lynne remember that she had forgotten to pick up her book of patterns. Hopefully Betty, Emma and Maggie would have another look at it and get in touch. Emma might decide she needed something new for Hannah's wedding. Thinking of the coming event reminded Lynne of Sam Walker. No doubt he would be there. Unfortunately he was likely to have Dorothy Wilson on his arm.

Fourteen

Dorothy was thinking of her mother as she heard a car draw up outside the hotel. She was also remembering giving birth and the agony of it. Her son had been a fair size, no doubt due to his father being a six-footer. She remembered her mother telling her that she had been a dainty baby with a head of blonde curls.

She went over to the window and gazed down into the road and her heart sank further. Last night it had snowed again. It would be the first day of spring on Mothering Sunday and the weather was the pits. She watched as Sam stepped out of the car and without wasting any time, she picked up her weekend bag and vanity case. Should she try and change his mind about going away? Of course, he might have already done so when it had snowed again, although somehow she doubted it.

She hoped fervently that if they did go that these two days away would not prove a mistake. Oddly, despite Sam being quite tough and no doubt ruthless with criminals, he was a romantic at heart. It could be that after their conversation at the Philharmonic pub, this weekend might not be exactly as she imagined it. She guessed he had given no thought to it being Mothering Sun-

179

day. Why should he? His mother was dead and Dorothy didn't know where he stood on sending a card to his stepmother. Would her own son have bought her a card if she had kept him? She felt the slightest of aches thinking of him buying one for another woman, proclaiming her the best mother in the world. She swallowed a sigh, knowing it was stupid to entertain such thoughts. She had her career and she was going to earn a decent amount of money and spend time in the sun this year. Goodbye snow!

As she reached the foot of the stairs, she saw the maid open the door and welcome Sam. He stamped his feet on the coconut mat and came through into the hall, stopping when he saw her standing there, waiting for him.

He smiled. 'Hello, love. You all set to go?'

'You obviously are,' she said brightly. 'D'you think it's sensible? Remember what happened last time we went travelling in the snow?'

'How could I forget? You criticized my driving all the way there! Anyway, the main roads aren't too bad, so let's get going.'

'If you insist, but if we crash and are killed, I'll blame you,' she said, handing her overnight bag to him but keeping hold of the vanity case. She turned to the maid. 'You don't have to bother making the bed, I've done it. I'll see you in a couple of days.'

'Look after yerselves,' said the girl, smiling. 'Yer can have fun in the snow, yer know!'

'My thoughts exactly,' said Sam. 'My sister has told me there's a sledge at the cottage.'

They hurried down the steps and as they reached the car, Dorothy looked up at the sky. 'Those clouds look a peculiar colour. It could snow again,' she said.

'Let's look on the bright side,' said Sam, opening the door for her before placing her bag on the back seat. 'They could blow away, the sun could come out and the snow could melt.'

'I hope you're right. It's not that long to Easter and Hester's wedding.'

'Three weeks,' he murmured. 'She was talking about a white Easter.'

'Is she serious? I was joking!'

He shrugged. 'You can ask her when you see her.'

Dorothy climbed into the car and settled herself. 'How's Jeanette or haven't you seen her lately?'

'She and Davy came one evening and she and Hester were nattering in the kitchen.'

'That's not unusual.'

'No, but Jeanette was upset. Betty has told her that she's thinking of leaving art school and not going to Italy and Jeanette says she's making a mistake.'

Dorothy raised her eyebrows. 'My goodness, why would Betty do that? I thought she loved her art as much as I love my acting!'

'Exactly,' said Sam drily, as he edged into the traffic. 'When I asked, the pair of them just stared at me and told me to go away.'

'I wonder if she's pregnant,' murmured Dorothy.

Sam shot her a glance. 'Don't be daft! She hasn't got a boyfriend. Her love is art and the trip to Italy has been her dream.'

Dorothy was silent a moment and then said, 'I wonder how Emma feels about it. Aren't they half-sisters?'

'Yes. I heard Hester say that Emma's going to be keeping her company at the cottage this weekend. Apparently she felt that she needed to get away. It means, too, that she'll be able to spend some time with Jared who's trying to get the renovations to the cottage finished before the wedding.'

'I see,' murmured Dorothy, wondering if they would see much of the two couples during the weekend. 'How's Hester's wedding dress coming along?'

'It's pretty well finished from what I've heard. Hester reckons Lynne Donegan has real talent.' Sam glanced at Dorothy. 'You remember who she is – the one I was talking to at the hotel that time.'

'Yes, I remember her but as I'm unlikely to meet her again, I can't say I'm interested in her.' She changed the subject, ignoring his sudden frown. 'So, how have things been in the police force this past week?'

His hands tightened on the steering wheel. 'We've had a spate of robberies and a couple of them involved nasty attacks on shopkeepers. One of the victims was a woman who was unconscious for over twenty-four hours. Fortunately she came round but was unable to give us a description of her attacker.' His expression was grim. 'But we'll get the swines eventually. They'll make a mistake and that'll be it. We do have our suspicions about who could be responsible.'

'Your Hester's going to miss all the excitement of her job after she's married,' said Dorothy.

'Probably, but she'll have plenty to keep her occupied and will soon get used to a different way of life. She'll be living close to Myra Jones whom she stayed with when she was evacuated. Myra's going to help her in the teashop that Emma set up during the summer.' He glanced at Dorothy as he stopped at traffic lights. 'I've never thought to ask whether you can cook.'

'A bit ... simple meals ... egg and chips, mince and potatoes.'

Sam grinned. 'Plain, simple food, but plenty of it will do me.'

'I like eating out,' she said.

'Can't do that all the time,' he replied.

The traffic lights changed and they crossed Islington, heading for Scotland Road and the north. 'You're never going to believe this but when Dad went to visit Grace the other day, they had pheasant for dinner.'

'Pheasant! What do they taste like?'

'Gamey, whatever that means, but he seemed to like it. Another thing he told me was that Grace is on the board of guardians at a home for unmarried mothers in the Cheshire countryside.'

Dorothy froze. 'Are you kidding me?'

'No, the subject came up because it's Mothering Sunday this weekend. Apparently the building used to belong to her family a couple of generations back and it was given over for that purpose after the Great War. Grace took over as a guardian after her mother died.'

Dorothy hoped it was not the same place where she and Lynne Donegan had their babies. It would be an unfortunate coincidence if it was and yet the names of mothers and their babies and the adopted parents were supposed to be kept completely hush-hush.

'What it is to have money and to be able to make such a gesture,' she said casually.

'The family probably had to get rid of it because of death duties,' said Sam. 'Anyway, they get a raw deal, some of those girls.'

'You think so?'

'Yeah, one little mistake and pow! We were bloody lucky that it didn't happen to you,' said Sam.

'Yes, weren't we,' said Dorothy, an edge to her voice.

He covered her hand with one of his for a moment. 'I would have married you.'

'I know but we were far too young,' she said.

'Even so...'

They fell silent.

Then Sam said, 'I know a couple of prostitutes who slipped up and got themselves pregnant.'

'Do you?'

'Part of the job, love. Last time it was due to a stabbing and we had to haul several of them in. Actually it was not that far from where Jeanette's living now. There's a Seamen's Club nearby.'

'Who was it who was stabbed?'

'A pimp. He nearly died,' said Sam, grim-faced.

'Tell me more! I'm not a wilting lily.'

He glanced at her. 'All grist to the mill, is it? You could make a film of it. A tart with a heart of gold gets pregnant. Pimp wants her to have an abortion but she's scared because she knew a girl who died, so she decides to have the baby and give it up for adoption. Whichever way you look at it, it has to be tough giving up your baby or keeping it and having to struggle to support it.'

'What if in your story she didn't give it up for adoption but kept it?' asked Dorothy, her heart beating fast.

'She'd need the help of a family and most prostitutes don't get such help. She'd have to carry on selling her body, catch a nasty disease and die.'

Dorothy shuddered. 'Really cheerful stuff! What happens to the child?'

'He's no longer a baby and is put in an orphanage and sent off to Australia or South Africa, works like a slave, makes his fortune and returns to England and marries an heiress who is the daughter of the man who got his mother pregnant in the first place.'

'No!' exclaimed Dorothy, impressed that Sam could make up such a tale. 'You're wasted as a detective! But tell me how would he know that he was the father?'

'He wouldn't. Only the cinema-goers would know because they see him at the beginning of the film.'

'They wouldn't like that. He got the girl into trouble and didn't marry her.'

'That's why you'd need a double twist. He

185

isn't the man but his twin brother, so not the real father.'

Dorothy groaned. 'Let's change the subject. The cottage, is it picturesque?'

'You'll be able to see for yourself. You do have a decent pair of shoes or boots you can walk in, don't you?'

She frowned. 'You're not really thinking of walking in the snow?'

'Why not? The inn that Hester's booked us in is not that far from Pendle Hill of witches fame. If the snow isn't too bad, it would bring colour to your cheeks,' said Sam, grinning.

Her eyes sparkled with annoyance. 'You have to be joking! I'm not walking up any hills at this time of year and that's definite,' she said firmly.

He said mildly, 'But it is my weekend. You have a week in London doing exactly what you want but you're not prepared to put yourself out for me. I wouldn't take you up the hills if it's risky.'

'I should think not. Anyway, I don't have boots suitable for walking up hills.'

'Why didn't you say that in the first place? I suppose I should have mentioned boots when I first broached the subject of a couple of days away.'

She felt like saying that it wouldn't have made any difference but decided best to just nod.

'We can spend the time snuggled up at the inn in front of a roaring fire or go and see a play that some amateurs are putting on at the village if you like?' said Sam. 'And if you get really fed up with me, you can spend some time with

Hester and Emma.'

She felt a twinge of guilt. 'I won't get fed up with you, Sam. I suppose we can walk around the village if I could buy a pair of walking shoes.'

'That's the ticket,' he said, looking pleased. 'We could also walk along the river or around the ruined abbey.'

She agreed, although she would have much preferred Blackpool with its hotels and theatres. One thing was for certain, it was obvious that despite his frustration, he was still prepared to wait until they were married before they slept together. Hester was bound to have booked them into separate rooms and rightly so. It was much wiser to play safe. One couldn't be too careful and she doubted he'd come prepared – and she certainly didn't want to get pregnant again. If this coming film proved a success there would be another one waiting for her in the wings.

The two days away could have proved to be just what the doctor ordered if either of them bothered with doctors. Dorothy joked that the inn, the village, the cottage and the surrounding countryside looked just like a Christmas card. Hester and Emma had travelled up by train the day before; Jared and Ally were already staying in the village. The two women showed off the new bathroom and the kitchen which Dorothy admired, despite her preference for modern houses.

On the Saturday evening the six of them had a meal at the inn and there was plenty for them to talk about what with Hester and Ally's coming wedding, Emma and Jared's baby expected the end of June and Dorothy's role in the film. She did not go on too much about the latter because of wanting to keep the peace between her and Sam. Several times during the evening she was aware of Emma placing a hand protectively over her bump and Jared smiling at her and squeezing her free hand. They were so content in their marriage that it made Dorothy feel depressed and restless, knowing that was how Sam would like them to be but she just could not see herself in that role. Sam was gorgeous and she wanted his happiness but could she make him happy? She had hated how she had looked when she was pregnant. She remembered how she had done her utmost not to draw attention to her increasing waistline. She had worn a corset, hoping that would conceal her condition and not only because she was unmarried.

'Hester tells me that you have a lovely frock for the wedding,' said Emma, rousing Dorothy from her reverie.

'Yes! I bought it in London. That's where you need to go to get anything really fashionable.' She reached for her cigarette case and took a cigarette before offering it around the table.

'I'm happy with the gown Lynne's made me,' said Hester, after refusing a cigarette. 'And it's not costing me a fortune.'

'I'm sure you'll look sensational,' said Ally, smiling across at her.

'I'm sure she will, too,' said Dorothy hastily, accepting a light from Sam. 'But clothes are very much part of my job. I have to look stunning to get important people in the business to notice me.'

'My sister, Maggie, is mad about clothes,' said Jared, reaching for his pint. 'She wants to be a model. What d'you think of that as a career for a young girl today? You've lived in London, haven't you, Dorothy? What advice would you give to her? She might listen to you if you warned her of the dangers she could encounter.'

Emma leaned forward. 'When we say anything to her about it, she gets a weed on and says we just want to spoil her fun. Jared is her guardian since their mother died and she left Maggie some money. It would be easier for us if she hadn't as she keeps saying, "It's my money. I can do what I want with it."'

'It's a heck of a responsibility,' said Jared ruefully. 'There's also my cousin, Betty, who has a weed on at the moment, too. She's gone and changed her mind about being an artist and going to Italy, which has been her dream for years.'

'We've heard a little about Betty,' said Sam, glancing across at Hester.

'Of course, your sister, Jeanette, shares the flat with her now,' said Jared. 'Now Betty's joking about working in the theatre.'

'Why should she want to do that?' asked Dorothy, startled.

Jared and Emma exchanged looks. 'It's too complicated to explain,' he said, 'even though both her father and mother were involved in the theatre at one time.'

'She's in a strange mood,' said Emma. 'If you

could persuade Betty that acting isn't all it's cracked out to be, we'd appreciate it.'

'And persuade Maggie that London is a dangerous place for young pretty girls,' said Jared.

Dorothy remembered her younger self and the struggle she'd had to become an actress. She had only got where she was today because she hadn't listened to those who had told her not to do it. She had been single-minded, her heart set on doing what she loved best and wanting success. If it had not been then she would have dropped out years ago. She was aware they were all waiting to hear what she had to say.

'I admire Betty's courage for daring to tell her family that she's changed her mind and wants to do something else,' she declared with a smile. 'Encourage her and if it's just a mood, then she'll soon realize what sheer hard work treading the boards is and give up.'

'You really believe that?' asked Emma.

'I wouldn't say it if I didn't,' replied Dorothy with a shrug. 'It's the same with Jared's sister. I understand your concern but let her have her chance. Otherwise, she'll hate you and might just run away. Much better if I were to give you the name of a boarding house in London. It's run by a woman I know, who gave up her career on the stage and took it over from her mother. She looks after her lodgers like a mother hen does her chicks.'

Emma glanced at Jared. 'She sounds a good person,' she said.

'The best,' said Dorothy warmly. 'I'll give you her full name and address and Maggie can mention my name to her.'

Jared thanked her.

Hester changed the subject, mentioning an amateur play that was advertised in the village. It was decided that they would go and see it the following evening and that's what they did. The others enjoyed it but Dorothy was not impressed by most of the performances and could see where the production could be improved.

Afterwards, as she and Sam strolled back to the inn, he asked her whether she could see herself getting involved in such a group after they were married. She experienced a sinking feeling in her gut.

'It's not the first time you've mooted that idea. Is it that you believe if you bring it up often enough I'll say yes? I don't want to play at acting! I want the real thing and if I can't have it then that's the end of it!'

'Don't be so touchy!' said Sam, kicking a pebble into the gutter. 'I was only asking. You spoke so wisely to Emma and Jared about Betty and Maggie. You could teach a group like that to improve their performance.'

Dorothy felt like stamping her foot. 'Let's drop it! I meant what I said.'

He scowled. 'OK! No doubt you'll be glad to get back to the city?'

'To be honest, yes! I'm a townie. I'm glad we're going home tomorrow and pleased that there's Hester's wedding to look forward to.'

'No doubt because once it's over, you can join your film-making pals down south,' said Sam.

'I'd be lying if I said I wasn't looking forward

to the filming.'

He looked grim and, without another word, strode on ahead.

She swore beneath her breath, thinking she could catch up with him if she put on a spurt, but she couldn't be bothered. Although she had enjoyed the break away, it had not really drawn them any closer to reaching an agreement about the future that would make them both happy.

Fifteen

It was Easter Saturday and the sun was shining as Lynne came out of Edie's hairdresser's next to St Alban's pub in Whitefield Road. She almost collided with Hester and Jeanette.

'You're early,' said Hester, eyeing her hairdo.

'I have to get Nan up and see everything is OK for her and Bobby,' said Lynne, smiling. 'They-'re both coming to see the wedding. How are you feeling this morning? Not a bag of nerves, I hope.'

'A bit jittery,' said Hester, pulling a face. 'Praying that everything goes off smoothly. At least I don't have to worry about traffic jams from here to Whalley preventing Ally from getting to the church on time. He was staying with my friend Wendy and her husband last night.'

'That's great,' said Lynne, 'and you have the sun, too.' She held her face up to its rays.

'We could do with the wind dropping,' said Jeanette, rubbing her arms. 'It's still a bit chilly.'

'Give it time,' said Lynne. 'By this afternoon, it could be a lot warmer.' She hesitated. 'Thanks for dropping my pattern book in the other week, by the way, Jeanette. How is Betty?'

'A bit glum-faced. I told her that she should have got you to make her a couple of frocks, even though she says she's not going to Italy. I don't know why she's allowed what Maggie said to undermine her confidence. She must know she's got artistic talent.'

'I certainly think she has,' said Lynne. 'I love her painting and have it in my bedroom. Bobby's a bit put out, says she never thought I'd go for modern art. She's done a rather nice sketch of that singer, Tony.'

'Well, Tony'll be singing at the do this evening and Betty will be there, too.' Hester paused. 'We'd best go inside. Our appointment is in five minutes. See you this afternoon, Lynne.'

'I'm really looking forward to seeing *your* outfit finished,' said a smiling Jeanette, fluttering her fingers at Lynne before following Hester into the hairdresser's.

As Lynne went on her way, she thought about the outfit she had made for the wedding and prayed that she had not overdone it. She had spent more than was sensible on materials and would hate Hester to think she was trying to outshine the other guests. Lynne's problem was that she needed more customers if she was to continue to be self-employed and she wanted to make an impression that said *See how talented I am*. As much as she hated to think of Nan passing away, it was a fact of life that when people grew old they died. Without Nan's pension and small savings, finances would be even tighter than they were now. Perhaps best not to dwell on that at the moment. Today was one of celebration. If the worst came to the worst then she could always pawn her mother's jewellery and accept her stepfather's offer to pay for Roberta to go to America.

To Lynne's delight and surprise when she arrived home she found a postcard on the mat of the Trevi Fountain in Rome. She turned the postcard over and read the small neat handwriting on the reverse. She slipped it into her jacket pocket and entered the kitchen with a smile on her face. She dumped the shopping she had done on the way home on the table and looked at her daughter. 'Guess what?'

Roberta, who was polishing the sideboard, glanced at her mother and did a double-take. 'Blinking heck, Mam, I hardly recognized you with your hair all wavy. You going somewhere?' she added with a cheeky grin.

'Very funny,' said Lynne, her eyes twinkling. 'Is Nan still asleep?'

'She was when I looked in on her. D'you want me to go up now and see if she's awake?'

'Take her a cup of tea up and show her this.' Lynne passed the postcard to her daughter.

Roberta gazed down at the photograph of the Trevi Fountain and heaved a sigh before turning the postcard over and reading the greetings from Stuart. 'He wishes we were there enjoying the sunshine with him,' she murmured. 'At least this means he was definitely serious about keeping in touch. You did notice that he mentions Betty and how much she'll enjoy Italy?'

'Yes,' said Lynne, starting to unpack the shopping.

'Perhaps he'll send a postcard to her at the coffee bar,' said Roberta, putting on the kettle. 'I wonder what Dorothy Wilson will be wearing for the wedding.'

'I guarantee it'll be something expensive,' said Lynne, not wanting to think about the actress and her relationship with Sam. 'D'you think you'll be able to make a pan of scouse for you and Nan?'

'What's difficult about it?' said Roberta. 'I just have to throw everything in the saucepan and let them simmer.'

'Not quite that simple. You'll have to put the meat in first and simmer that for about an hour. It's a cheap cut, so will be tough if you don't. Then add more water and your chopped vegetables, as well as salt, pepper and some dried herbs.'

'Do I add Oxo?'

'It's not necessary but you can if you want.'

'I thought I'd take her for a walk in the park after we've seen the wedding. It's not that far away from the church,' said Roberta.

'As long as you make sure Nan has her walking stick and doesn't get too tired,' said Lynne, pushing a paper bag across the table. 'There's two cream cookies in there for you and Nan.'

Roberta flushed with pleasure. 'Thanks, Mum,

you shouldn't have but I appreciate the treat.' She paused. 'I was thinking as soon as I'm four-teen, I'll get a Saturday job to help out with expenses.'

Lynne smiled. 'That's a good idea but you've ten months to go before then, so stop worrying. Now I'd better put the finishing touches to the hat I'm going to wear.'

Lynne was feeling a little shy as she entered the church, knowing that she would know few people there. Then she saw Sam, handing out books and directing people to pews and realized he must be one of the ushers. Suddenly he notic-ed her and she felt a rush of pleasure as those treacle-toffee eyes took her in. She wondered what he thought of her outfit. On her curling shiny auburn hair she was wearing a wide-brim-med hat trimmed with cream artificial roses and her trim figure was clad in a lace and satin straw-coloured Edwardian-style full-length gown with a fluted hem. On her small feet she wore a gleaming pair of cream crossbar shoes. Fortu-nately she had remembered to leave off the spectacles her daughter did not approve of.

'Can this really be Mrs Donegan, the dress-maker?' he asked in a jokey voice.

She told herself to be sensible. He probably smiled at everyone with such charm and besides, he was already spoken for. 'Yes, it's me,' she said awkwardly. 'How nice to see you again, Mr Walker.'

'Call me Sam,' he said, shaking her hand before handing her a prayer book and hymnal.

'You'll be with our lot and that's this side,' he indicated.

'Thank you.'

'Hester told me she'd invited you. You've made a great job of her wedding dress and you look very nice, too. Did you make that outfit yourself?'

'Yes. I don't get the opportunity to dress up often, so I'm hoping I haven't gone over the top,' she said in a rush.

'You know who you remind me of in that outfit?' said Sam. 'The Queen Mother when she was young.'

'If I do, then I've made a big mistake,' said Lynne ruefully. 'She was only a small girl during the Edwardian era when this style was fashionable.'

'I can't believe you'd make a mistake,' he said easily. 'It must be me. Anyway, don't fashions come and go? I mean not everybody stops wearing a favourite suit or dress because the fashion pundits dictate change.'

Lynne smiled. 'You're right! I'm sure there were plenty of women who carried on with this style during the Great War and its aftermath. The Queen Mother would have been nineteen in 1919.'

'I've seen her several times,' said Sam. 'The first time was during the thirties after the abdication when she and the King came to Liverpool before his coronation.'

'I remember that,' said Lynne. 'Everyone was cheering and waving flags because they admired them so much.'

'That was because the country felt let down when Edward abdicated,' said Sam. 'I admire people who do their duty by others. Next time I saw them was when I was a policeman on the beat and they came here for the Grand National.'

'Your job must be really exciting,' said Lynne.

He smiled. 'It has its moments but sometimes it can be as dull as ditchwater. Paperwork and the like.'

'I see what you mean.' She became aware that there were a couple of people waiting to talk to him. 'I'd best go and sit down,' she whispered, and made to walk away.

He took her arm and glanced down the nave. 'Can't have you sitting on your own.' And he walked her right down the aisle.

'I could have sat at the back,' she whispered.

'There'll still be room in the front pews for a small one, so stop worrying. You'll get a better view of your handiwork from there.'

She gave up arguing with him, not sure whether she felt embarrassed or flattered that he should be determined to take care of her. As they reached the two front pews, she noticed Dorothy looking slightly bored, sitting next to an old lady.

'Dot, can you look after Mrs Donegan?' he asked.

Dorothy's head shot up and she stared at Sam and Lynne.

There was such an expression on her face that Lynne said, 'I'll sit somewhere else.'

'That sounds sensible to me,' said Dorothy, her fingers curling on the handbag in her lap.

198

'You're forgetting, Sam, that your dad and Grace, as well as Beryl, will have to squeeze in here.'

'I hadn't forgotten them,' said Sam. 'Shove up, Dot! She's not going to take up much space and Grace will be in her wheelchair.'

Dot's mouth set in a stubborn line. 'What about you? You won't be at the back for the whole of the service.'

'Don't worry about me,' said Lynne, her cheeks rosy. 'I'm only the dressmaker and I've seen Hester's wedding gown from all angles already.'

'You heard her, Sam,' said Dorothy. 'She's only the dressmaker! You're embarrassing the poor woman.'

'Am I embarrassing you, Lynne?' asked Sam.

Lynne did not like being called *the poor woman*. There was no way that she'd feel comfortable sitting next to Dorothy and was tempted to tell Sam that but she did not like agreeing with Dorothy, so said, 'I know you're being kind but it is probably best I sit further back.'

He gave in. 'If that's what makes you happy, then I'll find you a seat a bit further back.'

She thanked him and with a short nod in Dorothy's direction, followed him to a pew two rows behind the family one. She wasted no time unhooking a hassock and kneeling on it. She lowered her head and clasped her hands and remained in an attitude of prayer, thinking of the scene that had just been played out. *Why did Dorothy Wilson not like her?* Lynne sensed it didn't have anything to do with her being only the dressmaker. There had been real dismay in her eyes when she had caught sight of Lynne with Sam. She remembered the way Dorothy had reacted when they had set eyes on each other in the hotel.

Of course, it could be that she resented Sam taking notice of any other woman. Lynne knew only too well how insecure some actresses felt but somehow she doubted Dorothy felt insecure. Of course, she was not as young as some of the British actresses on the scene these days and she could see the likes of Diana Dors as a real threat to Dorothy becoming a big star.

What am I doing thinking like that? I'm no threat to her acting career. It had to be that she didn't like Sam taking notice of any other woman.

Lynne remained on her knees until the organist launched into the music she always thought of as 'Here Comes the Bride'. She rose to her feet, as did the rest of the congregation, and caught a glimpse of Sam's profile and then that of Dorothy as she glanced round. Lynne received a sudden shock because, in a flash, that look of exasperation on the actress's face reminded her of someone she had come across years ago. Thirteen years and three months to be precise. Why had she only just recognized her? Then she remembered that she had thought Dorothy looked familiar. If the actress's behaviour was anything to go by, then it was obvious that Dorothy had immediately recognized Lynne.

Such thoughts were banished momentarily as Hester swept past on her father's arm in a cloud of ivory satin and veiling. Lynne was aware of the bouquet's spicy scent of pinks and carnations and the heady perfume of roses. Then came Jeanette, looking almost as lovely as the bride.

'Dearly beloved...' the vicar began.

Lynne had difficulty concentrating on the age-old words of the marriage service at first because she could not stop thinking of the younger Dorothy and Lynne and their babies in that home in the Cheshire countryside. Then she pulled herself together and forced herself to listen. Her throat tightened with emotion as she heard the bride and the groom exchange their vows to love and cherish each other, through sickness and health, for better, for worse, as long as they both should live. She found herself regretting deeply that she and Robert had never had the opportunity to speak those words. It would have been a memory to cherish forever.

What of Dorothy? What memories did she hold dear? What regrets did she have? Did Sam know of her past? Of course he didn't! And that was why she wanted to keep Lynne at a distance.

Suddenly she felt a need to get out of the church and half-rose in her seat, only to instantly sit down again. What was she thinking, drawing attention to herself? As it was Sam glanced over his shoulder and their eyes met. Her heart began to thud and swiftly she lowered her gaze and stared fixedly at the page where it was open at the next hymn: 'Love Divine, All Loves Excelling'.

She decided to leave as soon as the service was over rather than face Dorothy. She would need an excuse. It would be bad mannered just to vanish. Perhaps she could say she wasn't feeling well? Then it struck her that she didn't need to run away. She could just ignore Dorothy. Lynne had to admire the other woman. She had wanted to get on with her life and she seemed to have achieved what she had set out to do if she had wanted to be an actress. As for herself, she had succeeded in her aim to bring up her daughter herself and so could hold her head up high.

It was on the way out of the church that she collided with Emma. 'Are you all right?' Lynne put out a hand to steady the pregnant woman.

Emma pulled a face. 'Sorry about that. I'm getting so big now that I'm always bumping into people. I don't seem able to judge the distance between me and them, not to mention furniture and doorways.'

Lynne smiled. 'I can understand how you feel. Are you keeping well?'

Emma sighed. 'Fine but I'll be glad when it's over and I can hold my baby and see that everything's all right with it.' She changed the subject. 'You've made a lovely job of Hester's wedding gown and what you're wearing is lovely, too. When you think of Teddy Boys, their style is based on Edwardian male fashion, too. You could start a trend in women's fashion. You're really good at what you do, aren't you?' She babbled on. 'What about smocking and yokes? I didn't get much of a chance to finish our conversation at Betty's flat. D'you think you could make me a couple of maternity smocks in a pretty cotton material, as well as a couple of skirts? I'm fed up of wearing the same two outfits I have at the moment.'

Lynne's eyes lit up. 'It would be a pleasure. You'll want them pretty soon, I'd imagine?'

'Too right! Would you mind coming to my house for fittings and the like? You can charge me for travelling expenses.'

'No trouble. If you'll give me your address.'

Emma did so and they agreed on a date. Jared joined them and after being introduced to him and exchanging a few pleasantries, Lynne excused herself. She had remembered Nan and Roberta were supposed to be coming to watch the wedding and wanted a word with them. She looked towards where a crowd of well-wishers was milling about on the outskirts of the church grounds and spotted them. She began to make her way through the chattering wedding guests, only to suddenly be seized by the arm.

'I'd like to talk to you, *Mrs Donegan*,' said Dorothy.

Lynne did not like the tone of her voice. 'I can't think what you and I have to say to each other, Miss Wilson. For some reason you've taken against me. Now if you'd let go of my arm? I want to have a word with my daughter and grandmother.'

Dorothy released Lynne's arm. 'They're here?'

'Yes! Now if you'll excuse me.' She hurried over to where Nan and Roberta were standing, glad to get away from Dorothy, although it might have been interesting to hear what she had to say.

'Hester looks lovely,' said Roberta, her eyes

shining.

Nan nodded her agreement. 'Who was that glamour puss you were talking to a few moments ago?'

'That's Dorothy Wilson, Nan,' said Roberta. 'Did she admire your outfit, Mum?'

'You know what? She didn't,' said Lynne, smiling. 'I caught sight of you two and excused myself.'

'I wouldn't have minded a chat with her. What with us both having worked in the theatre,' said Nan. 'Anyway, you'd better not linger with us, love. You'll be needed for the group photograph. Don't forget to ask if you can have a copy of one of the bride and bridesmaid when they're developed, so you can put them on display for your next lot of customers!'

Lynne nodded and walked away, only to have her arm seized again but this time it was Sam who wanted to speak to her.

'Come on, Lynne Donegan, it's photo time,' he said, smiling down at her.

He wasted no time, ushering her into position next to Emma and Jared. As Lynne posed, she saw Dorothy talking to Sam and swallowed a sigh. But whatever she was saying it caused him to give a shrug before moving away and taking up a position the other side of a woman in a wheelchair. Lynne would have given a gold guinea to have heard his and Dorothy's conversation.

As soon as the photographer had finished, Emma asked if Lynne would like a lift to the Tudor Rooms where the wedding reception was to take place. She thanked her and found herself sharing the rear passenger seat with an elderly Welsh woman, Myra Jones. She also admired Lynne's gown and they chatted comfortably. Lynne discovered that Myra lived in the village where Hester and Ally were to make their home. She suggested that Lynne should visit the area during the summer months. Lynne replied that she would try but if she was honest would have said that she could not possibly afford to do so unless she were to manage to find some more customers.

On their arrival at the Tudor Rooms, Lynne took the opportunity to congratulate the newly-weds but as there was a line of guests queuing up behind her she did not linger. She helped herself to a glass of sherry and looked about her for somewhere to sit. She was aware that Dorothy was talking to the woman in the wheelchair and noticed Hester's father and Sam join them.

Lynne felt a little out of things and so was pleased when a voice said, 'You're Lynne Donegan, the dressmaker, I believe!'

Lynne smiled at the pleasant-faced woman of a similar age to herself. 'I am! Who are you?'

'I'm Hester's friend Wendy,' she replied, sitting on the chair next to Lynne. 'We were in the police force together until I married. She ordered me to make friends with you when she saw you sitting all alone.'

'That's good of her – and you, as well,' added Lynne hastily. 'But I'm fine, honestly! I enjoy watching people.'

'Me too!' said Wendy, smiling. 'Were you

watching anyone in particular?'

'The woman in the wheelchair. D'you know who she is?'

'Yes, that's Hester and Sam's stepmother, Grace. She went missing during the Blitz. It was only a few months ago that her daughter, Jeanette, managed to trace her.'

'Why was that?' asked Lynne.

'It's complicated but she was caught in an explosion and lost her memory for a short while and what with her ending up in a wheelchair she didn't want to be a burden on the family,' said Wendy. 'I wager that's why Sam's girlfriend is giving her so much attention.'

'Why d'you say that?' asked Lynne, sipping her sherry.

'Grace Walker's story would make a good film.'

'I thought you'd have to be famous to have a film made of your life?'

Wendy shrugged. 'It could be fictionalized. I can't see any other reason why Dorothy should want to spend time with Grace. Dorothy likes to be the centre of attention. In my opinion she's someone who puts her own needs first. She doesn't think about Sam's.'

'You know Sam well?' asked Lynne.

'He's a damn good detective and cares about people. I wouldn't be surprised if he was to make inspector this year. He's also a great dancer.' Wendy looked pensive. 'If our actress is not careful, she could lose him. A woman spending time away from a man like Sam who wants to settle down and have a family is just asking to

206

be dropped.'

'Surely she must realize that?' said Lynne, startled by how bitchy Wendy was towards Dorothy.

'You'd think so, wouldn't you? They've known each other for years, you know? She was the best friend of the first girl he loved but Carol was killed in the Blitz.'

'How sad!'

'Yes, it was. Anyway, he and Dorothy didn't see each other for years and then she came to Liverpool to appear in a play.'

'I suppose they fell in love,' said Lynne.

Wendy took a sip of her sherry. 'Are they in love? Besides, you need more than just being in love to make a marriage stick.' She paused. 'You lost your husband in the war, I believe?'

'Yes. Robert's ship was sunk with all hands lost.'

'War's a terrible thing,' murmured Wendy.

They both fell silent. Fortunately the call went out for guests to take their seats at the table and Lynne could escape.

She was pleased to find Myra seated on her left and a policeman friend of Hester's on the right. It turned out that he was a bit of a talker, so she did not need to say much, only phrases such as *Is that so? Fancy that!* and *Isn't that dangerous?* By the time he stopped talking, Lynne had finished her soup, and had the chance to look about her.

Instantly she became aware that Dorothy was watching her. Lynne allowed her gaze to drift past her and then turned to Myra and began a conversation with her about Whalley. Even as she listened, Lynne wondered how long Dorothy had been watching her. Surely Dorothy must realize that it was in both their interests for them to bury the past?

Once the speeches and toasts were made and the wedding cake cut, there came a break in the proceedings. Some of the men made for the bar and Lynne headed for the Ladies. The music group would be arriving at seven, when more guests were expected to join them for dancing and a buffet.

As Lynne washed her hands and renewed her lipstick, the door opened and Dorothy entered. Lynne's heart sank and she said the first thing that came into her head. 'If you're looking for Hester, she's not here.'

'Actually I was looking for you,' said Dorothy.

Lynne stared at her warily. 'Oh!'

'You must think I'm awfully rude.'

Lynne was silent.

Dorothy cleared her throat. 'Your appearance rather threw me in church as did Sam's behaviour. I put it down to that outfit you're wearing. I believe you made it yourself.'

'That's what dressmakers do,' said Lynne lightly. 'I'm sure you've seen better in London. Your outfit for example. Bond Street?'

Dorothy nodded. 'You've been to London?'

'No, but I read fashion magazines and my grandmother went to London when she was much younger. She used to be a dresser in the theatre but had to give it up because of age and ill health.'

Dorothy looked thoughtful. 'Have you ever thought of following in her footsteps? With your eye for detail and talent with a needle, I'm sure you'd do well. I could recommend you to a travelling company. You'd get to see more of the country and might even go abroad.'

Lynne could not believe what she was hearing. 'I have an ailing grandmother and a teenage daughter in my care. I can't just swan off round the country and abroad like yourself, Miss Wilson!'

Dorothy's eyes flared open wide. 'You know about that?'

'Of course! You're off to Italy to make a film. I hope it goes well for you.' Lynne put away her lipstick and made for the door.

'Wait!'

Lynne stared at her. 'What is it?'

'I feel we should talk.'

'About what?'

Dorothy hesitated. 'You don't think we have things to say to each other?'

Lynne was baffled by the whole conversation and thought that perhaps it would be good to have some light shed on it. 'I tell you what, Miss Wilson, if you feel like talking then perhaps you wouldn't mind popping along to our house and having a chat about the theatre to my grand-mother? She really misses it. Hester or Jeanette can give you the address if you can find it within yourself to make an old woman happy.'

Dorothy hesitated. 'I might be able to fit it in,' she said cautiously. 'It would have to be soon.'

'Monday evening?'

'Monday's a bank holiday. How about Tuesday evening?'

'That's fine. See you around.' Lynne left the Ladies, feeling slightly shaky, wondering how she had managed to keep her cool.

She was immediately pounced on. 'We've had so many compliments about our frocks,' said Jeanette. 'Hopefully you'll be inundated by women asking you to do sewing for them.'

Lynne flushed with pleasure, but even so she felt slightly alarmed. What if she couldn't cope with a sudden influx of work? For a few minutes she and Jeanette talked about clothes and the younger woman's hopes for a wedding next year. Then they were interrupted and Lynne was left alone once more.

Only three women came up to her and talked about dropping by at her house and seeing what patterns she had and asked what she charged so she gave them her card. Not for the first time did it occur to her that more and more people were beginning to buy off the peg and the days of dressmakers like herself being self-employed were numbered.

She decided to forget business and enjoy the wedding celebrations. She felt that in Emma she had made a new friend, as she had Hester, but just how much she would be able to see either of them in the future was another question. She had responsibilities as she'd told Dorothy and couldn't just flit off when she wanted. She thought of her grandmother and daughter, wondering what they were doing now and of the son that Dorothy had given away. Where was he now?

Sixteen

'Cruising down the river on a Saturday after-noon,' sang Nick, resting back in the rowing boat with his hands behind his head.

'You've the words wrong,' said Chris, wield-ing the oars expertly. 'It should be Sunday after-noon.'

'Yes, but it is Saturday, so don't be picky,' grinned Nick. 'You could have said we're not cruising.'

'So I could. You'd better watch yourself,' said Chris. 'We'll be coming to the bridge soon.'

'I don't think I'm going to bang my head,' said Nick, looking up at the bridge just ahead. As he did so he noticed a girl and an old woman on the bridge watching them. They waved to him in a friendly manner and he waved back but it was not until the boat shot under the bridge that he realized who the girl was. He twisted round as the boat shot out into the sunlight and looked up, wondering if she might have recognized him. It was as he thought and she had crossed to the other side of the bridge and was gazing down at him, waving madly.

'Hi, Nick!' she shouted. 'It's all right for some, messing about in boats.'

'I've done my bit of rowing,' he shouted. 'See

yer!'

'Who's that?' asked Chris.

'It's that girl from the coffee bar. The one called Bobby. I remember she said that she lived off West Derby Road, which isn't that far away,' said Nick. 'Watch out for that duck!'

'It can swim, can't it!' Chris rested on his oars. 'Anyway, we'll have to take the boat back soon. What do you want to do next? Or is your dad expecting you home early?'

Nick looked up at the sun and thought about the hours he'd put in at the shop earlier that day. His dad had given him a handful of change and told him to go and enjoy himself for a few hours. 'I think I'm OK for a while yet. How about getting some chips and going into town to the Tatler cinema?'

'If you like,' said Chris. 'But you can stop lazing about and take over the rowing again.'

'I don't mind if I do, although I was starting to get blisters.' Nick carefully changed places with his friend and rowed back to the landing stage where they had hired the boat.

They bought chips in Tuebrook, lavishly sprinkled with salt and vinegar, and ate them out of the newspaper as they waited at the bus stop to go into the city centre. At that time of day there appeared to be more people coming from town than travelling into it, so they were soon in the cinema and settled comfortably in plush seats, watching a Tom and Jerry cartoon. They roared with laughter as the mouse again managed to outwit the cat who, despite the punishment each meted out to the other, lived to fight another day. There was also a cartoon of Daffy Duck whose catchphrase *This means war* reminded Nick of what he had been thinking the other week when he had arrived home from the coffee bar.

He had gone in the back way and overheard his uncle suggesting that Kenny take Nick out of the Liverpool Institute and enrol him on a scheme for teenage boys to go to South Africa. *It'll be the making of him*, Dennis had said. *You don't want him to turn into one of those Teddy Boys and get into trouble. I bet they're behind the break-ins that you read about in the Echo. Do you know what Nick's doing right now?*

Nick had been furious and had burst in on them. 'I'm here now, Uncle Dennis. What was that you were saying about Dad not knowing where I am?' He had glared at him. 'And I was helping him in the shop most of the day! Isn't that right, Dad?'

'Yes, son,' Kenny had replied.

Of course, his uncle had blustered his way out of that by saying he only wanted what was best for Nick. Not for one minute had Nick believed that. He was a very unpleasant man, always seeking to undermine anything Nick was good at. He had never shown any kindness or thought for anyone other than himself before. Nick had told his father about Dennis hanging about outside the coffee bar. His manner had been really cool to his brother since then and Dennis had left pretty sharply after the exchange. Afterwards Nick had been told that the FOR SALE notice had gone up at the house in Wales and his father had made an appointment with a solicitor.

The cartoons finished and the newsreel flashed up on the screen with images of Sir Anthony Eden who was taking over from Winston Churchill as Premier of Britain and more about the disturbances in Cyprus and the latest on Princess Margaret's activities. Suddenly Nick noticed the time on the clock on the wall. It was later than he thought.

'I'll have to be going,' he whispered to Chris.

'Let's go then,' said his friend.

It was dusk by the time they parted on the corner of Balmoral Road where Chris lived. They exchanged tarrahs and Nick headed for home. The shop door was locked and the blinds down, so he made his way to the rear of the shop. To his surprise the yard door swung open at his touch. He could only presume his father had forgotten to latch it. He ran up the yard and came to an abrupt halt when he saw that the door was ajar. The wood around the lock and the door jamb was splintered and there were bits of wood on the step and the paving in the yard. He remembered an article in the *Echo* about recent break-ins.

His heart began to thud as he pushed the door wider and stepped inside. He was about to shout his father's name when it occurred to him that whoever had broken in could still be there. He froze and listened intently but could hear no sound coming from inside the building. He hoped to God that those responsible had not heard him coming and were waiting for him on the other side of the storeroom door. He made no move for what seemed ages and then when still there was no sound he decided he had to act. What if they were well away, having left his father lying there unconscious?

Cautiously Nick opened the door that led to the shop a couple of inches and, all being silent, he opened it wider. Despite the gloom due to the blinds being drawn, he could tell that the place was in a mess. He fumbled for the switch and light flooded the interior, illuminating the chaos the intruders had left the shop in. He looked towards the counter and his heart seemed to leap inside his chest as he saw his father lying across it. Stupidly, for a moment, Nick thought he was doing one of his stretching exercises and then he swore at his own foolishness. The blood was pounding in his ears and he thought he might faint. Somehow he managed to stumble across the room, tripping over lengths of wood and nearly going flying when he put his foot on some scattered nails.

'Dad!' he said hoarsely, placing a trembling hand on his back.

There was no answer, which really shouldn't have come as a shock because there was a chisel protruding from Kenneth's back. Choking back a sob, Nick turned and hurried out to summon the police.

Seventeen

When the music group struck up for the first dance with 'There's No Tomorrow', Lynne had few expectations of being asked to dance but she had not reckoned on Hester introducing her to a couple of her male colleagues from the police force. Lynne accepted their offers to dance but warned them that she was not much of a dancer. After treading on their toes several times, she was not asked to dance again.

She had been sitting alone for a short while when she saw Betty enter the room on the arm of a man who looked a few years older and she wondered who he could be. She watched the couple exchange a few words with Hester, and then Betty caught Lynne's eye and she and her escort made their way over to her.

'Hi, Lynne,' said Betty, smiling. 'Would you mind if Lenny and I sit with you?'

'No, I'd be glad of the company to be honest,' she said warmly.

'Good!' Betty hung her handbag on the back of the chair that Lenny had pulled out for her. 'This is my boss from the coffee bar,' she added.

'Good to meet you, Lynne,' he said, holding out a hand.

'It's nice to meet you, too,' she said.

216

'Can I get you both a drink?' he asked.

They both thanked him and asked for Babycham and he went off to the bar.

'So that's your boss,' said Lynne, smiling.

'Yes, Lenny's a decent bloke, even though he never listens to me. I've lost count of the times I've told him he should apply for a licence for live music and dancing.' Betty blew out a breath.

'So there's nothing serious between the pair of you?' asked Lynne with a twinkle.

'Hell's bells, no! I'm fond of him but he's a bit too old for me. Besides I'm not looking to go steady with anyone,' she said firmly. 'I was hoping that by bringing him here, he might change his mind when he hears the group play.'

'Is that your only reason?' asked Lynne.

Betty smiled faintly. 'I did want to apologize for not ordering anything from you. I mean it was one of the reasons I asked you and Bobby along to my flat and I didn't even give her the time that I intended to, to discuss her art.'

'You were distracted.'

'Too right I was.' She pulled a face.

'I was sorry to hear that you're thinking of giving up painting and not going to Italy,' said Lynne. 'What did your art tutor say about your decision?'

Betty sighed. 'That I should take some time off and give it more thought.'

'That sounds sensible to me,' said Lynne. 'We've had a postcard of the Trevi Fountain from Stuart.'

'I had one from him, too.' She sighed again. 'He wrote down his itinerary in very small

217

handwriting. I wish he hadn't. It made me feel...'
She did not finish her sentence.

Lynne felt a surge of concern for her. 'I imagine you've got some money saved?'

Betty nodded.

'Then why don't you go to Italy now?' urged Lynne. 'Don't think about work or the future. Have a holiday! See the sights. Relax in the sun and enjoy yourself.'

Betty gaped at her. 'But I can't do that!'

'Why not?'

'Because I can't just go abroad like that! Besides I'd be letting Lenny down.'

'I'm sure Lenny would be able to find someone else to take your place for just a fortnight. It would do you a lot of good,' said Lynne firmly, covering Betty's hand with hers.

Betty was silent for a long time and then she said, 'No, I can't do it. I was going to travel with Tony's family, stay with their relatives. They wouldn't be expecting me this early.'

'Have a word with Tony this evening and he could pass a message on to his parents and see what they have to say. Don't put it off or you'll probably think up another reason why you shouldn't go!'

'You mean it's a case of now or never?' said Betty.

'Yes!' Lynne smiled. 'What have you got to lose? You'll be spending less than you planned in the first place.'

'But the whole point of my going to Italy was because of my art,' said Betty.

'There's nothing stopping you enjoying art for

art's sake,' said Lynne. 'It's what most tourists do.'

Betty nodded and rose to her feet. 'You have a point. I'll just go and have a word with our Jared and Emma. I know they've been worrying about me and I want to reassure them that I'm OK.' She walked away.

'Where's Betty gone?'

Lynne glanced up at Lenny who held a tray bearing their drinks. 'She went to talk to Emma and Jared. I presume you know who they are?'

'Yes!' He placed the tray on the table. 'She's very fond of them and hasn't been a bit like herself and when she burst into tears because I made her favourite fried mushrooms and tomatoes in butter on toast the other evening, it all came out that there had been a family tiff. She wasn't even going to come to this do but I told her she was cutting off her nose to spite her face. I know she's been wanting me to listen to her friends' music, so I told her that I'd come with her.'

'That was kind of you,' said Lynne, reaching for her glass and thanking him before adding, 'And what do you think of the music?'

'Not my kind of thing but I can see how it appeals to the kids.' He downed half of his beer. 'She also mentioned that the actress, Dorothy Wilson, was going to be here and I thought I'd like to see if she's as attractive as her photo.'

'You're a fan?' asked Lynne.

He shrugged broad shoulders. 'I love film but I went to see her on stage when I read a review in the *Echo* and discovered she was a local girl and I knew her in the old days. Ages since I've seen her, mind, and her voice has changed. She's almost managed to lose the accent.'

Lynne could not help but be interested in his having known Dorothy in the past. She looked about the hall for a sign of her and spotted her on the dance floor with Sam. 'There she is with Sam Walker. He's the brother of the bride, if you don't know.'

'Oh, I know Sam from years back.' Lenny scanned the dance floor but couples were joining those already dancing, so it wasn't as easy to find Sam and Dorothy again. 'Would you like to dance, Lynne, then if you spot the pair, you could guide me in the right direction and we could bump into them accidentally on purpose?'

Lynne was amused. 'Do you think that's necessary? You could wait until the dance ends and then we could find them.'

'Nah!' He grinned. 'I'll make more of an impression if we do it my way.'

'All right, but I'm a lousy dancer,' she warned.

They took to the floor and she soon discovered that he was just as much a rotten dancer as she was. Miraculously they managed to avoid treading on other people's toes and more by luck than design they ended up close to Sam and Dorothy when the music came to a halt.

'I've been watching you,' said Sam, to their surprise. 'I couldn't see your feet but I could tell that neither of you were performing the same steps as everyone else.'

Lenny grinned. 'I confess that I can't tell a waltz from a tango.'

'I hope you're not going to say that you never know what your feet are gonna do?' said Dorothy, staring at him hard.

'Alma Coggan hit: 1954,' said Sam, staring at Lenny. 'I've a feeling we've met before?'

Lenny nodded. 'I used to live in Toxteth and played street football when I was a kid. Not only do I have a feeling that you were in the opposing team once but that your dad might have arrested me. I once ended up in court and had to pay a fine.'

Sam chuckled. 'Dangerous sport, street football! I remember you now. You had a bloody good left foot. You could have turned professional.'

'I remember you, too,' interrupted Dorothy. 'Your boot came off and went flying through the air and through Old Misery Guts' window.'

Lenny laughed. 'My dad almost scalped me alive for that. Ol' Misery got me by the scruff of the neck and dragged me to our house. My boot was in his parlour and he told Mam I wasn't going to get it back until Dad forked out for a pane of glass.'

'You didn't turn professional though,' said Sam, his eyes narrowing. 'I'm sure it would have been in the *Echo* if you had.'

'No, the war came along and I volunteered.'

Sam asked about his war and soon Lynne could see that Dorothy was getting fed up with the conversation.

'So what are you doing now?' she butted in.

Lenny glanced at her. 'I own the coffee bar where Betty Booth works. I came here with her.'

'Aren't you a bit old for her?' asked Dorothy.

Lenny stared at her. 'I don't see how that's any of your business, kid.'

Sam nodded. 'He's right, Dot. It's up to Lenny to choose whom he goes out with.'

'You would say that,' said Dorothy, sounding annoyed. 'I've had enough of this conversation.' And she walked away.

'She fancies herself, doesn't she?' said Lenny, gazing after her.

'No, you've got her wrong,' said Sam.

'She's bored of the talk about the war,' said Lynne.

'Pity about her,' said Lenny. 'She didn't have to listen.'

'No, but perhaps we went on a bit,' said Sam.

Lynne had an idea. 'Why don't you go and ask for her autograph, Lenny? She's bound to be flattered and forgive you.'

'I wouldn't bank on that,' murmured Sam.

'You could talk to her about film,' said Lynne.

Lenny's face lit up. 'You've got a point there.'

At that moment the music started up again and the three of them laughed because it was 'I Can't Tell A Waltz From a Tango'.

'Excuse me,' said Lenny, and walked off.

Sam stared at Lynne. 'D'you feel like dancing?'

She shook her head. 'If you had been watching me earlier, you wouldn't ask. I'll tread all over your toes.'

'Don't worry about it. I always know what my feet want to do,' he said lightly, holding out a hand to her.

222

She hesitated and then placed her smaller one inside his large one and felt a quiver go through her as he brought her against him. He glanced down at her. 'Don't be nervous.' She was silent and at first moved stiffly in his embrace. 'Relax!' he murmured against her ear. 'Just follow my lead and go with the music.'

She tried to do what he suggested but stumbled over his feet several times. Each time he hoisted her up against him until to her surprise she realized that her feet were resting on the top of his shoes. Partly due to embarrassment but also because of a giddy pleasure she made no objection. He was so tall and strong with big feet that she had no trouble balancing on them.

The song came to an end and he swung her to a halt so that her feet landed on the floor. She swept him a curtsy and he bowed from the waist before escorting her back to her seat. He sat down in one of the vacant chairs. 'Have you heard from the Yank?'

'Yes, he sent me a postcard from Rome. His father would like me and my daughter to visit him in America. Actually, he's my stepfather and has offered to pay for the trip.'

'And will you go?' asked Sam, frowning.

'My daughter would love to go and it would be interesting for both of us but...' Her voice trailed off.

'Have you ever thought of remarrying, Lynne?'

His question surprised her and she was almost tempted to tell him the truth that she had never been married but stopped herself in time. What

223

was she thinking of? She hardly knew him and beside what would it gain her?

'I don't really go places where I'd meet a prospective husband,' she murmured. 'I work from home and only occasionally go to the pictures with my daughter.'

Sam nodded and appeared about to say something else when Hester came over to him in company with another man. 'Sam, you're wanted,' she murmured.

Sam frowned and excused himself and walked away with his sister and the man. Lynne wondered what was going on and suddenly felt at a loss. She drank her Babycham and as there was no sign of Betty or Lenny returning to the table, decided that perhaps it was time to go home. She went over to Hester and thanked her for inviting her to the wedding.

'You're going already!' exclaimed Hester, startled.

'I'm just a bit concerned about Nan because she hasn't been well recently.'

'But we were just about to announce the buffet. It's bad enough that Sam had to leave.'

'Was it police business?' asked Lynne, taking a shot in the dark.

Hester hesitated and then nodded. 'A murder of a shopkeeper in Prescot Road apparently. There's been a number of robberies recently but this is the first time the burglars have killed.'

'That's terrible! But wasn't there anyone else they could have sent instead of Sam?' asked Lynne, toying with the stem of her empty glass.

'With it being the Easter weekend the force is

overstretched and so Sam has been hauled in. He's a good detective.'

'Your friend Wendy told me that he should make inspector this year,' said Lynne.

Hester smiled. 'The whole family will be thrilled if he does. Although, perhaps I should leave our great-aunt Ethel out of that. She and Sam have never got on and besides she's started going a bit doolally recently.' She paused. 'I'll have to let Dorothy know he's left. I wonder where she is?'

'She went off in a huff because of something Betty's boss said to her.'

'Really!' She touched Lynne's arm. 'Never mind them for now. I'll tell you what, I'll have some food wrapped up for you to take home, enough for you, Nan and Bobby's supper.'

Lynne was touched by her thoughtfulness. 'That's kind of you but you don't have to.'

Hester smiled. 'I'd like to. It would have been nice if Nan and Bobby could have been here. I've really enjoyed my visits to your house. When I'm settled in Whalley, you must come and visit me. It's really lovely countryside around there.'

Lynne remembered Myra Jones telling her the same thing, so she thanked Hester for the invitation. Perhaps if more work did come her way and the customers paid on time, then she would be able to afford a day off in the country.

It was on her way out of the building that she saw Dorothy and Lenny having a cigarette. 'Hester's looking for you, Dorothy. Sam's had to leave.'

'I know,' she said, dropping the stub of her cigarette and grinding it out with her heel. 'I spoke to him on his way out. Apparently murder's been done and it's not that far away from here.' She shivered. 'It's horrible!'

Lynne agreed. 'She also mentioned that the buffet would be getting served soon. I'm off to see how Nan is. You won't forget to come and see her on Tuesday, will you?'

'No,' said Dorothy. 'Goodnight, Lynne. You coming in, Lenny? Betty will be wondering what's happened to you.'

'Betty has her mates in the group to hang around with.' Lenny smiled at Lynne. 'Nice meeting you.'

'Goodnight,' said Lynne, and walked away.

She thought it appeared that Dorothy was no longer annoyed with Lenny and she had seemed friendly enough with her. She hoped that she would keep her promise. Maybe then the pair of them would get round to admitting to each other where they had met just over thirteen years ago. She thought fleetingly of Sam and what he might make of Dorothy having a son somewhere.

Eighteen

'This place really is in a hell of a mess,' said Sam, moving aside a plank of wood with the toe of his shoe and avoiding screws and nails that were scattered all over the floor as he moved out of the way of those removing the body of Kenneth Rogers.

'You can say that again,' said the beat bobby who had been first on the scene.

'They did it for the hell of it,' said the inspector, dusting off a chair and sitting down before taking out a briar pipe.

'It wasn't a factor in the other break-ins and it's not as if there's been a fight,' said Sam. 'No bruising on the face or abrasions on the victim's hands. The murderer came from behind and took him by surprise.' Sam changed the subject. 'Where's the son, did you say, Constable?'

'With a friend and his family who live on Balmoral Road,' he replied. 'Apparently they go to the same school. I thought it best he was out of the way and with someone he knew until we can get in touch with his next of kin. The mother says the victim's brother lives in Shotton in Flintshire.'

'Presumably the lad will have his address,' said the inspector, ramming tobacco in the bowl

227

of his pipe and lighting up. Once he had his pipe going nicely, he added, 'The sooner we get in touch with him the better, for the boy's sake.'

'There's something else that's different about this break-in from the others,' muttered Sam, prowling around.

'I presume you don't just mean the dead body and the mess,' said his inspector, who was due to retire soon and was happy to let Sam do all the work.

'I reckon the back door was forced from the inside,' said Sam.

The inspector removed his pipe from his mouth and pointed it at Sam. 'You're not suggesting it's an inside job and the son did it? Bloody hell, Walker, he's only a kid.'

'I wasn't suggesting the boy did it, sir,' said Sam.

The constable frowned. 'He seemed upset but he could be acting. Didn't like the way his father talked to him, perhaps. It's surprising how little it takes to make some of these kids react violently.'

Sam shrugged. 'I wouldn't deny what you say, Constable. We all know the trouble we've been having with juveniles. Remember that Teddy Boy who stabbed a doorman last year. The war's had a bad effect on many a youth.'

The constable nodded. 'He's no Teddy Boy. He's too young, just a pupil at the Boys' Institute. Mrs Nuttall tells me the boy lost his mother two years ago and was always a real help to his dad.'

Sam nodded and resisting, saying *See! She's*

given the lad a good character reference.

'I suppose we'd better go and talk to him, Walker,' said the inspector. 'Constable, you stay here.'

'Yes, sir,' said both men.

Nick stared miserably into space as he sat on the sofa in the lounge of Chris's parents. He was finding it difficult to believe what had happened. His father wouldn't have hurt a fly. He could only hope that the police would find his killer and the murderer would be punished.

'Would you like another mug of cocoa, Nick?' asked Chris's mother in a gentle voice.

'Thanks,' said Nick, handing his mug to her.

'What about something to eat?'

He shook his head, knowing he wouldn't be able to get food down him, even if his guts weren't tied up in knots like they were. God, what was going to happen to him now? He was sure those in charge wouldn't allow him to carry on living in the flat. Maybe he would be put in an orphanage and the shop and flat sold? *Don't be a clot!* said another voice in his head. *They're not going to put you in an orphanage. Someone will take you in! Perhaps Chris's mum and dad will let you stay here.* His spirits rose, only to sink again. *Why should they? They have three children already, so why take on another?* Then he suddenly remembered his uncle and his heart sank.

The doorbell roused him from his reverie and instinctively he stood up to go and answer it. Chris's father waved him down. 'You stay there,

229

Nicholas. I'll see who it is. Probably the police.'

Nick's spirits took another plunge and he could not keep still any longer and stumbled to his feet and headed for the bathroom, only to freeze when he saw the two men in the hall.

'Here he is, Inspector,' said Chris's father.

'I'm ... I'm just ... just going to the ... the bathroom,' stammered Nick.

'Then you go, lad,' said the inspector. 'We'll wait for you. We just want a few words. Nothing for you to worry about.'

Nick managed to drag himself upstairs and into the bathroom. He lingered as long as he could, not wanting to face the plain-clothes policemen downstairs. No doubt he would have to answer questions again about finding his father's body but guessed he wouldn't be able to get out of it. When he came out of the bathroom, he would have liked to have crept into Chris's bedroom but it was almost midnight and he didn't want to disturb him if he'd fallen asleep.

'Nick, are you all right?' called Chris's mother in a low voice.

'I'm coming!'

He went downstairs, holding on to the banister all the way.

Chris's mother placed her arm around his shoulders and ushered him into the lounge where the younger of the two men sat on a straight-backed chair, whilst the older one was occupying an armchair.

Nick sat on the sofa and was handed a mug of cocoa. He felt cold and warmed his hands on the mug and took a mouthful of the sweet chocolatey drink.

'I'm Detective Sergeant Walker,' said the younger man. 'So, Nick, do you feel up to answering a few questions?'

'I told the bobby everything earlier,' muttered Nick.

'We know that but we'd like to hear you tell us for ourselves,' said Sam.

Nick stared at the detective who had removed his trilby, revealing a mop of thick fair hair. He supposed women would think him good looking. He didn't wear glasses and his eyes were brown. Nick felt as if they could see right inside him. 'I haven't done anything wrong,' he blurted out.

'We're not accusing you of anything, Nick,' said Sam. 'Tell us about your day?'

The question surprised him and he did not immediately answer but sipped the cocoa before saying, 'I helped Dad most of the day in the shop, except for when I went shopping. I called in at the butcher's, the greengrocer's and the bakery after lunch. We were busier in the morning because a lot of men do jobs about the house and in the garden over the Easter weekend, so they were coming in for stuff and Dad was pleased that we were so busy.' He gulped.

'Take your time, lad,' said the inspector.

Nick nodded and drank some more cocoa before continuing. 'Then late afternoon Dad told me I could go out for a few hours, have some fresh air and buy myself a treat for working so hard. He gave me a whole pound in loose change because he said I was too old for an Easter egg.' A muscle in his throat convulsed. 'I – I was supposed to be back at seven o'clock to cook our evening meal but ... but I forgot the time. I went to Newsham Park with Chris. We hired a rowing boat, then – then we were hungry, so we bought chips. After that we went into town to the Tatler to watch the cartoons. I know I should have come home earlier but Dad ... Dad had told me to enjoy myself.'

'So what time did you get home?' asked Sam.

Nick turned his head to look at him. 'Not until after eight o'clock and that was when...' His voice trailed off and the colour ebbed from his cheeks.

There was a silence.

'Would you rather we left the rest until morning, Nick?' asked Sam, watching the boy struggle to regain his composure. He remembered how close to tears he had been after his mother died.

'It'll be Easter Sunday tomorrow,' said Nick. 'Dad and I were ... were going to put flowers on Mum's grave.' He swallowed.

'You must miss your mother,' said the inspector.

Of course he bloody does, thought Sam. *Poor kid!*

'Nothing's been the same since she died,' said Nick, putting down the mug and bending one of his fingers back and forward in an odd fashion. 'Now Dad's gone it's going to be different again.'

'Life changes all the time, son,' said Sam gently. 'It's the way things are.'

'It shouldn't be! I wanted it to be the same –

232

the three of us forever!' cried Nick wildly.

'Don't we all wish we could make time stand still,' said Chris's mother, who had stayed at the inspector's suggestion. She patted Nick's shoulder and he calmed down.

'Are you OK to carry on?' asked Sam.

Nick nodded. 'I came the back way because the shop door was locked and the blinds down. The yard door was open. I thought that was odd and then ... then when I went up the yard I realized the back door had been forced. The door jamb was splintered and there were bits of wood on the step and paving outside.' He frowned. 'That's odd!'

Sam stared at him intently. 'What was odd?'

'If it had been chiselled from outside it would have been damaged differently.' He stared at Sam. 'It could be that Dad let someone into the shop earlier and they tried to make it look like...' His voice trailed off.

'That is a possibility,' said Sam. 'Carry on, Nick.'

'I didn't immediately go into the shop because I thought the burglars might still be around, so I listened for a bit and when I couldn't hear any movement, I went to investigate...' Nick's voice cracked and he blinked back tears.

'Take it easy, lad,' said the inspector.

Nick breathed deeply and then told them how he had found his father's body. 'I ... I ... could make out that the shop was in a mess and then I saw Dad, lying across the counter. There was a ... a chisel sticking out of his back. I wanted to tidy up. Dad hated mess. Then I thought I should dial 999 and not touch anything.'

'So you didn't touch the till?' asked Sam.

'You mean did I check if there was any money in the drawer?' He frowned. 'I didn't have to because the drawer was open and I could see there was no money in it.' Nick fiddled with his finger again, bending it backwards and forwards.

Sam watched him, fascinated. 'You're double-jointed, aren't you, Nick?'

The youth didn't appear to hear him, saying only, 'I knew there wouldn't be any money there. I'd already worked out that a rotten murdering swine had broken in and robbed us and killed Dad!' His eyes were suddenly wet and he wiped them with the back of his hand.

'I think the boy's had enough,' said Chris's mother hesitantly. 'He must be exhausted.'

The inspector nodded. 'Can he stay here until we sort matters out for him?'

She nodded.

Sam stood up and he and the inspector thanked her and Nick and left. Sam felt wide-awake despite the hour. What a day it had been! A wonderful one for his sister and her new husband but a lousy one for the victim and his orphaned son. A bright lad who noticed things. Not everyone would have spotted that the door had been made to look as if it had been forced. Whoever had done this had gained free access to the shop. Posing as a last-minute customer perhaps? Sam hoped they'd catch the bugger who'd done this soon.

As he sat in the police car his mind went back over his day. It had been a peculiar day what with the wedding and then a murder. Interesting and fun meeting up with Lynne Donegan and Lenny Colman. Who'd have ever thought he'd have ended up owning a coffee bar? He had exchanged a few words with Dorothy and Lenny on his way out, explaining that there had been a murder. Lenny had said it had come as no surprise to him that Sam had joined the police force or that Dorothy had become an actress as she had always been good at pretending to be someone else – a comment which had surprised Sam, causing him to wonder just how well the two had known each other when they were kids.

Nineteen

'So, have you caught your murderer yet?' asked Dorothy, hoping to persuade Sam that she was really interested in his work.

It was one o'clock on Wednesday afternoon and they had little time to spend together. Dorothy had phoned the Walker household earlier that day to inform Sam that she had to leave Liverpool that evening after receiving a phone call from the film company. She had been fortunate to be able to speak to him. After the wedding, he had worked most of Easter Sunday and the bank holiday and ever since. Apparently there had been another break-in yesterday.

'We've arrested a couple of youths,' said Sam, opening the vestibule door of the hotel for her to go out. 'One of the neighbours noticed something suspicious when he was adjusting his television aerial and so had his wife phone the police straightaway.'

'So have they confessed?' asked Dorothy.

Sam shook his head. 'They completely deny having anything to do with the break-in and murder on Saturday and I believe them.'

'Why?' she asked, as they stood on the pavement.

'They don't seem the sort. I think they're new to the game. One was full of bluster but it was obvious that underneath he was terrified at being caught and about what his parents would say. The other admitted straightaway that it was his first time when I mentioned the other break-ins.'

'The son of the murdered man, what's happened to him?' asked Dorothy.

'His uncle came and took him back to his house in Flintshire,' murmured Sam, frowning.

'What's the frown for? Thinking it's a bit of a way to go if you have to question either of them again?'

'Something like that,' said Sam, although he was not thinking that at all but of Nick Rogers' expression when he saw his uncle. Despite Dennis Rogers' show of affection, Sam had sensed there was no love lost between the two. The couple who had been looking after Nick had been willing to have him continue living with them, but the uncle had been adamant that the boy should go with him as he was his legal guardian.

Sam changed the subject. 'What d'you want to eat? Chinese?'

'That's fine with me.'

She linked her arm through his and they cross- ed the cobbled road and took a short cut through into Renshaw Street where there was a Chinese restaurant not far from Sam's favourite book- shop. It was not until they were seated at a table and a waiter had taken their order that Dorothy said, 'So what was all that about, you dancing with the dressmaker in that peculiar way?'

Sam smiled faintly. 'I didn't know you saw us.'

Dorothy rested her elbows on the table and laced her hands together. 'I didn't but someone told me about it.'

'Who told you?'

'Hester's friend Wendy. I don't think she likes me.'

'You're imagining it.'

'No, I'm not,' she said crossly. 'Hester's told me that she's always had a soft spot for you. Thinks you're the bee's knees and you do seem to be putting yourself out for Lynne Donegan. What did you talk about?'

Sam's smile vanished. 'We scarcely spoke. I danced with Lynne in *that peculiar way* as you point out because it saved me from getting my toes trodden on. I think she enjoyed herself. I forgot to ask whether you gave Lenny your auto- graph?'

'He asked but I forgot because after he apolo- gized for upsetting me, we got talking about the old street and when we were kids. I asked him about Lynne Donegan but he said he'd only just met her.'

'Betty Booth introduced them.'

'I know that now! It was a relief, I must admit,' she murmured absently, taking out her cigarette case and putting a cigarette between her painted lips without offering him one.

'Why was it a relief?' asked Sam.

His question seemed to fluster her because she dropped her cigarette. 'Damn!' she exclaimed, bending to pick it up. 'I'm all fingers and thumbs this afternoon.'

'Excitement, I suppose,' drawled Sam, lighting her cigarette for her from his pocket lighter. 'Soon you'll be away from Liverpool and enjoying doing what you like best.'

'It's my job, Sam.' Her hand trembled slightly as she put away her cigarette case. 'The money's good and I've got to seize my chances while I can.' She smoked jerkily. 'Did she mention that I volunteered to go and visit her grandmother to make up for my rudeness?'

'Who?'

'Lynne Donegan, of course!'

'No, I told you we hardly spoke.'

'I'm surprised. I thought the pair of you might have had lots to talk about. You were so friendly with her in the church.'

Sam tapped his fingers on the tablecloth. 'I was being polite. She was all on her own. I thought you might have been kind to her.'

Dorothy sighed. 'So you didn't talk about me?'

'You mean because you're famous?'

Dorothy flushed. 'I didn't mean that.'

'So what did you mean?' asked Sam. 'You've got me wondering what this is all about.'

She reached for the ashtray on the table and stubbed out her cigarette and sighed heavily, thinking she would have been better keeping quiet about him dancing with Lynne. She should have had more sense because if Lynne had said anything, he would have asked her straight out if it was true. She only knew that the other woman presented her with a threat and she did not enjoy the feeling of dread that came over her just thinking about her.

'What's the big sigh for?' said Sam with obvious patience. 'I can't believe you're jealous of her.'

Dorothy sat up straight. 'I'm not jealous of her and that's the truth. I don't envy the life she leads. I like my life!'

'As it is, I suppose. You doing what you want and having me on a string,' said Sam grimly.

'You had your mind set on buying a car before Christmas and that's what you did!' Dorothy flung the words at him.

'I'd have bought you an engagement ring and set a date for our wedding but you didn't want that. Perhaps we should call it a day,' muttered Sam. 'You could be free to do whatever you wanted then and so could I.'

His words scared her because although she'd imagined what it would be like to be completely free of him, she didn't want to let him go. 'I can't believe you said that just because I mentioned you dancing in that peculiar way with our

239

little dressmaker.'

'It's more than that and you know it,' said Sam heatedly. 'You're going to be away for I don't know how long and when you come back I bet you'll change your mind and decide you have to make that documentary. That's if you're not asked to star in another film and you decide it would be crazy to refuse,' he said, tracing a pattern on the tablecloth with his fork.

She almost blurted out, *How did you know?* But, of course, he couldn't possibly know that there was a chance of that. He was only guessing. Even so she began to have doubts about whether he had told her the truth about Lynne. 'It's her, isn't it? She criticized me, didn't she?'

Sam stared at her incredulously. 'Are you calling me a liar?'

'I want you to promise not to see her while I'm away!'

'So now you don't trust me. I'm making no such promises.'

'Why not? Because you'd break them? I've a good mind to leave right now.'

'Don't let me stop you,' said Sam coldly.

She had not really intended walking out on him but pride and anger caused her to reach for her coat and handbag and, getting up from the table, she walked out of the restaurant without a backward glance. She half-expected him to come after her, to say sorry and that they mustn't part in such a way.

But he didn't.

She kept on walking, up Renshaw Street until she reached Lycee Street. She continued on up there, thinking to turn left at Roscoe Street or Rodney Street which would take her into Mount Pleasant where the hotel was but suddenly she remembered Lenny and his coffee bar. Why shouldn't she go in there and have a coffee and a snack?

As she pushed open the door she realized immediately that the place was full of teenagers; all appearing to be talking at once and from the jukebox came music that she recognized as Alma Coggan. She could not see an available table – or Lenny for that matter – and was about to leave when a voice said, 'It's Dorothy Wilson, isn't it?'

Oh no! she thought, having forgotten that Betty Booth worked here when she wasn't at college.

'Hello,' said Dorothy, clutching her handbag tightly. 'I see you're full up.'

'Pretty much! Didn't expect to see you here.' Betty smiled. 'Were you wanting to have a word with Lenny? He was telling me that you knew each other from yonks ago. You can go in the back if you like. I'm sure he'll be pleased to see you and I'll bring you in a coffee, shall I?'

'Thanks,' said Dorothy, thinking she couldn't very well refuse. It would appear unfriendly and she didn't have to stay long.

She followed Betty, squeezing between tables and chairs and went through a door that led into a kitchen. It was welcomingly warm in there and the smell of cooking reminded her that she had left Sam to deal with her chicken chow mein. She felt a twinge of guilt.

'Hello, Dot! What are you doing here?' asked

241

Lenny, placing two bacon butties on plates. 'Slumming it?'

'Why d'you have to say that as if I'm some kind of snob?' she retorted, her eyes flashing with annoyance.

'It was a bad joke. Why are you here?' he said mildly.

'I was just passing and thought I'd look in. I'm leaving Liverpool this evening.'

'So you came to say goodbye?' He sounded amused.

'You don't believe me?'

'No.'

She spotted a chair and sat down. 'You'd be right not to do so.'

He walked past her and, opening the door, shouted to Betty who came running, tore a page from her order pad and placed it down before carrying out the plates of bacon butties.

'My feet are killing me,' said Dorothy, easing off a black patent leather shoe decorated with a leather bow at the front. 'It's a bit of a climb up here.' She wriggled her toes.

'So why make the effort?' asked Lenny, gazing at her legs before glancing at the order. He took sausages from a refrigerator and placed several in a frying pan on a hot plate.

'I had an argument with Sam and walked out on him.'

'Hah! Had a feeling it would be something like that. Didn't argue over me, did you?'

'You flatter yourself!'

He grinned. 'Then go back to him and make up.'

'I should, I suppose. I left him in the Chinese with a beef curry and a chicken chow mein to eat.'

'That's mean. I know he's a big fella but even so...'

She got up from the chair. 'I'll see you then.'

'Yeah, see yer. Hope everything goes well with the filming. Get me some autographs of the rich and famous if you will?'

'Will do,' said Dorothy, and left.

As she made her way through the packed coffee bar to the outside door, Betty caught up with her. 'You going already?'

'Yes! I'm leaving Liverpool this evening to begin filming.'

'Good luck!' said Betty.

Dorothy thanked her and went outside and stood a moment, breathing deeply of air that was a little fresher since the new Clean Air Act had been passed. *Italy!* she thought with a rising excitement. Then she began to make her way back to Renshaw Street, hoping to find Sam still at the restaurant.

To her relief he was at the table where she had left him, drinking coffee. He raised his eyebrows when he saw her. 'Women! Always changing their minds,' he said in an emotionless voice. 'You're too late. I've eaten yours.'

Dorothy sat down opposite him. 'I'm sorry. I deserve that.' It took her a lot to say what she said next. 'If you want to see our little dress-maker, feel free. I know I can trust you. Just re-member that you're a very attractive man and she's probably desperate for a husband.'

243

Sam's eyes narrowed. 'Don't be ridiculous. Why would I have any intention of seeing her?'

Dorothy could not disguise her relief. 'I also have to ask you a favour. Would you mind popping a note through her door apologizing for me, saying I won't be able to visit her grandmother for a chat about the theatre after all.'

'I'll see it's done.'

She paused and looked about her. 'Now where's that waiter? I need to order another chicken chow mein, knowing that my boyfriend is a pig having eaten mine.'

'I lied. I didn't eat your chow mein because I cancelled it. Now tell me, where did you go when you left here?'

'I just walked round the block, looking in the shop windows,' said Dorothy, reluctant to tell him the truth about having dropped in on Lenny.

'I don't suppose you saw anything that you wanted to buy that matched up to Bond Street?' He lit up a cigarette.

'I've packed all I need,' she said.

Their parting was less strained than she thought it might be. At least he kissed her and told her not to work too hard on set and enjoy herself in Italy.

It was only as the train pulled out of Lime Street station that Dorothy thought of Lynne again and wondered if Sam would deliver her apology in person.

Twenty

Lynne looked up from embroidering a patch pocket on a skirt and glanced at the clock on the mantelpiece and saw that it had gone eight o'clock. For a moment her eyes rested on the corner of the envelope stuck behind the clock and then her thoughts returned to the guest they had been expecting. She doubted Dorothy was going to turn up now and had mixed feelings about her failure to do so. Part of her was relieved but she knew that Nan would be disappointed. There were few things her grandmother enjoyed more than reminiscing about the old days in the theatre.

'She isn't coming, is she?' wheezed Nan, shifting restlessly in her chair.

'She might yet,' said Lynne.

'I bet she's forgotten. Too busy to give an old woman some of her time.' She paused. 'And where's our Bobby?'

'She's gone on a message and should be back soon,' said Lynne.

No sooner had she spoken than there came a rat-a-tat-tat at the front door. Lynne wasted no time going to answer its summons and was surprised to see Betty standing on the doorstep.

'I hope I'm not too late?' said Betty hastily.

245

'Only I've a message for you. Dorothy Wilson had a phone call this morning and had to go to London.'

'How did you get to know?' asked Lynne.

'She came into the coffee bar to give her autograph to Lenny and mentioned that she was supposed to be coming here to talk to your Nan.'

'That's right. Thanks for letting me know. Come on in.'

The two went into the kitchen and Lynne introduced Betty to her grandmother. 'Nice to meet you, girl,' said Nan, shaking hands. 'We were expecting that actress, Dorothy Wilson. I was looking forward to talking to her about the theatre.'

'I know. What a shame!' Betty sat down opposite the old lady and glanced up at Lynne. 'I thought you'd be interested to know that after listening to the fellas play at the wedding, Lenny's giving serious thought to getting a licence and hiring them to play a couple of evenings a week.'

'Good for him and good for the group,' said Lynne, smiling.

'That's what I said,' said Betty.

There was a pause and then Lynne said, 'How about a cup of tea and a jam tart? Our Bobby made them this afternoon.'

'Thanks,' said Betty. 'And while I'm waiting, perhaps your gran would like to talk to me in place of Dorothy about her memories of the theatre.'

Lynne beamed at her and turned to the old woman. 'You'd like that, wouldn't you, Nan?'

Instantly the old woman nodded and shifted in the chair and eased back her shoulders. Earlier the lines of her face had drooped, but now her eyes were bright and she was looking so much more cheerful. 'If you're sure, girl?'

'Of course, I'm sure. My mum loved the theatre and worked behind the scenes and used to play the odd minor role. You might even remember her.'

Nan was about to ask her name when there was a sound at the door.

'That'll be Bobby,' said Lynne, placing a plate of jam tarts on the table.

A moment later her daughter entered the kitchen with a bulky brown envelope under her arm. She smiled at Betty. 'What are you doing here?'

'She's come to let us know that Dorothy Wilson can't make it,' said Lynne.

'I could have told you that. I met Jeanette at the top of the street. She was with her boyfriend. She was going to pop in to let you know that Dorothy couldn't be here before they went on for a meal. Sam phoned and asked her to do it. Apparently he's up to his eyes due to there being another robbery and couldn't come himself.'

'Thanks anyway, love,' said Lynne. 'Were you able to get what I needed?'

Roberta nodded and handed her the envelope. 'Instructions inside. By the way, Mam, you know that murder you mentioned. It's in to-night's *Echo*. It's blazoned all over the page.'

'What murder is this?' asked Betty.

'The victim was a widower called Kenneth

Rogers who owned a hardware shop on Prescot Road,' said Roberta. 'His son found the body. Guess who he is?'

'No idea,' said Betty.

'Nick who comes into the coffee bar!'

Betty's mouth fell open. 'You're serious! Poor Nick!'

'So who's this Nick?' asked Lynne.

'I know who he is,' said Nan. 'He's the lad Bobby and I saw in a rowing boat in Newsham Park after the wedding. She called out to him and later she showed me her drawing of him. What a terrible thing to happen. He looked to really be enjoying himself.'

'It's so sad,' said Roberta forlornly. 'Nick told me that he lost his mother a couple of years ago and now he's lost his dad, too. How awful to be an orphan.'

Betty frowned. 'He does have another relative. An uncle! Don't you remember he was hanging about outside the coffee bar.'

'I know who you mean,' said Roberta. 'Nick gave me the impression he wasn't his favourite person. I wonder if we can do anything to help.'

'I don't see what we can do to help,' said Lynne.

'If the police are involved, I bet Hester's brother will know about it,' said Betty.

'Of course he will,' murmured Lynne.

'I'll see what his friend Chris has to say next time he comes into the coffee bar,' said Betty. 'Although it's possible Nick could be with him.'

'No, it says in the *Echo* that his uncle lives in Shotton in Flintshire.' Roberta sighed. 'Shall I go and make some tea or cocoa?'

'Cocoa, love,' said Lynne.

As her daughter left the room, Lynne changed the subject. 'How's Emma been since the wedding?'

'I knew there was another reason why I came,' said Betty, taking a piece of paper from her pocket. 'She's written her address down in case she forgot to give it to you. Since she got pregnant she's become real absent-minded. She said that any day this week is fine if you want to visit her in Formby.'

Lynne smiled and took the paper from her and glanced at it. 'I have the address and we agreed Friday but I see from this note that she's written down instructions how to get to the house.' She folded the note. 'Now you relax and Nan can get on with telling you about her life in the theatre.'

For a while Betty just listened to the old woman talking and then she said, 'I have a couple of questions.'

'Ask away, girl,' said Nan.

'Emma's mother ran away because she wanted to be on the stage. I wonder if you ever met her.'

'What was her name?'

'Mary Harrison – she was from Whalley. Apparently she had a lovely singing voice and lodged in the same street as my mother and her sister in Liverpool. Mary and my mother, Lizzie, ended up marrying the same man, William Booth. He was an artist and his grandmother owned a theatre here in Liverpool.'

'Sounds familiar,' said Nan, puckering her brow. 'But my memory isn't what it used to be.'

Betty said casually, 'I believe before she was married, Mum had a boyfriend who was an actor called Johnny. Apparently he died of blood poisoning.'

Nan nodded and said that perhaps there was something in her memory box about them.

Over cocoa and jam tarts, Lynne broached the subject of Italy. 'Did you give any more thought to what I said about taking a holiday now instead of putting your trip to Italy off altogether, Betty? I'm sure even a week would do you good and although I get the impression the Italians don't seem to go in for modern art like the painting you gave me, and prefer the Old Masters, you'll probably find encouragement and inspiration once you're there. And you just might bump into someone you know,' she added in a teasing voice.

Betty licked a jammy finger. 'You make it sound as if I'd be a fool not to go.'

'No, I wouldn't say that but if you were to meet up with Stuart, I bet he'll know lots about the architecture. Then there's Dorothy Wilson who'll be filming there. You might just get an invitation to go on set and that would be interesting,' said Lynne.

'It's a bit of a long shot me meeting up with them,' said Betty, doubtfully.

'Didn't Stuart send you his itinerary?' asked Roberta.

'Yes, but—'

'And as for our famous film star, I bet Jeanette could find out from her brother where they're filming,' said Lynne.

'She could ask him at the same time about Nick,' suggested Roberta.

Betty smiled. 'You've got it all worked out! I'll see what Lenny has to say about my taking time off in the next week or two and what can be arranged if things fit into place.'

'That's the ticket,' chuckled Nan. 'There's nothing like a break from everything to make you feel a new woman, ready for anything life throws at you.'

Betty stayed another half hour and then she hugged them all and reminded Lynne not to forget to go and see Emma on Friday.

Lynne had no intention of forgetting because she was looking forward to the day out and seeing Emma again.

Friday morning was almost cloudless and after Lynne had placed the envelope from behind the clock in her shoulder bag, along with her purse, some material samples, tape measure, pencil and notebook, she wasted no time setting off for Exchange Station, leaving her daughter to keep Nan company for it was still the school Easter holidays. Lynne could not remember ever visiting the village of Formby before, although she knew the beach, sand dunes and pinewoods to be popular with Liverpudlians, especially during the summer months.

It was busy inside the railway station because folk were making the best of the fine day. She was soon on the Southport train heading north. There were mothers and children in the carriage, so it was quite noisy as the young ones chattered

251

excitedly but Lynne did not let it bother her; she was enjoying gazing out of the window at the dockyards, Tate & Lyle sugar refinery and the enormous Victorian tobacco warehouse. She found herself thinking of the orphaned youth, Nick, and whether Sam was any closer to discovering the person who had murdered the lad's father. She wondered whether the uncle had a wife. There had been no mention of one, so he could be a bachelor. If so, how would the nephew and uncle manage? Teenagers were not easy to handle, so would a man, unused to children, cope? It was not going to be easy for either of them.

Her thoughts drifted to the wedding and that dance with Sam and a smile played around her lips. Then she thought of Dorothy and lastly Lenny, Betty's boss. She found the idea of her calling in with her autograph for Lenny an unlikely thing to do on the day she had to leave for London to begin filming, so had she felt a need to inform him that she wasn't going to be around for a while? If so what would Sam have thought about that?

The train began to pass through fields until eventually it arrived at Formby station where she stepped down on to the platform. Following the pencil-written directions to Emma and Jared's house, she managed to find it without any difficulty. She was welcomed warmly by Emma and after a cup of tea and home-made scones, Lynne took out the material samples that she had brought with her. Emma finally chose a glazed cotton floral print and a polka dot one in green

and white for maternity smocks. Then she picked out a plain green gaberdine and a burgundy
twill for maternity skirts. That done, Lynne took
Emma's measurements and wrote them down
and then Emma suggested they sat in the garden
and relaxed.

'I phoned Hester this morning to see that
everything was all right with the cottage,' said
Emma, wielding knitting needles with an exper-
tise beyond Lynne's capabilities. 'She told me
that she'd had a phone call from Sam telling her
that he had already heard from Dorothy and that
she was in Venice.'

'Venice! Somehow I thought she'd be in
Rome,' said Lynne, feeling almost envious. She
held her face up to the sun and imagined gliding
along with Sam in a gondola. 'I wonder if he's
wishing he was there with her.'

'Not according to Hester,' said Emma. 'He's
too involved with a murder case to think of
much else.'

'You mean the shopkeeper?' asked Lynne,
opening her eyes and staring at Emma. 'I think
the surname was Rogers.'

'That's him! Apparently they hauled in a
suspect but while the man's admitted to several
other burglaries, he swore that he hadn't had
anything to do with the one involving the
murder. Hester says Sam reckons that there's
something odd about the whole thing.'

'Bobby told me that she knows the victim's
son. He's some lad that she met in the coffee
bar.'

'Betty hasn't mentioned him to me,' said

253

Emma, 'but then why should she when she's had other things on her mind?'

'Apparently he's gone to live with his uncle. I feel sorry for the lad but I don't know much about bringing up boys. I only know when you're the mother of a teenage daughter you can't help worrying when they become interested in the opposite sex.'

'I know what you mean,' said Emma. 'I worry about Betty going off to Italy despite her being eighteen. You know this American, Stuart Anderson – is he as decent as she seems to think he is?'

Lynne's face lit up. 'I think so. So she's definitely going?'

'Yes, she's booked a flight and all the arrangements are made, thanks to Tony's father and stepmother.' Emma frowned.

'I'm sure she'll be fine. She has a good head on her shoulders and it's not as if she won't have anyone to turn to if she needs help.'

Immediately Emma's expression lightened. 'You're right, of course.

There was a silence.

'I wonder if Sam feels he can trust Dorothy? Venice is such a romantic city and what with all those handsome film stars...' Emma let the words hang.

'If you don't have trust, then I think everything would fall apart,' murmured Lynne.

Emma nodded. 'Betty was telling me that Dorothy dropped by at the coffee bar to speak to her boss.'

'She told me that, too,' said Lynne, glancing at

Emma.

'I mentioned it to Hester when she rang up because she knows him, what with her having visited the coffee bar on more than one occasion. She's never mentioned, though, that she knew him when they were all kids growing up. It's strange the way life turns out, isn't it?' murmured Emma. 'Meeting those you haven't seen for years and probably haven't given any thought to after all that time.'

'That's life,' said Lynne, hesitating before adding, 'I met Dorothy years ago, too, but we were just like ships passing in the night.'

Emma stared at her. 'But you remembered her?'

'Not immediately.' She changed the subject by reaching into her handbag and taking out an airmail envelope. 'This is from my mother's husband, Stuart's father.'

'That was out of the ordinary the way your mother died,' said Emma, her hands stilling on her knitting.

Lynne agreed. 'It still makes me shiver when I think about it. Anyway, Stuart's father wants my advice about the wording for her gravestone. He's suggested several different verses from the Bible and wants me to choose one. All extolling her excellence as a wife and mother. I find it really difficult what with my mother and I having fallen out years ago.'

'What was it about, if you don't mind my asking?' Emma murmured. 'I know my mother didn't really want me because she believed it would ruin her singing career on the stage.'

Lynne hesitated and then decided to tell Emma the truth. 'I got pregnant. I met Robert when I was only sixteen and what with the war and knowing we might never see each other again, we got carried away and we didn't have time to get married before his ship sailed.'

Emma stared at Lynne. 'It must have been a terrible time for you!'

'Yes, it was. Mother told me never to darken her doors again or something like that. Robert's ship was torpedoed and I ended up in a home for unmarried mothers in Cheshire. If it weren't for Nan, I'd have had to give up my daughter for adoption like so many others did ... although, not everyone wanted to keep their babies,' added Lynne. 'Bobby does know the truth about her father, although it's only a couple of months since I told her we weren't married when she was born.'

'How did she react?' asked Emma.

'Pretty well, considering. I'd always talked about her father to her and all she seemed to care about was that he and I were in love when it happened.'

'And you were?'

'Oh, yes, but it was an adolescent love and I sometimes wonder if it would have survived if he'd come back from the war. We didn't really know each other that well.'

Emma leaned forward and patted her hand. 'My mother was married and still didn't want me. After she died, my grandparents brought me up. I never really knew my father. They didn't approve of him because he was an artist and discouraged him from seeing me. That's how he ended up marrying Betty's mother in Liverpool.'

'Betty told Nan that your mothers had married the same man. She hoped that she might have met them in the theatre.'

'And had she?'

'At the moment it's slipped her mind but she's searching through her memory box of newspaper cuttings and the like, so hopefully she'll find something.' She glanced at Emma. 'Is it important to Betty? I know I wish Nan would talk about my father more. He was her only son but he died before his time, rescuing some children from a fire. I suppose she finds it too painful.'

Emma sighed. 'I'm sure it is painful for Betty. Just like your daughter, she was told something recently about her parents that she didn't know and it came as a shock.'

'Do you want to talk about it?'

'In brief, we don't know for certain whether we do share the same father. It's possible her mother was already pregnant when she married him.'

Lynne thought about that. 'Was the other man an actor?'

'Yes.'

There was a silence.

Lynne said softly, 'I like Betty. She's kind and willing to help people.'

'She got pregnant once,' said Emma abruptly.

Lynne blinked at her. 'When?'

'Jared's uncle raped her. She was only fifteen.'

'That's terrible!' Lynne gasped.

'Her aunt arranged an abortion.'

'What happened to the uncle?'

'He's dead now. It's not only wicked step-mothers in fairy tales who do nasty things to children,' said Emma.

Lynne shivered. 'It puts things into perspective, doesn't it?'

'It damaged her and she doesn't find it easy making friends with men but I think she is managing to put what happened behind her.' Emma stared at Lynne. 'That's why it's so important this American is a decent bloke.'

'I can see that.'

'I don't think she'll ever forgive the uncle but it would be good for you if you could forgive your mother.'

Lynne hesitated. 'I can do that but when it comes to choosing one of these Biblical verses, I really find it difficult to agree to any of his choices.'

'Why don't you pick one that you'd choose if your mother had been the kind of mother you wanted. Someone like your grandmother. Make the man happy,' Emma urged.

Lynne smiled. 'I'll do it. Although my mother will never be worthy of rubies to me,' she said, referring to a verse from Proverbs.

With that settled she felt a lifting of her spirits and thought how good it was to have friends as well as family. It was only on the way home that she thought about what Emma had said about it not only being wicked stepmothers in fairy tales who did nasty things to children.

Twenty-One

'I don't believe you!' Nick's face drained of colour as he gazed across the kitchen table at his father's brother. It had taken less than a week to age the youth. Since he had come to live in Shotton, his features had matured so that he looked older than his thirteen years. 'You're lying because you want to keep the proceeds of the sale of this house all to yourself! You want me to be left with nothing! You're determined to steal Dad's share and take the shop and its contents, as well.' His voice cracked. 'Well, you can't! Dad made a will.'

'How dare you call me a thief!' Dennis Rogers' expression was ugly and a tic twitched at the corner of his left eye. 'And I'm telling you the truth about you being adopted, so don't you be accusing me of being a liar!'

'You are a liar!' flashed Nick, who deep inside had been scared ever since his uncle had come for him but he was not going to be bullied. That way lay even more misery. 'Mum and Dad would never have deceived me.'

Dennis smacked him across the head. 'It's true I tell you! Our Kenny and bloody Muriel adopted you when you were a baby. I'll be seeing our Kenny's solicitor today and I'll bring the document home with me. He's sure to have it.'

Nick's ear stung and there was a ringing in his head but he clenched his fists and said, 'I bet this document doesn't exist. I'm going with you.'

'It'll cost me more if I take you with me. And if anyone calls, you tell them they'll get their money as soon as the sale of the house is completed.'

'I–I thought you might have changed your mind about selling the house now.'

'No, I need to get away from here and I have plans for you, boyo.' He slapped Nick on the shoulder. 'Good plans! Have you ever thought of the kind of life you could have living in one of the dominions?'

Nick rested his hands on the table, remembering confronting his uncle after overhearing him talking about wanting to send him on a youth training scheme to South Africa. 'You want to be rid of me and you think you can do it by forcing me to emigrate.'

'What's wrong with emigration? You could have a great life. South Africa want the brainy boys. You could go into mining. Or what about Canada or Australia? It would be a great experience living on a sheep station in the Outback, wouldn't it?' he said persuasively.

Nick stared at him fixedly. 'What about my schooling? Mum and Dad had plans for me! What about the shop?' The timbre of his voice altered and went up an octave. 'We could go back there and open up again. You lost your job at the steelworks, so what's stopping us moving to Liverpool? Dad put his heart and soul into making the shop a success. He wanted me to follow in his footsteps and I'm willing to do that because it was what he wanted, even though Mum had something different in mind for me.'

'He wasn't your dad! Forget about the shop! I'm going to sell it lock, stock and barrel as soon as probate's gone through,' snapped Dennis, slamming his hand down on the table, causing Nick to jump. 'Do you think I'm a fool? Once in Liverpool you'd be off with your friends, telling them lies about me. Well, our Kenny's will that you mention names me as your guardian! And I don't want to ever set foot in that bloody shop again. Leaving here and going to Liverpool changed my brother. He should never have married Muriel and did what she wanted. Scouse bitch! Pity he ever met her. He should have stayed over here. Should never have adopted you. Only she miscarried and couldn't have another baby and her heart was set on having a child.'

'I don't believe you,' said Nick, but his voice wavered and he felt sick inside.

'It's the truth, I tell you! The shop originally belonged to her brother but he was killed in the war. After that, all our Kenny could think about was throwing bloody money at it – and for what? Just so he could leave it to you instead of his own flesh and blood.'

Nick still did not want to believe him but his conviction that Kenneth and Muriel Rogers would never have lied to him was weakening. Yet still he wished his mother was alive to tell him that Nick was her son. He would believe her

261

above anyone, even Dad, but neither of them was here. He thought of Chris's parents who had been prepared to foster him but he doubted they would know the truth. Then Nick remembered the detective sergeant whom he had first seen the evening of his father's murder and who had commented on his being double-jointed. He had seemed an observant bloke. The difficulty was that he hadn't seen him since his uncle had brought him here, so it could be that his uncle had already told him that he was adopted or the detective had been in touch with Kenneth's solicitor and he had shown him the evidence.

Nick's throat felt suddenly tight and tears welled in his eyes. 'I am his flesh and blood,' he gasped. 'You shouldn't tell lies.'

'Listen, boyo,' said Dennis, prodding him in the chest. 'I can tell you where you were born and it was in no hospital or comfortable semi-detached in West Derby.'

'Perhaps not, but there was a war on when I was born, so Mum could have been evacuated for the birth.'

Dennis looked annoyed. 'You have a bloody answer for everything, don't you?' He thrust his face close up to Nick's. 'You were born in a home for unmarried mothers in Cheshire. I was in the army and our Kenny, who was flat footed and had a damaged lung seared by the heat from the furnaces in the works, wrote to let me know all about you. I thought him a bloody fool taking on the responsibility of a child that wasn't his own!'

Nick felt hollow inside. What was he going to

do? Why was his father killed? Surely a common burglar would know he would hang if he was caught, so would rather have avoided such a crime? It had to have been an accident. Unless...

He looked at Dennis and remembered the arguments he had overheard between him and Kenneth. An idea occurred to him that frightened him almost out of his wits. If Dennis was to read his mind then God only knew what he would do to him. He might not be a tall man but he was broad and strong from having worked in the steelworks.

'Well, do you believe me now?' asked Dennis, that tic throbbing at the corner of his eye.

Nick nodded. 'But it means that you're not my uncle and because of that you see no need to take responsibility for me, even though Dad appointed you as my guardian.'

'That's right.' Dennis looked relieved. 'Muriel always said you were a clever boy. As soon as I've spoken with the solicitor, I'll be in touch with someone I've spoken to who helps orphans to find a new life away from war-damaged Britain. There are great opportunities for lads like you to climb the ladder and make their fortune the other side of the world. If you have sense, you'll take your chance at a new life.'

'It sounds ... exciting ... but aren't I too young to be working on a sheep station or in mining? I'd have liked to finish my education.'

'You will be educated, boyo,' said Dennis eagerly. 'It'll take weeks and weeks for you to get there on a ship. There'll be lots of other boys and girls so you'll have company and there'll be lessons. I've been reading up about it.'

'And what will you do when I'm gone?'

'It's none of your business, boyo,' said Dennis, slapping him on the back. 'But I can tell you one thing for certain, I won't be staying around here. Now why don't you write a nice cheery letter to your friend Chris, and I'll post it for you on my way to the solicitor's? I'll have to read it over, mind.'

Nick's spirits sank further. What was he to do? He wiped his eyes with the back of his sleeve and began to think hard.

Twenty-Two

'You off to school now, Bobby love?' asked Nan, who was downstairs before eight o'clock for a change and sitting beneath the window in the early morning sun. The fire had not been lit because there was a shortage of coal on Merseyside. The tug men had been on strike and now there was talk of the rail workers walking out, too.

'Where else would I be going, Nan?' asked Roberta, kissing the old woman on the cheek.

'Nowhere, I suppose,' said Nan, patting her face.

As Lynne handed a cup of tea to her grandmother, she thought about how they had all been woken early by the sun on that fine May morning. May was one of her favourite months with all the signs of spring to lift the spirits, and summer to look forward to with its long evenings of daylight.

She remembered how on the 1st of May, the young girls in her street would dress up in their mothers' frocks as it was a simple way of providing the girls with long dresses. Some had even borrowed a pair of their mother's high heels, and a touch of lipstick to parade around the block, rattling an empty tin can on a length of string in the hope of being given some coppers by adults. Some customs die hard, thought Lynne, remembering her daughter doing the same thing only a few short years ago.

'So what time will you be home this evening?' she asked, plucking a single strand of hair from the lapel of Roberta' s blazer.

Her daughter pursed her lips and then took a deep breath. 'I was thinking of calling in at the coffee bar to see if there's any sign of Chris, Nick's friend. I hardly know him but he might have heard from him.'

Lynne agreed. 'Maybe I should pay Emma another visit and see if she's had a postcard from Betty.'

'It'll cost you the fare, Mum,' reminded Roberta. 'Why don't you wait and see what I find out at the coffee bar? I thought we'd have had one by now. It must be that they take ages coming from abroad. It could be that either she's back or she's decided to stay longer.'

'All right, but don't be too late home.'

'I won't,' said Roberta.

With a wave of her hand, she hurried off to catch the bus. The day dragged by and it was a relief when school let out and Roberta could make her way to the coffee bar. She found the place half-empty and to her disappointment there was no sign of Betty or Chris but perhaps Lenny had heard from her. Roberta went to the rear of the cafe and after asking if she could come in, she entered the kitchen. The tantalizing smell of fried bacon and toast lingered in the air.

Lenny glanced up from the worktop where he was filling a bread roll with ham and sliced hard-boiled egg. 'Hello, Bobby, can I help you?'

'I wondered if you'd heard from Betty?'

He placed the filled roll on a plate and washed his hands, saying over his shoulder, 'I've had a letter. She's planning on returning after the Whit bank holiday. I got the impression she would be writing to you.'

Roberta frowned. 'I wonder when.'

He shrugged and rested his back against the table and folding his arms. 'How old are you? You wouldn't like a Saturday job working here, would you?'

She was surprised at the question and flushed with pleasure. 'I'm thirteen and I wouldn't mind at all working here Saturdays but I'd have to ask Mum.'

'I thought you were fourteen,' said Lenny, looking disappointed. 'Sorry, kid, it wouldn't be legal.'

She sighed. 'I'm sorry, too. I won't be fourteen until next February.'

'Well, if you still want a Saturday job, come back then. Somehow I doubt Betty will be working here.'

'Did she mention Stuart Anderson?'

'You mean the Yank?'

'Yes, he's Mum's stepbrother and was staying at the same hotel as the actress Dorothy Wilson.'

He smiled. 'I know. Dorothy met them in Venice and fixed it so they were allowed on the set.'

'Wow! That was good of her.'

At that moment there were footsteps and the other waitress came in. 'I'd best be going,' said Roberta. 'Thanks for the information, Lenny. Tarrah!'

She passed the waitress and went into the cafe and was about to leave when she caught sight of Chris sitting at the same table as Tony. Her heart gave a flutter and her legs seemed to turn to jelly. Two gorgeous looking lads at one swoop but did she have the nerve to go over and play it cool?

At that moment Tony glanced her way and must have recognized her because he signalled for her to come over. She hoisted her satchel higher on her shoulder and approached the table.

'I didn't know you two knew each other,' she said, slightly breathless.

'Only through coming here.' Tony pulled out a chair for her. 'We got talking about music. Chris plays the guitar.'

'I didn't know that,' she said, sitting down and placing her satchel on the floor.

'Why should you?' said Chris. 'We only met briefly that time you were sitting with Nick.'

267

She was glad he had mentioned Nick. 'Have you heard from him? I was shocked when I read that his father had been murdered and that he's now living with his uncle.'

'Not for long,' said Chris, frowning.

'Is he coming back to Liverpool?' asked Roberta eagerly.

'No, supposedly he's emigrating to South Africa!'

Roberta gasped in surprise. 'Why?'

'It's his uncle's idea. He thinks it's a marvellous opportunity for someone like Nick. Although, as it turns out, he's not his real uncle. Apparently Nick was adopted as a baby.'

'That must have come as a terrible shock to him.'

'As it would to anyone,' said Tony.

Chris nodded. 'I wouldn't argue but I find the whole thing weird. There's something odd about the letter. It doesn't sound like him. I know he's had a shock but even so ... I'm wondering whether his uncle dictated it to him.'

'Why should he have done that?' asked Tony.

'From what Nick's told me the uncle has always been a bit nasty to him, as if he resented him. If it's true he's adopted, then maybe that's the reason why,' said Chris.

'I think he wants Nick out of the way and I bet it's something to do with the house the grandfather left,' said Roberta thoughtfully.

They stared at her. 'What do you know about that?' asked Chris.

'I overheard you and Nick talking about his father wanting to sell it.'

There was a silence.

Roberta cleared her throat. 'I wish there was something we could do but I don't see what. Anyway, I'd better get cracking. Mam told me not to be late.'

'See you around!' said both youths.

She nodded and left. As she sat on the bus on the way home, she thought about Nick and what she knew of his situation. Should she mention it to her mother and see what she thought? Although, most likely Lynne would be more interested in what Lenny had told her about Betty and Stuart seeing Dorothy in Venice.

'So here you are at last,' said Lynne, switching off the wireless as her daughter entered the room.

'I've news for you,' said Roberta. 'Lenny told me that Betty and Stuart went to Venice and met up with Dorothy Wilson and she arranged for them to see some of the filming.' She took off her blazer. 'And Nick, whose father was murdered, has turned out to be adopted and so his uncle, who isn't his uncle, is sending him to South Africa!'

'What!' Lynne stared at her in surprise. 'Did Lenny tell you that, too?'

'No, Nick's friend, Chris, was there with Tony. You remember him, don't you, Mam? Italian with a fab singing voice?'

'Yes, I remember him,' said Lynne drily.

Roberta chewed on her lip. 'I'm worried, Mam.'

'No more than I am. These two lads...'

269

'Oh, Mam, don't be fussing just because I talk to boys. I only wanted to know whether Chris had any news of Nick and that's what he told me.'

'So why are you worried?'

'I don't trust the uncle. Apparently, he'd been arguing with Nick's dad over a house left to them by their father. I just have a feeling that the uncle wants Nick out of the way and it's to do with the house.'

'This Nick, is he the one in your sketch book?'

Roberta blinked at her. 'Have you been looking at my drawings?'

Lynne nodded. 'Obviously. You've nothing to hide, have you? You haven't been meeting him before all this happened, have you?'

'If you mean sneakily – no! I've only ever seen him in the library and the coffee bar.' Roberta frowned. 'Anyway, I thought you might mention about Nick being adopted and sent away to his uncle, to Hester Walker's brother, the policeman.'

'I'll see,' said Lynne, reaching into her apron pocket and taking out an envelope. 'You didn't really need to talk to Lenny. This is a letter from Betty and Stuart. I can't say that either of them has wasted any time getting together and making plans.'

Roberta smiled. 'You mean they've had a whirlwind romance and are getting married?'

'No-oo!' Lynne handed her the envelope. 'Read it and you'll see. I'm wondering what Emma and Jared will make of it.'

Roberta took the letter out of the envelope and

began to read. Her eyes widened as she came to the part that her mother had referred to and then she looked at Lynne. 'She's going to go to California with Stuart to paint! She's going to get herself a job over there.'

'Yes, although she'll be coming home to Liverpool before then. She wants to be here when Emma's baby arrives and Stuart will be staying in Europe a bit longer.'

'D'you think they plan on getting married eventually?' asked Roberta.

'I've no idea. She'd need Jared's permission because he's her guardian and she isn't twenty-one yet,' Lynne murmured.

'I hope they do get married,' said Roberta happily, handing the letter back to her mother. 'What's to eat? And where's Nan?'

'With the weather being so nice, she decided to go for a walk to the park,' said Lynne, frowning. 'I would have gone with her but she told me not to bother and get on with sewing. I'll go and get your dinner out the oven and then take a stroll that way and see if she's fallen asleep or is talking to someone.'

'You get going now, Mam. I can get my own dinner out of the oven,' said Roberta, shooing her mother out of the kitchen.

Lynne put on her cardigan and headed for the front door. 'I'll be back soon,' she said.

But Lynne did not return as quickly as she would have liked because when she reached West Derby Road there was still no sign of Nan. She crossed to Sheil Park, passed the prefabs and the children's play area, still without catch-

271

ing a glimpse of her grandmother. Her concern increased and she continued walking towards Sheil Road and crossed to the road that led to Newsham Park on the other side.

The park consisted of a large area of grassland where children and adults alike played ball games or picnicked and occasionally listened to a brass band playing at the weekend. At the far end of the park there was the boating lake where Roberta and Nan had seen Nick and Chris rowing the day of the wedding. Lynne told herself that it was possible that her grandmother had managed to walk alone this far with having her walking stick. Of course, she could have also met a neighbour who had lent her an arm and both could be sitting on a bench, resting.

Suddenly Lynne spotted the green-coated bulky figure of Nan on a bench several yards away. She appeared to be asleep in the evening sun but a feeling of foreboding caused Lynne to run the last few yards. Reaching out a trembling hand, she touched her grandmother's wrinkled cheek. It still felt warm but Lynne knew that the dear old woman was dead because there was no familiar sound of her laboured breathing.

She sat next to Nan and took her hand in hers and felt for a pulse but could not find one. Tears rolled down her cheeks but she made no move to get up. Eventually she knew that she would need help. She glanced about her. Where was the park keeper when you needed him? Certainly nowhere in sight and she couldn't see anyone else either. But then it was tea time. Then she spotted a youth standing on the bridge, gazing down at the lake's surface.

'Excuse me!' she called. He appeared not to have heard her, so she raised her voice. 'Hey, love, could you give me a hand here?'

His fair head turned and he looked her way. She signalled for him to come over. He left the bridge and came towards her. She had a feeling that she had seen him before but that wasn't important now.

'What is it, Missus?' he asked.

'I need help with my grandmother. She's died.'

He stared at the old woman and Lynne with a stricken expression in his brown eyes. 'What ... what d'you want me to do?'

The sight had obviously upset him, thought Lynne. 'It's all right, love. She's not going to harm you. It's only the living that can hurt you. Could you find the park keeper for me, and if you can't, could you go to the police station and explain the situation? I can't leave her, you see.'

The youth swallowed and then nodded and took off at a run. She watched him go, hoping he would do what she asked and not just abandon her.

Within half an hour, she heard the ringing of an ambulance bell in the near distance. Five minutes or so later, a middle-aged policeman approached her, followed by two men carrying a stretcher.

'Are you all right, Missus?' asked the police sergeant.

Lynne recognized him. 'You're Hester's father!' she blurted out.

He stared at her. 'And you're...?'

273

'The dressmaker. I'm Lynne Donegan and this is my grandmother! She...' Tears welled up in her eyes again and she couldn't go on.

Immediately the three men took over and did all that was necessary and later Lynne was taken home in a police car.

She found Roberta outside the house talking to a neighbour and her daughter seized hold of Lynne's arm as soon as she stepped out of the police car. 'What's happened? Where's Nan?'

Lynne told her the sad news and Roberta cried in her arms.

The following days were difficult ones and it was not until a week after the funeral that mother and daughter experienced any semblance of normality in their lives. They had a visit from Jeanette who brought condolences and letters from Emma and Hester, and Sam called round. He sat with Lynne in the kitchen, drinking tea and eating jam tarts.

'I'm sorry I never met your grandmother,' he said. 'Jeanette and Hester said that she was quite a character.'

'She was and I'm going to miss her terribly,' said Lynne huskily, absently breaking a jam tart in half. 'She had a very interesting life but there was sadness in it, too. She married late and lost her husband within a few years. My father, her son, died in his thirties and that grieved her deeply. He was a hero, though. A fire bobby, he rescued some children from a fire, only to lose his own life. At least Nan lived to a ripe old age. She was always there when I needed her.' Lynne blinked back tears.

274

Sam put down his cup and took out a large white handkerchief and offered it to her. 'She was also fortunate having you to take care of her in her old age.'

She mumbled a thank-you and wiped her eyes. 'I'll wash it and return it to you,' she said, placing it in her pocket.

They were both silent for a few moments and then Lynne said, 'You know I had to make a real search for her birth certificate. Fortunately I found it in a box with all kinds of memorabilia to do with the theatre. She was nearly ninety-one.' She gave him a watery smile.

He took her hand and squeezed it gently. 'You were fortunate getting on so well with your grandmother. I never knew mine but my great-aunt has lived with us for years and she and I never have got on. Now she's going senile I can't believe that I actually feel sorry for her. I could do with Jeanette living back home but, maybe when Dorothy returns...' He sighed. 'But that wouldn't be fair on her.'

Despite finding real comfort in the feel of his strong but sensitive fingers holding hers, Lynne withdrew her hand. 'You mean the pair of you will be getting married when she comes home?'

His brow furrowed and he toyed with his fingers, bending them back and forth. She watched him, fascinated. 'Are you double-joint-ed?'

He nodded but didn't expand on the subject. Instead he said, 'I don't know anything for cer-tain where Dorothy's concerned. She has a mind of her own and makes no pretence that it won't

275

be difficult for her to give up her career. She's talked about producing and directing a film about women of Liverpool, so maybe she will stay in Liverpool for a while.'

'I should imagine a lot of Liverpudlians would find such a film interesting,' said Lynne. 'It's a pity she had to cancel her visit to Nan. I'm sure she would have found more material for her film.'

'Yes, it was a nuisance that she had to leave in a rush.' He frowned.

She remembered what Betty had said about Dorothy seeing Lenny that day and wondered if Sam knew about it but decided it was none of her business. 'You'll have heard from her, of course,' said Lynne.

He nodded. 'A couple of postcards and she telephoned the other evening. Apparently she met Stuart Anderson and Betty Booth and they had a great time watching scenes being played out.'

'So I heard. How long will it be before the film hits our cinema screens?'

Sam's brown eyes met hers and he gave a wry smile. 'Now you're asking me something! I've no idea. I doubt she knows herself.'

They both fell silent and then Lynne remembered what her daughter had told her to mention to Sam. 'Do you mind me asking you about one of your cases?' She did not wait for his answer. 'The shopkeeper who was murdered ... his son ... did you know he was adopted and that his uncle is planning to send him to South Africa?'

'It's news to me,' said Sam, frowning. 'How

276

did you get to know?'

'My daughter told me and she had it from a friend of the boy. I assume the uncle must have told him he was adopted after he went to live with him.'

'Why should he want the lad to go to South Africa? If he didn't want to have him live with him, his friend's parents would have fostered him but he turned their offer down.'

Lynne hesitated before saying, 'My daughter thinks he wants him out of the way. Something to do with the uncle and the boy's father arguing over a house that had been left to them.'

'I see,' murmured Sam, remembering how he had thought the victim had most likely known his murderer. 'Thanks for this information, Lynne. I must admit I felt sorry for the lad. I had a feeling he wasn't fond of the uncle but my superior didn't see anything wrong with that.'

'Glad to be of help.' She smiled. 'Another jam tart? I find baking relaxing when I'm stressed out.'

He smiled. 'Your pastry's good. Our Hester's got light hands with pastry, too. You should go up and visit her in Whalley sometime.'

'I have had an invitation. Perhaps when I've finished all the sewing I have on at the moment.'

He hesitated before saying, 'Are you all right for money, Lynne? If things are tight we do have a fund...'

Hastily she replied, 'I'm fine. I had no diffi-culty paying for the funeral. Nan had paid tup-pences and sixpences for insurance weekly with the Liver and the Pru over the years and there was also some money in her post office savings book. If I'm careful I'll have enough to pay for coal and gas and electricity for a year or more, as well as have the odd day out.'

He nodded and then left, saying that he hoped to see her again before too long. 'I'll let you know when I find out more about the Rogers case.'

She thanked him and, after he had gone, found herself hugging the thought of seeing him again to herself. She washed his handkerchief and hung it on the line, considering his handsome face with his thick mop of fair hair, brown eyes and charming smile. He seemed so strong and caring. She told herself she should not be thinking about him in such a way but then he and Dorothy were not officially engaged, although a wedding definitely appeared to be in the offering. Even so, she could not wait until their next meeting and hopefully it would not be too long before he discovered more about the boy, Nick, and the so-called uncle.

Twenty-Three

The following morning, after telling his inspector what he had discovered and asking what his superior had found out after speaking to Kenneth Rogers' solicitor, Sam consulted a couple of maps, filled up with petrol and headed for the Mersey Tunnel. Shotton on the Dee was approximately an hour's journey away, as long as the traffic kept flowing and he wasn't caught up in the notorious bottle neck that was Queensferry. Fortunately, the bank holiday was not yet upon them and the roads were not overly busy. Eventually he took the turning for Shotton and drove along Chester Road West and turned into a street on the left of what he took to be Victorian terraces. He drew up at the kerb in front of the address he had taken from the files. There was a notice in the garden saying 'Sold, subject to contract'. It took only a couple of strides to reach the front door and ring the doorbell.

A woman working in the front garden next door glanced at him. 'He's not there,' she said.

'Do you know where he is?' asked Sam.

'I've no idea.'

Damn! thought Sam. 'What about his nephew?'

'Kenneth's boy? Me and my husband thought

he'd be staying here until he left school but we haven't seen him for about a fortnight.'

Sam frowned. 'What about Mr Rogers?'

'It was a couple of days after we stopped seeing Nicholas that he vanished. It's all very strange.' She stared at him. 'What's your interest? Are you a debt collector? If so, you're not the first.'

'No, I'm a detective with Liverpool Police Force.' Sam produced his ID.

She gasped. 'Is this to do with the murder? I'll help you if I can. I liked Kenneth. He was a really nice man.'

'So I've been told,' said Sam. 'I'd like to get into the house – do you have a key?'

'I do that, but Dennis has probably forgotten about it. His father gave me it a while back. I used to go in and do a bit of cleaning when his wife took ill.'

'I can see you're a good neighbour,' said Sam in a friendly voice. 'You can accompany me if you like to make sure I don't steal anything.'

She laughed and told him to wait a mo' and returned with the key shortly after. She opened the door and he stepped inside with her hot on his heels. 'Dennis has been out of work for a while. According to my husband, who works at the steelworks too, he was sacked for going in drunk and being belligerent. His mother would have been so upset if she'd lived to see it. His father had worked there most of his life, too.'

'You're talking about the Shotton steelworks, of course?' said Sam, pulling on a pair of gloves.

'That's right. The works prospered during the

280

war, making corrugated steel sheets for Anderson air-raid shelters. They saved many a life during the Blitz. But there was a shortage of the zinc they needed to galvanize the sheets, so they had to stop making them and that's how the Morrison indoor shelter came into its own.'

'That's very interesting, Mrs...?'

'Gertrude Williams.'

She told him of the layout of the house in a hushed voice as they went into a back room. The furniture was heavy and dark. *Probably belonged to the parents*, thought Sam. Newspapers were piled up next to the hearth and a window overlooked a yard containing a narrow flower bed that had been allowed to run wild. There were ashes and cinders in the grate and charred paper. The mantelshelf held a photograph. The couple were dressed in what was probably their Sunday best, circa the Edwardian era. The man had a carnation in his button hole and the woman held a posy.

'That's Mr and Mrs,' whispered Mrs Williams.

Sam nodded and went over to an ornate sideboard, which had a half circular mirror set at the back of it, and opened a drawer. Unlike the room, which was tidy and well swept, its contents were higgledy-piggledy. Obviously Dennis or maybe Nick had been looking for something in a hurry. The other drawer was in the same condition. The hunch he'd had earlier was growing and he hoped he was right. He opened the cupboard doors but they contained only crockery and finely embroidered tablecloths.

'I'd like to take the papers and documents with

me,' he said. 'I'll write you a receipt which you can give to Mr Rogers if he should return.'

'D'you think you might find a clue to the murderer in all that?' she asked.

He smiled. 'Possibly. Is there a sideboard in the parlour?'

'No. Dennis was pawning stuff after he lost his job at the steelworks and got rid of it.' She hesitated. 'He was a bit of a gambler and my husband suspected he got in over his head.'

Sam believed it. Single man, living with his parents and working that long, should have had some savings to show for his time at the steel-works.

He went upstairs and found the drawers turned upside down on the bed, their contents scattered on the bedspread in the front bedroom. There were no clothes in the wardrobe. One of the other bedrooms was completely bare, whilst in the small box room boy's clothes hung in the wardrobe, including a school blazer. There were also some underwear, shirts and jumpers in the chest of drawers. If Nick was still alive, he had left in a hurry.

'I wonder what he was looking for?' asked Mrs Williams.

'Is there a cellar to this house?' asked Sam.

'No, there's a coal bunker in the yard.'

Sam was relieved. One of his fears was that he might have found Nick's body buried in the cellar. 'I've seen all I want to see here. I just need a bag for the papers downstairs.'

'I've a brown paper carrier bag you can have,' she said.

He thanked her and while she was fetching the bag, he took out his fingerprint equipment and set to work on a few likely objects.

When she returned with the bag, she asked if he would like a cup of tea. He thanked her but said he had to be on his way. He wrote down his name and phone number on the back of a card and handed it to her. 'Do let me know if Mr Rogers or his nephew returns.'

She nodded. They shook hands and he thanked her again.

As Sam drove back to Liverpool, he knew that he needed to revisit the site of Kenneth Rogers' murder. He glanced at his watch. If he was quick enough, then he would have time to make it there and be home in time to have a word with his father before he left for work.

Out front of the hardware shop there was a For Sale notice as Sam expected after visiting the estate agent to get the keys. Once again he took out his fingerprinting equipment, believing now that he was dealing with no professional thief but one who had seen enough films and read enough crime books to know to wipe clean the handle of the murder weapon and the surface of the till if he was not wearing gloves. Hopefully he had not thought of the edges of shelves and beneath the racks holding the chisels. He tried for prints and ... Bingo! If they proved a match for those he had taken in the house in Shotton...

Sam put everything inside the bag he had brought for that purpose and then inspected the back of the shop to see if there was any sign of another attempted break-in. Upstairs there was a sash window that was slightly open. He went back inside and upstairs. The bed had been stripped but there was an army blanket folded neatly at the bottom of a single bed in the smaller room, as well as a change of clothes. In the bathroom he also found a recently used tablet of soap, a damp flannel and a hand towel but no sign of shaving equipment. In the kitchen there were a few crumbs on the floor and a couple of tins of baked beans in a cupboard.

He would bet his bottom dollar that Nick had climbed over the wall and shinned up the drainpipe and somehow managed to get through the partially open window. But why had he come to Liverpool and not met up with his friend Chris? If Nick suspected his uncle of murder, why hadn't he come to the police? Of course, he might have thought they wouldn't believe him. Or maybe he didn't suspect his uncle of murder but just wanted to get away from him?

But where was Nick at this moment and where was the uncle? Could Dennis Rogers possibly have left the country? Would he have done so without getting his hands on his share from the proceeds of the sale of the house and the shop premises? Sam decided to go back to headquarters and return later. He didn't want a constable on watch, in case he frightened off Nick.

He doubted the youth would return before dark, so he should have time to reach headquarters and be back here before then. It was then he thought of checking the time and realized his father would have left for work, having expected Sam to return home to keep his eye on

Ethel. He decided to give Jeanette a call and ask her to do him a couple of favours.

'So who am I looking for and what are the dates he might have sailed?' asked Jeanette, chewing on the end of a pencil. 'I won't be able to do it until tomorrow, by the way. I'll be leaving in ten minutes.'

'A Dennis Rogers and it will have been some time in the last ten days if he has left the country but you might not find anything; he could just be lying low somewhere,' said Sam.

'OK! See you when I see you.'

'I've another favour to ask,' said Sam.

She gave a sigh. 'What is it now? If you want me to go and look after the old witch this evening you're not on! I've a date with Davy. I'm meeting his ship.'

'Damn!' There was a silence and then he said, 'Could you drop by at Lynne Donegan's as soon as possible and ask her if she could keep Aunt Ethel company this evening until I get home?'

'Lynne! Why should Lynne keep the old witch company? Why can't you or Dad do it?'

'Dad will have left for work and I'm still at headquarters but I'm heading for the hardware shop on Prescot Road,' said Sam. 'Could you accompany Lynne to the house if she agrees? Thanks, kid.'

She groaned. 'I'm meeting Davy's ship at eight! It's going to be a bit of a rush.'

'Well, get a move on and you'll still make it,' said Sam, putting down the phone.

'Brothers!' exclaimed Jeanette, placing the receiver on the cradle. 'What would you do with them!'

The other typist smiled across at her. 'You know you love your Sam. What's he up to now?'

'I'm guessing he's on the trail of a killer but I'd best keep that under my hat.' She glanced at the clock on the wall and then reached for the cover for her typewriter. 'I'll have to get a move on. I've a lot to do before I meet Davy.'

Lynne opened the door and to her surprise found Jeanette standing on the doorstep. 'Hi, Jeanette! What can I do for you?'

'I've brought a request from our Sam, although you mightn't want to do what he asks. Truthfully, I think he's got a nerve asking you.'

'You'd best come in,' said Lynne, holding the door open wider.

'I'd best not,' said Jeanette, grimacing. 'I'm tied for time and if I wasn't, I'd be keeping Aunt Ethel company. That's what he wants you to do. Neither he nor I can, and Dad's gone to work.'

'Where is Sam?'

'He's at headquarters but has had to go to that shop in Prescot Road where that shopkeeper was murdered.'

Lynne's jaw dropped and then she took a deep breath. 'Did he say why?'

'No, just that I was to do some research for him and I was to ask you to keep Aunt Ethel company until he gets back. I wouldn't blame you if you said no. It's such short notice.'

'It's OK,' said Lynne, smiling. 'I don't mind. I'll just leave a note for Bobby, so she'll know where I've gone when she comes in. Then I'll get my coat and I'll be with you.'

Lynne was as good as her word and soon they were both on their way to Jeanette's old home.

It was not the first time Lynne would be meeting Ethel but when they came face to face, it was like speaking to a stranger.

'You're a new face here,' said Ethel, hunched in a chair in front of the fireplace.

'Yes, I am, but we did meet at Hester's wedding,' said Lynne.

Ethel jutted out her bottom lip. 'She had no right to get married and leave me. All the years I've looked after her – and the other ones are as bad. Grace's mother went to prison, you know? Had Grace there. They force fed her. I told that other one all about it. Now what was her name? Where did she go? Pretty kid, had a magic box that took pictures.'

Lynne wondered if she meant Dorothy.

Ethel glanced around the room. 'There's no one here except us. That's the trouble. They come and they go, they never stay.' She stared at Lynne. 'Who are you? I don't suppose you'll be staying either.' And tears welled in her eyes.

Lynne was glad when the telephone rang. It was Sam's father and he wanted to speak to him. 'He's not here,' she said. 'Can I take a message?'

'Who are you?'

'It's Lynne Donegan. I'm sitting with your aunt because Sam had to go somewhere.'

'Well, tell him there's been a lad here asking after him but when told he wasn't here, the lad vanished. He looked familiar to me. Fair haired, brown eyes.'

Lynne felt a stir of excitement. 'I'll see that he gets the message.'

No sooner had she put down the telephone than there came a knock on the front door. Lynne excused herself, wondering if it was Sam, but it was her daughter.

'I found your note,' said Roberta, smiling. 'So I thought I'd come and keep you company. I brought my sketch pad with me. How is the old woman?'

'Confused and in need of company,' said Lynne, pulling her inside. 'You can do me a favour. Make her a cup of tea and sit with her until I get back. I need to go to the hardware shop where the murder took place and take a message to Sergeant Walker.'

Roberta's eyes widened. 'Is he on the trail of the murderer?'

'I hope so.'

'Then hurry up,' urged Roberta. 'But be careful, Mam!'

Lynne lifted her coat from a hook in the lobby and left before her daughter could delay her further.

Sam was gazing out of the upstairs front window while spooning baked beans out of a tin when he heard a sound below. He put down the tin and spoon and headed for the stairs. His descent was brought up short by the sight of the youth who had begun to climb up. Sam knew the moment when Nick caught sight of him and stopped in his tracks.

288

'Don't be frightened,' said Sam, raising both his hands so the palms faced outwards.

'I'm ... I'm not frightened. How ... how did you know I'd come here, Sergeant?'

'Guesswork! I went to the house in Shotton today.'

Nick stiffened. 'You spoke to *him*?'

'If you mean your uncle—'

'He's not my uncle and Dad wasn't my real dad!' Nick's voice broke on the last two words.

Sam's face softened. 'I know. I discovered you were adopted from Mrs Donegan. I think you know her daughter, Bobby, and she had the information from your friend, Chris.'

'I see. So is that why you went to Shotton today?' said Nick. 'To see me?'

'Look,' said Sam. 'Let's not stand here on the stairs but go up and sit down. We can talk more comfortably there.'

Nick nodded and followed Sam upstairs. They sat across from each other at the table in the kitchen. 'I was told your uncle intended sending you to South Africa.'

'That's right! I pretended to fall in with his plan to allay his suspicions. I think he ... he did Dad in and I was scared he'd kill me too, so I ran away!' Nick's voice shook.

Sam reached out and patted his hand. 'It's all right, Nick. I'll make certain he doesn't harm you, although I have a feeling he's more concerned about protecting his own skin. According to the neighbour, Mrs Williams, he disappeared shortly after you left, and there's a debt collector on his tail. I think it's possible that once he knew you were at large, he decided to make a run for it.'

Nick's fair head shot up and he stared at Sam from damp brown eyes. 'Where d'you think he's gone?'

'I honestly don't know. It could be that he headed for Holyhead and took the ferry to Ireland or maybe he decided he would be safer as far away from this country as possible.'

'South Africa or Australia, maybe!' exclaimed Nick.

'Could be. It's possible that he's still in Britain but somehow I think not,' said Sam. 'D'you have any idea of the kind of money he might have on him? Mrs Williams thought he was hard up but it could be that it was he who emptied your father's till and any other cash he had hidden away. Your father's solicitor was obliged to advance him some money on your behalf because Dennis Rogers was named as your guardian in the latest will he had.'

Conflicting emotions showed in Nick's face. 'So why murder Dad?'

'Tell me a bit about Dennis and Kenneth. Why do you think he could have killed him?'

Nick told him everything he had overheard of the brothers' conversations and of the relation-ship between himself and Dennis, ending by saying, 'I knew Dad was seeing a solicitor and I did wonder whether he planned to have a new will made. Whether that was to do with the pro-posed sale of the house or me, I don't know.'

'Most likely it could have been a bit of both,' said Sam. 'Your adopted father must have known his brother could be violent when crossed and perhaps decided he wasn't suitable to be your guardian if anything happened to him.'

Nick took a deep breath. 'Maybe Dad told him of his plans and Dennis lost his temper and picked up the weapon nearest to hand. I can't prove it but I feel it in my gut.' He swallowed and tears filled his eyes.

Sam nodded and patted his shoulder. 'My superior spoke to your father's solicitor today and he seemed to be of the opinion that your father was considering making a new will but he never finalized it.'

'And that's why he killed Dad. He wanted him dead before he could do so.' Nick frowned. 'It doesn't make sense. Uncle Dennis would have still had half of the proceeds from the house coming to him.'

'Maybe your father knew something that his brother didn't? I brought a pile of papers back with me from the house in Shotton. Perhaps I'll find something there.'

Nick nodded and then a thought occurred to him. 'There was this piece of furniture that my grandfather had left Dad. We were going to fetch it just after Easter. I wonder if there was anything in that which could shed light on all this?'

'Maybe. If you could describe the furniture we could have a look inside it,' said Sam.

Nick nodded. 'It'll be in Grandfather's will but I don't know if that's still around.'

'Maybe that's what Dennis was searching for?' said Sam softly.

'You think he found it?'

Sam shrugged. 'I can't say but presumably your grandfather had a solicitor and we can ask him.'

Nick nodded. 'So what do we do right now?'

Before Sam could make a suggestion, there came the noise of someone hammering on the door below.

They looked at each other.

Sam thought he could guess what was on going on in Nick's mind. 'Don't you worry. Everything's going to be all right.'

He headed downstairs but Nick was not letting him go on his own and followed close behind. Sam looked out of the side shop window and his heart lifted when he recognized Lynne and he opened the door to her. 'It's good to see you but what are you doing here? Has something happened to Aunt Ethel?'

'My daughter's sitting with her. Your father phoned. He had a message for you about a youth wanting to speak to you...' Lynne paused as she caught sight of a shadowy figure. 'Who's that?'

'Lynne, meet Nick,' said Sam.

The youth moved out of the shadows and the light from a street lamp fell on his face.

'Oh,' she said, her eyes widening. 'We've met before.'

Sam looked at her in surprise. 'When?'

'When I found Nan dead in the park.' She smiled at Nick. 'I never had a proper chance to thank you but I'd like to thank you now. I thought I recognized you then, although we'd never met before, but I remember now, I've seen a drawing of you that my daughter sketched.'

'That would be at the coffee bar.' He looked embarrassed, jerking the fingers of one of his hands backwards and forwards with the other. 'I was glad I was able to help you.' He glanced at Sam. 'I went to the nearest police station and spoke to the sergeant there. He gave me a funny look and I just got scared because I'd only just escaped from Uncle Dennis. Seeing the dead old lady reminded me of finding Dad and I wasn't reasoning sensibly. I thought Uncle Dennis might have got in touch with the police and told lies about me. I even thought he might be having a watch kept on Chris's parents' house and the coffee bar, so I stayed away from both places. I reckoned he wouldn't come here because he told me he hated the place.'

'But what are you doing here, Nick?' asked Lynne. 'I presume it was you who wanted to see Sam at police headquarters earlier.'

'Yes, but I started feeling sick and they didn't seem to know for sure where he was.'

Sam said, 'Let's not worry about that now. We've found each other.' He stifled a yawn. 'Beg pardon! I'm feeling a bit tired as well as hungry. Let's get out of here.'

'Where are you taking me?' asked Nick.

'I suggest that you come home with me. I bet you're as hungry as I am,' said Sam, smiling faintly.

Nick nodded.

They all left the shop and Sam locked up.

Once in the car and on the way home, Sam told Lynne about his trip to Shotton and after that he asked Nick why he had wanted to speak to him specifically.

'I decided, after being unable to make up my mind what to do, that you had looked like you understood what I was going through the night of the murder,' said Nick hesitantly. 'I made up my mind I could trust you to take my suspicions seriously. Grown-ups don't always listen to what us young ones have to say.'

Sam felt touched and slightly guilty at the same time, knowing that what Nick said was often true. At last he brought the car to a halt outside the family home and the three of them got out. Sam opened the front door and they went inside to be immediately greeted by Roberta.

'You're back and you've Nick with you,' she said delightedly, putting down her drawing pad. 'Am I glad to see you, Nick. Chris will be made up, too.' She glanced at her mother. 'I'll go and put the kettle on, shall I? By the way, don't make too much noise, everyone. The old woman is asleep.'

Sam told Roberta to leave putting the kettle on for the moment and gave her a ten-shilling note and asked her to go and buy some fish and chips from Garnett's chippy. 'Perhaps you can go with her, Nick?'

Nick nodded and the two teenagers left the house.

Lynne and Sam looked at each other and smiled. 'It's been quite a day,' she said softly.

'You can say that again.' He ran a hand through his tawny hair. 'I'm glad Nick managed to escape dear Uncle Dennis.'

'D'you think he would have hurt Nick if he hadn't done?' asked Lynne, dropping her voice, aware of Ethel stirring.

Sam hesitated. 'We'll never know. If he believed Nick was prepared to go to South Africa, most likely he wouldn't see any reason to do so. I'm of the opinion Dennis didn't come over to Liverpool with murder on his mind the night his brother died. He probably hoped he could get him to lend him some money until the sale of the house was completed.'

'D'you think you'll be able to trace him?'

'I hope so,' said Sam, sitting down wearily. 'I'm going to have to go along to headquarters.'

Lynne was startled. 'You mean this evening, after the day you've had?'

He grimaced. 'There's stuff I need to sort out.'

She was disappointed but told herself that a man had to do what a man had to do. She put the kettle on and cut some bread and butter to have with the fish and chips. 'I presume you will eat first?'

He rose from the chair and came over to her and placed both his hands on her shoulders. 'Yes. By the way, I really do appreciate all your help, Lynne. Especially when you're going through a bad time yourself at the moment with losing your gran.'

She reached up a hand and placed it over one of his. 'I know you do.'

'If there's anything I can do for you...' His voice trailed off.

'Dancing lessons?' she suggested, tossing a smiling glance over her shoulder at him.

'Will do,' he said, managing to resist a sudden urge to kiss those smiling lips. 'No time like the present,' he added, sliding a hand down her arm and taking hold of her wrist.

Slanting him a bemused look, she allowed herself to be led over to the wireless. He fiddled with the knobs until he found some dance music. Then he slid an arm around her waist. 'Now just follow my lead and go with the music,' he said, a twinkle in his eyes.

She giggled and then nodded obediently. 'I'll do it, though I think you're crazy, risking your toes like this.'

The music, 'The Trish, Trash Polka', was fast and lively. Ethel had her eyes open and was staring at them as if she had never seen anything quite like them before as Sam began to whirl Lynn around the room, narrowly avoiding chairs and table and sideboard and steering her out into the lobby. They danced its full length before he danced her into the parlour and back into the kitchen in time to hear the music come to an end.

Lynne was breathless and clung to the front of his shirt. 'Thanks for that,' she gasped.

'See, you can dance,' said Sam, his hands clasped behind her waist. 'You only trod on my toes about a dozen times.'

'You're underestimating my talent,' said Lynne, her eyes smiling into his.

'Who's that woman, George?' asked Ethel.

Sam pulled a face and released Lynne. 'I'm Sam, not Dad, Aunt Ethel. You need glasses.'

The words were scarcely out of his mouth when the knocker sounded. Lynne hurried to open the front door and welcomed the two youngsters with the words, 'I'm glad you didn't waste any time. Sam is starving and he has to go back to headquarters.'

The three of them hurried into the kitchen.

The smell of fish and chips had Sam salivating and he wasted no time, grabbing hold of the parcel and unwrapping it. He told Lynne not to bother with plates so she didn't, thinking it would save on the washing-up.

The four of them sat round the table and the two males ate greedily with their fingers, making no effort at conversation, while Lynne made chip and fish butties and Roberta picked up her pencil and pad and began to sketch swiftly. Lynne handed a butty to Ethel who wolfed it down. While Lynne watched with amused tolerance, Sam and Nick demolished the food in front of them much more slowly but with obvious enjoyment.

When he had finished every last crispy bit, Sam rose from the table and looked at Lynne. 'I'm going to have to go. Will you be all right with Aunt Ethel?'

She nodded. 'You get going. I'll stay here until you or your dad gets back.'

'Thanks. You're the best and so is your daughter.' He smiled at them both and then turned to Nick. 'There's two spare bedrooms that used to be my sisters'. Use whichever one you want and if you feel like a bath, don't hesitate. There's towels and bedding in the airing cupboard on the landing. Tomorrow you'll have to come with me to headquarters but don't be worrying, I'll see to it that nobody forces you to do anything you don't want to.'

Nick stumbled to his feet. 'I don't know how to thank you.'

Sam touched his knuckles lightly under Nick's chin and then left.

After he had gone, Lynne poured herself another cup of tea and made Ethel one as well. Then she stared at Nick for at least a minute until he shifted uncomfortably on his seat and then glanced at Roberta. 'You didn't tell me that there's something wrong with my face,' he joked.

'There isn't anything wrong with your face,' said Lynne.

'Then why are you looking at me the way you are, Mrs Donegan?'

She smiled. 'I'd embarrass you if I told you that I like your face. You're a good-looking lad.'

He flushed. 'I wish you wouldn't, Mrs Donegan.'

Lynne dropped her gaze to his hands on the table. He was doing that funny little trick with his finger joints again. 'So, you're adopted, Nick,' she said abruptly.

He jerked a nod. 'Yes, I've seen the document that says so and I brought it with me, along with my post office savings book, and baptismal certificate. I decided I had a better right to them than bloody Dennis. Forgive me for swearing.'

Lynne hesitated before saying, 'What about your original birth certificate?'

'I haven't the actual one with my birth parents' names on it. The document I have, which I suppose replaces that, is the one given to my adoptive parents. Dennis showed it to me and said that it was given to Kenneth when they took me from the home in Cheshire. The date on it isn't really the date of my birth but the date when they adopted me.'

'You do realize that, even if you had the original birth certificate, it would not tell you the name of your natural father?' said Lynne.

'No, I didn't.' He looked disappointed. 'I thought I'd be able to go to Somerset House in London where the records are kept and find out who my birth parents are.'

'Your father would have needed to be aware of your existence and agreed for his name to have been registered as the father, Nick.'

He blinked. 'Are you saying that my natural mother never told him that she was having me or he didn't want to own up to me?'

Lynne hesitated. 'At a guess I'd say that she never told him.'

Nick was silent for several seconds and then said, 'You're thinking that's because there was a war on and he could have been killed, just like Bobby's father was?'

Lynne darted her daughter a glance. 'I thought it might help him,' said Roberta.

Lynne nodded and gave her attention once more to Nick. 'I hope it does help you to understand? During the war so many couples thought they might never see each other again and decided that it was now or never for them to be together.'

He nodded. 'I suppose he could have even

been a Yank.' A sigh escaped him. 'I bet I'll never find out who they were.'

'Perhaps it's best that you remember the couple who brought you up as their son. I think they made a good job of doing so,' said Lynne firmly. 'Now shall we change the subject? Are you going to have a bath, Nick?'

'I will,' he said, squaring his shoulders. 'You think Detective Walker really meant for me to stay here tonight?'

'Of course he did,' said Lynne.

'Only I don't want him to feel that he has to help me,' said Nick, his lean face set.

'It was obvious to me he meant it,' said Roberta.

'Perhaps you'd like me to run the bath for you, Nick, in case you're feeling a bit shy about going upstairs in a strange house?' said Lynne.

He shook his head. 'It's kind of you but I'm not scared of going upstairs on my own.'

Lynne nodded and watched him leave the room. 'You think he's going to be OK?' asked Roberta.

'He's a cheeky monkey,' said Ethel stridently, startling them both.

'Why d'you say that, Ethel?' asked Lynne.

'Because I say he is,' said the old woman, glaring at her. 'I can lock him in the cellar and it makes no difference. He still looks at me in that way of his. He's not like his father in manners.'

Roberta exchanged glances with Lynne. 'She's going doolally!' mouthed the girl.

'You're another cheeky one,' said Ethel, taking a swipe at Roberta, who drew back, so the blow

300

did not land.

'That's enough now,' said Lynne. 'Unless you want to be left here all on your own.'

Ethel stared at her and then she looked away, her mouth working. 'Don't want to go in the workhouse,' she mumbled, trembling.

'Who said anything about the workhouse?' said Lynne, feeling sorry for her now. 'How about another cup of tea?'

'Cocoa if you please?' said Ethel.

Lynne glanced at her daughter who stood up and went in search of a tin of cocoa in the unfamiliar back kitchen.

They had finished drinking their cocoa by the time Nick came downstairs. His fair hair was damp and tousled and he looked much more relaxed.

'You want a cup of cocoa?' asked Roberta.

'I can make it myself,' he said hastily. 'I'm not used to being waited on.'

'That's what I like to hear,' she said, smiling. 'A member of the opposite sex who can do things for himself.'

He grinned and collected the dirty cups and took them outside.

Roberta looked at her mother. 'You know, he reminds me of Sam.'

Lynne said smoothly, 'It's the fair hair and the brown eyes.'

Roberta nodded. 'OK if I go home? I've got homework to finish.'

Lynne nodded. 'Don't work too hard.'

'Will you be very late?'

'I hope not.'

Roberta went out, whistling noisily.

Lynne stared at Ethel but she'd dozed off again and Nick was still in the back kitchen. Lynne leaned back in the chair and closed her eyes. Gosh, she was tired but she had a lot of thinking to do.

'I could watch her if you want to go,' whispered Nick suddenly.

Lynne's eyelids fluttered open and she stared up into the youth's face and fought the urge to pat his cheek and say *I think I know who your parents are.* 'No, it's all right,' she said, sitting up straight. 'I'll stay a bit longer. You sit down and drink your cocoa.'

He sat on the sofa, cradling the mug of cocoa. 'I see they've a telly,' he commented. 'Chris's mum and dad have a telly.' He sipped his cocoa. 'What d'you think will happen to me, Mrs Donegan? If I was a few years older, I'd have Dad's money and could be independent. I could get a job or go on to further education. Mam wanted me to be a doctor or a teacher.'

'And what do you want?' asked Lynne.

'I'd like to be a detective like Sergeant Walker. To catch criminals and make Liverpool a safer place.' His brown eyes gleamed with enthusiasm. 'I'm sure Mam would believe it a worthwhile job if she was still alive.'

'Of course she would,' said Lynne warmly. 'I'm sure, when the time comes, that if you have a word with Sam – Sergeant Walker, I mean – he'd tell you how to go about becoming a police detective.'

'He's one of the good guys, isn't he?' said

Nick.

Lynne agreed. Then she leaned back and closed her eyes, effectively bringing the conversation to an end, but she was thinking that it was good for a son to admire his father, even if he didn't know it.

Twenty-Four

'So how do you feel now, Nick?' asked Sam, as they stood outside the solicitor's office in North John Street a week later. 'Are you happy with the decisions that have been made for you for the present?'

'Yes, Sergeant,' said Nick hastily, shooting a glance at Chris's mother and the woman from the Welfare who had both accompanied them to the meeting with the solicitor in charge of Kenneth Roger's business affairs.

Sam smiled. 'Good. Then I'll bid the three of you a good day. I need to get back to headquarters.'

Nick guessed why. There had been a report in the *Echo* about a watchman who had died of a fractured skull and murder was suspected. He hesitated before saying, 'Will I be seeing you again, Sergeant Walker?'

'I'll keep you posted,' said Sam. 'I presume you'll be going along to the coffee bar in Hope Street?'

Nick nodded. 'You'll pass a message on through Bobby or Betty?'

Sam nodded and, with a wave of the hand, he walked away.

'What a nice man he is,' said Chris's mother.

'Yes, he is that,' said the woman from the Welfare. 'So are you happy with the arrangements, Mrs Nuttall?'

'Everything's fine,' she said, smiling at Nick. 'I'm sure we'll all get along like a house on fire. It's not as if we're strangers to each other.'

The woman returned her smile. 'Well if there is anything that worries you at all, do get in touch. Although I will pop in and see you and Nicholas during the next month.' She held out her hand and shook hands with them both. 'See you soon.'

Nick watched her walk away, thinking how swiftly everything had been settled once he had plucked up the courage to seek help from Sergeant Sam Walker.

'So, Nick, do you want me to come with you to school or would you prefer making your way there on your own?' asked Mrs Nuttall, who had taken on the role of his foster mother. She would be paid from his adoptive father's estate which would include the money from the sale of the house in Shotton.

Astonishingly, Kenneth's father had left the house to his eldest son, who was to use his discretion when it came to how much money Dennis should be given when it was sold. It transpired that ever since Dennis had been demobbed, his mother had been handing over money to him whenever his gambling got him into difficulties. Mr Rogers senior only discovered this when his wife was dying and, deciding that their younger son had bled them long enough, changed his will.

'I'll manage fine on my own, thank you, Mrs Nuttall,' said Nick.

She smiled. 'You can call me Aunt Amelia, if you like. It's friendlier and I can't see you wanting to call me Mam.'

'I'd like that.'

'That's settled then,' she said, giving him a friendly pat on the shoulder. 'I'll see you and Chris this evening.'

He nodded.

They did not immediately part company but walked together in the direction of Church Street before splitting up. Nick headed in the direction of Renshaw Street and the Boys' Institute on Mount Street, thinking about the couple of days he had spent at Sergeant Sam's house before moving to Chris's parents' home. It had been odd the way the old aunt kept mistaking him for Sam when he was younger. Even Sam's father had stared at him oddly. Nick had been tempted to ask if there were any photographs around of Sam when he was his age, just to see if they were alike at all. He couldn't see it himself but thought it was probably due to them both having fair hair and brown eyes, which wasn't all that common.

He thought about the telephone call from Sam's sister, Jeanette, who worked in Cunard Building. Apparently she had checked out the passenger lists for ships departing around the time Dennis had vanished and found his name on the *Carinthia* sailing for Canada. Enquiries were in progress. Dennis was wanted to help with police enquiries, the fingerprints found at the house in Shotton having matched those found on the chisel rack in the shop. Nick's admiration for Sam had increased and so had his determination to be a detective. In the meantime summer would soon be here and without having to worry about Dennis being a threat to him, Nick's heart was feeling lighter, although he still grieved for his adoptive father. Hopefully he would be able to meet up with Bobby at the coffee bar in the meantime.

Roberta's thoughts were running along the same lines as Nick's and so shortly after four o'clock one fine afternoon, she strolled along Myrtle Street in the direction of Hope Street. She was wearing a blue and white gingham frock, white ankle socks and black shoes as well as her blazer and school hat. The latter she planned on removing once she reached the coffee bar. It was a rule of the school that the hat had to be worn going to and coming from school. If seen without, punishment meant one had to wear the dreadful hat all day in school.

She entered the coffee bar and was pleased to see that Nick and Chris were already there and seated at a table. As she made her way towards them, she could hear Alma Coggan's latest hit, 'Dreamboat', coming from the jukebox and she began to hum the tune. She spotted Betty talking to Lenny the boss and noticed that they were glancing over at Nick and Chris. No doubt they were discussing Nick's affairs. Betty would have heard from Jeanette about Dennis Rogers having skipped the country and gone to Canada.

Nick stood up and pulled out the vacant chair for Roberta and she sat down. 'Thanks! Is everything OK with you two?'

'Great,' said Chris. 'Nick's part of our family now.'

'That's fab!' exclaimed Roberta, removing her hat and resting her arms on the table.

'Yeah, I've always wanted a brother instead of two sisters,' said Chris. 'Not that I'm saying there's anything wrong with girls, mind,' he added, grinning.

'I should think not,' said Nick, smiling at Roberta. 'I wish I'd had sisters. How's your mam?'

'Fine,' she replied. 'Come Friday, she's hoping Sergeant Sam will be giving her a dancing lesson.'

Chris stared at her. 'Sergeant Sam?'

'She means Detective Sergeant Walker,' said Nick. 'It got confusing when I was staying with him saying Sergeant Walker because his father is a Sergeant Walker, too.'

'Right! Now what kind of dancing?' asked Chris. 'I bet it's ballroom. All the oldies are still doing ballroom. It's time they got with it.'

Roberta frowned. 'Mam's not an oldie and neither is Sergeant Sam. They're getting on but they're not old. Mam was only seventeen when she had me, which means she's thirty, not fifty. I bet Sergeant Sam's not much older.'

'Mum said the war made them all look older than they are. It was the worry,' said Chris.

'Are you three ordering?'

They looked up at Betty.

'Yes,' said Chris. 'I'll have an espresso and an iced bun.'

'I'll have a hot chocolate,' said Roberta.

'Same here,' said Nick.

Betty said, 'Two things. I'm sorry to hear about your Nan, Bobby. I'll drop by and see your mum tomorrow evening if that's OK. And Nick, it's great that you're back in Liverpool.'

'Same with you,' said Nick, smiling. 'I bet you had a good time in Italy.'

She nodded. 'So what was the worry Chris was talking about?'

'No worry,' said Nick with a shrug. 'It was Chris telling us that his mum thinks the war aged people.'

'I reckon that's true. This morning Jeanette and I were discussing the war but we were talking about how many babies were born then and that probably twice as many were born in 1947. You were a war baby, weren't you, Nick?'

He nodded, adding, 'Yes, born 1942, although what with being adopted I don't know the exact date.'

'Now there's a surprise! Every family has its secrets, I suppose.'

'I'd agree that most families have a skeleton in their cupboard,' said Roberta.

'I wonder where that phrase "skeleton in cupboard" comes from. I just wish I knew the exact date of my birth. It gets me that I've never seen my real birth certificate,' said Nick.

'Actually,' said Roberta casually, 'I've never seen mine either. I must ask Mam about it.'

'I'd better go and get your orders,' said Betty, hurrying away.

Roberta noticed that Lenny, who had been hanging around, had already gone into the kitchen and instead of preparing their drinks behind the counter, Betty had gone in there as well. Perhaps she had an order for a hot meal.

The following evening Lynne had just posted a letter to Emma and another to Hester, belatedly thanking them for their messages of sympathy, when Betty arrived on her doorstep. She hugged Lynne tightly and expressed her condolences on her bereavement. 'She was a really interesting lady and I'm glad I had the opportunity to have a good chat with her about her theatrical days as a dresser.'

Lynne kissed her on the cheek and pressed her into a chair and sat opposite whilst her daughter put the kettle on. 'I've a box of memorabilia that Nan left that you can borrow if you want. There's copies of old posters and *The Stage* as well as snippets of news and photographs of performers cut out of the dailies.'

Betty's face lit up. 'I'd enjoy taking a gander at them.'

'Right, I'll get the box before you go.' Lynne leaned forward in her chair. 'So tell me all about Italy and meeting up with Stuart?' she said.

'It made such a difference having his company,' said Betty, resting her chin in her hand. 'He's so knowledgeable about architecture – the different periods, you know.'

'As you'd expect of an architect,' said Lynne, looking amused.

'Yes, but he knew his paintings, as well,' said Betty. 'And he can dance and catch a waiter's eye when a restaurant is busy.'

'Now that sounds useful.'

They smiled at each other. 'I tell you what he said that surprised me,' murmured Betty.

'What?'

'That Liverpool has some great buildings. I reminded him that the Luftwaffe had destroyed quite a bit of the city centre.'

'Including the old Customs House,' said Lynne.

'Stuart said that we should be thankful that the Liver Building is still standing as well as St George's Hall.'

'Well, I am thankful,' said Lynne. 'So what about California?'

Betty said hesitantly, 'What do you think about my travelling out there with him?'

'I think it's a wonderful opportunity. I hope you have a lovely time and do some of the best painting you've ever done.'

Betty chuckled. 'That shouldn't be difficult. I'm glad you don't think I've gone off my nut. There are those that do! Our Maggie for instance. I told her the light will be different in California and there's the Pacific Ocean and San Francisco and Hollywood to visit. Lenny said he envies me. His ambition has long been to visit

310

Hollywood and gawk at all the film stars.' She hesitated. 'I've told Stuart that I'm not sure how long I'll be able to stay. We're just really good mates at the moment. I know that might sound odd because there are those who believe men and women can't be just good friends, but Dorothy Wilson seems to think it's possible.'

Lynne was surprised. 'Honestly?'

'Yes! She says that in the theatre you get to know lots of men who are just good friends who don't see you as a potential wife or lover.' Her eyes twinkled. 'I had the impression that Stuart didn't quite believe her. Maybe he thought she was just saying it because she has Sam back here in Liverpool.'

'Of course.' Lynne sighed.

There was a silence and Roberta entered the room carrying a tray. 'I made cocoa. I believe there's few things as comforting as a decent mug of cocoa.'

Betty agreed and after drinking half her cocoa began to talk about the different places they had visited in Italy. By the time she paused to draw breath, it was doubly obvious to Lynne that she was a much happier person than last time she had seen her.

After exhausting the subject of Italy, they talked about Emma's expected baby and whether it would be a boy or a girl. 'As long as it's healthy is the main thing,' said Lynne. 'At least Emma won't have to worry about diphtheria, whooping cough and consumption and paying doctor's fees the way I did. Vaccination is a wonderful thing.'

311

'You're forgetting about polio, Mam,' said Roberta. 'That's still around.'

'Not for much longer. I read the other day in the *Echo* that there's a hope of protection against that scourge too.' She gave her attention to Betty once more. 'So you'll be staying in Liverpool until after Emma's had her baby and Stuart returns?'

Betty nodded. 'Yes, I know she'd rather I was staying here but she wants me to be happy.'

'Of course she does,' said Lynne warmly.

Betty sighed. 'I'll have to be going soon.'

'I'll get that box for you.' Lynne left the room.

Roberta smiled at Betty. 'I wish I could go with you to California. I'd fill my sketch book.'

'How are you getting on with your drawing?' asked Betty.

Roberta went over to the sideboard and took her pad from it and handed it to Betty. 'See what you think?'

Betty flipped open the cover and began to turn the leaves of the pad, making comments about the different sketches and then she came to one that gave her cause to pause. 'This is of Hester's brother.'

'Yes, it's Sergeant Sam eating fish and chips. Mam likes him. I can tell the way she looks at him.'

'Yes, he's a very attractive man. I notice you have several drawings of Nick.'

'And a couple of Tony,' said Roberta hastily. 'And even one of Chris, although his face is so mobile, it's difficult to catch the actual expression I was after.'

312

Betty closed the pad. 'You're good.'

Roberta flushed with pleasure. 'Thanks, tell Mam that.'

'What's Betty to tell me?' asked Lynne, entering the room. She handed the large chocolate box of memorabilia to their guest.

'That I've talent, Mam!' cried Roberta.

'I know that,' said Lynne, giving her daughter a hug. 'Anyway, we must let Betty go. She'll be wanting to get back to her flat.'

'Yes, I must go,' said Betty, jumping to her feet.

'Give my love to Emma when you see her. I have written but you might see her before she gets my letter,' said Lynne. 'I'll be praying that the birth goes smoothly.'

'So will I,' said Betty, hugging her. 'I'm so looking forward to being an aunt.' She did not know how she had managed to resist drawing Lynne's attention to the sketches of Sam and Nick. At the same time she wondered how Bobby had not noticed the likeness between the two either. Maybe it was because it had not occurred to her to look for it?

Betty would not have done so if Lenny had not made a comment when she had told him that Nick was adopted. Apparently Lenny had been looking out some old photographs and come across one of the schoolboy Sam playing in the street with some other lads. He had not drawn any conclusions, just commented on it.

What of Lynne? Surely she must have seen the drawings and should have noticed the similarities between them? And what of Sam – how was

313

it he had not noticed it? Could it simply be because he was one of those men who spent scarcely any time looking at themselves in a mirror?

Anyway, it really was none of her business what Sam Walker had got up to during the war – if he had got up to anything! Who was to say Nick's father wasn't a relative of his?

Twenty-Five

'I hope you don't miss the train, Mam! You keep fiddling about,' said Roberta. 'What you're wearing is fine.'

Lynne glanced in the mirror once more and then at her daughter. 'If I miss the train, I'll just have to get the next one. At least all the strikes appear to be over.'

The recent disputes on the railways and docks had disrupted everything. She wondered if it had anything to do with the Conservatives having done so well in the elections throughout the country.

'But that would make you late for the connection at Manchester,' said Roberta.

Lynne raised her eyebrows. 'Stop worrying about me! If the worst comes to the worst, I'll just have to ring Hester and tell her I can't make it and return home.'

She picked up her bag and left the house, thinking of Sam and how he had cancelled their dancing lessons, apparently due to pressure of work. She had to confess that she had been deeply disappointed. Still, that was life.

She hurried up the street towards West Derby Road and it was while she was waiting to cross to the bus stop on the other side of the main road that she heard the beep of a horn and then her name being called. She glanced in the direction of a car nearby. The driver signalled to her and she realized it was Sam. She went over to see what he wanted.

'I believe you're going to Hester's! D'you want a lift?' he asked.

'You mean to Lime Street station?'

He smiled. 'No, to Whalley! I'm going there, too.'

She hesitated and he coaxed, 'Come on, Lynne. I'd like to make up for letting you down over the dancing lessons I promised you but, honestly, I have been up to my eyes in work. My inspector is retiring any day now and I'm in line for promotion after catching those responsible for the break-ins that have been going on.'

'OK!' She smiled and walked round to the passenger side and got in. 'This really is good of you.'

'No, it isn't. I'm going that way, so it's no hardship for me to take you as well.' He moved out into the traffic. 'And, as I said, I want to make up for those dance lessons we never had.'

'How did you know I was going?'

'Our Hester mentioned it when she phoned to

315

tell me that Emma had given birth to a baby boy.'

Lynne's face lit up. 'That's wonderful news! Are they both well?'

'Yes! Anyway, I now have a day off, so I invited myself to our Hester's, saying I could do with a trip to the country.'

Lynne smiled. 'I really appreciate the lift.'

'It's a bit of a journey having to change trains three times.'

Lynne agreed. 'But I've been wanting to accept Hester's invitation to see the cottage for ages.'

He glanced at her. 'The outing will do you good after what you've been through losing your gran.'

She agreed. 'I thought she'd die at home with me at her bedside, not on a park bench.'

'There's worse ways to go,' said Sam, his expression sombre.

Lynne agreed, thinking of Robert and her mother and the murder victims Sam must have seen. 'Have you had any news about Dennis Rogers?'

Sam frowned but did not say anything, giving the traffic all his attention. Once they were moving swiftly again he said, 'No, and I wish they'd find him.'

'Canada's a big country,' she murmured.

'Yes, and with great swathes of wilderness where a fugitive can lose himself.'

'But is he the kind of man who could cope in such wilderness?'

He glanced at her. 'Whether he is or isn't we

might never get to know.'

Lynne thought that Sam did not have to spell out what he meant because she had a mental image of her mother being killed by a bear. No doubt there was other wildlife in Canada that could prove dangerous to an unwary traveller.

Sam's voice broke into her reverie. 'Of course, he could be in a big city somewhere doing casual work with no questions asked.'

'Or he could be killed by a snake or a hungry pack of wolves.'

Sam grinned. 'I wonder if Nick has thought of that.'

'He might think it a fitting end but perhaps he'd rather just forget him,' said Lynne.

Sam's expression changed. 'No, Nick believes he killed his adoptive father and wants him punished. I can understand that because I would feel the same.'

Lynne glanced at him. 'I think that's under-standable but perhaps I'd best let you concentrate on your driving until we're out of the city.'

He nodded. 'And you can relax. We've a fair way to go yet.'

Lynne leaned back in the seat and tried to do what he suggested but she could not deny that being in his company was having a disturbing effect on her. Especially with them talking about Nick and her suspecting he could be Dorothy's son. A sigh escaped her.

'What's the sigh for?'

'Contentment,' she lied, adding, 'It's so good to have a day out. I can't remember when last I had a whole day off.'

'Last time I was in Whalley was with Dorothy before the wedding. It wasn't really her scene. She'd have preferred to go to Blackpool to see a show and check out the shops. Although, thinking about it, I couldn't see her doing much of that when she's shopped in Bond Street.'

What a fool Dorothy is, letting him see that she didn't share his liking for the countryside, thought Lynne. 'Have you ever been to London?' she asked.

'Once. I had this yen to see Scotland Yard for myself, not just on the screen in black and white.' He smiled. 'Is there anywhere you'd really like to visit?'

'Yes, Paris. I'd like to sit outside a cafe and watch people go by. See if the Parisian women are dressed as stylishly as I've read about in magazines and newspapers.'

He chuckled. 'That makes sense because it's your business. When our Jeanette mentions Paris it's in connection with romance. I took her to see that film *American in Paris* with Gene Kelly a few years back and she loved it.'

'He's a great dancer,' said Lynne.

'I much prefer him to Fred Astaire.'

'And he's better looking,' said Lynne. 'Does Dorothy like dancing as much as you do? Will there be music in this film she's making?'

He pulled a face. 'I'm pretty sure it's not a musical because she's not famed for her singing voice. I suppose I should have asked more questions but I don't have a place in her acting world. She laments that I'm not there with her but the truth is that if I did as she suggested and had a week over there, I'd be hanging around having to amuse myself while she worked most of the time.'

'When is she due back?'

'August maybe. I'll see her briefly and then she'll be shooting up to Scotland and then more filming in the studios down south.' He paused. 'My stepmother is looking forward to seeing her again because Grace is convinced that the film Dorothy wants to produce will get made. Dorothy also interviewed Aunt Ethel for it but I doubt she'll remember who she is when she gets back.'

'The woman with the magic box that took pictures,' murmured Lynne.

'What's that?' asked Sam, slanting her a gaze.

'Just something your Aunt Ethel said to me.'

He grimaced. 'You and Bobby are good with her. Dad feels guilty about leaving her to live on the Wirral.'

'Couldn't your father take her to the Wirral with him?'

'Not a chance! He's been parted from Grace since 1941 and now they've found each other again, I think he's entitled to some happiness.'

'What parted them?'

He told her, finishing with the words, 'The Blitz caused so much disruption and heartache but only those who lived through it know how truly bad it was.'

'I met Robert in a shelter during the Blitz,' said Lynne softly.

Sam glanced at her with interest. 'What was he like?'

'Full of life and he made me laugh. It seems so

319

long ago now and yet it isn't that long. I sometimes think that if I didn't have a photo of him then I'd forget what he looked like.'

'I feel like that about Carol. She was my girlfriend and was killed in the Blitz. I was heartbroken.' He glanced at Lynne. 'You know what it's like when you're young and in love.'

'How old was she?'

'Seventeen! And what made it more difficult was there was no need for her to die. If she'd stayed at her aunt's place in Ormskirk, she'd probably still be alive. Sometimes I think about how different my life would have been if she'd lived.' He stared at Lynne. 'You must feel the same about your husband?'

Suddenly Lynne wanted to be honest with him. 'We weren't married.'

Sam shot her a startled look but did not speak.

She took a deep breath. 'I just pretended for my daughter's sake. We hadn't known each other long but we fell madly in love. We had such a short time together. Then his ship was torpedoed with the loss of all hands and I never saw him again. I had no contact with his family; they lived in Ireland and I didn't have their address.'

She glanced at him, wondering what he thought of her, but he was gazing straight ahead and so she could not read his expression. Then she watched him remove a hand from the steering wheel and he clasped her right hand and squeezed it gently.

They drove on in silence and, after a short while, Sam freed her hand. 'I will give you dancing lessons. It will take you out of yourself and it's good exercise.'

'You think I need exercise?' she asked, a smile in her voice.

'If you're sitting at a sewing machine all day, you must get stiff, especially about the shoulders. I know I do when I'm at the desk too long, writing up reports. You don't have a radiogram or a record player, do you?'

She laughed. 'Be serious! You've been in my house. You must know they're beyond my pocket. There's the wireless. Anyway, I thought you'd be teaching me at your house because of your Aunt Ethel needing an eye kept on her.'

He smiled. 'You're right, of course. I'd forgotten. We could practise in the parlour and look in on her now and again.'

'I could always look in on her during the day if that would help, if a neighbour couldn't do it?' she said seriously.

'That would be great!' Sam's expression was warm. 'Are you sure you don't mind?'

'I'm used to old ladies,' she murmured.

They both fell silent but it was a comfortable silence as the car wended its way along a lane with hedgerows on each side and flowering honeysuckle and cow parsley in the narrow grass verges.

Eventually they arrived in Whalley and Sam drew up at the kerb outside a cottage. A notice was displayed in front of the house, saying open for teas and light meals. An arrow pointed in the direction of the side of the building.

The pair of them followed the arrow into a

321

garden where tables and chairs were set out. A couple of tables had the convenience of a large umbrella. Several people were already taking advantage of what was on offer.

Lynne recognized Myra Jones who was serving a couple of customers. She spotted them and smiled and signalled to Hester who came over. 'Hi, Lynne! So my brother managed to catch you before you left.'

'She was already on her way but she hadn't gone far,' said Sam, kissing his sister on the cheek. 'Didn't expect to find you so busy.'

'The good weather brings people out to visit the abbey ruins or for a walk on the fells,' said Hester. 'You've never seen the ruins, have you, Lynne?'

'No,' she said, smiling.

'I have,' said Sam, 'but I don't mind showing them to Lynne. By the look of things we'd be best out of your way for a while.'

'You've arrived at lunch time which is our busiest time of the day,' said Hester. 'You'll probably be glad to stretch your legs after the journey. Come back in an hour or so and we'll be ready to give you lunch and have a chat. Ally will be here then.'

'If you don't mind I need to use the facilities first and I bet Lynne wouldn't mind a cup of tea,' said Sam.

Lynne agreed. 'I could make us both one if you don't mind, Hester? I won't get in your way.'

'That's fine,' she said.

'You go on ahead, Lynne,' said Sam. 'I just want a word with my sister.'

Lynne went into the kitchen, expecting Sam to join her within a minute or so but the kettle had boiled before he came in. He excused himself and went to the newly installed downstairs lavatory. By the time he reappeared she was gazing out of the window and had finished her drink.

Sam picked up his cup and came and stood beside her. 'Hester was just telling me that you knew Dorothy from years ago.'

Lynne stilled. 'I suppose Emma told her.'

'Yes. Are you annoyed? Is there something between you and Dorothy that the pair of you want kept quiet?'

Her heart began to thud. 'Why should you think that?'

'It's obvious I'd say. She's never mentioned having met you before.'

'She could have easily forgotten me. I certainly didn't recognize her immediately when we met earlier this year. Although, having said that, I did think she looked familiar but I put that down to her being famous.'

He nodded. 'That makes sense.'

'Is that all you spoke about to Hester?' Lynne knew that she shouldn't really be so inquisitive.

Sam did not seem put out by the question. 'No, I wanted to discuss a case with her. Hester was an excellent policewoman. She has a good head on her shoulders.'

'A pity she had to give up her job when she married,' said Lynne.

'You think that, too?' He drained his cup. 'Anyway, she's been a help to me and I'll set my *leetle grey cells* to work on the suggestion she put forward.'

'I thought real policemen found Hercules Poirot a pain in the neck.'

'I read him when I was much younger,' said Sam, taking her cup from her. 'So where did you have your baby, Lynne?'

The complete change of subject caught her by surprise and her mouth went dry. 'What made you ask that?'

'I suddenly thought about you not being married and Nick Rogers being adopted. No doubt his mother was unmarried as well.'

'Probably.' Lynne looked down at her feet in their sensible shoes. 'My mother threw me on the streets and Nan was on tour with a repertory company and I didn't know exactly where to find her. So Roberta was born in a home for unmarried mothers in Cheshire. I remember being at my wits' end, thinking that I'd have to give her up for adoption. Fortunately Nan turned up in the nick of time.'

'Were many babies given up for adoption while you were there?'

'The majority of them.' She felt fidgety. 'Anyway, it's your day off. Can you stop behaving like a police detective for a few hours! I want to stretch my legs.'

'OK!' He emptied the tea leaves from the cups into the waste bin before washing the cups under the tap and then placing them on the draining board. 'You said that your grandmother was on tour...'

She clicked her tongue against her teeth. 'Yes, that's right. She was a dresser and taught me a lot about what I know about dressmaking. When Bobby was a baby we used to travel around with her. I probably met Dorothy then,' she said lightly. 'I'm sure I've told you all this before. Now shall we go?'

'I'm sorry. Forgive me?' He smiled.

'I suppose you can't help yourself but no more questions.' She rubbed her hands together and then clapped them. 'Right! Are you ready for that walk?'

They went out the front way and made their way along the main street. 'Do you really want to see the abbey ruins or would you prefer a walk along the river?' asked Sam. 'I reckon we'd be falling over people at the ruins. There's a path behind the abbey grounds. It's a pleasant stroll.'

'OK, I suppose I do need the exercise as much as you do,' teased Lynne, remembering what he said earlier. She twisted from the waist in an attempt to see the size of her bottom.

'I wasn't saying you were fat! You've a neat little posterior.'

She blushed. 'Are you sure about that?'

'Sure I'm sure,' he said, grinning. 'You've a trim figure and I like the colour of your hair as well.'

Her lips twitched. 'You don't have to go overboard with the compliments.'

'Why can't women take compliments gracefully?' he protested. 'I was going to add I like the way you smile, too.'

She laughed. 'Stop it!

They walked on in silence. Lynne's thoughts returned to thinking about the home in Cheshire and Dorothy and that meant she wasn't looking where she was going and stumbled over the root of a tree. Sam reached out a hand and grasped hers. He did not release it when she was steady but walked on. She was intensely aware of the feel of his fingers against hers but she did not drag her hand away. It was not as if he was kissing her; most likely he was simply making sure she did not slip again.

As they came to a bridge he released her hand and they both rested their elbows on the wall and gazed down at the water. 'I noticed you have little indentions on the balls of your fingers,' said Sam idly.

'I'm always pricking my fingers with pins and needles, that's why,' said Lynne. 'Next time you have a murder suspect, if she has fingers like mine, then you'll know what her occupation is.'

He smiled. 'I suppose I'd notice if I was taking her fingerprints.'

'Do you do much of that?'

'Years ago I did but it's something you don't forget.'

'I suppose most criminals wear gloves now?'

'If they've got any sense, but some still make mistakes.' He paused. 'Did you see that rise?'

'I saw a fish coming to the surface. Was it after a fly?'

He nodded. 'I bet there's a few fish in here. I used to go fishing, but never have the time now.'

'Where did you go?'

'When I was very small, I'd take a net to the lake in Newsham Park. When Dad gave me my first rod, I'd go to Carr Mill Dam, by St Helens,

326

for freshwater fishing. Then when I reached my twenties, sometimes I'd travel out to Conway or Anglesey for sea fishing.' He straightened up. 'I took Dorothy fishing once but she hated it. It's a very restful hobby. I've always thought if I had a son, we could go fishing together.'

Lynne thought of Nick. She did not really want to believe that Dorothy could be his mother. Yet she and Sam had known each other a long time.

They left the bridge and walked on in silence. The sun was shining through the trees, dappling the surface of the river. She thought of what Hester's friend had said at the wedding. *Dorothy was taking a chance following her dream and leaving Sam to his own devices, so she only had herself to blame if they parted.* Suddenly Lynne felt such a sense of peace and happiness come over her. She had not felt such emotions for a long time and it was due to being with this man in this restful place. It was so easy just to be with him.

By the time they arrived back at the cottage, the lunchtime rush had abated and so they were able to eat outside in the sun. The two men talked about the merits of different cars whilst Lynne and Hester discussed clothes, youngsters, crime and houses and Emma's baby.

It was on the way home that Sam said, 'I couldn't help overhearing part of your conversation with Hester. I hope what she said didn't frighten you, talking about young criminals. We are having some trouble with youths at the moment but most of them are no different from how we used to behave when we were young.'

'Can you honestly say that about Teddy Boys?' asked Lynne.

'Not all Teddy Boys are criminals and not all girls are ladylike. Some like to cause fights, egging on the lads for a bit of excitement. A lot of the powers that be blame the war but you can't blame it for everything. Yet the fact that so many haven't got fathers has to make a difference.' Sam glanced at Lynne. 'Don't you agree?'

'I wouldn't argue, although I don't think young Nick is the kind to get into trouble,' she said.

'Strange, I was thinking of Nick, too.'

Her heart began to thud in that uncomfortable manner again. 'Yes, but he has a foster father.'

'That's true.' Sam sighed. 'And a family now.'

'And that will probably help to keep him on the straight and narrow,' said Lynne, her heartbeat steadying. 'Thinking of girls, your sisters have been fortunate in having a father and a brother. It must have helped them understand men better. More so than myself.'

'They can still make mistakes.'

'We all make mistakes. We don't live in a perfect world,' murmured Lynne, closing her eyes.

'Why don't you doze?' suggested Sam. 'It's been quite a day.'

'I will if you don't mind,' said Lynne, stifling a yawn. 'I'm feeling really sleepy. It's all that fresh air.'

She drifted off and eventually found herself dreaming that she was waltzing with Sam to the Blue Danube and their steps were in complete harmony. Then suddenly she got into a muddle and began to tread on his toes and felt frightened. She couldn't think why until she sensed they were being watched and she just knew that it was Dorothy standing there, laughing.

Twenty-Six

Dorothy stepped off the train in Lime Street with her arm in a sling and headed towards the exit. Her forehead was damp with perspiration. She had not expected it to be so hot in Liverpool and could have coped with it better if she had not been dressed for a north of England summer. Still, she was here now, having phoned the hotel when she was in London to reserve a room for one night only and telling them about her accident.

She had returned to England sooner than she had reckoned on. The filming had gone smoothly until just a few days ago, but then she had caught her heel in the cobbles during the scenes in Rome and fallen, breaking her arm. There had been some swift rewrites of her part but at least they'd had a wrap and even the film crew were now back in Britain.

They and the other actors needed for the scenes in Scotland had caught the overnight train from London to Edinburgh and taken most of her luggage with them, but she had asked for time out to visit Liverpool. She had tried to get in touch with Sam but the phone in the Walker household had been engaged every time and she did not like phoning him at work. Still, she was hoping to surprise him before catching the train to Scotland and persuade him to take a couple of days off and travel north with her.

As she passed the Adelphi Hotel and walked up Mount Pleasant with her overnight bag, she considered paying a quick visit to Lynne Donegan, as well as Sam. Stuart Anderson, whom she had seen only a few days ago, had spoken to Betty on the telephone and mentioned that Sam was giving Lynne dancing lessons. The news had stunned Dorothy because despite having given Sam leave to see Lynne in a casual way, she had not meant it. She did not trust the other woman, having noticed the way she looked at Sam, and would not put it past her to tell him the truth about where they had met during the war. She felt certain Lynne would play the sympathy card, having lost the father of her child in battle. Well, Dorothy planned to play on his sympathy, too, with all her might.

Sam decided to call it a day. He placed the cap on his fountain pen, threw it down on the desk and yawned and stretched before reaching for the telephone. He had phoned earlier but it had just rung and rung and he had decided that perhaps Lynne was upstairs taking Aunt Ethel to the bathroom and had not heard the telephone ringing.

He had been disappointed because he liked to hear Lynne's voice. She talked about the little everyday things in a way that he found soothing and she also listened to what he had to say without jumping in too quickly with something she wanted to say. She always sounded amused by his jokes even if they weren't that funny. He dialled and felt himself tense as he got the engaged signal. He put the phone down and, removing his jacket from the back of his chair, he shrugged it on.

'You off then, sir?' asked the WPC as he headed out of the door.

'Yes, goodnight!'

As he made his way to where his car was parked, Sam found himself mulling over the trip to Whalley. Lynne had impressed him with her forthrightness in telling him that she was an unmarried mother. What a tough life she'd had, being rejected by her mother, losing the man she loved but having his baby and keeping it. He admired her for bringing up her daughter with just her grandmother for help, knowing that few would have attempted it.

Since their return from the outing to Whalley, he had enjoyed teaching her how to dance and their conversations afterwards. It was so much easier to be with her than Dorothy and they seemed to have more in common in terms of family values. None of the bickering, which was so often a feature of his dates with Dorothy, who was always so determined to live life her way. Of course, she had every right to do that when she only had herself to think about. But she didn't! Her suggestion that he go to Italy for a week's holiday had somehow stuck in his gullet. It was as if he was a pet dog and she was tossing him a bone. What had also annoyed him most was those words she had used the last time he had seen her. *If you loved me, you would do anything to please me.* No, he had to add the proviso: 'within reason'. Did that mean he didn't love Dorothy or he didn't love her enough to move heaven and earth to spend a few hours with her? As he opened his car, he realized that was the sticking point in their relationship.

After greeting Kathy at the hotel and having her bag carried up to her room, Dorothy managed with difficulty to have a quick wash down and change her blouse, as well as renew her make-up. Thank God, it was her left arm she had broken and not her right and it was a simple break. She tried phoning the Walker household again but the telephone was still engaged. Was it possible it was off the hook? She left the hotel and hailed a taxi.

It seemed no time at all before she was knocking on the door of the Walkers' house, hoping to catch Sam. If he was not at home, then she would go to Lynne's house, warn her off, and then take a taxi to police headquarters. If she telephoned and he was busy then she feared that he might just tell whoever was manning the phones that he was not in the office unless it was urgent.

The last thing she was expecting was that the Walkers' front door should be opened by Lynne.

For several moments both women could only stare at each other. Then Lynne said, 'What have you done to yourself, Dorothy? You'd best come in.'

'Got your foot in the door good and proper, have you?' said Dorothy, who was feeling not only hot and sticky again but thoroughly fed up and, she had to admit, as scared as when she'd had the accident.

'I suppose you would think that,' said Lynne, letting out a sigh. 'Sam's not here if you were expecting to see him.'

'Then why are you here? Getting ready for your dancing lesson?'

Lynne smiled. 'I am enjoying them. He's a good teacher is Sam, and a gentleman. I suppose you're not going to come in if Sam's not here? Although I can make you a cup of tea. This heat's getting to everyone and Ethel and I were just going to have a cuppa.'

Dorothy frowned and stepped over the threshold. 'You and Ethel?'

Lynne nodded, leading the way up the lobby. 'Shut the door behind you. She needs someone to keep an eye on her; she really can't be left alone for too long now.'

'I did phone several times. Is the phone off the hook?'

'I'll check. Sometimes Ethel lifts the receiver, listens and then drops it.' Lynne found the receiver off the hook and replaced it. 'No wonder I haven't heard from Sam. He generally rings to ask after the old lady and tell me he's on his way.'

Dorothy frowned and followed her into the kitchen, glancing at Ethel who was snoring noisily in her favourite armchair. 'Good God, she's aged!'

'That's what Hester said when last she visited. Do make yourself at home,' said Lynne, remaining standing with her back against the table. 'How did you break your arm?'

'A stupid accident! I caught my heel in the cobbles.'

'Tough luck,' said Lynne sympathetically. 'So what's happened about the filming?'

'Fortunately we were well on with it and they rewrote my accident into the script. I've more location work to do up in Scotland and then we're at the film studies down south.' Dorothy sat down and opened her handbag and took out a silver cigarette case and lighter. 'I can't remember if you smoke or not.'

'No, my grandmother had a bad chest and cigarette smoke would have only made it worse. She died not so long ago.'

'You must miss her.'

'Yes, I do,' said Lynne, watching Dorothy take out a cigarette. 'Can I help you with that?'

'It's OK. I've got the hang of managing now.' Dorothy lit up and dropped lighter and cigarette case in her handbag.

Lynne opened the window wider. 'I'll go and make a cup of tea.'

She went out into the back kitchen and put on the kettle. Dorothy followed her. 'What's your game, Lynne?'

Lynne glanced over her shoulder. 'I won't

pretend I don't know what you mean but I'd rather not discuss Sam as if he was a bone for us to bicker over. We were talking about my grandmother. She was really sorry when you didn't come the day you left for London. Sam said you were in a hurry but Betty told me that you dropped in at the coffee bar and spoke to Lenny.'

Dorothy raised her eyebrows. 'What of it? Sam and I disagreed about something and Lenny's an old friend. I'm sorry I disappointed your grandmother. Betty told me that she was quite a character.'

Lynne spooned tea leaves into the pot. 'I'll never forget her.'

'Because she turned up trumps when you were desperate to keep your baby?'

Lynne looked surprised. 'I didn't think you'd want to talk about those days.'

'Well, I do.' She smiled faintly. 'I thought I'd tell Sam all about it. How the baby's father died at Dunkirk.'

'That would be daft! Dunkirk was in 1940.'

Dorothy gave a twisted smile. 'I was never any good at dates.'

'Sam's the father of your son, isn't he?'

Dorothy stiffened. 'How can you possibly know that? I didn't tell you anything about the father.'

'Because...' Lynne folded her arms across her chest and stared at her. *Should I or shouldn't I tell her?*

'What were you going to say?' asked Dorothy.

'If Sam isn't the father, then why bother telling him anything about that period in your life?'

'Because I don't trust you to keep quiet about it,' said Dorothy abruptly.

'It's only my word against yours. Don't you think he'll believe you if it came to choosing one of us to believe?'

Dorothy drew on her cigarette and blew out a perfect smoke ring. Lynne continued to stare at her in a way that made Dorothy feel furious at her.

'I've told Sam that I gave birth to Roberta in a home for unmarried mothers and that her father was killed before we could marry,' Lynne burst out.

The half-smoked cigarette dropped from Dorothy's lips. 'Bloody hell, why?'

Lynne bent and picked up the cigarette and threw it in the sink. 'I could say because I didn't trust you not to tell him when you discovered he was teaching me to dance but, to be honest, I didn't think you'd raise the subject with him. I didn't regard myself as a threat to your relationship because you're so beautiful. But you obviously do. Perhaps you have far more to lose than I at first realized. The scandal of being an unmarried mother wouldn't do much for your career I imagine.'

Dorothy's face hardened. 'Are you threatening me?'

'No. I'm just telling it as it is.' Lynne hesitated. 'Thinking about what you said about Sam not being the father of your son. We both know that you knew each other years ago. I also know that he was in love with a girl called Carol and she died in the Blitz, so I know she couldn't be the

336

mother of his son.'

Dorothy stilled. 'He ... he told you about Carol?'

'Yes, I think it was after I told him about Robert.'

'You have been having a heart to heart, the pair of you!'

Lynne shrugged. 'I find him easy to talk to and my daughter likes him, too. She calls him Sergeant Sam but that's going to have to change. He's just been made an inspector.'

'Has he by God! So he's achieved his dream.' Dorothy closed her eyes and then opened them wide. 'Tell me, how did Sam react to you being honest with him?'

'He understood why I pretended I was a widow, though I could see it came as a shock at first. In return he told me about Carol.'

Dorothy frowned. 'I suppose you're in love with Sam?'

'Yes, I love him. Do you?' asked Lynne, gazing at her squarely.

A slight smile lifted the corners of Dorothy's mouth. 'You're wishing I'd stayed away. I bet you're worried that I only have to snap my fingers for Sam to come running.'

'You're not right for him, you know you're not! Why don't you just go away and play at being someone else and leave us in peace!' snapped Lynne. 'You'll mess him all up again if you stay. Even if you did make a baby together, it doesn't make you the perfect couple!'

Lynne's words struck Dorothy like a blow and she was gripped by the same fear she had felt

337

when she'd had her accident and when she had been unable to persuade Sam to come to Italy or to get in touch with him earlier. 'And what if I don't go away? You'll tell him I had his son adopted? Well, it won't work because he won't want to believe it. He loves me and would prefer to believe what I tell him!'

Lynne thought of Sam and his desire for a family. She thought of Nick and his finding his adoptive father murdered and how he must have worried about what his horrible uncle might do to him. What a relief it must have been when Sam sorted matters out for him! Had Sam finally recognized Nick as another lad like himself? Had he been hurt?

Anger surged through her like a tidal wave. 'You'd do anything to get what you want, wouldn't you? I want Sam to be happy and I believe we can be happy together with you out of the way.'

'You're deluding yourself!'

'Is she?' Sam's voice caused the two women to whirl round and stare at him standing in the doorway. For several tense moments none of them spoke.

Then Dorothy said, 'Sam darling, I broke my arm!' She held it up.

'So I see.' His brown eyes were unfathomable. 'It's not the only thing you've done, is it?'

She hesitated. 'How much did you hear, Sam?'

'More than you'd like. I don't think I need to ask why you never told me you were pregnant.'

She took a deep breath. 'I suppose not. But I wasn't only thinking of myself but you, too.'

'I'd like to believe that but I'm not sure I do.' His expression was grim. 'Not that it matters now. It's all over between us.'

A muscle in Dorothy's throat twitched. For a moment she could not speak and then she managed to say, 'I thought this would happen as soon as I saw Lynne with you at the hotel.'

'Did you? Yet you never said a word to her, whereas you could have befriended her. I can assure you that she never said a word against you behind your back.'

'I was tempted,' Lynne put in.

He flashed her a smile. 'I wouldn't want you perfect.'

'No, perfection would be difficult to live with,' she said wryly.

'Oh, stop it!' cried Dorothy. 'Don't you two realize that I could lose everything? Not just you, Sam, but my career! I have to do well with this film and breaking my arm meant rewrites. It wasn't the first thing that went wrong and they might decide I'm a jinx. They could change their minds about featuring me in their next film.'

'Truthfully, my dear Dorothy, I don't give a damn!' said Sam, his eyes glinting. 'It's time you thought of someone else besides yourself. What about the film about Liverpool women you made such a hoo-ha about? You've interviewed members of my family as well as others who got all excited about it. Obviously you've stopped caring if that goes up the Swanee as long as you can be a big star!'

'That's not true,' said Dorothy weakly.

'Liar!' said Sam scornfully.

'Don't you two start bickering,' said Lynne hastily, turning off the gas under the kettle. 'You'll be waking Aunt Ethel up.'

Sam reached out to Lynne and brought her against him. 'You're right. It's not worth the effort of arguing; it's all over now. I'm hungry, is there any food on the go?'

'It's all this upset,' said Lynne, pressing her lips against his. 'But I'm sure we can work things out.'

'Oh, this is marvellous,' said Dorothy crossly. 'Now the pair of you are behaving as if I no longer exist. Well thank you very much! I thought I meant something to you, Sam. You said you loved me. God knows you were desperate enough to get me married and playing the role of the little woman at home for you. You've changed your tune pretty quick. Well, I can tell you now, I'd no intention of marrying you, Sam. You were nothing more than a diversion and a mildly entertaining one at that. Now, if you'd just phone for a taxi, I'll leave you and the little dressmaker to plan your visions of domestic bliss.'

These last words were delivered with an imperious tone but they failed to hit their mark. Reluctantly, Sam released Lynne and looked at Dorothy. 'It's your left arm that's broken, not you're right. Make the phone call yourself.'

But, for all her acting skills, Dorothy was having trouble maintaining this performance; her bottom lip trembled and tears filled her eyes. 'I always thought you were a gentleman, if nothing else.'

'I don't trust you not to say something bitchy to Lynne, once I'm out of the room,' he said.

'I'll make the call,' said Lynne, and left the back kitchen.

Sam turned his back on Dorothy and poured hot water into the teapot. 'I don't suppose you want a cup of tea?'

'Do you hate me? Really hate me?' asked Dorothy, a tremor in her voice.

'Knowing what I do now, I think that hate is perhaps too strong a word. Forgiving you for not making me aware earlier that I had a son is a more difficult question to answer. I would have been even more angry and hurt if I had known say six months ago that you'd had my son and had him adopted.'

'Why, what's changed? Is it Lynne? You think she can give you a son? You don't understand what a difficult choice it was for me to do what I did but then I didn't have much in the way of choices.'

'You could have told me and I'd have married you.'

'I knew that and I think I still made the right decision.'

'Little as I hate to agree with you, I do so now,' said Sam. 'I hope it all works out for you, Dot.'

'I believe you mean that.' Her eyes glistened. 'Tarrah, Sam. Good luck.'

In the kitchen Aunt Ethel was still asleep.

Dorothy reached for her handbag and delved inside and by the time Lynne put down the phone, Dorothy had lit a cigarette. 'I have a question to ask,' she said.

'What?' asked Lynne.

'How did you manage to sound so certain that Sam was the father?'

For a moment Lynne just stared at her and then asked, 'Where are you going when you leave here?'

'What's that got to do with anything?'

'Why don't you go and eat at Lenny's place?'

'Lenny won't be open at this time of evening.'

'Want to bet?' said Lynne softly. 'Go and have a look. You'll get a surprise.'

Dorothy stared at her. 'You think there's something between me and Lenny?'

'I hear you believe men and women can be friends. I think you're in need of a friend,' Lynne said. 'I wish you luck.'

Dorothy murmured, 'Thanks. I'd wish you the same, only I do believe you have all the luck you need right now.' She stood up. 'I'll wait outside for the taxi. Goodbye.'

'Tarrah.'

Lynne returned to the back kitchen and Sam. 'You all right?' she asked.

'Yeah!' His tight expression relaxed.

'Now you must be really hungry. I've a casserole with mutton chops, sliced potatoes and other vegetables in onion gravy in the oven. Will that do you or is there anything else you'd like?'

He brought her close, thinking how he had always been careful not to overstep the mark but now he sensed that Lynne was as hungry for him as he was for her, so he kissed her with a lack of restraint.

After a delicious interlude during which not

342

one word was spoken, she said huskily, 'I take it that was for starters.'

'You bet! Now let's sit down and eat. We've a lot to discuss,' said Sam. 'Such as will you marry me?'

'Yes, please,' Lynne answered, looping her arms around his neck and kissing him. 'Tell me, do you think there's a possibility that Nick is your son?'

He stilled. 'You've seen the likeness, too? When I did, I thought I was imagining it. Especially as no one else said anything and I couldn't think how to broach the subject with you. Anyway, when I discovered he was adopted and I had already noticed that he was double-jointed the same as me, and had my colour of hair and eyes, what else could I suspect but that Dorothy had got pregnant and kept it a secret from me?'

Lynne nodded. 'Yes, I understand that.'

'Let's eat,' he said abruptly. 'We'll talk some more later.'

They were silent as they ate the first course. Sam was extremely appreciative of her cooking as she cleared the plates. Then she took a rice pudding from the oven.

'This looks great!' He gazed down at the crispy brown skin on the pudding and sniffed the nutmeg sprinkled on it with satisfaction. He picked up his spoon. 'You definitely know the way to a man's heart.'

Lynne smiled. 'It's good to be appreciated.' She kissed him before dishing out the rice pudding. 'Thinking of Nick, he and Bobby were born within minutes of each other, you know. I

343

remember he was a lovely baby and he's a good-looking and charming youth,' she added softly. 'And he'll grow into a handsome man like his father.'

Sam cleared his throat. 'Flatterer.'

'It's true!' She paused and picked up her spoon. 'What are we going to do about him?'

Sam sighed. 'He seems happy with the Nuttalls.'

Hearing that sigh, Lynne said, 'He could be happy with us. We could adopt him. But if you think it's best if we leave things as they are, then, of course, we will.'

'I'd like to claim him as my son but how do I go about it? He's bound to ask questions – and can I ever take the place of the man who was a father to him until a few months ago?'

'There's no question of that! I'm sure Kenneth Rogers will always hold a special place in his heart. Your position is different. Nick already admires you tremendously and wants to follow in your footsteps,' said Lynne. 'He'll have asked himself questions and...'

Sam paled. 'He'll ask me who his mother is! Oh my God, let's think about this.'

Twenty-Seven

Even before Dorothy reached the coffee bar she could see teenagers dancing on the pavement to the sound of music coming from inside. Loud music! The kind that she reckoned could damage your eardrums if you listened to it long enough. *Mambo Italiano!* She hesitated outside the open door before taking a deep breath and going inside.

The place was jammed with youngsters. Crammed into a corner were the music group whom she recognized from Hester's wedding. Then to her dismay she spotted Jeanette dancing with Davy and she wanted out of there. But before she could turn and leave, she felt a tap on the shoulder.

'What are you doing here?' shouted Lenny. 'I thought you were still in Italy.'

'I broke my arm!' She held up the plastered limb. 'I've only just got back. We've finished shooting over there.'

'That's tough.' He looked sympathetic. 'What about Sam? Does he know you're here?'

'What?' She put her hand to her right ear as if she could not hear what he was saying. She had heard him all right, but wanted to get him alone.

Lenny grabbed her right arm and forced a way

345

through teenagers, tables and chairs to the kitchen. The heat hit her in the face and she felt sweat prickle out all over her body. She thought she was going to faint and then he was leading her through a storeroom to the open door that led into a yard where there were crates, some containing empty bottles and cardboard boxes.

'Is that better?' he asked, sitting her down on an upturned crate.

She nodded. 'I'm all mixed up, Lenny.' She delved into her handbag and took out her cigarette case. She offered it to him but he shook his head.

'Do you want me to light your cigarette for you?' he asked.

She thanked him.

He flicked her lighter and held her hand steady while he lit her cigarette, then dropped the lighter into her handbag. He upturned another crate and said, 'Why are you here?'

'Lynne suggested I came.'

His eyes narrowed. 'Lynne! I see.'

'Do you?' Her face crumpled and tears filled her eyes. 'I thought this film was going to be my big break but then to go and break my arm was such a stupid thing to do,' she said, prevaricating.

'Are you telling me that they chucked you off the set?' he said in disbelief.

'No!' She puffed jerkily on her cigarette. 'But it wasn't the first stupid mistake I've made and I'm worried they'll see me as a jinx.'

'Surely it was an accident and their insurance will cover it?'

'Yes, but even so...' She sighed.

'You mentioned Lynne.'

'Yes, Lynne.' She flicked ash from her cigarette. 'She's felt like a thorn in my flesh since I set eyes on her again. Now I feel I'm at a crossroads in my life. I had hoped Sam would take a few days off and come up to Scotland with me, but...'

Lenny gave a twisted smile. 'Hah! We're getting to the nitty-gritty now, are we? I'd heard that he and Lynne were enjoying each other's company. You've only yourself to blame if you really wanted to hang on to him. I bet you lost your temper when you saw them together. I thought you'd learnt control.'

'I have!' She pouted.

'I remember when you were a kid, clouting one of the lads because he got you out in a game of rounders.'

'Trust you to remember that.' She drew in a shuddering breath. 'I could do with a drink.'

'That won't solve your problems but I've some sherry.'

'Sherry! Haven't you any gin?'

He shook his head. 'I hate the taste of gin. And I can't stay out here long because of the kids inside.'

'I thought you'd help me! I thought you'd listen and understand and give me some advice. I think he'll marry her now and I'm left feeling all mixed up.'

'Why don't you tell me the whole story? But you'll have to be quick about it,' he warned. 'I've a business to run and having live music is a new venture.'

Dorothy did not know whether she wanted to laugh or cry. 'My life is falling apart and all you can think of is live music!'

'Don't be melodramatic!'

She gulped. 'Lynne knows something about me that could ruin my career if it came out,' she said in tragic tones.

'And that would be a shame,' said Lenny, his tone gentling.

She opened her eyes. 'I'm glad you feel like that. I need a friend but I've always found it difficult making friends of women. Carol was the only close friend I ever had.'

'Sam's girlfriend?'

'Yes, and it was terrible for both of us when she was killed.'

He fixed her with a stare. 'And so you comforted each other and we know where that can lead.'

She found herself blushing. 'I don't know what you mean!'

'Don't come the innocent with me! You know what I mean.'

'OK, so I know what you mean.' Dorothy dropped her cigarette stub and ground it out with her heel. 'I had hoped I'd never meet her again!'

'Then the only thing I can think of is that you got yourself into trouble. Had a baby and you gave him up for adoption,' said Lenny bluntly.

She let out a squeal. 'How d'you know? And keep your voice down; someone will hear you!'

'I doubt it with the racket in there. So it's true,' said Lenny, getting up. 'I'd better get back inside or the kids'll be dancing on the tables next.'

'Is that all you can say?' she whispered, following him inside and plonking herself down on a chair in the kitchen.

'What else do you want me to say?' asked Lenny. 'I presume you and Lynne met when you were in hospital giving birth?'

'Near enough! What am I going to do? What if it were to get out?'

'I can't see Lynne spreading the word.'

She sighed. 'No, you're right. What's really upset me is what Sam said about me letting people down over the film about Liverpool women I was going to make.'

'I see. Why can't you make it?'

'Because there's a clause in my contract that they have the option on my being in the next film they make and they could go into production almost immediately after this one is finished.'

He stared at her in disbelief. 'But you were going on before about them thinking you a jinx! Surely they wouldn't want you if that were true, and so you could make your film here in Liverpool if you've got the dosh?'

'But I want them to want me! I still want to be a famous international actress but I feel I should do what I set out to do and make that documentary.' She gnawed on her lip. 'After all, I've done the interviews with the women of today. There's some real good stories there.' Her eyes lit up. 'Honestly, Lenny, real good.'

'And Liverpool could do with a boost,' he said. She nodded. 'So what do I do?'

'Stop presuming they see you as a jinx and won't want you for the next film. You're still going up to Scotland, aren't you?'

'Yes, they rewrote the script to cover the accident.'

He smiled. 'There you are then, they want you. What they probably won't want is you appearing with a broken arm in the next film.'

'It could have mended by then.'

'Still, I bet they'll be prepared to give you some time out and you can spend that in Liverpool.'

'I hope you're right.' She returned his smile. 'I think I'll have that sherry now.'

He nodded but before he could get out the Bristol Cream, they were disturbed by Betty entering the kitchen. 'Lenny, you'd better come—' She stopped and stared at Dorothy. 'I didn't see you come in. Gosh, you've broken your arm?'

Dorothy said, 'That's why I'm wearing this sling, sweetie. I'm surprised Stuart hasn't mentioned it.'

'No doubt he'll tell me next time he's on the blower. Anyway, he'll be back soon and California here I come! Shouldn't you be on your way to Scotland?'

'Tomorrow.' Dorothy darted a glance at Lenny. 'It's a pity you can't have a holiday and come and collect some autographs.'

'I thought you were getting some for me,' he said.

'I did, but they're in my luggage which is on its way to Scotland,' she said wryly. 'Anyway, I'd best go. I can see you're busy and I've had a long journey and another one ahead of me tomorrow. Bye, Lenny. Betty!' She left the kitchen, thinking she'd had enough emotion for one day.

She paused in the doorway leading to the pavement and looked back at the crowded coffee bar. Suddenly she recognized Lynne's daughter, having seen her outside the church at Hester's wedding. The girl was dancing with a fair-haired lad and they were laughing. She felt a pang of envy. What it was to be young and have your whole life before you! She smiled wryly and left the building. She would drop Lenny a line from Scotland, enclosing the signed photographs she had for him and provide him with the name of the hotel where she would be staying, so he could keep her in touch with what was happening in Liverpool until she got back.

Twenty-Eight

Roberta raced from school to Mount Street where the Boys' Institute was situated. Youths were streaming out of the building and she prayed that she had not missed Nick, whom she had not seen for several days. It was September and she had only been back at school for a week. She had hoped he would turn up at the coffee bar after school yesterday because Betty was back

351

from America and had painted some fantastic pictures. But Nick had not been there and she was bursting to tell him her news.

She stood on a corner, scanning faces. Then unexpectedly she felt a tap on her shoulder and looked around and there he was. 'How did you get there without me noticing you?' she demanded.

Nick grinned. 'You were looking in the wrong direction. I was one of the first out and went into the sweet shop. I saw you walk past as I was paying.' He offered her the paper bag and she took a toffee chocolate eclair. 'Thanks.'

'So what d'you want me for?' he asked.

'I've big news! Mam and Inspector Sam are getting married.'

Nick's hand froze halfway to his mouth. 'When?'

'In a fortnight! I've been waiting for them to say something for the whole of the summer holidays but not a peep from them. Then suddenly last night they broke the news. Apparently they see no reason to wait. *It's not as if we're teenagers.*' She mimicked Lynne's voice. 'I said I didn't know what had kept them from marrying earlier. Anyway, I'm going to be the bridesmaid.' Roberta removed the wrapper and popped the sweet into her mouth. 'Fortunately Mum already has the pattern for my frock and she's shown me some material samples and I've picked peach figured satin. You're invited.'

'Let's go and have a milkshake,' said Nick, his eyes alight. 'My treat.'

Roberta cocked an eye in his direction. 'You

352

come into money?' she teased.

He smiled faintly. 'I have an allowance.'

As they made their way to the coffee bar, she told him that she had his invitation in her satchel. 'I know it's short notice but I hope you can come. Although, I've a feeling that Chris's parents will already know about it. I overheard Mum and Sam talking when he had Sunday dinner at our house last week.'

They arrived at the coffee bar and went inside. They found a table and sat down and almost instantly Betty came over, pad in hand. 'Hello, you two, what can I get you?'

'Two milkshakes,' said Nick.

'Banana and strawberry flavoured,' put in Roberta.

'Not in the same glass,' said Betty, winking at Nick. 'All well with you?'

'I'm OK!' he murmured.

'You look like you've something on your mind.'

He shrugged. 'I've homework that's a killer.'

'Perhaps I can help,' said Roberta, leaning forward.

'Oh yeah, brilliant at Algebra, are you?'

She looked at him with concern. 'I'd surprise you if I said yes, wouldn't I?'

The corner of his mouth twitched. 'Art's your thing, not Maths.'

'How do you know? You've never had a proper look at my sketches.'

He rested his elbows on the table. 'Show us your pad then?'

'You open your invitation first. I guarantee

you'll get a surprise.'

He slit open the envelope with a finger while she delved into her satchel. He read the card and shot her a glance. 'They're having the reception here!'

'Something wrong with that?'

'Nooo! Just surprised. It says there'll be dancing from seven o'clock and Jimmy Miller's group will be providing the music.'

'Don't you think that sounds good? Tony will be singing.'

'I'm surprised Chris hasn't mentioned it now he plays with the group the odd time. Will Lenny be doing the cooking?'

'Not single-handed,' said Betty, who had been listening. 'My half-sister, Emma, and Sam's sister, Hester, are going to help out. They are super duper when it comes to food. You have to be there!' She walked away.

'You will come, won't you?' said Roberta earnestly. 'We count you as one of the family.'

'But I'm not, am I? Besides I've never been to a wedding. They're for girls, really. They go all gooey-eyed when they hear "Here Comes The Bride", so Chris says.'

Roberta frowned. 'You have to be there! You wouldn't have an invitation if Mam and Sam didn't want you there!' She slapped her sketch book down on the table. 'Anyway, have a look at that. Mam thinks I've really improved. I reckon when she sees Betty's paintings, she'll make the decision to let me go to California next time she goes to visit Stuart. After all, I do have an open invitation from my step-grandfather.'

'It's OK for some,' murmured Nick, flicking open the sketch book.

'I'm sure you could go as well. You could save up your allowance.'

He did not answer but carried on turning the pages of drawings. Then he stopped and stared before turning a few pages back and looking intently at a sketch of Sam glancing up from reading a newspaper with a half-smile that twitched the corner of his mouth.

'Mam really likes that one,' said Roberta. 'She says I've caught him perfectly. I'm going to have it framed for her birthday.'

Nick made no comment but appeared to be staring into the distance.

'Nick, can you hear me?'

'I thought...'

'What?'

He left the pad on the table and dropped some money beside it and stood up. 'I'll see you!'

Roberta stared after him. 'Nick, where are you going? What about your milkshake?' she called.

She was about to get up and follow him when Betty approached with the milkshakes. 'What's up with Nick?' she asked, placing the tray on the table.

'He was looking at my sketches and suddenly went all peculiar,' murmured Roberta.

'Ah!' exclaimed Betty, gazing down at the open pad. 'That's Sam Walker, isn't it?'

'Of course!'

'Ever noticed how similar they look?'

'You mean they're both fair-haired and have brown eyes.'

355

'I'd say more than that and I'm surprised at you, Bobby, for not seeing it,' said Betty. 'Are you going to drink both milkshakes?'

Roberta frowned. 'What d'you mean you're surprised at me? I have noticed they're alike. I even said so to Mam but she said that it was just the fair hair and brown eyes.'

'Mmmm!' Betty picked up the money for one milkshake and walked away with the other one.

Roberta reached for the tall glass and sucked on the straw while at the same time staring down at the drawing of Sam before flicking over the pages to one of Nick. She experienced a surge of excitement and, shooting to her feet, she grabbed her possessions and ran out of the coffee bar.

'Sir, there's a lad wanting to speak to you,' said the sergeant. 'I tried to fob him off, asked him to tell me what he wants but he's not having any. He keeps saying he must speak to Inspector Walker.'

'Did he give his name?' asked Sam, putting down his pen.

'Nicholas Rogers.'

Sam stiffened. 'Send him in to me.'

But the sergeant did not have to because Nick had followed him and now he brushed past him and entered the room. Sam could tell he was all worked up about something and wondered for a moment whether by some fluke Dennis Rogers had managed to slip into the country without being noticed.

'What is it, Nick?' he asked.

'Could you be my natural father?' said Nick

356

fiercely, not beating around the bush.

Sam placed his hands on the arms of the chair and pushed himself upright. He could see the youth was trembling and knew how he felt, needing to hold on tightly to the edge of the desk. 'Possibly, but I have no legal proof.'

Nick flinched. 'Is it that you're glad about that? You'd rather not own to it?'

'Bloody hell, son, it's nothing like that! I never suspected I was a father until a few months ago and I was blown away by the thought. As I just said, I had no proof.'

'But when you first saw me...?'

'I saw similarities but not for one minute did I think you could be my son. I thought it was a coincidence. Besides, I didn't know then that you were adopted. Not until Bobby's mother told me that was so ... And, as I've just said, your birth was kept from me until very recently.'

'What about my natural mother?' asked Nick hoarsely.

Sam had seen that coming but, as it was, he hesitated. 'I can't give you her name.'

Nick looked taken aback. 'Why? Could I have more than one mother?'

'Bloody hell, no! It was war time and I was only seventeen!'

'You mean I wasn't wanted!' Nick gave a twisted smile. 'I'd already worked that one out as soon as I knew I was adopted.'

'If I'd known about you I would have married your mother. As it was she had other plans.'

'Do you ever see her?'

'Very rarely. We'd lost touch.'

'Then it's not Bobby's mother.'

Sam thought his son sounded relieved. 'Of course not.'

Nick sat down on the chair the other side of the desk. 'Bobby told me you and Mrs Donegan are getting married.'

'That's right.' Sam began to relax because it was obvious his son had accepted what he had told him as the truth.

Nick flushed. 'Does she know I might be your son?'

'She was the one who raised the prospect with me! She spotted the likeness before I did.'

'I suppose she saw the drawings,' said Nick. 'That's what happened to me. I left Bobby in the coffee bar. She probably thought I'd gone off my rocker. I left her with two milkshakes to drink.' He grinned.

Sam smiled. 'Then you'd better get back there. You will come to the wedding? We'd like you to be there. We've also invited the Nuttall family to the evening do, so you won't be on your own.'

Nick stood up. 'I don't suppose you've spoken to them about me being your son?'

'As it happens, we've thought of doing so but were undecided because you seemed happy with them.'

'They're OK,' said Nick casually, 'but things will change soon. I mean Chris is a couple of years older than me and will be leaving school next year. He's always wanted to be a newspaper reporter even though he likes playing the guitar.'

'What are you saying, Nick?' asked Sam, staring at him intently.

Nick took a deep breath. 'Bobby seems to be of the mind I'm like one of the family. Hers I mean. I'd like it to be true.'

'Then maybe we can do something about making that official,' said Sam, his voice uneven as he came round the desk and placed a hand on Nick's shoulder.

Epilogue

Liverpool: 1957

'Hi, Miss Wilson!' Roberta held the door of the coffee bar open to allow Dorothy through.

She smiled at the girl. 'Good morning, Bobby! How's the family?' It was nearly two years since she had seen Sam and Lynne but Lenny had let her know when their wedding took place and she had sent them a telegram wishing them the best. Then he had told her how they had discovered the child she had given away and adopted him and she knew she should be glad because he would be secure with them. She had felt the same when he told her they'd had a baby.

'All very well, thank you,' said Roberta, now fifteen and a Saturday girl at the coffee bar. 'The baby's thriving.'

'A girl, wasn't it?'

'Yes! Anna! She's a cutie, blonde with brown eyes ... and when she chuckles it makes you laugh, too.'

Dorothy felt a twinge of envy, thinking it would be nice to have a daughter to dress up and take about but she did not regret a moment of her life so far and one couldn't have everything. 'Is Lenny in the kitchen?'

'Yes, he's been expecting you since your

phone call. We're all looking forward to your play. I know we saw the documentary on telly last year but this performance is going to be special, isn't it?'

'You can say that again,' said Lenny from the kitchen doorway.

Dorothy turned her head and stared at him. 'I've brought you a complimentary ticket.'

'I should think so,' he said laconically, winking at Roberta. 'Make us two coffees, love?'

'OK!' She hurried to do his bidding.

Dorothy went over to Lenny and kissed him on the cheek. 'So you have some good ideas, my man! Poppy even agreed that it would do me more good than harm to return to the Liverpool stage briefly, what with the new film coming out soon.' She thought how it was her third in two years and how she was in need of a break.

'Come into the kitchen,' said Lenny.

She linked her arm through his and they went through into the back. She stopped in the middle of the kitchen and her eyes slowly took in the room. 'You've had this place revamped! Why didn't you mention it in your letter?'

'Didn't see it as important in your scheme of things,' he said, removing her hand from his arm, raising it to his lips and kissing it before dropping it.

She frowned. 'I'm interested in what you do, Lenny. You've been a good friend to me. Keeping in touch, encouraging me and giving me ideas. I'd have never thought of doing anything for the seven hundred and fiftieth anniversary of the signing of Liverpool's Charter if you hadn't

361

suggested "Outstanding Women of Liverpool" would go down a treat here. Of course, I had to revamp it for the stage. As Poppy pointed out, it's a completely different medium. As if I didn't know!' She was so glad she had found time between the first two films in fifty-five and fifty-six to make her documentary. Sadly Aunt Ethel hadn't lived to see it.

'Sit down,' said Lenny abruptly. 'You hungry?'

She pulled a face. 'I don't know if I could eat. I feel wobbly inside, just like I did the first time I stood on the stage at the Pivvy.'

'That wasn't the first time,' said Lenny. 'You're forgetting the performances you put on as a kid in your mam's backyard for us other kids in the street.'

'So I am!' Dorothy's eyes softened with reminiscence. 'How could I forget those early days? I was so happy then.'

'Because you're away from your roots and too busy thinking of the here and now and letting Poppy plan your future,' said Lenny.

She nodded. 'She's talking about my booking passage on the *Queen Mary* for New York, and meeting this American agent she has contact with and then going to Hollywood. I do begin to wonder if she's aiming too high for me.'

'That doesn't sound like the old Dorothy. She had lots of ambition and wanted to climb to the top,' said Lenny.

'I'm tired, Lenny.'

At that moment Roberta entered and placed their coffees on the table in front of them. 'Any-

362

thing else I can get you? A doughnut? An Eccles cake?'

Dorothy shook her head. 'It sounds quiet out there.'

'Won't be for much longer,' said Roberta. 'The normal crowd will be in, including Nick, but not Tony, who's working with his dad, and Chris, who has a job on the *Daily Post* now.'

Dorothy's heart lifted at the thought of seeing her son. 'Will your stepbrother be coming to the theatre?'

'Mam insists on it, despite him saying it wasn't really his thing and he's seen it on the telly.'

Dorothy was disappointed, but told herself not to be ridiculous. The boy could never know she was his mother. Even so...

'Well, you can tell him this production will be different, a proper live performance from me, not just a commentary.'

'Oh, he knows; he's seen the posters. You're famous, Miss Wilson.' On those words Roberta hurried out.

'Famous,' muttered Dorothy.

'That's right you're famous, Dot! Doesn't that make you happy?' asked Lenny.

She sighed. 'Of course, I know it should, but I'm not at the top of the tree, am I? Will I ever be, despite all my hard work? And after this play, I don't suppose going to America will be a holiday.'

'And all for what?' said Lenny softly. 'I've been asking myself, how long before cinemas start closing down? On a winter's evening will people prefer to sit at home watching television, rather than go out in the cold?'

'I don't believe it!' exclaimed Dorothy, shocked, wondering why she had not thought of that. 'Everyone loves a night out at the pictures or the theatre!'

'Most just love being entertained and television can do that. It's not going to happen overnight, of course,' said Lenny thoughtfully. 'But it's on its way. People said that the talkies would never catch on but they proved to be the end of the silent movies.'

'You're frightening me!' Dot put down her cup.

'What's there to be frightened of?' he asked. 'You only need to be ahead of the game or quit and settle down.'

She hugged herself. 'I'm not ready to settle down. I've a few more years in me yet!' She noticed he looked disappointed.

'If that's how you feel. Your face has already been seen on the telly, so all you've got to do is build up your presence and you could become a household name in no time.' He reached across the table and took her hand. 'When that happens, the theatrical impresarios and film producers will be beating a path to your door. No need for you to go to Hollywood, although you could possibly end up on Broadway. If that happens I'll come with you. It would be worth my making the effort to see your name up in lights on the Great White Way.'

'Would it, Lenny?' she said wistfully. 'I never thought I'd be able to winkle you out of your comfy nook here and accompany me abroad.'

'I'll do it for you, Dot. No one else! And when you're ready to call it a day, you can share my cosy nook.'

'You're on!' said Dorothy, planting a kiss on his lips.

She was surprised by the sense of joy she felt and began to laugh.

He joined in.

They were still laughing when Roberta came in with an order for two bacon butties.

CPSIA information can be obtained at www.ICGtesting.com
Printed in the USA
BVOW05*1657190215

387738BV00002B/3/P